WITHOUT
COMPROMISE

Sarah-Jane McDonald

COPYRIGHT

DEDICATION

This book is dedicated to my sister, Patti the Brave.
She has been my friend and confidant all my life and
has survived her own encounter with breast cancer. I
thank God for her, and for our love and friendship.
We share about life openly, with guns blazing, and are
seldom tentative with each other. True love can take
it all and still come out intact. That's what makes our
bond so special. I love you sis.

ACKNOWLEDGEMENTS

I'd like to thank my loving Heavenly Father who
continues to amaze.
I'd also like to thank my husband, sons and extended
family for their constant support. Finally, thanks to
Gina for the beautiful cover and to Leila my faithful
editor and friend.
I love you all.

DISCLAIMER

The events in this book are a work of fiction from the author's imagination. Any likeness to any person or event is coincidental.

AUTHOR'S NOTE

This book is filled with suspense and drama but is a complete work of fiction. I created Elite One and the protocols surrounding the Department to facilitate the story and took liberty and artistic license to bring in details to enhance the storyline. To my knowledge, nothing like this exists in real life. With that in mind I ask you to extend me a little grace and read this novel with an open heart and strictly for the purposes of entertainment. I hope, however, that you will learn about God in the little nuggets along the way. Those parts of the book are absolutely true and real.

Happy reading!

Sarah-Jane

CONTENTS

PROLOGUE

He stepped over the woman's body and went about searching the small two-bedroom house, looking for any evidence that could link the victims to his boss. He went through each room methodically, ripping the place apart as quietly as possible. Eventually he found what he was looking for, a small packet of envelopes with a rubber band around it, and he carried it out to the kitchen and the deep metal garbage pan there. He lifted out the garbage bag, separated the contents from their envelopes and opened them all out, dumping them in the bottom of the pan as he finished each one. When everything was ready, he set fire to the lot, making sure that every last piece of paper was burnt and only ashes remained.

When he was through, he went back into the bedroom where the child lay and with sadness in his callous heart and infinite tenderness, he lifted her and carried her into the living room and laid her beside her mother, right in the crook of her arm. The regret at what he had done nearly suffocated him, and he knew with certainty that this was his last job. He just couldn't kill anymore.

When Constantine had asked him to do this execution, he had vehemently protested, but his boss wouldn't relent. He had planned, therefore, to do away with the mother and carry the child to a convent he knew of without Constantine's knowledge, but when he had seen Jimmy Wexler, Constantine's other enforcer tailing him, he knew if he didn't carry out his employer's orders to the letter, the child would die by Wexler's hand and so would he.

He left out the back door, and when he reached his car which he'd parked a block away, he sat for a few minutes, guilt and remorse weighing heavily on him. He knew Jimmy would be at the house making sure he'd carried out his task, so pulled the small black notebook from the pocket of his pants, put it on his lap and with profound sadness discreetly wrote up his latest job. When he was done, he replaced the book, started the engine, put the car in gear and drove off. He maneuvered unseeingly through the suburbs of L.A. and eventually into the City, heading back to his motel, the picture of Lucinda's face and the child's clearly imprinted on his mind.

He remembered the mother's fright when she had stumbled upon him in the living room, just after he'd jimmied the back door and entered. He'd shot her straight through the heart just as she opened her mouth to scream, the silencer on his weapon muting the usually loud explosion to a mere whisper. He'd then gone in search of the toddler and found her in her bedroom playing on the floor. She looked up at him when he came through the door and showed no fear whatsoever, even though he was a stranger. As he pointed the gun at her, her eyes held only trust, and that was what distressed him the most.

As he drove, he couldn't get her look out of his mind and was so distraught he missed seeing the traffic light ahead turning from green to red. He drove straight through, and it was only at the last moment he caught sight of the transit bus out of the corner of his left eye, but it was too late. It plowed into him and in turn his car plowed into a crowd of pedestrians standing at the crosswalk. The world began to fade around him and he hoped in his heart he was dying. Then he wouldn't have to live with the painful memory of what he'd just done. There'd be no more orders, no more killing, no more little girl's innocent eyes to haunt

2

him.

****

Dr. Marissa Sparks put on her jacket, removed her handbag and a small package from her locker, then closed and secured it. She'd done two surgeries that morning, had just finished her rounds and was looking forward to going home early for a change. She'd been working flat out for the last three days and had a full surgery block slated for the rest of the week, so she'd decided to take what was left of the day and recharge her batteries. She had one brief stop to make in the E.R. to leave something for her friend and fellow doctor, Megan Wallace, who would be on duty later, but she was tired. As a cardiac surgeon, she had times when there just didn't seem to be enough hours in the day and that had been the case for the last two weeks.

She emerged from the elevator and entered the E.R. to what looked like utter chaos. The place was swarming with doctors and nurses, and there were gurneys with patients along the walls as the cubicles appeared to be full. A mini triage had also been set up in the small inner waiting area.

"What's going on?" she asked one of the nurses as she hurried by.

"A bad accident involving pedestrians, Doctor," she said.

Marissa went over to the Nurses' Station and handed the package for Megan to the young nurse there, asking her to give it to Dr. Wallace when she came on duty. She turned away and hesitated a moment, wondering if she should stay and lend a hand. The staff seemed overwhelmed and she knew they could do with her help.

Just then she saw the paramedics bring a patient in, one of them saying, "We need a doctor urgently!"

She quickly opened her handbag and removed her stethoscope before she closed it and handed it over the counter to the nurse, then she hurried over to the gurney they'd brought in. The paramedics gave her their report then told her that the patient had apparently been driving a car that had been involved in the accident and had gotten the full impact from a transit bus.

When they'd gone, she examined the man who appeared to be in his fifties and his injuries were devastating. She knew there was nothing she could do for him. He was unconscious, and she didn't expect him to live much longer, but she got a dose of morphine and administered it in the intravenous line to alleviate his pain and so ease his passing.

She was writing up some paperwork for him when, to her surprise, he opened his eyes and looked at her. He had the kind of face only a mother could love. Even though it was covered with blood from a horrible head wound he'd received, it was apparent he'd seen many fights, and the scars around his mouth, eyes and a particularly gruesome one along his jawline told the tale of his life better than words.

He opened his mouth and began to speak softly, so she bent over and put her ear close to his lips so she could hear what he was saying.

"Am I .... going ....to die?" he asked.

"Yes, I'm afraid so," she told him honestly, but with compassion in her tone. She could see he wasn't the type who would want a soft answer.

He nodded as if resigned to the fact then asked with hope in his eyes, "Is there…. a priest?"

"He's upstairs," she replied. She'd seen him ministering to a little boy's family just as she was leaving. "Let me ask someone to get him for you."

"No time," the man said. "Need to …… tell you…… something. Don't want to…... die with it…... on my conscience."

"I'm no priest," she told him concerned.

"No matter," he said. "I'm…..… Giovanni Russo. I killed a ……a woman and her child before I…… hit the bus," he confessed. The minute she heard what he said, she reached into the pocket of her slacks and pulled out the recorder she had placed there earlier and had used as she'd seen each patient during her rounds. She turned it on then held it to pick up the sound of his voice and asked him to repeat what he'd said.

"I'm …… Giovanni Russo," he repeated. "I just killed…… a woman…… Lucinda Gray…… and her …… child," he said. "I work for…… Constantine Antonelli. Do you…… know him?" he asked.

"No, should I?" she asked, completely shocked by what she was hearing.

He gave a slight smile, his lips lifting to one side, "Guess not," he replied. "Big drug...... king pin," he informed her. "I've offed more than ......fifty people for him," he grimaced, then continued. "Kept a record. My kill book...... in my pocket. Take it. Give it to...... the right person...... for me." Marissa was speechless. What on earth had she gotten herself into?

"Why are you telling me all this?" she asked. "Let me get a police officer and you can tell him instead."

"No," he said. "Constantine has....... people working for him...... all over," his breath came in quick short spurts and he had to pause before he could speak again. "government..., police.... everywhere. It needs ...... to go...... to the right...... person or...... he'll get away. Take the book...... now." Marissa was still bending over him and when she looked down, she could see the book he spoke of almost falling from the left pocket of his pants. The left pocket of her jacket was right next to it, so she discreetly slipped it from one to the other.

"Do you...... have it?" he asked.

"Yes," she replied, and he gave another slight smile.

"Good," he replied. "Don't trust...... anyone. Get it to...... the right person. Watch out...... for Jimmy."

He opened his mouth to say something else, but he began to gasp, obviously passing away, then within seconds he took his last breath and was gone, his face taking on a relaxed countenance. Marissa was trembling from head to foot, completely shocked by what she'd heard. She turned off the recorder and put it in her jacket pocket automatically before checking his vitals to confirm his passing. She pulled

6

the sheet over his head and turned away, then made her way over to the nurses' station to tell them he was deceased.

They gave her more paperwork and she began to fill it out, her hands trembling so badly she had to take a minute before she could continue. The E.R. was still a beehive of activity, and several times she was jostled by one person or another as the medical staff hurried about. She didn't pay any attention, however, as all she could think about was what the man had told her. Because of it, she had to keep reigning in her thoughts to focus on what she was doing, so she took a while to finish her task.

When she'd finally completed everything and looked around, she saw that much of the chaos had ceased. The place was still very busy but in better order as staff had been pulled from other departments to assist. She heard the head nurse advise that there were no more incoming victims, so she asked the nurse for her handbag and the young woman handed it over to her.

She opened it, pulled the stethoscope from around her neck and put it inside, then reached into her pocket to put the recorder in as well but found to her shock it wasn't there. She patted both of her jacket pockets and could feel the little book was still in the left one, but the right was completely empty. She began searching around, looking on the ground to see if it had fallen out but didn't see it in her immediate vicinity.

She took up her handbag, put it over her shoulder and went back over to the gurney which was still against the wall with Russo's body. She'd been so rattled by what he'd told her she thought she might have forgotten to take up the recorder. She was sure she had, but she searched the surrounding area just to make sure. She stood for a few moments, trying to think. She remembered the jostling then and began to wonder if someone had taken it from her pocket.

As she considered the possibilities, she looked up and saw a man in tight jeans and a white t-shirt leaning on a far wall watching her. He had big muscular arms that strained the fabric in his sleeves to the limit and his hair was slicked back with gel. She was instantly uncomfortable but couldn't understand why his stare struck a wrong cord in her. He didn't look particularly creepy, but she suddenly felt afraid.

She'd just begun to look away when he lifted his hand and she glanced back to see the recorder firmly between his fingers. Instantly, a feeling of dread came over her and she again looked at his face. He slowly smiled at her and in that moment, she had only one impulse and that was to run. Just then a group of people, about eight in all, rushed in through the E.R. door. They were obviously from the same family, some of them sobbing uncontrollably, and it was apparent they were looking for one of the accident victims. They came between Marissa and the man and she didn't waste a second. She quickly used the opportunity, turned around and ran down the corridor through the E.R., looking behind her as she went. She could see him trying to make his way through the crowd, so she used her ID card to grant her access into one of the doors that had 'NO ADMITTANCE' printed across it and disappeared inside.

Within a minute she had negotiated a complicated maze of corridors and was outside. She had parked just by the door where she exited, so she quickly got into her car and was out on the street within seconds. Her first instinct was to run home for her passport and get out of the country. Then she thought to go to the police but dismissed the idea.

8

She was in an absolute panic and didn't know what to do.

After ten minutes of driving aimlessly, she decided to pull over and try to calm down. Her fear and the myriad of emotions she was feeling was ruling her brain, so she parked and as she sat there, she took several deep breaths to calm her racing heart. Thankfully, after a short while, she felt her whirring emotions coming under control.

When she began to think more clearly, she decided the first thing she needed to do was get rid of the book. To keep it on her would be a death sentence. If the man with the recorder worked for Constantine Antonelli as she suspected, the sooner the evidence was no longer in her possession the better. She thought to throw it away but didn't think that would save her. Then she realized with sudden clarity that the book was her insurance policy. As long as she had it and they couldn't get their hands on it, she'd be okay. The idea came to her then to put it in the safety deposit box she had shared with her grandparents, Jim and Patty Drummond, who were now deceased. It was the only place she could think of which the criminals wouldn't have easy access to.

Her decision made, she pulled out into the street and headed to her bank a few blocks away. When she had completed her task, she decided to call the FBI. She couldn't handle this on her own and needed to bring in the authorities to protect her, so she pulled out her cell phone as she drove and called the operator, asking her to put her in touch with the Federal Bureau of Investigations.

****

Marissa parked outside her house in a quiet Los Angeles

suburb after checking once again to make sure she hadn't been followed and, getting out, she hurried over to her front door. She let herself in, closed it quickly, turned the deadbolt, then put on the security chain for good measure. When she was done, she leaned back against it and closed her eyes feeling frightened and vulnerable. She'd been told two agents would meet her at her place, so she waited anxiously for the authorities to arrive.

Within fifteen minutes a car pulled in behind hers and two men in suits got out. She watched from behind the living room curtain as they made their way over and rang the doorbell, but she needed to get confirmation before opening up.

"Who is it?" she asked.

"We're with the FBI, Dr. Sparks?" one of the men addressed her, and they both held up their badges with their identification so she could see them through the peephole.

She opened the door in relief, and the taller of the two addressed her.

"I'm Agent Walker, Dr. Sparks, and this is Agent Senior. We're here to take you into protective ….," but Agent Walker got no further with his explanation. Suddenly, the world around them erupted in a hail of semi-automatic gunfire and within seconds all three of them went down.

CHAPTER 1

Jonathan Peoples opened the front door and walked into his home located outside the suburbs of Atlanta. Even though he'd lived there for a little over a year and a half, he was still unaccustomed to its size. He had decided when he'd sold his two-bedroom apartment near Santa Monica Beach in Los Angeles that he wanted to have something a little bigger to putter around in but hadn't intended to purchase anything as big as the four-bedroom three-and-a-half-bathroom home he now owned. The price of real estate in Georgia was vastly different from that of L.A., however, and he had been able to acquire his new place for half of what he'd sold his apartment in California for and still have a tidy sum left over.

He had actually been looking for a small house when he'd taken up his new assignment on the other side of the country, but the huge lake where he now lived had been the draw for him. It was the only property for sale on the water, so he decided to purchase it, even though it was a little too big for a bachelor. The lake was connected to several others in a sprawling expanse of water that covered many miles and was perfect for his needs. He missed the ocean which had only been a few blocks from his place and afforded him easy access to all the water sports he loved. Atlanta was far away from the sea, but the lake was the next best thing. Here he was able to take out his boat, which he kept at a slip nearby, and even enjoy water skiing when his best friend Gabriel Michaels was available to go with him.

Gabe had been the one who'd put him onto the place, having purchased the same model on the same lakefront

11

three doors down from him. He too missed the ocean, but not for the water sports Jon loved. The beach was his thinking place, and he liked to walk along the shore in the early morning hours when the place was quiet and uncrowded.

A few weeks after Gabe had bought his place, the house Jon now owned had come on the market. When Gabe saw the realtor's 'For Sale' sign, he'd told Jon and he quickly gobbled it up. They each had swimming pools in the back yard with large patios surrounding them and unobstructed views of the wide sandy beach and the expansive water beyond.

Jon dropped his keys on the hall table, set the case with his laptop down in the office to the left of the entryway and went upstairs. He changed into a t-shirt and a pair of jogging pants then went back down into the kitchen. He fixed a sandwich and a bowl of canned soup for himself then sat on one of the bar stools at the kitchen island to have his meal. He wasn't a big eater in the evenings, preferring to eat out for lunch then have something light for supper. He usually ate on the patio, but it was cold out, so he remained indoors and had his meal while looking at the stunning view of the lake through the sliding glass doors that gave access to outside. As he ate, his thoughts took him back to the events that led to him moving to Atlanta, and he replayed the memories in his mind.

For many years the FBI had had a mole in their organization who sold information to several mob families. His activities had brought about the death of more than nine government witnesses in fifteen years, and he'd also given his underworld contacts a slew of information which they'd used to aid them in carrying out their nefarious schemes. Finally, Ralph Logan, a twenty-year veteran of the Bureau had been given up by one of the mob bosses, Stella Rivera, just before her death, and once investigators knew where to look, they had stopped him in his tracks.

Jon would never forget the day the Bureau took Logan down. He'd asked to be allowed in on the bust when they'd traced the mob informant to his beach house in Ventura north of Los Angeles. Jon and several specially selected agents had staked out the place, keeping a low profile through the night and into the next morning. At around eight o'clock, they saw the garage door open and the reverse lights of a car come on and watched as a brand-new Italian made convertible moved into the bright California sunshine. It had the top down and still sported the paper dealer plate on the back. Gordon Lightbourne who was the agent in charge of the take down, pulled his car in behind Logan's while the other agents who'd been in hiding surrounded the vehicle with their weapons drawn.

Jon got out of the car with Lightbourne, and together they walked over and looked down into the driver's seat at the man who had brought so much grief to so many.

Then Jon said to him, "Nice wheels, Ralph. Antonelli and Rivera must have paid you well."

He remembered how Logan had sat stunned for several seconds, not saying a word. It was apparent they had caught him completely off guard, probably because he'd felt he had covered his tracks so well, and he had. If not for Rivera's information, he would have gone on doing his lucrative sideline for years. Jon then remembered how Logan had looked up at him in misery, knowing what prison would mean, and in a gesture that spoke of his complete despair, he'd closed his eyes, slumped forward in his seat, rested his

13

head between his hands on the steering wheel and allowed his peers to take him into custody.

Logan's malfeasance had caused the Bureau to take a long hard look at how they conducted business in the Witness Protection Division, and it eventually led them to form a new branch which they named Elite One. It was so highly secret that only the very top brass and the small group of hand-selected agents involved knew of its existence. They handled cases directly related to the mob, those involving government officials or anything that was high profile in nature. The new division was located in Atlanta, but very few people knew where the office was or any details about the cases under their control.

The Bureau had appointed Travis McAllister, Jon and Gabe's good friend as director of the new unit, and he'd immediately asked the two men to join him. Travis wanted excellent and experienced agents who he could trust, and Jon and Gabe fit the bill. Things had been very quiet of late, with only one team of agents deployed. Jon hadn't had a case in over six months, but Travis had promised him that the next protection assignment would be his.

Jon's thoughts again drifted to three years before, but this time to a more personal event in his life. In a park in Billings, Montana, in the company of his two long-time Christian friends, Philip Abrahams and Jacob McIntyre, he'd given his heart to the Lord and his life had changed completely. At times he couldn't imagine how he'd lived without the Lord for so long, and he'd grown exponentially in his faith during the last few years. Philip and Jake kept in touch with him and they also prayed for him daily and he did the same for them, so glad for their mentorship and guidance.

He attended a church not far from his home, but because his job was so fluid, he wasn't able to volunteer as he would have liked. He had recently promised himself, however, that he would start praying for God to show him a ministry he could serve in that didn't always require his physical presence. Two years before he had also started pursuing a degree in Theology as he felt the Lord was leading him into missions, and he wanted to be prepared. He had no idea how it would all come together, but he was trusting his Heavenly Father to guide him all the way.

His cell phone rang just as he was about to get up and put the empty plate and bowl in the dishwasher, so he dug it out of his pocket and answered.

"Peeps," his friend Gabe said soberly without preamble, "has Travis called you?"

"No," he replied. "Are you home yet?" he asked, knowing Gabe had worked late. They usually carpooled, but Gabe told him to leave him at the office and he would drive a company car home.

"About fifteen minutes away," Gabe said. "He must have gotten held up. He said he was going to call you as soon as he hung up from me, but that was ten minutes ago."

"What's up?" Jon asked. Just then his phone chimed, and he saw Travis' name on the Caller ID. "Call you back in a second," he said, "he's trying to get through to me now," and he swapped over to speak to his boss.

"Hey, Jon," Travis said, sounding distracted as if he was doing something else and talking at the same time. "Hold on a minute let me finish this," and Jon waited patiently until

15

Travis joined him again. "Okay," he said, "all done," then he continued. "I have an assignment for you and Ice, pal," he said, using Gabe's nickname, "mob related and very high profile. I need you to come on back to the office right away. You'll be flying out tonight to collect our witness. Pick your safe house. You have the lead on this one. I was talking with Ice when the information started coming in about fifteen minutes ago, so I told him to go grab his gear and get back here with you as soon as possible. Make sure you have enough stuff for several weeks," he added. "I'm not sure how long this detail will last."

"Give us a couple of hours and we'll be there," Jon said. "Gabe's not home yet."

"Okay," Travis said, knowing both men lived nearly an hour from the office. "Be as quick as you can."

"We will," Jon replied before hanging up.

He dialed Gabe's cell while dealing with the dishes, and made arrangements for him to pick him up, then went around securing the house both inside and out for an extended stay away. When he was done, he went upstairs and put a few essentials and several extra pieces of clothing in his 'go bag', then got dressed, and within forty-five minutes he heard Gabe tap on his horn and he was locking his front door.

As they drove into the City, Gabe was quiet as usual and that gave Jon the opportunity to think about the safe house. He knew that for Travis to assign himself and Ice to the same case it was something big. He and his best friend seldom worked together. They were regarded as two of the best the Bureau had and were usually leads on different cases. Reading between the lines, therefore, Jon made his decision quickly and picked just about the safest place he could think of.

"Where are you thinking?" Gabe asked as he drove.

"Jacob's Mountain," Jon replied. "It's March so I know Jake isn't using it right now."

"Have you been there since he finished the house?" he asked.

"No, I've only seen the plans and pictures of it," Jon replied, even as he was busy dialing Jake's number.

He'd asked his Christian mentor and friend if he would mind loaning his place to the Bureau on occasion when they needed a safe house and Jake had agreed. He'd told Jon, however, that during the summers months it wasn't available as that was when he and his family used the house the most. It was located high in the mountains of Washington State and the property had breathtaking views. Jon had been there only once, before it had been developed, and couldn't help but like the location. It was remote and well hidden.

Jacob McIntyre owned and ran a private investigation and security firm in Billings, and he was not only well respected by members of law enforcement but was well versed in the confidentiality aspect of the business. Jon knew he would keep quiet if the house was in use, but this was the first time he was making the request of him, so he hoped he would agree.

"Are you…...?" Gabe began to ask, but just then Jon

held up his finger for him to hold on as Jake's voice came on the line.

"Jake how are you buddy?" Jon asked.

"Jon," his friend replied, "good to hear you, pal."

"How are Jess and Josh?" he asked, referring to Jake's wife and young son.

"We're all great," he replied, "just holding our breath you could say. Jess and I decided to try for another little one and she's just approaching twelve weeks, so we're entering that critical phase when she lost the first two. She's on complete bedrest for now, but she's in good spirits. How are you?"

"I'm good," Jon said, "and I'll keep Jess and the baby in my prayers for a safe delivery," he added.

"Thanks, Jon," he replied, "we really appreciate it."

"Are Philip, Gabby and their kids okay?" he asked then.

"They're all doing fine," Jake said.

"Please tell them hi for me," he added.

"I will," Jake replied.

"Jake, I need to ask a favor," Jon continued, getting to the point of his call, "but I know things must be stressful for you right now with Jess and the baby."

"It's no problem at all, pal," Jake replied. "Shoot."

18

"Can I use your place for a while?" he asked.

"It's all yours," Jake answered. "We won't be doing any traveling for a while, at least that's our hope. I'll tell the Colonel and Mary to expect you," he added, referring to his neighbors and very good friends the Jamisons who Jon knew well. "You know you can rely on them for complete discretion."

"I know," Jon said. "Thanks a lot, Jake. I really appreciate it. I'm not sure how long I'll need it, but if and when you're ready for it, just let me know and we'll move. Don't worry about the place either, pal," he added. "I'll take good care of it."

"I know you will my friend," Jake replied. "By the way, how's Gabe?" he asked.

"Same here," Jon responded vaguely.

"He's still the same and he's there with you," Jake surmised.

"That's right," Jon said.

"We'll keep praying, Jon," he said. "Take care and call me if you need anything."

"I will, Jake," Jon replied, "and thanks again for the use of the place."

"No problem," Jake said, and they both hung up.

****

Jon and Gabe stepped into Travis' office exactly an hour and forty-five minutes after Jon got his call. They found him on the phone and on his cell doing two things at once, and the whole office was buzzing with the usual activity that surrounded them getting a new witness. Travis completed both calls then asked Gabe to close the door for him and handed off the office phone to Jon.

"Have you chosen your safe house?" he asked, busily looking up another number in the contact list on his cell phone.

"Yes," Jon replied. "We're going hiking," he said vaguely.

"Great choice," Travis replied with his phone to his ear. "Call and take care of the flight arrangements for me while I deal with this last detail. Gabe could you fill these out for me?" he directed, handing him some paperwork. "When we're done, we'll talk," he said. After a flurry of activity, all three of them finished their tasks and Travis was finally able to fully brief his two friends on their latest assignment.

"This one is big, guys," he said. "Antonelli's enforcer, Giovanni Russo, murdered a model and her daughter in L.A. earlier today. He got into an accident after leaving the scene and died at the hospital but not before spilling his guts to our witness, Dr. Marissa Sparks. She's a cardiac surgeon who was helping out in the E.R. Apparently Russo connected with a transit bus and subsequently plowed into a crowd of pedestrians, killing three people and injuring many.

"When the Doctor called us and our guys went over to her place to take her into protective custody," he continued,

20

"they only got as far as identifying themselves before a drive-by shooter sprayed the place with bullets. Our agents were shot but returned fire and the shooter fled. One of our guys has since succumbed to his injuries, but the other is going to be okay. The Doctor was partially shielded by both men but took a bullet in her left side. It was deeper than a graze, but went right through, so she assured our agents and the attending physician at the hospital that she was more than capable of looking after herself. When she was released, they took her to one of our places there and have a small army of agents guarding her.

"Talk about the biggest fish in the pond, Trav," Jon said. "This is the break we've been waiting for regarding Antonelli."

"It sure is," Travis agreed. "This is the closest we've been since he executed his accountant for coming to us. Excellent job on the safe house, by the way," he added. "I take it you've already checked its available."

"Yes," Jon replied. "It's ours for the next several months if needed."

"Okay, good," Travis said. "I'll make arrangements for them to move her to our connecting city and have a car waiting for you. You can stay overnight at one of our places there, then leave early tomorrow morning for your final destination."

Ever since they'd formed Elite One, safe houses and their locations were only spoken of in vague terms, as reading notes and listening to conversations were two of the ways Logan had been able to get the information his clients needed. Nothing of that nature was spoken of openly in the

21

office anymore, and Travis insisted that as few people as possible know the complete details of each case. Agents might know one or two things which they needed to carry out their duties, but usually only Travis and the agents directly involved with the witness knew their location or all the facts. This was done not only to protect the witness, but the other Elite One agents as well.

"Is Anne back from vacation yet or is Gloria coming with us?" Gabe asked, speaking of two of the three female agents they used on cases, usually involving women and children. The third, Jennifer Harrington was recovering from surgery and would be off for four more weeks so he knew she wouldn't be assigned.

Anne Peterson was a hard as nails fifty-three-year-old African American Air Force veteran who had been with the Bureau for over eighteen years. Her black hair was liberally sprinkled with gray and her expressive dark brown eyes either flashed with anger or sparkled with amusement, depending on the situation. She was an excellent agent who had been with Elite One from the beginning, and Jon, Gabe and Travis liked her immensely.

Gloria Escoffery who was thirty-six, had been with the Bureau for thirteen years but was a recent transfer to Elite One. She had blonde hair and hazel eyes and was a highly trained agent. She had one fatal flaw, however, and that was a serious crush on Gabe. He in turn couldn't stand her. Just to mention her name brought a pained expression to his face which caused Jon and Travis to grin.

"Don't worry, pal," Travis said. "I'm sending Anne with you," and they watched in amusement when Gabe relaxed in relief. "She was preparing to leave Denver when the call came in," Travis explained, "so we put her on a plane almost immediately, and she just got into LAX."

"Good," Jon replied. "I'm glad she's already there."

"Here's what we have on the Doctor so far," Travis said, handing over a sparse file folder. "Both of you familiarize yourself with the details while I finish up here," he advised, and all three busied themselves with their various tasks.

This case was the biggest their new division had ever handled, and they needed to take care of every detail to ensure their witness' protection and safety. Antonelli's tentacles were far reaching, so the sooner they got Dr. Sparks to a more secure location, the easier they would all feel.

CHAPTER 2

By one o'clock in the morning, Pacific Time, Jon and Gabe were in Seattle and at the safe house where they would stay for a few hours before leaving for Jacob's Mountain. When they got there, the agent on duty informed them that Dr. Sparks had been in pain, so she'd taken some pills and gone to bed early, while Anne had gone shopping and returned only a short while before their arrival. She too had retired for the night. He also informed them that he had the watch until they were due to leave and gave them a detailed report regarding the position of the agents around the perimeter of the house, assuring them that everything was secure. Jon wanted to leave by three-thirty in the morning, and although he and Gabe had gotten some sleep on the flight over, they decided to try and catch a couple more hours' rest. It would be a long day and they wanted to be fresh and alert.

****

Marissa lay awake in bed long before the pre-arranged time when she knew she had to be up. The pain pills she'd taken had knocked her out from early evening, so now she was bright eyed and ready to go, even though it was only two o'clock in the morning. How quickly her life had been turned upside down. Even now she couldn't believe the chain of events that had led to her being here.

She loved her job and was very good at what she did, at least that's what her fellow surgeons and the nurses said. People she knew outside the medical profession, however, told her they didn't understand why she loved surgery so much, but when she held a scalpel, it was similar she thought to what an artist felt like with a paint brush. It became an extension of her hand, almost as if her thoughts and her movements were one.

She thought of the two agents who'd been shot and felt deep sadness that Agent Senior had since passed away. She'd asked about Agent Walker just before she'd retired, and they told her he was in stable condition, and the doctors were optimistic he would make a full recovery. She hoped so. She'd tried to help both men, even though she was frightened, bleeding and in pain, but there wasn't much she could do. Agent Senior was losing a lot of blood and had lost consciousness, and Agent Walker was alert, but in serious condition.

She had given them what assistance she could while waiting for the paramedics to arrive and was thankful they were there within a few minutes. Not long after, her house was swarming with police and FBI agents, as she'd indicated to the nine one one operator when she had made her frantic call that two of the Bureau's agents had been shot and so had she.

Now here she was, hundreds of miles from home and without one personal item to her name except her handbag and what she wore. She had no cell phone, as hers had been taken from her by the agents involved in her protection, no laptop or tablet and no clothes or toiletries. The one item that mattered to her was in the safest place possible, however, and that was the most important thing. As long as Russo's kill book was secure, it would ensure she stayed alive. She hadn't told anyone about it and had decided that until she knew who she could trust, she would keep its existence and its location to herself.

At three o'clock there was a knock on her door and Anne, the agent she'd met just before leaving L.A., asked her if she could come in. Marissa had already gotten out of bed, done a quick face wash in the attached bathroom and used the small brush she carried in her bag to try and bring some order to her hair. She found it painful to raise her left arm to help with the task, however, and using one hand didn't do a great job, so she decided to leave it until she had a little more time and help. When Anne came in, she was carrying a large new suitcase with inline skate wheels which she laid on the bed, and she opened it to reveal a complete wardrobe along with some other items Marissa would need.

"I guessed you to be about a size eight, is that correct?" she asked.

"Yes," Marissa said in surprise. "When did you go shopping?"

"When you were asleep," Anne said. "Thank goodness for twenty-four-hour big box stores," she added as she started taking out the things for her to see.

There was underwear, three pairs of jeans and a pair of black pants, four long sleeved t-shirts, two of which were fleece, two flannel button-down shirts, and two cotton blouses. There were also socks, tights, a thick winter jacket, a fleece hoodie, a lighter jean jacket, tank tops and soft bottoms for sleeping and a pair each of low-heeled pumps, moccasins lined with lamb's wool, and flip flops. Lastly there was a set of towels along with toiletries and the first aid items she would need to dress her wound.

"How did you know what size shoes?" Marissa asked in curiosity.

"I came in and peaked at your heels while you were sleeping," she said. "It was clearly written on the inside."

"Oh. Thank you so much," Marissa said gratefully.

"You're welcome. They're not the quality I'm sure you're accustomed to," Anne replied, "but they'll do the job. I'll be back for you in ten minutes," she said before leaving the room.

Marissa would have loved a shower but knew she wouldn't have the time. She hadn't had one since early the day before, but at least she didn't have on the same blouse and slacks she had worn to work. They'd been a bloody mess, but before she'd left the hospital for the safe house in Los Angeles, they'd given her a change of clothes so at least she didn't have to walk around in the ruined items. She determined that as soon as she reached wherever they were taking her, she would shower first thing, so she repacked the suitcase and waited patiently for Anne to return for her.

Eventually, Anne came and led her outside and into the kitchen where she gave her coffee and two Danish pastries. Marissa ate hungrily as she hadn't had any dinner the night before. Within fifteen minutes, she was led out into the living room and she noticed not only her new suitcase but other suitcases, groceries and two large coolers were standing in the foyer by the front door.

"Dr. Sparks," Anne said, "meet Jon who will be the agent in charge of your protection, and this is Gabe," she pointed to two men individually as she called their names.

Anne had explained earlier that for their agents' safety, only first names were used. Marissa looked at both men as she shook hands with them. Jon was fair with closely cropped light brown hair and had the softest pair of blue eyes she'd ever seen. He looked like he laughed often too, judging by the laugh lines at the corners of his eyes. She figured him to be in his late thirties or early forties and he was extremely good looking.

Gabe was about the same age and was also striking, but his hair was dark brown, and she estimated it reached his shoulders. It was hard to tell, however, as he had it in a neat ponytail at the back of his head. His eyes were also blue, but the color reminded her of the blue in the glaciers she'd once seen on a trip to the Alps with her grandparents. He had a pleasant face, but there was no warmth in his gaze. He looked cold, stoic and sad, as if he found very little joy in the world around him.

Just as she was taking in the two men, there were doing their own assessment of her. There was no doubt that she was an attractive woman. She was petite, no more than five foot two with chestnut colored hair and arresting green eyes, the color of the sea near to shore. She was a little unkempt, with her hair only brushed back into the bun she must have had it in from the day before, and her clothes were wrinkled, but Travis had stressed to Anne that they needed her to be ready by three thirty, so she probably hadn't had time to do much with herself. She also walked slowly and carefully, favoring her left side, and she looked stressed and in pain.

"Dr. Sparks," Jon said, "it's nice to meet you, even under these less than ideal circumstances. We'll be leaving now for a safer location," he explained. "Once there, we'll debrief you and let you know where things stand regarding your safety."

28

"Thank you," she said, and followed them out to a large SUV they had waiting.

The windows were tinted almost black and when she entered the back seat, she found there was no way to see through the tint in the rear portion of the vehicle to outside. There was also a partition between the front and rear seats, which was lowered at the moment, but when raised it essentially blocked off the occupants in the back from those up in front.

They left immediately, the suitcases, groceries and coolers having been put in the back of the vehicle while she was being introduced to the agents. With the partition raised, they drove through the quiet streets of Seattle using a convoluted route until eventually they came onto the highway. As they drove, Marissa couldn't tell where they were heading, she only knew what Anne had told her as they drove out of the City and that was it would take several hours to reach their destination.

She didn't feel much like talking, so she closed her eyes and determined to try and catch up on some sleep. She was uncomfortable and in pain, so she'd taken more pain killers before leaving the house and knew they would put her out in short order.

CHAPTER 3

When she awoke some three hours later, Marissa felt more rested despite the less than ideal sleeping conditions. She was surprised, however, when she opened her eyes and saw that the partition was still raised. Anne was reading, as the space was brightly lit by several LED lights in the roof.

Marissa sat quietly for a few minutes observing the woman beside her. She was tall, at least five ten, with big brown eyes and salt and pepper hair done in long braids down her back. Marissa guessed her to be in her late forties or early fifties, as despite her graying hair, her skin was smooth and unwrinkled. She shifted into a more comfortable position, and Anne looked over at her.

"Had a good sleep?" she asked, putting her finger in the book she was reading to mark the page.

"Yes, thank you," she replied. "Why the coffin-like experience?" she asked, nodding to the partition. "I thought they would have put it down after we got out of the City."

"The location is highly secret," Anne explained. "Not even I know where it is. It ensures safety for the next witness we may need to use the same facilities for," and Marissa nodded in understanding. She could see the logic in that.

"Do you know how much longer?" she asked.

"I'd say less than an hour," she replied. "You're welcome to borrow one of my magazines if you'd like," she added, offering Marissa a few choices. She chose one and browsed through it to pass the time.

Fifty minutes later, they felt the vehicle slow, make a sharp right turn and stop. Within a minute, they were driving again, but this time in a steep winding climb.

"If this is a driveway, it's certainly long," Marissa thought.

They had been going around many such curves and steep climbs ever since she'd woken up and she wondered where on earth they were taking her. Several minutes later, they were on flat terrain and the car stopped. They could feel both men get out and they waited for several minutes before they felt them get back in and the car began moving again.

Within moments they were in a steep descent and when they were on the road after another brief stop, it was only for a short distance before they felt the car make another sharp right and come to another stop just like before. Marissa surmised that both times it was so that gates could be opened and closed because, within a minute, they moved forward for a few yards, stopped again, and waited. The car soon began another steep and winding climb, this one taking even longer than the first. Eventually, the terrain leveled off once again and they came to a stop.

The partition lowered and Jon, who was driving, turned and said, "Welcome to your home away from home, Dr. Sparks. Let's hope your stay will be a short one."

He hadn't yet driven up to the house, but had stopped the car just over the rise, so it lay before them in all its splendor. Marissa did a double-take when she got her first look at it. It was a log home, but unlike any she had ever seen. This one was a combination of field stone, logs and glass, modern to the hilt and absolutely beautiful.

"Now this is what I call a safe house," Anne said, and they all nodded in agreement.

Jon moved the SUV forward, and they made their way around a sweeping circular drive before stopping under a portico. He and Gabe exited the vehicle and told the ladies they needed a few minutes before they could come in, then both men left them there. Jon got some keys out of his pocket and opened the front door, then he and Gabe disappeared inside.

"What are they doing?" Marissa asked.

"This safe house has been borrowed, so they're sweeping it for weapons and removing any traces of the owners and the location from view," Anne explained. "It wouldn't be much of a safe house if you had guns hanging over the fireplace or if you or I could identify where we are."

"Oh," Marissa said, "I guess not."

Fifteen minutes later, Jon and Gabe returned to the car and invited the ladies to go inside and look around but advised that the master suite was locked and off limits. He and Gabe then went about unloading the SUV, carrying everything in and placing them in either the bedrooms or the kitchen. Marissa and Anne went exploring and to say the interior of the house was lovely was an understatement. All the rooms including the formal living and dining rooms and the four bedrooms and four and a half bathrooms that were open were tastefully decorated. The kitchen was a cook's dream, with a granite island that seated six and stainless-steel appliances.

The absolute star of the show, however, was the outside terrace which opened off the family room. It had a large covered porch from which extended a massive open patio area complete with an outdoor kitchen, a spa, a dining table and chairs and a lounging area with six chairs arranged around a firepit. There was also a double lounge chair angled to one side, yet despite all that, there was still ample room left over, giving the place a spacious and uncluttered look. Everything was covered for the winter, but the view was breathtaking with lovely snow-capped mountains and large drifts of evergreens, cliffs and valleys.

"This place is what you call top drawer," Anne said, as they made their way back inside.

"It certainly is," Marissa agreed.

"Dr. Sparks, would you come with me please," Jon addressed her as she stepped into the family room, and he led her back to the formal living room. He indicated she should go down the passage on the right that led to all the bedrooms except the master suite and instructed her to go to the very end. "We've put you in here," he said, showing her the last room at the back of the house. It had an attached bathroom as did all the bedrooms, and she saw her suitcase had been put on the bed for her convenience.

He left her then, and Marissa went over to the large window which was securely locked with key-only access. The house had obviously been built to follow the line of the cliff on one side of the property, and outside the window there was just a lip of land about fifteen feet wide. It was enclosed by a high wrought iron fence ostensibly to prevent anyone from falling over the side. There was a sheer two-hundred-foot drop to a gorge and river below and Marissa now understood why the window had a key, especially if the owners had children. The view looked out on the spectacular mountains and Marissa didn't think she would ever tire of the beauty around her.

She turned away and opened the small walk-in closet then the dresser draws to see if she would have space for her clothes. They were totally empty, so she opened her suitcase and slowly unpacked her new things. When she finished and had put her toiletries in the bathroom, she went outside and asked Anne if she would come and assist her in wrapping her waist to prevent the wound from getting wet. After she left, Marissa finished undressing and went into the shower. She couldn't stand directly under the water as she would have liked but stood back and used the washcloth to channel the soap, then the water over her body. She was thankful she had washed her hair the evening before her life turned upside down, so she tried not to get it wet. She would ask Anne if she could wash it in the sink for her in a couple of days.

When she was dry, and in her underwear, she sat on the bed with the first aid products and tended to her wound. The bullet had gone through the soft flesh at her side, just below her ribcage, and she knew her mother would have said that God had been with her. A few inches over to the right, and she might not have been here at all. It had caused a painful wound, but had missed all her vital organs, and had only needed disinfecting and stitching.

She finished her task then slipped on a pair of thick black fleece pants which Anne had purchased for her to sleep in.

She needed something warm she could wear outdoors with a soft waist she could roll down below her wound and this fit the bill. The jeans could be worn once she had healed. She put on one of the fleece t-shirts and slipped her feet into the soft warm moccasins then called Anne and ask her if she could assist her with her hair. Anne brushed it for her and left it hanging free, then told her she was going to have her own shower before leaving her alone.

Marissa wondered out into the family room and saw Gabe busy in the kitchen. Whatever he was cooking smelled heavenly, and she watched as he moved around with sure movements as if cooking was second nature to him. She looked over and saw Jon working on his laptop nearby, and when he saw her, he finished his typing and shut it down.

"You look much better," he said. She looked a lot less stressed, and he couldn't help admiring her lovely features. "How are you feeling? he asked.

"A little sore," she replied, "but I'll survive. I am starving though," she added. "What's for lunch?"

"I have no idea," he said, as they made their way over to the kitchen island which was already set for the meal, "but whatever Gabe gives us will be a treat. He's been cooking since he was a kid, helping his parents in their restaurant."

"You can have a seat, Dr. Sparks," Gabe said at that moment, indicating one of the elegant bar stools, and Jon sat down beside her.

Gabe filled four plates from the pots on the stove, covered one and put it in the microwave for Anne, then brought two over and placed them in front of Jon and

35

Marissa. He went into the fridge for the salad and dressing he'd prepared earlier, then got his own plate which he put beside Jon. He had made a heavy meal as they all hadn't had much to eat since the day before. As soon as he sat down, he and Marissa sprinkled freshly grated Parmesan cheese on top of their food and began eating the delicious spaghetti and meat sauce right away. Jon, however, spent a few moments to give God thanks for the food before him, and Marissa watched him with interest.

They were all silent as they ate, each with their own thoughts. When they finished, Jon took the plates over to the sink and proceeded to put everything away before doing the dishes. A few minutes later Anne came in, and when she saw the food Jon had taken from the microwave and set on the island for her, she smiled.

"I always like assignments with you, Ice," she said to Gabe taking a seat.

"What an appropriate name," Marissa thought to herself. His disposition reminded her of frost, and she wondered if he'd earned the nickname because he was always so sober, or if it was in relation to the color of his eyes.

"I second that," Jon said, agreeing with Anne. He finished wiping down the counter, then turned to Marissa and said, "Dr. Sparks, do you feel up to talking with us for a while?"

"Sure," she said.

He left the room and moments later came back with her thick jacket and the ones belonging to himself and Gabe which he had taken from the coat closet by the front door. He then opened the patio door and invited her outside. They all sat under the shelter of the covered porch, and she noticed that the protective covers had been removed from the furniture and put away, making the place look even lovelier than before. It was cold, but not unpleasantly so, and the sun was shining as well, so they were quite comfortable.

Jon pulled a recorder like hers from his front pocket, turned it on and introduced the conversation he was about to have, while Gabe sat in a chair facing her with a laptop computer which he'd turned on.

When they were both ready, Jon spoke, "Dr. Sparks, please tell us in your own words what happened yesterday?" he asked as he sat back after placing the recorder on the coffee table in front of her.

Marissa began to give her account as comprehensively as possible. She described the man she had spoken to and outlined his injuries, then proceeded to tell them what he had told her, but only to a point. She mentioned the recording she had made but said nothing about the kill book she had taken from Russo's pocket or its location. She couldn't get out of her mind the warning he had given her to tell the right person as Constantine Antonelli had people working for him in all areas of government.

She didn't know these men, and until she was able to determine she was safe, she wouldn't give them everything. She did tell them, however, about the man who had been watching her after Russo had died and described him to them in detail before telling them how uncomfortable he made her feel. She went on to describe how he had shown her the recorder and her flight to get away from him then, finally, she outlined the events that had taken place outside her house and her frantic call to nine one one.

When she finished, Jon said, "Thank you, Dr. Sparks. There's just one more piece of information we need from you," he continued. "Could you give us a list of your closest relatives? We need to know who may be in danger from Antonelli because of what you heard."

"I have no relatives," she replied with finality. "My father and grandparents are dead, and my mother disappeared nearly twenty years ago. I haven't seen or heard from her since. I don't have any siblings or any other relatives," she added, "at least none that I know of."

Jon nodded, then as it seemed they were through, Marissa asked if she was free to roam around the house and grounds.

"Out on the terrace here is fine," Jon told her, "but I would prefer if one of us goes with you if you want to go out front. I'd also like for you to just keep to the immediate area outside the front door and garden and not venture any further than that," he advised, and she nodded.

"Is there somewhere close by where you could get some things for me?" she asked.

"I think it depends on what you need," Jon said.

"Well, I would like to get some knitting supplies," she said. "I can't imagine what I'll do while I'm here for an indefinite period and knitting is something I enjoy."

"That's no problem," Jon said. "Just write a list and give it to Gabe. He's planning to take a trip to town tomorrow and will be happy to bring back what you need. While you're at it," he added, "write down anything else you think you'll need in the foreseeable future. We may as well prepare for a few weeks stay here."

"Do you have any idea how long it will be before I can get back to normal?" she asked next.

"Things are still a little fluid right now," Jon said. "Give us a few days to investigate what's happened and maybe I can give you a clearer answer then."

"Okay," she said. "If there's nothing else," she continued, "I think I'll just go and have a better look at that magnificent view.

When she had gone, Jon said to Gabe, "When I speak to Travis, I'm going to ask him to look at the surveillance tape they pulled from the hospital and see if he can pick up the man she said was watching her."

"Okay," Gabe said, making further notes on his laptop as he and Jon talked, and they went on to wrap up the debriefing of their witness.

Marissa, meanwhile, went out to the stone fence surrounding the patio. As she stood looking out at the mountains with their caps of snow, she thought of Jon, and for some reason she felt drawn to him. He seemed like a kind man and had a warmth about him the other two agents lacked. Yes, Anne was kind and had looked after her needs well and Gabe had cooked a delicious meal, but they were otherwise detached and in Gabe's case, remote. She once again thought of the color of his eyes which were a unique and beautiful shade of ice blue and wondered what would happen to his face if he smiled.

"He's so frigid it would probably shatter," she thought.

She was continuing her assessment of the trio when she heard footsteps and within a few moments she was joined by Jon.

"Lovely view isn't it, Dr. Sparks?" he commented.

"Yes, it is," she replied, then continued, "Jon, can we dispense with the formalities and go to using my first name. I much prefer being called Marissa or even Rissa," she said, "that's what all my friends call me."

"That would be fine," he said.

"I have to admit I'm still a little shell shocked over what's happened," she said. "I had a full roster of surgeries slated for the remainder of this week and a busy life outside the hospital. Now I'm stuck here all because I took a short cut through the E.R. yesterday afternoon."

"Life's like that isn't it?" Jon commented "It can take you and throw you for a loop when you least expect it."

"I guess you work with people who've had their lives disrupted all the time," she said. "How long have you been an agent?"

"Over ten years now," he replied. "Gabe and I served in the military before that."

"What branch of the military?" she asked

"I'm sorry, but I can't say," he said.

As agents in Elite One they kept just about all their personal information confidential except for broad generalities. He and Gabe had both served in the Green Berets before joining the FBI, but information like that wasn't something he could convey to his witness.

"I understand," she said. "My uncle, my mother's brother, was in the Marine Corps. He died in combat during Desert Storm."

"I'm sorry to hear that," Jon said soberly. "Whenever we lose anyone, no matter what branch they serve in, it always brings sadness to those of us who are left behind," and she nodded.

"I don't think my grandparents ever got over it," she said. "He was so young, and they were so proud of him. I guess he knew the risks and so did they when he joined the military" she continued, "but you always hope that death or injury won't happen to you or your loved one. They told me they prayed for him constantly and were expecting him to come home. I could have told them that was a complete waste of time."

"You don't believe in God then Marissa?" he asked.

"Why should I?" she asked him directly. "I noticed that you pray before meals, Jon. Are you a religious man?" she asked.

"I'm a born-again Christian," he said without apology.

41

"I accepted Jesus as my Savior over three years ago."

"Each man to his own convictions I suppose," she said flippantly.

Jon was sad to learn of her unbelief. She had no idea what she was missing or how her lack of trust in Jesus could affect her eternal soul. He decided right then and there to start praying for her. He found that with some people, only a personal encounter with God could bring about their conversion and that was what he'd pray would happen to Marissa Sparks. He would pray and ask God to make Himself so real to her that she wouldn't be able to deny His existence.

"That troubles you as a Christian doesn't it?" she asked, turning from the view to look him dead in the eyes, "that I don't share your faith."

"Of course it does," he replied. "You mightn't believe that God exists, Marissa, but I know He does," he said with passion. "I know. I don't just have some belief I haven't examined," he explained. "I know and have experienced His Presence in my life."

"Have you ever heard of the evangelist Adrian Sparks?" she asked then, stirred by the sincerity of his beliefs.

"You mean that fire and brimstone preacher who got himself killed in South America about two or three years back?" he asked. When she nodded, he continued, "Yes, I've heard of him. He was killed near to Thanksgiving. I remember reading about it. Was he related to you, another uncle perhaps?" he asked.

She chuckled. "I wish he had been my uncle," she said. "Wouldn't that have made life easier. No, Jon," she said, "I'm the P.K., the preacher's kid," and Jon's mouth fell open in shock.

"You've got to be kidding me?" he said when he'd recovered somewhat. "You're his daughter?"

"The one and only," she confirmed. "One day I'll tell you the story" she continued, "but if your God and his are one and the same, then I want nothing to do with Him."

She turned and headed back into the house, leaving Jon dumbstruck. One of the most difficult people to convert, was an unbeliever who knew all the answers yet still refused to submit to God. He had his work cut out for him if he was going to pray her into the fold, especially if her father was as objectionable to her as he had been to the tribe in the jungles of South America who had eventually killed him.

He stayed outside for a long time after Marissa had gone. The view drew him in, and he stood at the fence praying about his latest assignment and for her. He also prayed for Anne and for his friend Gabe who was still only a shell of himself after five years without his precious Gina. Jon had worn out his knees praying for him, and he knew that his friends Jake and Philip had also been praying for Gabe for years, even before Jon's conversion. He had told them the story just after it happened, and they had been interceding for Gabe ever since.

"How long, Lord?" Jon asked his Heavenly Father now. "So many prayers for such a long time. How long before we see him come to You? How long before he starts to live again?"

Sometimes he became frustrated over the situation, but he knew God was listening and was attentive to his prayers. He would continue until his last breath to pray for his friend. They'd been through a lot together, especially in the army, and had saved each other's lives several times. That kind of bond wasn't something either of them took lightly.

As if thinking about him made him appear, Gabe came up beside him.

"You could still do recon for the army, you know that?" Jon said to him. "You're worse than a leopard." Gabe grunted. "What do you think of Dr. Sparks?" he asked.

Out of all the men Jon knew, Gabe could sum up a person after only a short conversation, and Jon valued his opinion and insight.

"She's a nice person," Gabe said, "but she's not as confident as she would like everyone to think. I don't mean in her profession," he added, "but in her personal life. She's also scared to death."

"Which is understandable," Jon said, and Gabe nodded. "Anything else?" he asked.

"I think she's hiding something," Gabe said. "She knows more than she's telling us."

"You're sure?" Jon asked.

"Positive," Gabe confirmed.

"How on earth do you do that?" Jon asked shaking his head in amazement.

"It's a gift," Gabe said, not as a boast or even jokingly. He just stated it as a fact and left it at that.

"One I appreciate, believe me," Jon said. "I'll have Travis ask the agents looking over the surveillance tapes to do a close-up of when she's talking to Russo. Maybe we can pick up something from that," and Gabe nodded. "Do you know who her old man was?" Jon asked, as they continued to look out over the scenery. They could just make out a corner of the Colonel and Mary's house as the deciduous trees were still bare, their spring foliage having not yet begun to fill in the spaces between the evergreens.

"No clue," he replied.

"Do you remember Adrian Sparks?" Jon asked.

"The name sounds familiar," Gabe said, "but I can't recall where I know it from."

"He was that preacher who was killed in South America about two or three years back," he said.

"Yes, I remember the story now," Gabe said. "He'd been working there as a missionary and made himself so offensive to the tribe he was assigned to, that one night two of the tribesmen went into his tent, took him out into the jungle and cut his throat. The report said it seemed they were hoping he would have been ripped to pieces by wild animals to hide the murder, but his remains were found before that could happen."

"Exactly," Jon said. "We got into a discussion about me praying over lunch and she told me that Adrian Sparks was her father. She also told me that if his God and mine were

45

the same then she wanted nothing to do with Him. Seems he not only incurred the wrath of the tribe in South America, but that of his daughter as well."

Gabe shook his head. "He must have been a piece a work to leave a legacy like that," he said. "Any idea what happened to her mother?" he asked.

"No," Jon said, "but I'll find out."

Gabe nodded, "I'm going out front to familiarize myself with the grounds," he said then turned and headed inside, while Jon pulled out his cell phone and made his call to Travis.

CHAPTER 4

Five weeks passed, and the men continued their investigation long distance while Anne helped Marissa with her personal needs. The wound was healing nicely, and she had removed the stitches herself when the time came to do so. She was still in a little discomfort, but knew she was well on the way to recovery, so the week before she'd told Anne she could manage on her own. She still found it painful to lift her left arm above her shoulder, but she was managing to brush her hair, it just took a while.

She had been able to start her knitting right after she'd gotten her supplies, and it was helping her pass the time. She was in the middle of making a beautiful afghan as a surprise for Anne to thank her for all her help, and her needles were flying through the project. She had also begun teaching Anne how to knit at her request, partly the older woman admitted because she was bored to tears. Marissa had her working on a simple scarf to practice her knits and purls which was coming along nicely, and her student actually seemed to enjoy the relaxing pastime, much to Marissa's surprise.

Anne didn't strike Marissa as the type who would be interested in a creative hobby. She was usually on her laptop working or reading and was a diehard Science Fiction fan, but she'd told Marissa she loved using her hands, she'd just never had the time to learn anything. She also told her she would be welcoming her first grandchild soon and that was the other reason she wanted to learn the craft. She wanted to make a baby blanket as an heirloom gift for her precious grandbaby, and Marissa promised to help her.

What had also surprised her was how well Gabe had done in shopping for the items she'd asked him for. He had not only bought her what she'd had on her list at the hobby store but had included a few things she'd forgotten. When she had smiled, thanked him and asked him how he knew to add what she'd neglected to put down, he simply told her without a smile that he had younger sisters who had all knitted at one time or another, and he had bought similar things for them. Then he'd turned and walked away leaving her standing there.

"What a frigid fish," she remembered saying to herself. It was hard to believe he came from a family which included girls, and she wondered if he treated them as coldly as he did everyone else.

Jon on the other hand was his usual pleasant self and she secretly found herself attracted to him. He had a wonderful personality and was the one who kept the balance among all of them. They would both sit and talk, usually while she knitted, and she told him about her life with her grandparents, although she didn't share much about her mother and father. She'd only told him that her mother had left her father one day and had disappeared, never to be seen again, and that she'd spent the last few months before college living with her grandparents.

Jon shared some of himself too, but there wasn't much by way of family interaction for him to tell her about. Both his parents had retired and lived abroad along with his brother and sister and their families. He didn't get to see them much, but they constantly stayed in touch via the computer. It was then she learned that his father wasn't originally from America, but his mother was, and although Jon had been born here, he'd visited his father's homeland and had spent time with his uncles, aunts and cousins there many times during his childhood. He told her he hadn't been back in over seven years, but he was hoping to make a trip soon.

This day found her in her usual spot under the covered patio knitting and talking to Jon who was busy trying to fix the blender which had stopped working the night before. He had it partially disassembled and was looking it over to see if he could find the problem.

"You're sure you know what you're doing?" she asked as her needles were busily turning out stitch after complicated stitch with seemingly no effort on her part.

"Actually, I do," Jon said. "It's a hobby of mine to fix stuff. Whenever my mother had an appliance problem, she'd just hand it over to me," he explained. "I had a job after school at a repair shop and learned a lot while I was there."

He paused a minute from his industry and looked over at her. She was busy counting stitches, so her eyes weren't on him but on her work. He'd been praying constantly for her in the five weeks since they'd met but found that the strangest thing was happening to him. He was starting to look at her not as someone who needed the Lord, although there was no doubt she did, or as someone who was just his witness, but he'd started looking at her for the lovely woman she was.

Her rich chestnut hair was long, silky and gorgeous and flowed down to the center of her back in wonderful waves. Her face was truly beautiful and her eyes, her loveliest feature, were the light green of the sea, just tranquil and soothing. She had a sweet smile and laughed often at his

49

jokes and his tales about his childhood, and as he looked at her now, he realized with sudden clarity that he was falling for her.

The discovery shocked him so much that the part he'd been holding fell from his hand to the floor with a clatter, causing her to look up. He quickly lowered his eyes so she couldn't see the truth in them, and proceeded to pick up the piece which, to his relief, hadn't been damaged by his clumsiness. He set it down on the table and asked her to excuse him, then he got up and went through the house and out the front door. He shut it behind him, leaned against it and closed his eyes.

"This isn't happening," he said to himself. "I must be mistaken."

In all his forty years he'd only come close to marrying once, and in the end when she'd turned him down and returned to her old boyfriend, he had considered himself lucky. Since then, he'd made sure to keep out of the marriage fray. What he was feeling now, however, was unlike anything he had ever experienced, and he knew he was in deep trouble. First and foremost, she wasn't a Christian; that put her out of his reach as nothing else could. Second was the fact that she was his witness. Romance and witness protection were two things that just didn't mix.

He took a deep breath and began to pray, desperately needing his Father's guidance and help. "Lord," he said, "I know this relationship isn't from You. I know You wouldn't have me fall in love with an unbeliever, and I know You wouldn't have me fall in love with a witness. This must just be my hormones talking to my body, Lord," he said, "that's all. Please God," he pleaded, "take these feelings away from me. I want to honor You in every way, and I know You would be disappointed in me if I went against Your teachings. Father," he continued his earnest petition, "please help me stay true to You. Crush these feelings I have for Marissa under Your feet I pray, in Jesus' name I ask, amen."

Feeling marginally better, Jon took a deep breath and had just turned to open the door to go back inside when his cell phone rang, and he saw it was Travis.

"Hey, Trav, how are you?" he answered.

"Doing great, Jon," his friend replied. "I'm just calling to let you know that Ice was right on the money as usual," he said.

"How so?" Jon asked.

"She was hiding something," Travis said. "I just got the report from our boys regarding the compromised surveillance tape."

They had gotten tape from two cameras located at opposite ends of the Emergency Room at the hospital and at different angles; but one, the one which would have shown Marissa and Russo talking had been damaged, and it had taken the technicians all this time to lift the footage from it. The first camera had picked up Jimmy Wexler, one of Constantine Antonelli's enforcers without difficulty and had shown his activities in detail. It had even picked up when he had filched the recorder from Marissa's pocket as she stood filling out her report. It had also shown when he tried to take off after her when she ran down the corridor but was blocked by the crowd.

51

"What did it show?" Jon asked.

"She slipped something from his pocket into hers," Travis said. "It was so subtle that if we weren't looking at it closely, we would have missed it."

"Could you tell what it was," Jon asked, unable to believe that Marissa had been holding out on them all this time.

"It looked like a small black book," Travis said, "but our guys weren't a hundred percent sure. You'll need to do another debrief, pal," Travis instructed, "and this time don't pull any punches."

"Okay," Jon said. "I'll do it as soon as Gabe comes back from town and let you know when we're through."

"Right," Travis answered. "When we know what we're dealing with, we'll take it from there," and they both hung up.

Jon felt his blood beginning to boil. Here it was he was falling for a woman who thought nothing of hiding evidence and who knew what else, and it brought into sharp focus just how little he knew about her and how different their values were. He became really upset and felt his anger building, but knew he had to take control of his temper before he went back inside to confront Marissa.

A myriad of thoughts ran through his mind as he tried to come to grips with what Travis had told him. Why on earth was she hiding the book from them? What had she done with it? Was it at her house? Had she tossed it away? He was in the middle of trying to reason things out when he heard a vehicle and looked out to see Gabe top the rise and the SUV make the sweeping curve before coming to a stop under the portico in front of him.

His friend had made a run into Chandler's Crossing that morning and was just returning. The very large town, which was almost a city, was located about seventy-five miles away, and had just about everything they could want. There was a tiny enclave called Refuge an hour's drive down the mountain, which was much closer, but it only had a few businesses that included a small supermarket, a diner and a bank and post office. It had very little to meet their needs, so most times they drove through and headed to the larger town.

"What are you doing out here?" Gabe asked as he went to the rear of the vehicle to begin unloading the things he'd bought.

"Er…. Travis called," Jon said, skirting the question. "Let me help you, then we can talk," he offered, and they both went about taking the things inside.

Marissa was still on the porch knitting and Anne was in her room reading, so Jon and Gabe unpacked the groceries, placed the things Gabe had bought for the ladies at their request in the family room, then he and Jon went back out the front door.

"What's up?" Gabe asked.

"The technicians were finally able to lift the footage from the second surveillance camera and you were right," Jon told him. "She was holding out on us."

"What did they see?" Gabe asked curiously.

"She took something from his pocket," Jon said, his anger starting to build once again. "It looked like a small black book, but our guys couldn't be sure."

"Have you spoken to her?" Gabe asked then.

"No," Jon said. "I was waiting for you; I'd just finished the call anyway. I can't believe that all this time she's been holding out on us and knitting up a storm like some modern-day Aunt Gertrude." Jon bit down on his vexation and surveyed the scenery in front of him.

Gabe looked at him, inwardly surprised that Jon was upset. His best friend was one of the most level-headed men he'd ever known, and even in dangerous or frightening situations he could always be counted on to keep calm and think clearly. He rarely lost his temper, and to see him respond like this over something that wasn't unusual when it came to a witness baffled him.

"What's the matter with you?" he asked. "I've never seen you get upset because a witness holds something back. Most times they do it because they're scared."

"Yeah, well her little omission has probably set us back weeks in our investigation," Jon argued with temper. "We could have been much further along by now if she'd just come clean with us."

"That's true," Gabe acknowledged. "Depending on what she has, it could also explain why Antonelli's disappeared."

The mob boss was nowhere to be found and according to word on the street, he'd put out a hefty finder's fee for anyone who could give him Marissa's whereabouts.

"She's been stringing us along like idiots all this time," Jon said, his anger getting the better of him, "and I'm going to get to the bottom of it right now," he added then opening the front door, he charged inside before Gabe could stop him.

He went through the house and out onto the patio then said to Marissa, "Dr. Sparks, I'd like a word with you." Marissa looked up in surprise, wondering what was wrong. Jon never spoke to her with anything but kindness, so she was taken aback by his tone of voice. She still had her knitting in her hand looking at him with a startled expression when he completely floored her by saying, "And put down that silly knitting."

Just then Jon felt Gabe's hand on his shoulder and his friend told him he needed to see him inside. Jon opened his mouth to protest, but Gabe's hand tightened on his shoulder, so he turned around and followed him through the family room and into the formal living room at the front of the house.

"Peeps," Gabe said, "I don't know why you're so peeved, but let me handle this until you cool off. You're in no condition to do anything right now. Frankly, I think she'll be much more forthcoming with me than she'd be with you," he continued. "I'm already a dragon in her eyes, and she feels intimidated by me so give me a chance to do this, okay?"

Jon took a deep breath, looked at him somewhat calmer and nodded. "I'm sorry, you're right," he said. "For some reason, I'm just really angry right now and my perspective isn't where it should be. I'll listen in, but I won't interrupt," he added. "Go get her."

They made their way back out to the patio and Marissa looked up uncertainly. "What's wrong?" she asked, truly perplexed. What had she done? She and Jon had been having a pleasant conversation and now, suddenly, he was very angry with her.

"Dr. Sparks," Gabe said, he had never addressed her as Marissa, "do you know what the term withholding evidence means?" She went red in the face. "Do you understand the penalty for lying to a federal agent?" Somehow they'd found out that she hadn't told them everything, and now she understood why Jon was upset and angry.

"Yes," she finally responded.

"Good," Gabe said. "I'm going to ask you only once for the complete truth," he continued, "and if you lie or omit anything, I'll bring the full weight of the law to bear on you, do you understand what I'm saying?" and she nodded. "You get one chance," he reiterated, "so make sure this time you don't leave anything out, do I make myself clear?"

"Yes," she replied.

Gabe went inside for his laptop and brought out his own recorder. He introduced the conversation into it, set it on the coffee table between them then went over and sat in the armchair opposite her. She looked up at Jon who stood with his back against the wall beside the now closed patio door with his arms folded, looking out towards the mountains in the distance. He looked like a solid immovable force, and she was sorry she was on the receiving end of his wrath. He was usually so mild-mannered that she knew it was an unusual thing for him to be this angry.

Gabe cleared his throat and she looked away from Jon and back to him. "Tell us what happened on March twenty-third when you went to the E.R," he stated with steel in his voice.

She repeated verbatim what she'd said before, but when it came to her conversation with Giovanni Russo, she filled in the missing pieces. "He told me he'd killed more than fifty people while he'd been employed to Constantine Antonelli as I told you before, but he said he'd kept a record and that his 'kill book' as he called it was in his pants pocket. He asked me to secure it and give it to the right person," she continued. "He said I needed to give it to someone I could trust as Antonelli had people working all over. It was almost falling out of his pants anyway, so I discreetly slipped it into the pocket of my jacket." She went on to relate the rest of her conversation with him and described his death and the events after.

"Where's the book now?" Gabe asked.

"It's in the safest place in the world," she said but didn't elaborate.

"Dr. Sparks, you didn't answer my question," Gabe said with a bite in his tone. "I told you before you'd only get one chance, and it seems you think I'm joking."

"With all due respect, Gabe," she said, "I'm well aware of what you said, but as I told you before, Russo stressed that Antonelli has people working for him everywhere, even in the government and with the police, and I can't be sure you're not on his payroll."

"It may very well be true that he has connections all over," Gabe said, "but you can trust us implicitly with the evidence you have."

"How do I know that?" she asked. "We're here in the middle of nowhere and if either you, Jon or even Anne is working for him, you could easily get rid of me when I tell you where the book is. It's the only insurance I have right now," she added.

"I understand your concern," Gabe said, "so let me tell you a little about us. Our section of the Witness Protection Division is highly secret and confidential," he explained. "Did you notice that the agents at your house, and at the safe houses in Los Angeles and Seattle didn't ask you any questions regarding your case or for any information?" She nodded. "And did you notice that not even Anne is privy to our location?" again she nodded. "It is precisely for the reasons you're concerned about. Only three people know where we are," he said. "Jon, our boss and me, that's it. Our office, its location and even the agents who work there are known only to a few people because of the sensitive cases we handle, so believe me when I tell you, Dr. Sparks, you are perfectly safe in telling us what you know."

Marissa looked him in the eye for a long time and all she saw there was complete sincerity, so she nodded and told them what they needed to know. When she was done, he asked her one more question.

"Making sure you heed my earlier warning," he said, "is there anything else you need to tell us before we wrap this up?"

"I can honestly say there isn't," she said. "If I think of anything else, I'll let you know right away. I have no intention of going to jail for some drug king pin or any of his cronies. I was only trying to protect myself, that's all."

Gabe nodded. "We understand," he said, his tone marginally softer. "Just remember you can tell Jon and I anything or come to us if you're concerned about anything. Anne is a highly trained agent, and knows who you are, why you're here, and quite a bit about the investigation, but she doesn't know everything. This isn't because we don't trust her," he hastened to add, "but it's to cut down on the number of people who have full knowledge about your case. People may know one or two things as it pertains to their job, but very few know all the details, another security precaution; therefore, please refer all matters of that type to Jon and me."

She nodded and asked if she could be excused. When he told her yes, she picked up her knitting and disappeared into the house.

Jon turned from his position and came over to sit on the chair she'd just vacated. "We've wasted five weeks because of her little stunt," he said to Gabe. He was still upset, but much calmer.

"Yes," Gabe replied, "but we could have pressed her. In truth we'd only have been going off my hunch so….," he left the sentence hanging.

"We need to get this to Travis right away," Jon said. "I'll go and call him now."

"You go ahead," Gabe said. "I'll just finish writing this

59

up and send it to him then go start on dinner."

****

Marissa went into her room and closed the door. She felt like a whipped pup after Gabe's interrogation and was unsure she should have shared everything with them, but it was done and out of her hands, so she decided to put it behind her.

She went over to the window, looked out over the valley and mountains and thought about what she'd just been through. When she was a little girl, she would always run to her mother whenever she was hurt or upset, or she would run to God. How she had loved her Heavenly Father back then. He had been her Friend and Confidante and she shared things with Him that no one else knew.

The day her mother left her, however, was the day she turned her back on Him. She had needed her mother so desperately. She had been the buffer between Marissa and her father and with her gone she'd felt vulnerable and at his mercy. True, her mother had given her enough bus fare to get to her grandparents, but they'd been complete strangers to her at the time. She'd also never taken a bus across town much less across the country, and she'd never felt more lost and alone in her entire life. In that moment, she not only felt abandoned by her mother, but abandoned by God as well, and she determined that she would never speak to Him again.

She had given her life to Christ when she was eleven years old. Her mother had patiently taught her about her loving Savior, and she'd soaked it all up. Her father on the other hand made her feel as though she was never good enough. She could never do anything right for him, and he always threw God's displeasure at her, making her feel like a bolt of lightning would come down from Heaven at any moment and strike her dead.

"Gracious," she said, as she stood looking out at the snow-capped peaks and vast stands of evergreen forest, "how stupid I was to believe all that nonsense," and with that she turned away and carried her knitting over to sit on the bed.

They called her to dinner a few hours later, but she told them she wasn't hungry. She wanted to be alone, so she knitted until quite late then got ready for bed. She was tired and stressed and unsure of what tomorrow would bring, even so she climbed in between the sheets and was asleep as soon as her head touched the pillow.

CHAPTER 5

Marissa came awake around two o'clock in the morning and found she was intensely hungry. The last meal she'd eaten was breakfast the day before as she hadn't felt hungry at lunchtime.

"Serves me right for letting pride get in the way," she whispered.

She decided to make herself a sandwich and a cup of something warm to drink, so she got out of bed and, feeling cold, she pulled on the fleece hoodie over her tank top, thankful she had worn the long fleece pants to bed. She slipped into her flip flops, opened her bedroom door and padded her way out to the kitchen. She paused when she saw that a light had been left on in the family room and was surprised to see Jon sitting on the sofa reading what looked to be a Bible. He must have sensed her presence because he looked up, took off his readers and closed the Book.

"Hungry?" he asked, his voice sounding much more receptive than earlier.

"Yes," she replied simply. "What are you doing up?"

"It's my watch," he said, and she frowned as she didn't understand what he meant. He must have seen her puzzled expression because he went on to explain, "Gabe, Anne and I stand watch each night. It's Anne's night off so Gabe will relieve me in a little over an hour."

"You've all been doing this every night?" she asked

incredulously.

"Every night since we've been here," he confirmed, coming to his feet and making his way into the kitchen. He went to the fridge, brought out some leftover chicken and vegetables and took some bread out of the storage container on the counter. "Want a sandwich?" he asked, "or would you rather have them separate?"

"A sandwich please," she said and proceeded to put the kettle on to make herself some instant decaf coffee to go with it. "Want some?" she asked, going to the cupboard that held the cups.

"Sure," he replied.

He expertly sliced the chicken and lay it on the bread before adding lettuce, tomato, mayo and a little relish. He made another for himself then cut both sandwiches in half on the diagonal. The water boiled quickly, so she made the two cups and carried them over to the kitchen island where he was waiting for her. They sat on the high barstools and she proceeded to work at her sandwich with gusto while he took his time to thank the Lord before he started eating his.

When they were finished, he went over and made more coffee for them and brought it back to the island. They hadn't talked much during the meal, but now Jon decided to see if he could get a conversation going.

"I'm sorry for the way I spoke to you earlier," he said, looking down into his cup as if it could tell him the meaning of life. "I was upset, but I should have been more understanding."

"I'm sorry I didn't tell you everything from the beginning," she said, "but I was afraid. I was just trying to protect myself."

"I know," he said, sipping his coffee as he avoided looking her way. His eyes rested instead on a beautiful painting that hung on the wall just off to his left in the family room. "That must be one of Gabby's pieces," he thought to himself as he examined it. She was his friend Philip's wife, and she was one of the most successful painters in the country. "I'll look at it later to make sure," he decided.

"It's set you back in your investigation, hasn't it?" Marissa asked interrupting his musings, the thought having just occurred to her.

"Yes, it has" he said simply, and she nodded. "Want to tell me a little more about your parents?" he asked. They were both uncomfortable and he wanted to see their easy comradery return.

"Is that because you're interested?" she asked, "or is it part of your job to pump me for information?"

"A little bit of both I guess," he replied honestly, "but I'm leaning towards the, 'I'm interested' part more than the job right now."

She nodded. "In that case," she said, "I'll tell you the story. My father was the most controlling, pious Pharisee who every walked the face of the planet," she began, unable to hide the bitterness in her voice. It softened considerably, however, when she said, "and my mother was the gentlest, sweetest human being you could ever hope to meet.

"Over the years, I've often wondered why she ever married him. He imposed a set of rules on her that was tantamount to slavery. She wasn't allowed to associate with certain people in his congregation or have anyone in the house when he wasn't there, not even a repairman. He had to approve all her friends and she could only speak to them when he was present. He insisted she give him every receipt for whatever she bought, even the groceries, and kept a strict record of how much he gave her and made sure everything tallied at the end of the week.

"He went shopping with us and selected all her clothes and mine. We weren't allowed to cut or style our hair or even wear lipstick because, according to him, we were vain enough as it was. He would also beat us if he felt we'd done the simplest infraction. Jon," she added, "you have no idea what living with that man was like," and he nodded in understanding.

"One day, a little before my eighteenth birthday and on my last day of high school, I came home and found her gone. She left me a note she had hidden in my Bible. My father demanded that I do my devotions directly after I came home from school each day, so she knew I would find it there. She told me she just couldn't take it anymore. She said she was leaving and she wanted to take me with her, but she wanted me to continue my education, so she'd arranged with her parents to take me in and left enough money for bus fare to get me from Cincinnati where we were living to Silicon Valley in California. My grandfather was a big vice president at one of the computer firms there.

"Just after she and my father got married, he forbade her from communicating with them as, according to him, they were nothing but 'heathens'. She told me she did call them, however, despite my father's edict, and they knew how difficult things were for both of us. They had begged her time and time again to leave him and moved back in with them, but my mother wouldn't do it. She didn't want to bring any problems with my father to their door. She knew he'd never leave her in peace. She explained in her note that was why she wasn't going to them. She knew it was the first place he'd look, so she was going to try and find a job somewhere far away. She also told me my grandparents were arranging for me to stay with a friend of theirs for a few weeks until things quieted down.

"Anyway, I immediately started packing and had just finished when my father came home. He was much earlier than usual so I was surprised when I heard the door and him bellow my mother's name. Anyway, she had apparently left him a note on the kitchen counter, and after he read it, he called out to me. I left the suitcase I'd packed and went to him. I couldn't get out the door with him there, anyway, so I decided the minute he left I'd leave too.

"When I went into the kitchen, he accused me of knowing her plans and not reporting it to him and he started taking off his belt. I knew what was coming and Jon," she said looking him dead in the eye, "a surge of anger went through me that I'd never experienced before in my life and I've never experienced since. He doubled the belt and came towards me and when he was close enough, I reached behind me and picked up a marble rolling pin my mother kept in a stand on the kitchen counter and I let him have it. I hit him in the face and heard his jawbone snap. He screamed in agony and crumpled to the floor and there was blood everywhere.

"I fled up the stairs, locked the door to my bedroom then I tossed my suitcase and backpack out the window and climbed down the trellis that hung on the side of the house;

almost broke my neck doing it too. Anyway, I made my way to the bus station and from there to my grandparents, and the rest is history. I never saw my father again until I heard he'd been killed. I had to go and identify his body and arrange the funeral.

"As for my mother," she continued, "I never heard from her again. I don't even know if she's alive or dead. I've tried searching for her many times on the internet and even hired a private investigator when I could afford it, but neither he nor I could find any trace of her. One last thing," she said, "and this to me was the icing on the cake regarding my father. I learned some time later that he'd sent a letter to his congregation the same week Mom and I left him saying that his wife had run off with another man and taken me with her. He said the shame of it was more than he could bear, so he was going on the mission field and wouldn't be pastoring the church anymore. How's that for melodrama?" she said with a bark of laughter.

"I owe everything to my grandparents, Jon," she added. "I loved them so much. They took me in, put me through medical school and loved me unconditionally. Once I'd started college and was settled, my grandfather retired, and they moved to L.A. to be near to me. I moved off campus and went to live with them because we'd become so close.

"Three years ago, they died of food poisoning. They were on a trip to the Far East at the time, and I can't tell you how devastated I was. I was alone in the world without a single soul I felt I could call family, and that just made me work and work to compensate for the huge void that was left in my life. I miss them and my mother to this day," she concluded.

"You had a tough childhood," he said, shaking his head.

"Yes, I did," she replied, "but in a lot of ways it's made me stronger," and he nodded.

They had finished their coffee by then and sat facing each other as she told him her story. Now that she was through, Jon rose and picked up the dirty plates and cups and carried them to the sink.

"Let me wash those, Jon," she offered. "I know you must be tired," and she went over and did the dishes.

When she was ready to go back to bed he said, "Can I offer you a little advice before you turn in, Marissa?" he asked.

"Sure," she said.

"Don't allow the experience you had with your earthly father to rob you of the wonderful relationship you can have with your Heavenly One," he said.

"My lack of relationship with God has nothing to do with how I see my father, Jon," she said surprising him. "I loved God once," she continued much to his shock, "my mother's God. I loved Him with all my heart; but the day He allowed her to abandon me was the day I abandoned Him, and I'll never look His way again. Good night," she said and walked away.

Jon had a big smile on his face as he watched her head out of the kitchen, his heart lifting within him. Knowing Marissa believed in God but was simply angry with Him made him feel a whole lot better. Now he knew exactly how to pray, and he was thankful to God for showing him what was at the heart of the matter.

He saw someone emerge from out of the shadows the moment Marissa disappeared into the passage leading into the bedrooms and realized Gabe had been listening in all along.

"Will you quit doing that," Jon said to him in quiet exasperation. "One day I'm going to take you out by mistake if you don't give me some kind of warning you're around."

Gabe only grunted before heading into the kitchen to make a strong carafe of coffee. Jon had nicknamed the brew 'diesel oil' and smiled whenever he remembered Mimi, Gabe's mother-in-law. She used to remark that his brew was so potent, he could stick a spoon in the middle of the cup, and it would stand up straight.

"I'm glad she had her grandparents to go to," Gabe said as he measured the grounds into the coffee filter.

"Me too," Jon replied. "I think I'm going to ask Travis to try and find her mother," he continued. "If Antonelli has a clue about her disappearance, he might think to find her and use her as leverage against Marissa; besides, I'm not sure why, but I feel an urgency in my spirit that we need to locate her. From the first day Marissa told us she'd disappeared, God has put it in my heart to pray for her mother. I can't seem to shake the feeling we need to hurry."

Gabe looked at Jon without surprise. Ever since he had come back from Montana three years before and told Gabe he was now a Christian, he'd seen a dramatic change in his friend. Previously, Jon had a girlfriend for every day of the week. He was constantly at the beach when time permitted or partying and always lived as though if he spent one minute being quiet, he would miss something important.

These days he was much more settled. It wasn't that he didn't enjoy his water sports or being with others, but there had been no more girls or partying until all hours. He had, in fact, started pursuing a Theology degree two years before and spent most of his time doing work related to that. He'd told Gabe once that he hadn't met a girl he could relate to anymore or who had the same values he now had. Gabe also noticed that whenever Jon got those feelings of urgency in his spirit as he called them, he was usually one hundred percent on target. It had wowed Gabe many times, but he didn't really comment on it. He just let it go as a hunch, but deep down he knew it was a gift.

"Gabe, I wanted to ask you something," Jon said hesitantly.

"What's up?" he countered.

"I wanted to know if you'd mind if I made some of the runs into town?" Jon said out of the blue, surprising his friend.

"Sure, no problem," Gabe said, looking at him curiously.

Gabe knew Jon preferred being close to any witness he was protecting; he always had, so he found it strange that he would want to leave his post for the long stretch of time the drive to Chandlers Crossing and back would take. "Do you want to go tomorrow?" he asked, "the things we were expecting yesterday should be in by then."

70

"That would be fine," Jon said, not looking Gabe in the eye.

He thought it might be best if he distanced himself from Marissa until he could sort out his feelings, and that had been the reason for his unusual request. He seldom left any witness in his protection, but his heart felt easier knowing Gabe would be here in his place.

"You okay?" Gabe asked then.

"Yeah," he replied. "I just have something on my mind, and I need a little space to pray and think about it," he added so as not to arouse Gabe's suspicions.

"Anything I can help with?" Gabe asked.

"No, pal, but thanks for asking," Jon replied.

"Okay," Gabe said. "If you need a sounding board, you know where to find me," and Jon nodded, told Gabe goodnight and left him to get some sleep.

Gabe watched him leave and frowned, and as he waited on the coffee he ran through the previous day's events in his mind. Ever since Jon's uncharacteristic anger at Marissa, he'd been concerned for his friend. He knew something was up, so he decided he would keep a close eye on Jon in the coming days. He had been unusually quiet all afternoon, and Gabe hoped that whatever was bothering him would be straightened out soon.

****

Marissa woke up the following morning to find Jon

71

nowhere in sight. She was curious as to where he'd gone but didn't ask. As she sat down to breakfast, however, she heard Gabe tell Anne that he'd gone into town to get the things they'd ordered and would be back that afternoon. When they'd eaten, Marissa offered to do the dishes then went out on the patio with her knitting. As her fingers worked, she realized she missed Jon. He'd been with her constantly over the nearly six weeks they'd been on the mountain and had acted as a buffer between herself and the others. It wasn't that Gabe or Anne were difficult to be around, but they weren't as social or personable as Jon.

She continued to knit and although she paid attention to her work, she allowed her mind to dwell on him. He had the most wonderful blue eyes and a pleasing smile that just about lit up his entire face. He had a delightful sense of humor too that had her and Anne laughing from time to time, but he also had a serious side and exhibited a confident, self-assured and protective attitude that made her feel safe and secure.

She paused her work and looked out over the vast display of mountains before her, and it was in that moment she realized she was attracted to him; not only attracted to him, but she was falling head over heels for him. He was the first person she thought of when she opened her eyes in the mornings and he was still in her thoughts each night just before she went to bed. One would think the circumstances which had brought them together would be first and foremost in her mind; and yes, it was always there, but she spent more and more of her time these days thinking about her protector and not so much about what he was protecting her from. That was why she knew her attraction wasn't a passing thing. He was exactly the kind of man she knew in her heart she wanted as a husband, one she could trust and who could be her confidante, lover and friend.

She reigned in her thoughts and put on the brakes, admonishing herself for going overboard and telling herself she needed a reality check. She reasoned that her feelings were too strong after only knowing Jon for six weeks and was probably due to the fact that he was her temporary guardian and nothing more. There was no hope for a relationship between them anyway, so it was best she put him out of her thoughts and look elsewhere for a mate.

She had no idea what her future held or if she would even be able to resume her life, so she'd best keep romance on the back burner for now. She looked back down at her knitting then and continued with the complicated stitch pattern she was working on, determined to put her thoughts aside. As she sat there, however, she pondered her new discovery in her heart and had a hard time dismissing Jon from her mind.

Towards the afternoon he returned, and she was not only glad to see him, but was pleased he'd been able to get the things she'd asked for. She had actually given the list to Gabe the morning before expecting he would be making the run as usual. She had told Jon she wanted to do something outdoors, so she'd asked Gabe to get her some seeds and bulbs she could plant for the homeowners. It would be nice to leave something like that as a thank you, and she vowed to start the following morning.

CHAPTER 6

Three more weeks passed, but they were still unable to get a location on Antonelli. He had gone deep underground since Russo's death, and all attempts to locate him had been unsuccessful. His men were also ramping up their efforts to find Marissa and news on the street was that he had upped his original finder's fee to two hundred and fifty-thousand-dollars. The reward would be given to anyone who could give him a location on her or bring him her body. Jon and Gabe kept that information between themselves and Anne, but they were even more vigilant in their care of her.

The 'kill book', it was discovered, held a treasure trove of information. Russo had kept meticulous records with names, dates, times and the reason for each execution. Murders that had gone unsolved for over twenty years were finally explained and the evidence against Antonelli was stacked. Marissa was the key to the case, however, as they needed the trail of evidence from Russo to her with regard to the book. The surveillance tape and her signed statement wouldn't be enough. She would have to testify about her conversation with the enforcer. It was the only way to make the charges stick.

With Anne's help, Marissa did her gardening around the fountain that occupied the center of the circular driveway, and now she was busy guiding Anne through the blanket for her grandchild. A friendship had developed between them in recent weeks, and they enjoyed spending time together on the project. Marissa kept an eye on her progress while she worked on socks and knit caps for the men for next winter. She intended to make each of them warm scarves to go along with the other pieces too, that is if she was with them that long. By the looks of it, she felt she might be.

The week before, she had given the afghan to Anne, thanking her as she did so for looking after her, especially when her side had been healing. Anne had been absolutely delighted with the gift, and throwing protocol to the wind, she gave Marissa a heartfelt hug and told her it had been a pleasure protecting her. She said she'd gotten all kinds on her protection details and, as agents, they were instructed to keep a professional distance from their witnesses, but Marissa's kindness, cooperation and their close proximity over the weeks made that impossible.

She also told Marissa she had probably been the least difficult witness they'd ever had, and Jon and even Gabe, who had seen the exchange, had to agree. They knew she was concerned and fearful of the future, she'd confided that much to Jon, but she'd exhibited great patience in light of the length of time she'd been in their custody and had shown tremendous fortitude despite the uncertainty.

Jon, meanwhile, was spending as little time with her as possible. He found every excuse to avoid her company but being in such close confines didn't make it easy. He caught her looking at him a few times, almost as if she was wondering what she'd done wrong, and he was sorry he couldn't explain.

He knew with certainty he had fallen in love with her, and the magnitude of his feelings left him stunned. He just couldn't understand how it had happened so quickly. He'd had many women in his life before he gave his heart to the

Lord, so many in fact that it shamed him. Some of them he knew only briefly and some even longer than he'd known Marissa; but none of them, not one had done to his heart what Marissa had.

He'd taken to calling her Sparky when he had her in his thoughts, which was almost a constant thing, because every time he looked at her, she ignited a fire in him he couldn't put out, no matter how hard he tried. He prayed daily for the Lord to remove the feelings he had for her, but God had chosen not to, and he just couldn't understand why. She was not a practicing Christian and very likely would have to be put into permanent witness protection after Antonelli's trial, so Jon just didn't see them having any future together.

****

One morning, just as they were entering their third month on Jacob's Mountain, Jon awoke with a sore throat and tightness in his chest and knew he'd picked up a bug. His head and body also ached, leaving him miserable and out of sorts. He hated being sick. It was five o'clock in the morning and it had been his night off, but he was feeling so lousy he decided to get himself a cup of coffee and take a couple of pain pills. He was cold and shivering when he got out of bed, so he slipped on a long-sleeved fleece pullover to cover his naked chest and left his room.

Gabe was just coming in through the front door after his recon of the grounds when he saw Jon heading into the kitchen.

"You're up early," he said, as he joined him at the island.

"Yeah," Jon replied hoarsely. "I'm as sick as a dog."

"It's all that putridly weak coffee you drink," Gabe said matter of fact. "When last have you seen me sick?" he asked.

"Practically never," Jon said. "The germs take one look at all that battery acid traveling through your pipes and high tail it outta there," he added in an attempt at humor. He poured some of Gabe's brew into a cup, added hot water from the tap, and fixed it to his liking.

Gabe then saw him shake the pain pills into his palm, but he stopped him from taking them. "Sit and let me make you some breakfast before you swallow those," he advised, even as he went into the fridge and brought out some eggs. "It's best you don't take them on an empty stomach."

Jon had the food Gabe prepared, took the pills and went back to bed, but when he woke three hours later, he felt even worse. He had his shower and went out to join the others who were just finishing breakfast.

"You look like roadkill," Anne commented dryly as she carried her plate over to the sink and began doing the dishes.

"I feel like it," Jon replied, going over and pouring himself a cup of coffee. "I have a cold," he added, barely able to talk because his throat was so raw.

Marissa came over to him and laid her hand on his cheek, startling him as she did so because his back was turned, and he hadn't seen her coming. "You're running a fever," she said. "Is your throat sore?" she asked.

"Yes," he replied, moving away from her and going to sit on a stool at the island. Even in his sick state her touch had affected him.

77

"Is your chest tight?" she asked, following him over to where he sat.

"Yes," he said.

"Headache and body ache?" she asked, naturally slipping into her role as a medical professional.

"Yes," Jon answered.

"Let me take a look at you," she said, and Jon immediately came off the stool and backed away.

"I'll be okay," he said. "I don't like being fussed over."

"I'm not fussing over you," she replied reasonably. "Maybe I can help you."

"If I need you, I'll call," Jon said, before he left the room and went out on the patio.

Gabe, Anne and Marissa all looked at him in surprise. Jon was always so mild-mannered that it was unusual for him to be so abrupt.

"He must really be feeling lousy," Anne commented as she finished the dishes and dried her hands on the towel.

Marissa nodded, but Gabe didn't respond. He'd noticed Jon was making a concerted effort to avoid being around Marissa. He'd taken to spending more and more time on his online classes for his degree, using that as an excuse to work at the table in the formal dining room and away from the kitchen, family room and terrace which were the hubs of the house. A thought had begun forming in Gabe's mind in

78

recent days, and Jon's reaction just now began to cement his musings even further, causing him to frown at the implications. If his suspicions were correct, Jon had a whole lot more on his mind than a simple cold, and he promised himself to keep an even closer eye on his best friend and on their witness.

****

Two nights later, Gabe could hear Jon coughing in his bedroom and so could everyone else in the house. The cough was heavy, and Gabe didn't like how it sounded at all. His friend had adamantly refused Marissa's repeated offers of help, but Gabe knew he needed to see a doctor. He would have told him to go down to Mary and have her look at him, but he knew she and the Colonel had gone to Chandlers Crossing for a few days to do their big monthly shopping and attend to some appointments they had there.

He was just thinking of carrying some water in to his friend when Marissa came into the family room and Anne joined them from the kitchen.

"Gabe," Marissa said, "I don't like the sound of Jon's cough at all," and Anne nodded her agreement.

"I've never seen him so sick," Anne said, with a worried expression.

"Would you please see if you can get him to let me examine him?" Marissa asked, concerned. "If he doesn't get some antibiotics and proper medical attention soon, that cough could turn into pneumonia."

"I'll go talk to him," Gabe said. "Give me a few minutes

and I'll let you know what he says," he added, and she nodded as he left the room.

Gabe knocked on Jon's door and asked if he could come in. When he didn't answer, Gabe took the initiative, entered the room and saw Jon sitting on the side of the bed with his head in his hands.

"You look like death warmed over, Peeps," he said without preamble, "and that cough needs some serious attention." Jon only nodded but said nothing. "Marissa wants to have a look at you," he stated, "and Anne and I want her to have a look at you too. Would you please stop being stubborn and give her a chance to examine you?"

Jon looked up at him and knew he couldn't hold out any longer. He felt awful and the cough was almost a constant thing.

"Okay," he said weakly, his voice barely above a whisper as the infection had given him laryngitis. "I guess it's my only option."

Feeling relieved, Gabe went back into the family room and told Marissa Jon had agreed, so she went to her room for her stethoscope which was still in her handbag from that fateful trip to the Emergency Room. She went into Jon's room with Gabe and saw him sitting on the side of the bed, so she went over to him, and the first thing she did was put her hand to his brow.

"He's burning up," she said to Gabe, as she proceeded to listen to his chest, unconsciously putting her hand on his bare shoulder as she did so and telling him to take a deep breath. Her request resulted in a round of coughing and when she put the stethoscope on his back and he coughed again, she frowned. "You're at the beginning stages of pneumonia, Jon," she said to him, then turning to Gabe she added, "he needs to get a course of strong antibiotics right away and some prescription medication for his cough and other symptoms. Can you arrange it if I tell you what to get?"

"That's no problem," Gabe said. "Just give me the name of the drugs he needs and the dosage, and I can have them here by mid-afternoon tomorrow."

He knew the Colonel and Mary would be returning then and would be more than happy to pick up what was needed at the pharmacy. Mary had told him once that she and her doctor were very good friends, and he usually gave her whatever she needed to treat anyone she was taking care of. She was the closest thing to medical aid the residents of Refuge and the surrounding area had, so on rare occasions when someone was sick and couldn't get to Chandlers Crossing, they would call and ask her to come down and see them.

Gabe had gotten to know the Jamisons quite well. Whenever he was going into Chandlers Crossing, he usually passed by to see if the older couple needed anything. On his return, he would stop for a few minutes to drop off their items and talk. It was very difficult for him to develop any sort of relationship with people these days, but the Colonel and Mary had been the rare exception.

"Good," Marissa said. "Meanwhile, Jon, I want you to stay in bed. You're in no condition to be out and about." He was only too happy to comply as he lay back down and swung his feet up from the floor. He was as weak as a kitten anyway and even the thought of having to get up was too much for him. "Gabe would you get a shirt for him, please?" she asked, "He needs to stay warm," and Gabe went over to the chest of drawers where he searched around until he found a gray long-sleeved t-shirt. He brought it over and Jon put it on. "That's better," Marissa said. "Could you also hunt up some extra pillows for me?" she asked. "I want to see if I can elevate him a bit, and if you don't mind, please ask Anne to bring in some pills and a glass of water to help with the aches and fever," and he nodded and left the room.

When he had gone, Marissa sat on the side of the bed facing her patient.

"You're so stubborn," she said looking at him. He just stared back and said nothing. "Why wouldn't you let me look at you? You wouldn't be in this sorry state if you'd given me a chance to examine you and prescribe something earlier."

"It wouldn't be appropriate," he whispered hoarsely. "You're my witness."

"Jon," she said reasonably, "we're in the middle of nowhere. If circumstances were different and you could see another doctor then I'd understand, but we're stuck here, and this is the least I can do after all you guys are doing for me. I'm happy I can do something to help," and he nodded in understanding.

Just then Anne came in with the pills and Gabe came in behind her with the pillows. Marissa got up from the bed, told Jon to sit up then put the extra pillows behind him. When she was finished, he lay back and felt much more comfortable. She gave him the pills to take then told him she would check on him in a little while before leaving the room with Anne.

Jon followed her out with his eyes then closed them and felt the tension leave his body on a sigh. She had wreaked havoc with his flesh while she'd examined him, even as he tried to fight his feelings in his heart. He loved her. The attraction he'd first felt whenever he looked at her had settled into a steady, unyielding throb, and he struggled daily to hide what he was feeling.

He was aware of just about everything she said and did, and he couldn't sleep for stretches of time at night because he was in such turmoil over the situation. The one good thing was that no one knew of his dilemma, only he and God knew what was going on, and he clung fiercely to his Heavenly Father. Jon wanted more than anything to be in God's will in everything he did; therefore, he vowed to continue to fight his feelings so he wouldn't compromise his relationship with the Lord.

Gabe silently watched Jon as he interacted with Marissa, his friend's every gesture confirming to him what he'd already begun to suspect. He knew Jon was fighting his feelings, and that was probably why he'd taken so long before allowing Marissa to examine him. He left the room a few minutes after the ladies, collected the prescription information which Marissa had written out for him, then made his way through the front door and onto the porch to place his call to the Colonel and Mary, his expression troubled. He didn't know what would happen over the coming weeks, but one thing was clear, he and Jon were traveling in uncharted territory and the last thing they needed was to run into the storm he saw brewing.

CHAPTER 7

It took Jon two full weeks to recover, but by the beginning of the third he was back to his usual self with only a slight residual cough as a reminder of his recent illness. He had asked Mary when she returned from Chandler's Crossing with the Colonel, if she would be kind enough to take over his care, and she had willingly agreed. He drove himself the short distance to her morning and evening so she could listen to his chest, and Gabe could see the wisdom in his actions. Marissa was curious as to where he went twice a day but didn't ask. She was just glad he was doing better and accepted the fact that he didn't need her help after the first few days. She didn't know he was being treated by someone else, she just assumed he was keeping his distance and observing the appropriate boundaries between agent and witness.

She had also become quiet in the days following her examination and care of him. Her feelings had blossomed into love for her protector and she spent her time knitting and thinking about him and about their relationship or rather the lack thereof. She was under no illusions that her growing infatuation was foolhardy. She didn't see it leading to anything but heartache for her; even so, Jon was constantly in her thoughts and her feelings for him deepened with every passing day.

She had noticed that, for quite some time, he had been keeping her at arm's length, even before he'd gotten sick, and she wondered if he had somehow perceived that she had fallen for him. It would explain his actions of late, and she was embarrassed to know he could read her so well. She had also noticed Gabe watching her more intently than usual when he thought she wasn't aware of it, and she made sure to tread carefully around both men, not wanting to give either of them fuel for what she believed they may already suspect.

****

The first Friday night in July, Anne sat out in the family room reading. It was close to three in the morning and she was feeling tired. This protection detail had been a long one with no end in sight, but she had to admit it was one of her better assignments. The location was beautiful, and their witness gave absolutely no trouble. She closed the novel and rubbed her eyes, glad that Gabe would relieve her in a little less than an hour.

Her thoughts drifted then to her daughter Leann and her expected baby and Anne couldn't contain her excitement at becoming a grandmother. Her daughter and son-in-law Derek, who was in the navy, had gotten married two years before and she had to admit she liked Leann's choice for a mate. He was polite and helpful and called her Momma, just as Leann did. She in turn treated him like the son she'd never had, and they got along very well.

She got up from the couch, stretched and decided to pour herself one last cup of coffee before washing out the container for Gabe to use, so she made her way into the kitchen with her empty cup. She had just placed it on the counter and was reaching for the carafe when she heard a noise outside. It startled her, and she quieted her movements to listen, thinking it was nothing. It came again, however, and her adrenaline kicked. She hurried into the family room and turned off the lights, pulled her weapon from its ankle holster where she preferred to carry it, then went into the living room and over to the front door. It had a peephole which gave a wide, panoramic view of outside, but she didn't see anything. The noise came again somewhere off to her right, just outside of her line of sight, and she was certain she heard footfalls on the porch. She waited a few moments, heard them recede and swiftly went into action.

She ran quickly and quietly through to the bedrooms and knocked softly on Gabe's door. He answered within a few seconds and Anne could see he was already dressed. Quite often he would come out and relieve her early, so she wasn't surprised.

"What's wrong?" he asked without preamble.

"I think we have company," she said. Gabe immediately came out into the passage.

"Go back out front," he instructed. "I'll wake Jon."

Anne went back into the living room while Gabe went over and knocked on Jon's door. When there was no answer, he knocked again, and when his friend finally opened up, it was clear from his rumpled appearance that Gabe had roused him from a deep sleep.

"What's wrong?" Jon asked, using the exact words Gabe had used to Anne.

"We may have trouble," Gabe said.

"I'll be there in a second," Jon said, instantly alert, and turned back into his room while Gabe hurried out to the living room.

Jon pulled on a t-shirt, took his weapon from his shoulder holster, then slipped on his shoes and quickly went out to the living room. He met Gabe and Anne over by the front door just as the noise came again. Jon looked out the peephole but couldn't see anything.

"I can't see a thing out there," he whispered to Gabe. "I'm going to slip through the service door in the garage and have a look." There was a door located at the side of the three-car garage to outside, and they used it all the time.

"Let me go," Gabe said. "I'm quieter than you."

Jon acknowledged the truth of his friend's words. When they were with the Green Berets, Gabe was always given assignments where stealth was of the utmost importance.

"Okay," Jon said. "I'll cover the front and stick close to Marissa." He knew one of them had to be their witness's last line of defense. "Anne, go wake her and tell her to lock herself in, then go with Gabe as back-up."

Their plan made, Gabe went through the family room and out the door leading to the laundry and garage while Anne hurried out of the living room and down the passage to Marissa's bedroom. She knocked then went in.

Marissa was startled when Anne shook her awake. "What's wrong?" she asked sitting up. She was so accustomed to being roused from bed at all hours that she was alert the minute she opened her eyes.

"We may have visitors," Anne said quickly. "We need

87

you to stay here and lock your door, and don't come out until one of us comes for you, okay?"

Marissa nodded. Her heart began racing in panic, and she was alarmed by the suddenness of what was happening. As she was about to voice her concern and ask more questions, however, Anne turned and quickly went out the door. Terror gripped Marissa and she was afraid to be alone, so despite what she'd been told, she left her room and made her way quietly into the living room. Jon was by the front door with his weapon in his hand and was startled when he saw her enter out of the corner of his eye.

"Didn't Anne tell you to lock your door and stay put?" he asked concerned, leaving the door and meeting her in the center of the living room.

"Yes, but I want to know what's happening," she said, and he could see she was terrified.

"Marissa," he said in a firm but understanding tone. "I need you to lock yourself in your room now and don't come out again or let anyone in. I'll come for you when its safe."

"Okay, but….," she said, he didn't give her a chance to finish.

"I know you're scared, but I can't talk to you right now," he said hastily, then seeing her uncertainty and vulnerability he tried to reassure her. "Don't worry, okay? We won't let anything happen to you." She nodded, and he walked her to the entrance of the passage then watched as she went down to her bedroom and closed the door, before he went back to the front door to resume his vigil.

Gabe waited for Anne, and as soon as she came, he cracked the door and looked out into the darkness with his semi-automatic pistol in his hand. He paused to listen, but the place had suddenly gone quiet. The area further out from the house was almost pitch black as there was only a quarter moon, but he was still able to see his immediate surroundings from the light coming from the large solar powered fixtures located strategically around the house.

He turned to Anne and whispered, "Go cut the security lights for me," and she went quickly back into the laundry to do as he asked.

When she returned, Gabe bent low and slipped into the darkness, moving quietly along the side of the house. There was a wide cobblestone pathway against the outside wall, and he made sure to stick to it with his soft rubber-sole shoes making no noise. He went around to the front and pass the three large garage doors then paused to listen again. The place was still quiet, so he moved up the stairs at the side of the porch and was by the front door within a few seconds. Jon had obviously seen him in the dim light, because he opened the door a few inches.

"Anything?" he asked, his voice at barely a whisper.

Gabe shook his head and was about to continue to the other side when they heard a crash come from the area around the utility shed which was located about fifteen feet out from the door where he had left Anne. He took off in that direction but stopped as he reached the corner by the garage and peeped around it.

The place was very dark, and the noise had stopped, so he bent low again and made his way back to the door. It was open a crack and Anne was there, but when Gabe asked her softly if she'd seen anything, she shook her head and whispered no. Just then they heard what sounded like a deep "woof", heavy breathing and more noise, before they saw a large bear saunter from behind the utility shed in the dim light and begin making his way towards them.

Gabe slipped inside, closed and locked the door and heard Anne release a sigh.

"Thank goodness it wasn't anything more serious," she said as they holstered their weapons and made their way back into the house.

"What was it?" Jon asked when he saw them enter and Gabe turn on the lights.

"A bear," Gabe said, and the relief in the three of them was palpable. "I just left him to do his foraging and came back inside."

"Thank You, God!" Jon said to his Heavenly Father with heartfelt gratitude. He'd been praying up a storm and was glad it was nothing more than an animal. "I'll go tell Marissa everything's okay," he said and went down the passage while Gabe and Anne went into the kitchen.

"Marissa," he said, and she opened the door immediately. "Everything's okay," he said. "It was a bear." He saw her melt with relief then to his shock, she fell into his arms, trembling from head to foot.

He held her for a few moments, understanding that she had been truly frightened and needed to be comforted. When he pulled away and stepped back, she looked at him

90

and said, "Thank you, Jon. Thank you, Gabe and Anne so much."

"That's why we're here," he said soothingly. "Try and get some sleep."

"I don't think I'll be able to sleep again tonight," she said with a wan smile and he smiled back.

"Do a little knitting or reading," he suggested. "It will help you to relax then maybe you can get some shut eye."

"I will," she said. "Thanks again," and he stepped back even further so she could close the door.

He tried to put the tender moment out of his mind as he made his way to the kitchen, but he knew it would come back to haunt him later. She had felt so good in his arms and he'd wanted her to remain there forever. He joined the others, and they spent a few minutes winding down while rehashing the incident, but in short order Anne told them with a grin that she could 'barely' keep her eyes open, so she was heading off to bed. Jon groaned at the pun while Gabe just gave her a pained look and shook his head. She gave a laugh, told them goodnight and headed to her room.

Jon was wide awake, so he talked with Gabe who was busy putting on the carafe with his strong coffee to brew. Eventually, Jon decided to head to his room too, but just as he was about to tell Gabe he was going back to try and get some sleep, his friend asked him to come into the family room so they could talk. The request was unusual for Gabe, so Jon followed him there and sat down in an armchair close to where Gabe usually set himself up during his watch.

"Want to tell me what's going on with you and Marissa?" Gabe blindsided him by asking quietly, and Jon was so floored he just stared at him before his shoulders slumped in defeat.

"How long have you known?" Jon asked, unable to believe that Gabe had picked up on what he'd been trying so hard to hide.

"A while now," Gabe replied.

"Is it obvious?" Jon asked in apprehension. "Do you think Anne knows?"

"I don't think so," Gabe said. "It's probably not obvious to her, but I know you too well," he added, and Jon nodded.

He leaned forward and, placing his elbows on his knees, he rested his chin on his steepled fingers, deciding to be honest with his best friend. "I don't think anything's going on with Marissa where I'm concerned," he said, "but I'm in love with her, pal," he declared, finally admitting what he had been concealing. "You know my history with women, Gabe," he continued. "I've had more girlfriends, or should I say acquaintances, than I can count. I don't even remember the names of half of them, and that's to my shame; but this," he said with a shake of his head, "this is a first for me. I'm so in love with her I can't think straight. All the others were just casual relationships, that's how I know this is the real deal. I've never felt this way about any woman before."

Gabe nodded in understanding. "You need to tread carefully, Peeps," he warned him. "This is new territory for you and me. Nothing like this has ever happened on a case

92

before."

Jon ran his fingers through his hair in obvious distress. "I know," he acknowledged. "I've been praying about it ever since I figured out what was happening, and I'm hoping to be able to get her out of my system, but I don't know, Ice. My feelings are pretty strong."

Gabe thought about Jon's earlier comment that nothing was going on with Marissa regarding him and knew his friend was mistaken. She was as ga ga over him as he appeared to be over her. The way she looked at him was clear evidence of that, but he didn't mention it to Jon. He was distressed enough over the situation as it was, and Gabe didn't want to burden him further.

"I've noticed you've been distant with her lately," Gabe said. "I assume that's why?"

"Yes," Jon answered. "I've been trying to spend as little time with her as possible."

"Tell you what," Gabe said, "let me do most of the interaction with her from now on, and you make most of the trips to town. That way we can limit your contact with her even further until this is over. What do you think?"

"I think that's a great idea," Jon said readily. "I just need to keep my distance until I can work this thing out." In a way he was relieved Gabe knew. He would at least have someone to talk to who could help him with the situation.

They sat quietly for a few moments before Jon decided to broach a subject with Gabe he almost never did. "Since we're sharing honestly, pal," he said, "can you tell me how you're doing, and I don't want any pat answers like you're fine. Try to tell me the deep truth from your gut for once."

Gabe was quiet for a long time, so long in fact that Jon thought he wasn't going to respond. "To this day I miss her, Jon," he finally said with his head down. "Gina lit up my entire world. In many ways she was my entire world."

"I know, pal," Jon said with compassion.

"You remember Charlie Gooding, don't you?" Gabe asked then out of the blue.

"Sure I remember Charlie," Jon replied. "He always used to lament when it was time to go home because he couldn't stand his wife and the ruckus with their six children," Jon smiled. "What was it he used to call her again?"

"Nag-nag," Gabe said, running the two words together quickly as their co-worker used to.

"That's right," Jon said. "What about him?" he asked curiously, not sure where Gabe was going.

"I used to feel sorry for him," Gabe admitted. "I was always so on fire to get home to my wife, while he would ask for extra assignments just to stay away from his."

"Yeah," Jon said, "I remember. I can't tell you how happy I was to hear that Lauren led Gina to Jesus the night before it happened, Gabe," he continued, referring to Travis' sister, Lauren McAllister. "It didn't mean that much to me at the time because I wasn't a believer then, but now I'm so glad she's with the Lord."

"We were up until the wee hours talking about it," Gabe said quietly. "I can still see her as she was that night," he continued, in quiet reflection, much to Jon's surprise. Gabe rarely spoke about his precious wife, and Jon was happy that he was finally opening up about her. "Her whole face was shining with excitement, and there was a peace about her that was contagious. It's not that she was ever restless," he explained, "but this peace was different."

"I know how she felt," Jon said, recalling when he had given his life to the Lord. "There's nothing like that peace, Ice, I can tell you. I've been praying for you a long time now, pal," he continued. "Don't you think it's time you forgive yourself? You know Gina would never want you to blame yourself as you've been doing all this time. Tell me something," he went on to say, taking a risk to voice his thoughts, "if the roles had been reversed, and she'd been the one working at the Bureau and that car bomb had killed you instead of her, would you want her to blame herself the way you've been doing?"

"No," Gabe said immediately, "No, I wouldn't. Trouble is, I don't think I know how to live any other way anymore. Only work and my friendship with you and Travis have gotten me through so far, Peeps," he added. "I can't thank you guys enough for sticking with me. I know sometimes I'm hard to deal with and understand," he continued, "but you've both been good to me and I appreciate it."

"We've been through a lot together, buddy," Jon said. "I'm not giving up on you, and I know Travis isn't going to either. Ever think about giving Jesus a try?" he asked, truly wanting to talk to his friend about his faith.

"Once or twice," Gabe admitted, "but I'm just not ready.

You better get some sleep if you're going to make the run into town later this morning," he added. "I'm sorry the stuff we ordered didn't come in yesterday."

"Sounds like a plan," Jon said rising from his seat, knowing that Gabe was done talking. "See you in a few hours."

He left his friend and headed for bed, but Jon felt good about their conversation. Gabe had said more words about Gina in the last few minutes than he had in the years since her death, and Jon hoped this small beginning would lead to more conversations of its kind. Gabe had locked up his feelings tighter than a drum and that was part of the problem. Jon knew for certain that if he could get him to turn to his Savior, then Gabe would truly be able to heal and find peace, and he determined to continue praying for his friend.

Marissa hurried back to her room the second she heard the men coming to the end of their conversation. She'd come to get a glass of water and was just about to enter the kitchen when she heard Jon ask Gabe how he was doing, and she had paused to listen. She knew it was wrong, but she was curious to know what had happened to make this man so morose and cold. When she realized that a car bomb had killed his wife, her fingers had gone to her mouth in shock and she'd had to stifle a gasp.

She lay in bed now thinking about Gabe and she felt tears running down her cheeks. To lose a loved one in such a horrible way would traumatize just about anyone. She had always talked about him to herself in derogatory terms, calling him Mister Ice or Agent Freeze, not realizing that his sober and standoffish attitude was born out of a deep sorrow he was unable to overcome.

As she lay there, she acknowledged that she'd learned a valuable lesson. Just because you didn't understand someone didn't give you the right to judge them. You could never tell what was happening in their life or what they were going through. She dried her tears and turned over to try and sleep, vowing as she did so that she would show Gabe a little more kindness in the future. She wouldn't do it in an obvious way that would make him suspect she knew, but just enough to take the sting out of anything she might say.

CHAPTER 8

Jon shut down his laptop after finishing his college assignment and prepared to hand the watch over to Gabe. It was three forty-five in the morning and by this time they had been at Jacob's Mountain for just two weeks shy of five months. In the weeks following the bear's visit, he kept remembering how good it felt to have Marissa in his arms, and it heated him up so badly, he had to firmly put the moment from his mind and turn his thoughts in another direction. He also made sure to keep his distance from her and couldn't understand why God hadn't answered his prayers and cool his ardor towards her.

He sighed and packed up his things, went into the kitchen and washed out his cup as well as the carafe for Gabe, then went back into the family room to read. Within a few minutes, Gabe arrived and bid him good morning before he went over to the counter to begin making his coffee. Jon roused himself and they had a brief conversation before he told Gabe goodnight and made his way to his room. He was tired and was glad he didn't have to get up until much later. He usually woke around ten thirty after taking the first watch which had always been his preference. Gabe liked the second, so on the rare occasion they worked together, they always got the time they wanted.

Jon went into his room and closed the door, stripping off his holster and t-shirt as he did so. He placed the holster on the roomy night table beside the bed, then went into the bathroom and finished disrobing, tossing the things that needed laundering in the dirty clothes hamper. He brushed his teeth, rinsed and dried his mouth then pulled on the pair of long drawstring knit pants he usually slept in. He came out of the bathroom, stretching his arms above his head as he did so, looked up and stopped short. Marissa was standing just inside the closed bedroom door dressed in short knit shorts and a tank top that left nothing to the imagination.

He lowered his arms slowly and swallowed. "Is there something you want, Marissa?" he asked quietly, stepping fully into the room and making his way over to where she stood, stopping with about five feet of space between them.

"Yes," she said softly, coming towards him, "actually there is."

"Gabe's in the family room," he said, backing up even as she advanced. "If you need something, you can check with him."

Very soon he found himself up against the bed with nowhere to go, so he stood there and watched as she came and stopped right in front of him.

"I don't need to see Gabe," she said, running her eyes over his body and he felt heat rush through him.

"Err, you shouldn't be in here alone with me you know," he said.

"Well if we aren't alone," she stated boldly, "how am I supposed to make love to you."

Jon just stared at her totally floored. He couldn't find one word to utter if his life depended on it.

"Marissa, you need to leave," he said firmly when he finally found his voice, but at that moment she reached out and placed her palms flat on his stomach before sliding them up his naked chest and around his neck.

Jon momentarily closed his eyes at the ecstasy her touch brought to life in him and he felt himself sinking fast. He held onto her hands and began to pull them from around his neck, but she held them firmly in place and asked provocatively, "Do you want me as much as I want you Jon?" and he swallowed again. "Aren't you interested in having a little of this?" and she took her tongue and ran it from one corner of his closed mouth to the other in such a blatant pass that it undid his resolve and he lost the battle that had been raging within him for weeks.

He reacted without thinking and pulled her fully into his arms, kissing her with such a passionate invasion that Marissa felt she'd been branded. She began kissing him back with the same wild abandon that he was kissing her, and many moments passed as they were totally consumed by their heated exchange.

Eventually they came up for air, and when he pulled his lips away, he trailed kisses down her neck and across her shoulders. "You're so sweet," he said softly as he roamed, then he paused and looked into her eyes. "I love you, Marissa," he declared. "I love you and I've wanted you for so long." He kissed her again and when he was through, he made his way back to her neck, but this time his lips continued down to her décolleté, setting her ablaze with longing.

"I love you too," she whispered. "Oh, Jon, I love you so much. Please make love to me. I want to know every part of you and for you to have every part of me."

What she said inflamed his senses so completely that he lifted her into his arms without hesitation and carried her to the bed. Every instinct of his flesh had taken over, causing him to shove his Christianity aside as it dominated his thinking, his body and his passion. He lay her down, got in beside her and pulled her on top of him. She ran her hands up into his hair then claimed his lips in another fiery onslaught that drove Jon's senses wild, causing him to ignore the warning bells going off in his head. He ran his hands down her body and it heated him even more. She was so soft and warm and willing, and he hadn't been intimate with a woman in over three years, much less one he loved as much as he loved her.

He rolled her over until he was on top of her and kissed her lips again, his brain foggy with the passion and desire their fiery encounter had stirred in him.

Jon heard the familiar Voice of his Heavenly Father telling him to stop, but he totally ignored Him. "She's your witness," God came again, but he was beyond caring. Marissa began softly telling him what she wanted, and it inflamed him even further so he paused in his love making and eased himself up slightly, so he could help her pull off her top. At that moment he heard God's loud command in his spirit, "Get up, Jon! Flee right now!"

Jon looked at Marissa and realized with sudden clarity what he was doing, his Heavenly Father' urgent directive bringing him to his senses as nothing else could. He knew if he stayed he would be lost, so obeying God immediately, he rolled off Marissa, got to his feet and ran out the door. He hurried through the living and family room, past a startled

Gabe and, pushing the drapes aside, he opened the sliding glass door and rushed out onto the patio, not stopping until he was at the stone fence. It was piercingly cold, and the wind that had been present since the evening before buffeted his heated body and began cooling off his ardor.

Gabe was just getting into the meat of his book when he heard the hurried footsteps coming from the direction of the living room. He quickly reached for his pistol which was on the table beside him, and had just gotten it in his hand, when he saw Jon rush past him and make his way out onto the patio without a word.

"What the....?" Gabe left the question hanging and rose quickly to his feet. "What's going on?" he asked himself. He went to the patio door to see what was wrong, saw Jon standing out by the fence and knew instinctively this was nothing to do with the job, but something to do directly with his friend.

Instead of heading outside, however, Gabe put his gun into his shoulder holster and went towards the front door to retrieve his jacket and Jon's from the coat closet. It was absolutely frigid outside. It had been unseasonably cold and windy for the last two days, and Gabe knew it wasn't wise for Jon to be outdoors in only a pair of knit pants. He had just passed the entrance to the passage leading to the bedrooms when he heard soft footfalls, so he stopped and slipped into the shadows. Just as he'd concealed himself, he saw Marissa pop her head cautiously out of Jon's bedroom, look right and left to make sure no one else was present then make her way silently to her own room, going in and closing the door behind her.

"That little....," he clamped down on the unflattering

remark that sprang to his lips, instantly knowing what had happened to Jon. With a shake of his head, he reached into the closet for the two jackets, put his on and made his way outside.

He saw Jon with his hands stretched out in front of him, his palms resting on the fence, his head hanging down between them.

He made a slight noise to let him know he was behind him then spoke, "Here, Peeps," he said, touching his shoulder to get his attention. "Put this on." Jon roused himself slowly and straightening up, he took the jacket from Gabe and slipped into it. "You okay?" Gabe asked him concerned.

Jon didn't answer. He simply pulled up the zip and looked out into the darkness.

"What was she doing in your room?" Gabe asked, startling his friend and causing him to turn and face him. "Did you arrange to meet her there or did she come on her own?"

Gabe already knew the answer because he knew this man so well, but he needed to hear him say it.

"She came on her own," Jon said in a dull voice. "You know you don't have to ask me that Gabe."

"I know," he replied. "The bigger question is, how far did it go?"

"I was only out of your sight for ten minutes," Jon said defensively, "so it didn't go very far. She came in when I

103

was in the bathroom. I only saw her a few minutes before you saw me."

Gabe nodded. "Did anything inappropriate happen in those few minutes?" he asked next.

Jon ran his hand through his hair then down to grasp the nape of his neck, before looking up at the starlit sky. "She made a pass at me that was so blatant, Gabe, I lost it," he confessed. "It was like dangling a carrot to a starving man, believe me when I tell you. I kissed her within an inch of her life and before I knew it, I had her in the bed. I was just about to make love to her when God brought me to my senses, and I ran out the door. That's when you saw me." He hung his head in shame. "I can't do this anymore," he continued. "This whole thing has been torturing me for weeks on end, and now I've compromised not only my job but my faith. I'm going to call Travis later this morning and ask him to put you in charge and send in another agent," he said, "I'll have no choice but to resign. What I did was inexcusable."

It pained Gabe to hear the despair in Jon's voice. His friend was a fine man and a superb agent. His record was exemplary and to have him leave over something like this just wasn't right.

"Jon," he said reasonably, "it isn't like you went looking you know. She sought you out, not the other way around. Don't do anything until you can make the decision without emotion," he advised. Then wanting to give Jon the opportunity to think things through he said, "The Colonel told me the other day that there's a good fishing spot a few miles up the road from here. Why don't you go there tomorrow and spend the day? Anne and I will hold down

104

the fort here. I know you're going to want to spend some time in prayer over this." Gabe knew that whenever Jon was troubled, he would take himself away to a quiet place to 'seek the Lord' as he called it. "When you come back," he continued, "let me know what you decide, and I'll abide by it, okay?"

Jon nodded, "Okay," he said. "I should know better than to make a decision before talking to the Lord first," he added. "Thanks, Gabe. I think I'll make myself some coffee and keep you company for a while if you don't mind."

"Fine by me," Gabe said.

He didn't know what Jon's decision would be, but for the first time in his life he wished he could pray. It was the first in a long time he felt emotion for anything outside of his own personal agony, and as they both turned and headed into the house, a longing started coming into his heart that hadn't been there in five years. It was a longing to be at a different place in his life from where he was now. It was a longing to be whole again.

****

Marissa lay awake in her bed for the rest of the night. She had crept back into her room and cried bitter tears of regret into her pillow. She felt humiliated, but more than that, she felt ashamed. Why she had gone into Jon's room and provoked him like that she would never know. She had been feeling rejected by him in recent weeks. He had spent very little time with her, and she'd wondered if she had inadvertently done something to him, given away her feelings for him or if he just wasn't interested in her.

105

His response to her when she'd gone to him, however, had been anything but indifferent; in fact, he had declared that he loved her, and she knew him well enough to know he wouldn't lie. Nevertheless, she was unsure if he was simply overcome by lust or if it was truly how he felt in his heart. She knew for her part that she loved him completely and nothing would ever change that, but now she'd made a total mess of everything, and she didn't know how she was going to face him in the morning.

At around six o'clock she finally fell asleep and didn't emerge from her room until mid-morning after a long hot shower. When she went out to the kitchen, she saw Gabe and Anne in the family room playing a game of chess. Jon was nowhere in sight and she was relieved. She gave them a brief good morning, poured herself a cup of coffee, put on her coat which she had left over one of the stools at the eating counter and went out onto the patio to stand at the stone fence. Five minutes later, Gabe came up beside her with his own cup in his hand.

"Good morning, Dr. Sparks," he said. He still addressed her by her formal title, even after so many months.

"Hello, Gabe," she said soberly. "Where's Jon?" she asked. "Did he go to town? I didn't know he was going again today."

"No, he didn't go to town," Gabe said. "He went to find a quiet place to pray." She turned to looked at him and deciding to give her a little dose of reality he added, "You see, he needs to decide whether or not to resign from the Bureau after what happened between the two of you earlier this morning."

Marissa's eyes opened wide in shock. She couldn't believe what she was hearing. She just gaped at Gabe for a few moments unable to put two coherent thoughts together. "How did you know about this morning?" she asked when she finally found her voice, her face suffused with color, "and what do you mean he has to resign? I never meant for anything like that to happen." She was suddenly filled with remorse, and tears starting to gather in her eyes.

"Dr. Sparks…. Marissa," he finally made himself say, "one thing you need to know about Jon is that he strives to be, 'a man after God's own heart', I think is how he phrases it. He is also a man of integrity and he feels, and he is correct, that he broke some serious rules last night; therefore, he believes the only honorable thing to do is resign."

"But I did what was wrong, not him," she said, beginning to cry in earnest. "Oh no, what have I done?" she added in despair, dropping her head in her hands and weeping.

Gabe didn't touch her, he only went over to the covered patio, pulled some tissues from the box which sat on one of the tables there, carried them out to her and allowed her to cry her eyes out. Anne came out on the patio to see what was wrong, but Gabe told her it was okay, and he would deal with it, so she went back inside, but her expression was troubled. As he watched her go, he decided he'd smooth things over with her later. Anne wasn't privy to what had taken place, and he wanted it to remain that way. The fewer people who knew what was going on, the better.

When Marissa had spent her tears and quieted, she turned to Gabe and asked without thinking. "Have you ever

107

been so in love with someone, Gabe, that you can't think of anything else but them from the time you wake up in the morning until you go to bed at night?"

He pulled back as if she had struck him, then taking a deep breath said with quiet sadness, "Yes, yes I have."

When she realized what she'd said, she started crying all over again. "I'm sorry," she sobbed. "I shouldn't be asking you something so personal." She hoped he didn't read anymore into her thoughtless remark than that. Knowing his history, how could she have even asked him such a thing? What was the matter with her? She was putting herself in deeper trouble with everything she said and did.

"You need to leave Jon alone, Marissa," Gabe said with steel in his voice. "He's a fine agent and a good man. He doesn't need you tempting him away from his faith and distracting him from his job. You've put him in a position where he now has to choose between you and everything he has committed himself to for years. If you love someone," he continued, "you don't try to rob them of who they are, instead you embrace them as they are," and she nodded that she understood. "I think it would be best from now on if you only have contact with him when either Anne or I are present."

"Will you please allow me to talk to him privately when he comes back?" she begged. "I want to try and convince him not to resign. I promise I won't make any more stupid moves like the one I made last night," she said, "and I'll stay away from him. I just need to clear the air between us. You can watch us talk if you like," she added. "I don't mind."

Gabe thought about it for a few moments then finally

relented, "Okay," he said. "One conversation alone then you direct everything to him after that with me or Anne present, is that clear?"

"Yes," she agreed. "Thank you, Gabe. For what it's worth I only did what I did because I love him. I don't usually go around throwing myself at men. It's not my style."

He nodded. Except for the incident with the 'kill book' she had been completely honest with them, and he knew she was speaking the truth this time.

He left her there and made his way inside to start lunch. Jon had said he would be back with dinner by five o'clock if the fish were biting, and Gabe hoped he not only brought in a good catch, but also an answer to his prayers they could all live with.

CHAPTER 9

Jon left the house at six in the morning. The sun had already risen, and it was cold, but he knew the temperature was expected to moderate that day and become warmer. He was worn out by his tumultuous emotions and the fact that he hadn't gotten any sleep, but the fresh air was revitalizing and a stimulant to his tired body.

He made the trek on foot and it took him a while. Once he had gotten to the bottom of the driveway, it was mostly uphill, but eventually he found himself at the spot Gabe had described by the side of the road. It was directly opposite the gated entrance to another house called Belle Haven, so it was easy to find. He went over the embankment, down a short path then through a thick forest of trees. He travelled for about a mile before he came out onto a grassy slope that led down to a river. It was so far in from the road that only someone who knew the area well would have known of its existence.

The first thing he did when he reached the tranquil spot was to put his fishing gear aside, get down on his knees and bow his head with his face in his hands. At last he could come before his Heavenly Father. What he had to do he couldn't do at the house of even as he walked, he needed privacy and peace to get into a posture of repentance and pray.

"Father," he began, "please forgive me. I don't deserve Your mercy, Lord, but I'm humbly asking for it," he said. "What I did was inexcusable. I just don't know why I lost control like that. Please forgive me, God," he pleaded again. "I'm so sorry I let you down and compromised by faith. I'm

110

so sorry, I'm so sorry."

Jon continued to pour himself out to his Heavenly Father for a long while. He knew he'd been forgiven even before he had uttered the first word, because he knew God saw the regret in his heart and how contrite he was. He continued to pray, however, asking God to help him to forgive himself and to remove the feelings he had for Marissa once and for all.

He then turned his prayers towards her, and he asked his Heavenly Father to let the outcome of the investigation be such that Marissa could live in freedom without having to look over her shoulder and to help her find her way back to Him once more. Jon continued to pray for her then he asked God to direct him whether to resign or not.

He remained quiet to hear if God would speak to him, then came the peaceful Voice he knew so well, "Stay." That was all. Nothing more came to him, but he felt God's peace invade his soul, and he knew he had his answer.

He spent some time praising and worshipping his Heavenly Father, and when he ended his time with Him, he got to his feet with a calm and grateful heart, took up the rod and bait and began setting himself up to fish.

Around mid-morning, he had just reeled in and unhooked his fifth catch, a large one pounder, when he heard footsteps behind him. His weapon was in his hand within seconds, and he spun around while seated on the bank in readiness for he knew not what.

"Jon, put that thing away," the Colonel said, shaking his head and continuing to advance. "I'm sorry I startled you."

111

Jon relaxed and put his gun back into its holster under his jacket before getting to his feet. "I'm sorry, too, Colonel," he said, going over to meet him and extending his hand. "I wasn't expecting anyone."

"No harm done," the older man said, giving Jon's hand a firm shake. The Colonel was a giant of a man, at least six foot seven, with a completely bald head and laughing brown eyes.

"How's the fishing?" he asked, as they walked back to the bank together.

"The fishing's good," Jon said, pulling up the string with his catch out of the cold water for the Colonel to see.

"Mary sent me out of the house so she could put together a special evening for us," he explained. "I don't know what she has planned, but I'm looking forward to it."

"What's the occasion?" Jon asked as he resumed his seat and began baiting his hook again.

"We've been married the big five O today, Jon," he replied as he took a seat beside him and began setting himself up to fish. "I'm a blessed man. My Mary wanted to make the day special for us, even though we'll be leaving here for a two-week vacation at the end of the month to celebrate," he said. "We are taking a cruise to Alaska the first week, then head to Billings to spend the second with Philip and Gabby, Jake and Jess, David and Alaina and all the grandkids," he elaborated, speaking of Jon's good friends.

He, Philip and Jake had gone to college together, and he had met David and Alaina Kendal who owned Belle Haven up by the road on several occasions. The Colonel and Mary didn't have any children but referred to the three couples as their adopted sons and daughters and their children as their grandbabies.

"That's wonderful, Colonel," Jon said. "Congratulations. Please give Mary a hug and kiss and tell her the same for me."

"It will give me no end of pleasure to do that, my boy," he said chuckling. "What brings you here?" he asked. "You have the day off?"

"It's more like I took the day off," Jon said. "I just needed a quiet place to pray," he added pensively.

"Am I disturbing you?" the Colonel asked quickly. "I can always go downstream."

"No sir," Jon assured him. "I've finished, and God has answered, so I'm just trying to put dinner on the table. Actually, I have enough," he added, "but I think I'll catch some more so we'll have enough for a few meals."

"You look a little downcast," the Colonel observed. "Anything you want to talk about? I'm a good listener, and I can keep a confidence, even from my Mary."

"I don't know, Colonel," Jon replied hesitantly, then decided to share his dilemma with the older man. He knew the Colonel would keep things to himself, so he felt safe telling him what was going on. "I kind of got myself into some trouble, and I needed to seek the Lord and ask Him if I should resign from my job."

113

The Colonel turned to him and raised his eyebrows in surprise. "What on earth could you have gotten yourself into to make you want to do a thing like that?" he asked. "You're a good man, Jon, and a fine Christian," he added. "Why do you feel you need to resign?"

"I'm in love with my witness, Colonel," Jon said bluntly, causing the Colonel to drop his jaw in shock.

"Oh," he said, recovering from his momentary loss for words.

"I'm in love with her and last night I lost control and almost made love to her." He again hung his head in despair and shame at what he'd done.

"Oh," the Colonel said again, clearly blown away by Jon's confession. "Why couldn't you have given me something easy," he said, trying to lighten the moment.

Jon smiled sadly then said, "Life's not easy my Dad always says".

"Isn't that the truth," the Colonel confirmed, throwing in his line. "Did you initiate the encounter, Jon, or did she?" he asked, wanting to get a better perspective on the situation.

"She did, sir," he replied and explained what had happened. "She said she loved me," he continued, "but I don't know if it was just for that moment or if it's really a heart thing." The Colonel nodded in understanding.

"Have you asked God for forgiveness, son?" he questioned.

114

"Yes, sir," he said. "I guess I just need to forgive myself."

"Ah," the Colonel said, "that's the hardest part, isn't it? But you know, Jon, if God has forgiven you, then it's a done deal," he declared. "You beating yourself up over a momentary lapse isn't going to alter what happened or change how God sees you. When you ask Him for forgiveness, all He sees is the blood of His Son when He looks at you. He sees you righteous and His, nothing more. As far as the east is from the west is how far He has removed your transgressions from you, Jon, so hold on to that."

The Colonel felt a nibble, yanked on his line and began to reel in his first catch. "As for your witness," he continued as he unhooked the fish and tied it to a line, "you need to tell her you're sorry about what happened, even though she was the one who initiated it. I take it she's not a Christian?" he asked, as he dropped a line with his catch into the water.

"She was once," Jon said, "but she had a rough childhood and feels the Lord abandoned her, so she's turned her back on Him." He was careful not to give the Colonel any more information than that. Even though Jon knew he could trust him, it was against the Bureau's policy for him to discuss his witness with anyone. "I've been praying she'll find her way back to Him," he added.

"I'll pray with you too," the Colonel promised, throwing his freshly baited line in once more. "I'll also pray for God's will in your relationship," he said. "Sometimes we limit God by what we see," he continued. "With you, it's her unbelief and the uncertain future she faces since she's in protective custody. You never know how those things will turn out, but God sees all of it," he said. "Have you ever stopped to think, Jon, that when the disciples saw Jesus hanging on the

115

cross, they were living in the moment, thinking it was all over. It's not like us now who know the whole story. They were living it. They had no way of knowing what would happen in the future.

"It's the same with us," he explained. "God's plan sometimes doesn't make a lick of sense to us, but when we look back on our life, we realize He was working everything out for us all along. Trust Him, son," he implored, "and don't believe your witness mightn't be the one for you. The Lord has a way of surprising us with how He works things out."

"Thanks, Colonel," Jon said, truly grateful for his wise counsel. "I know God wants me to stay and not quit, so I'll trust Him to work out the rest."

By mid-afternoon, they had gotten enough fish for at least three meals each, so they packed up and once they reached the road, the Colonel gave Jon a lift to the gates of Jacob's Mountain. He knew not to drop him at the front door. They bade each other good-bye and Jon walked the rest of the way to the house. He'd had a good day and running into the Colonel had been a blessing to him as he was able to soak up the wisdom of the older man. God had truly looked out for him and given him just what he needed, and as he rang the doorbell, he thanked his Heavenly Father for His goodness, mercy and grace.

Gabe opened the door and came out onto the porch. "Let me just drop these in the sink and come back," Jon said to him. "They're already scaled and gutted."

He went in and deposited his catch. Anne was in the family room with her knitting and waved to him, but

Marissa was nowhere in sight. He went back outside and closed the door then said to Gabe, "I ran into the Colonel and we fished together. I think God arranged for him to be there for me today."

Gabe nodded. "That's good," he said. "That old man has more wisdom in his little finger than you and I have in our entire body."

Gabe had spent time talking with the Colonel and Mary on several occasions which was something he rarely did with anyone, and he appreciated their counsel and friendship.

"Isn't that the truth," Jon said. "I'd already prayed and gotten my answer, but I was still feeling pretty bad, so he straightened me out. I'm staying," he added, much to Gabe's relief. "I know God told me not to resign."

"Good," Gabe responded. "That's a load off my mind. She wants to talk to you," he continued. "I told her she could have the one conversation with you, then she's to have no more private contact with you."

"I need to talk to her too," Jon said. "You have the first watch tonight, don't you?" he asked.

"Yes," Gabe said. "Anne takes over from me at four." Both he and Anne preferred the four o'clock watch, so whenever they were on assignment together, they swapped out with each other, so they could both have a little of what they wanted.

"Okay," Jon said. "When Anne goes to bed, I'll talk to Marissa. I'll probably take her out onto the patio, and you can monitor things from the family room if that's okay?"

117

"That's fine," Gabe agreed. "Let's get inside," he said. "I have a hankering for fried fish and hush puppies for dinner. It'll be nice to have fish for a change," he added, as they both turned and went into the house.

****

Later that night, Jon sat in one of the armchairs on the patio. He hadn't seen Marissa since he'd returned. Gabe told him that she had spent most of the day in her bedroom, only coming out to have lunch. She'd declined dinner, so Jon told Gabe to put it in the microwave for her, sure she would be hungry later. Gabe, however, was thoroughly disgusted with the idea. Fried fish and hush puppies were always best eaten right after they were cooked.

An hour after Anne went to bed, Gabe made his way down the passage and knocked softly on Marissa's door. When she answered, he invited her to go and talk with Jon, so she went with him. As Jon sat waiting for her, he was still feeling ashamed of his behavior the night before. Even though he hadn't initiated what had happened, he felt he should have been responsible enough as a Christian, as an agent and as a man to nip things in the bud before it had gone as far as it had. He felt embarrassed that he hadn't been able to exercise his usual self-control and instead had acted like a love-starved teenager. He heard a noise, looked up from his musings and saw Marissa standing in the doorway. Gabe, as they'd agreed, was sitting in the family room out of earshot, but in full view of the patio.

"Hi," he said to her sadly. "Are you hungry?"

"Not really," she said, coming over to sit in the chair opposite to where he was. "I'm still full, with regrets

118

mostly," she confessed.

"Me too," he replied. "I want to tell you how sorry I am for what happened," he continued. "If you want to file a report with my superiors, Gabe will tell you how to do it."

"Don't be an idiot," she said bluntly. "Do you think I didn't know what I was doing when I came into your room or didn't know what might happen?" she asked. "I'm a doctor, Jon," she said. "I probably know how a man's body functions even better than you do, at least from a physical standpoint; besides, I'd never do that to you."

"Thank you," he said.

"Are you going to resign?" she asked.

"No," he replied, and saw her melt with relief. "I feel God wants me to stay, so I'm going to walk in obedience to Him."

"I'm so glad," she said. "I had no idea my stupidity would have led to something like that. Can you please forgive me, Jon?" she asked. "I'm so sorry. I can't believe I did what I did. You've been so distant lately," she explained, "and I just wanted….," she paused, "I don't know what I wanted," she said in despair. "I just……" she paused again and didn't finish her sentence but looked at him instead. His eyes met hers and it was written there for him to see. She loved him. He nodded, hoping she would know that he understood. It seemed she did because she said, "Do you feel the same or was it just….," again she didn't finish what she wanted to say.

"I feel the same," he admitted, "very much so."

The tears came into her eyes then. "Is that why you've been so distant?" she asked, and he nodded. "Do you think there can be a future for us?" she voiced the question that was foremost in her mind.

"No," he said with brutal honesty, "but I'm only looking at it from a practical perspective," he explained. "You're not walking with the Lord, Marissa, and that's the most important thing to me right now, but there's something else," he added. "I'm going to be as honest and fair to you as I possibly can, based on what I know, is that okay?" he asked, and at her nod he continued. "It's highly unlikely you'll be able to return to your old life or your home or your job," he said. He was trying to be as gentle as possible, but he knew the kind of truth he was conveying would hurt. There was just no easy way to say it.

"That has been my greatest fear," she said, the tears really flowing now. "I just want to go home and pick up where I left off, but I've been feeling more and more lately that's never going to happen." He nodded and handed her the box of tissues that was on the table beside him.

"I know a lot depends on the outcome," he said, "but whether you get a chance to testify or not, you'll more than likely have to go into permanent witness protection. It would mean a new name, a new place to live in a new state and a new life," he explained. "You'll probably be able to keep practicing medicine, but more than likely we'll have to work at changing your appearance. You wouldn't be able to contact your friends either. In essence, Dr. Marissa Sparks would be dead, and you'll experience a physical rebirth as someone completely different."

She nodded in understanding. "When will I know?" she

asked sadly with her head down.

"I suspect in a few months," he said. "Antonelli has gone deep underground, and we haven't been able to find him. He also has a bounty on your head that has been steadily rising."

"How much am I worth?" she asked quietly.

"Half a million dollars," Jon said.

"That much," she said dryly. "I guess I should be flattered."

"Marissa," he said, "all I'm saying may not happen, but as things stand now, I don't see any other recourse. I want to say something else to you so that you can know my heart," he added, and she looked up. "I've never felt about any woman the way I feel about you," he confessed. "If things could have been different…," he left the sentence hanging. "I love you completely," he admitted, "and whatever happens I don't think that will ever change. I've been praying for a better outcome to what I can see ahead," he continued, "so maybe God will answer my prayers and we can be together. One thing I want you to know is that I'll never stop praying for you. As long as we both live on this earth, no matter what the future holds, I'll be praying," he said, and she could see the sincerity in his eyes. "I want to see you give your life back to the Lord, Marissa," he said. "That is going to be my prayer for you."

She couldn't answer for the tears his beautiful confession brought. She just put her head in her hands and wept. "I love you too, Jon," she said when her emotions were once again in check and she could talk. "I love you so

121

much. There's something I want you to know," she added, "I don't want you to think I'm some sort of loose woman who jumps into bed at the drop of a hat. I made a promise to my mother when I was a little girl," she continued. "I promised her I would never give myself to any man who wasn't my husband. Over the years, I've changed that promise a bit," she confessed. "I promised myself that I'd never sleep with anyone I didn't love."

"And how many men have you loved in your life, Marissa?" he asked, knowing it was inappropriate, but wanting her to see what that new promise had meant over the years, how much not waiting had cost her.

"In my whole life I've only ever been in love with one man, Jon," she said, seeming to know what he was thinking and rising to her feet. "Only one," she reiterated, "and that man, Jon, is you." She watched as his mouth fell open in stunned disbelief, then without saying another word she turned and walked into the house, not stopping until she went into her room and closed the door.

CHAPTER 10

A little over a week later, they were all in the kitchen helping Gabe fix dinner. Anne was making a salad, Jon was setting the table and getting the drinks ready and Marissa was making a quick dessert. Gabe was peeling a piece of butternut squash over the garbage can to add to some soup he had cooking on the stove. He had already sautéed the vegetables and Italian sausage for a dish he planned to serve with it and was just waiting for the pasta to finish boiling to put it together. They were talking intermittently, each concentrating on their task when they heard Gabe wince and drop the knife he'd been using. He grabbed for the towel on the counter in front of him, but not before the others noticed blood dripping from his left hand into the trash.

"Don't use that towel, Gabe," Marissa warned quickly and was beside him with a wad of paper towel before anyone else could react. "Here," she said, handing it to him. "Apply some pressure," she instructed. After a moment she said, "Let me see."

Gabe held his hand away, however, and wouldn't let her look at it. "I'm okay," he said.

"You can't be okay and bleeding like that," Marissa replied reasonably. "Let me have a look." She tried to reach for his hand to see how bad the cut was, but Gabe pulled away.

"Just leave me be," he said. "I'll take care of it."

"With one hand?" she asked, raising her eyebrow. "How stupid is that. When the bear was outside that night and we didn't know what was happening, you didn't make me to go out there with your gun to defend myself did you?" she questioned. "I'm a doctor," she stated. "Why don't you let me do what I do best and help you? If it's nothing, I can at least bandage it for you."

"I said I'll take care of it," Gabe said through gritted teeth, obviously in pain.

"Of all the stubborn, pigheaded, ridiculous......," she paused in her string of adjectives. "Now you listen to me, Gabriel," she said in an exasperated but firm tone, "you sit in this chair right now and don't tell me anymore nonsense."

"Leave me alone," Gabe enunciated every word. He was standing staring at her and she was staring right back.

"Fine," she said flippantly, with a flick of her hand as if she didn't care. "I'll just wait until you bleed yourself unconscious, then I'll look at you."

Jon was struggling with all his might not laugh, and so was Anne. Gabe had finally met his match, and it was amusing to watch the war taking place in front of them. "She has a point you know, pal," he said, and Gabe gave him a thunderous look. "Well she does," he stated again with a grin.

Anne coughed to cover her laugh, then said, "Why don't you just let her look at you, Ice? She's probably been hankering to get back to work. You can at least give her a chance to do a little doctoring."

Finally, Gabe relented and held out his hand for her inspection. The minute he eased the paper towel away so she could see, however, he started bleeding profusely again. She noticed a gash in his left palm by the meaty part of his thumb about an inch long. She asked Anne for more paper towel, and after wadding it up into another pad, she gave it to him and told him to put it back on the wound and apply pressure once again.

"That hand is going to need stitches," she said. "If I had my bag here I'd do it, but as it is, you're going to have to go to an emergency room; that is, if there's one anywhere near here."

Jon came to her then and said, "I have an idea. Give me fifteen minutes." He grabbed up the keys to the SUV and headed out the door. He wanted two agents to be with Marissa at all times, and knew Gabe couldn't drive himself to Chandlers Crossing, so he decided to go down to Mary and see if she had what Marissa needed.

He was soon back and had brought a little kit with him with just about everything she could have asked for to do the job.

"This is perfect!" Marissa said in surprise, as she pulled out the contents and set them on the counter. It had everything, right down to the disposable gloves. "I don't know where you got it, but I'm glad it was nearby."

Jon was glad too. Mary kept herself well stocked for anyone who required help and was only too happy to give him what he needed. Her only concern was who would be doing the stitching and suggested to Jon that maybe Gabe should come to her. Jon assured her, however, that they had

125

someone with them who was more than capable in that area, so she wasn't to worry.

Marissa cleaned the wound and used her expertise to neatly suture the gash close. Gabe sat there without flinching and allowed her to do it, but she saw the beads of sweat above his lips and forehead and knew he was in pain.

"I'm sorry," she said with professional compassion. "I know it's painful, but I'm almost finished." Gabe just grunted and said nothing.

Within another minute the job was done, and she cleaned the blood from his hand and wrapped it expertly with the bandages provided.

"Keep it elevated for a while," she admonished, "and don't get it wet."

She took off the disposable gloves and deposited them and the items she'd used in the trash, then went into her room to wash her hands at the sink. She came back a few minutes later with one of the pain pills she'd been given for her own wound and held it out to him saying, "Here, take this."

He began shaking his head when she looked at him with a raised eyebrow and said to Anne while looking him dead in the eye. "Anne, please pour a glass of water for Gabriel." When Anne put the glass before him, Marissa said firmly, "Take this pill right now and don't argue with me." They stared at each other for a full minute before Gabe obediently took the pill from her and swallowed it with the water. "Good boy," she said, and at his glare she said in a placating tone, "Tell me how to do the dish you were making, and I'll finish it for you."

Gabe sat on the bar stool and gave her instructions on how to complete the pasta dish. The soup was already done. He had only decided to add the squash at the last minute, so he told her to forget about it and just stir the contents in the pot occasionally. She finished the pasta, then proceeded to stir the soup. She took a sip with a spoon and added a bit more salt, much to Gabe's distress.

"What are you doing?" he asked and made as if to rise.

"You stay right there," she said. "It needs more salt," she added.

"It does not," he said in aggravation.

"Does too," she replied before closing the lid. She heard him say something she was sure was unflattering under his breath, but just took it in her stride. Her medical colleagues didn't call her 'Sparks the firecracker' without good reason.

Jon, meanwhile, continued to watch the tableau with amusement. This was a side of Marissa he'd never seen before, and it delighted him no end to see her in action. Later, Anne whispered to him that she hadn't had that much fun in a long time, and Jon couldn't help grinning and nodding his head in agreement.

****

The following week, Jon stood out on the patio in his usual spot by the fence looking out over the lovely morning. It had been a slow few weeks and whereas the views and the atmosphere were peaceful, the turmoil in his heart was

127

anything but. He had finally given up fighting his feelings for Marissa and just accepted things as they were.

The confession she'd made to him the last time they'd spoken together privately had both shocked and distressed him too, not that he wasn't glad she was still as pure as the driven snow. It just made him more ashamed than ever about his actions the night she'd come into his room. When he realized he would have unknowingly taken her innocence if his Heavenly Father hadn't stopped him, it made it even more difficult for him to look her in the eye.

He continued to pray unceasingly for God to remove the love he had for her, but God had chosen not to. She loved him too. He knew it as surely as he knew his own name. Sometimes, in an unguarded moment, she would look at him across the room with such longing that it caused his heart to race triple time. He knew that, for his part, Gabe felt like a referee watching the two of them eying each other. It was just too stressful for the three of them. Anne seemed oblivious to the tension. She did her job, and she and Marissa spent a lot of time together either knitting or in the garden which helped somewhat.

This day marked five and a half months since they'd all been together. It was for Jon, Gabe and Anne the longest protection detail they'd ever been on. There were no other agents available to relieve them, but in any event they'd all agreed they wanted to see this case through to the end. Antonelli had been in the Bureau's sights for years, but he had eluded prosecution every time the authorities had gotten close. Everyone was anxious to see him pay for his crimes. This opportunity was golden, and Marissa was the key, so her location was kept strictly between Jon, Gabe and Travis. Not even the higher-ups knew where she was, it was that closely guarded.

Jon sipped the last of his coffee and was preparing to go inside when his cell phone rang. He looked at the Caller ID, saw it was Travis and answered right away.

"Hey, buddy," he said. "How are things on the home front?"

"Busy as ever, pal," Travis replied, "but your case just got a little more interesting."

"I'm all ears," Jon said, truly hoping they had gotten the break they needed.

"It's taken all this time, but we've finally found her mother, Jon," Travis said.

"You're kidding," Jon replied in surprise. "That's great, Trav. I wasn't sure you would have been able to."

"It wasn't easy, let me tell you," Travis said, "but there's a problem."

"What?" Jon asked, knowing something had been wrong all along.

"She's dying," Travis said. "She's been living in Tennessee and working for a Judge and his daughter. She's changed her name too, so it took a little while to track her down."

Travis went on to give him the details and they spoke for some time, deciding to see if they could bring about a reunion between mother and daughter before it was too late. Eventually Travis told him he had to work out some logistics and get back to him, so Jon let him go.

Within two days, Travis called him back. He had decided to move them from Jacob's Mountain to the Judge's home in Tennessee. Anne would go back to Atlanta while Jon and Gabe would continue as they had been. He told Jon that the transfer of Marissa into permanent witness protection had already begun, but her appearance would have to be changed to complete the process. Jon listened intently to all the information and eventually hung up after a lengthy forty-five-minute conversation with Travis. He saw Gabe come out onto the covered patio just as he'd finished, so he called to him, and they met by the patio's kitchen.

"We're moving," he said without preamble as Gabe sat on one of the stools next to him by the eating counter.

"Tennessee?" Gabe asked, knowing what was happening.

"Yes," Jon said.

He filled Gabe in, and they decided to call Marissa outside and speak with her there. When she joined them, she knew something was up. She could feel it in the atmosphere surrounding the two men.

"Marissa," Jon said. "We've got something to tell you. Maybe you should sit down for this," he invited.

"I'm okay, Jon," she said, taking a deep breath. "Just tell me what it is."

"We're making some major changes," he stated, "but for a very good reason." She looked at him expectantly, so he continued, "Marissa, we've found your mother." She gasped and her fingers went to her mouth, clearly shocked by what

Jon had revealed. "There's more," he said.

"Tell me," she said, seeming to sense that whatever was coming wasn't good.

"She's very sick, Marissa," Jon said gently. "I'm sorry," he added, "but she's dying."

"No!" she exclaimed. Her eyes immediately filled with tears which spilled down her cheeks and she turned away from them. Gabe went over to the covered patio and brought back some tissues which he handed to her. "Where is she?" she asked, turning back to face them when she could speak, her tears still flowing.

"She's been living in the south," he said, not wanting her to know the exact location until they got there. "We're now taking steps to move you from here so you can be with her during this time."

"When do we leave?" she asked anxiously, her breath catching on a sob.

"It will take us a day or two to pack up and set this place to rights," Jon said, "then we'll go, but Marissa there's something else."

"What?" she asked, and he could see she was bracing herself for whatever was coming. Jon wanted so badly to take her in his arms and comfort her, but instead he said, "We've already begun the process of transferring you into permanent witness protection. It's the only way to ensure your safety since we're leaving this place.

"What does that mean exactly?" she asked, her emotions

once more in check.

"It means a new identity as we discussed before," he said, and she nodded. "We'll need to do something to change your appearance too, like give you colored contacts, maybe cut and color your hair," he added. "When we leave here, things should be finalized enough with your transfer for you to have your new name, so we'll only have to deal with your appearance before Gabe and I get you to our new location."

"That I can live with," she said. "Right now, I just want to see my mother," and he nodded his head in understanding.

"We're also making arrangements for your house and car to be sold and your finances will be transferred into a new bank account with your new name. We take care of all that to ensure the funds can't be traced," and she nodded.

"I have a few questions," she said.

"Go ahead," Jon replied. "I'll do my best to answer them."

"Will Anne be coming with us?" she asked.

"No, Anne won't be coming with us," Jon said. "She'll be heading back to our headquarters."

"Will I be living where my mother is permanently?" she asked next.

"No," he replied, "only for the time being. We'll make alternative arrangements for you after your time there."

"One last thing," she said. "Do you know what my mother is dying from?"

"She has breast cancer," Jon said. "She had the lump removed, but she has been reacting badly to her chemotherapy treatments. She nearly died when she did the last one," he explained. "The doctors feel that, without them, it would only be a matter of time before the cancer would recur," and she nodded in understanding

"I don't care what the doctors say," she said, and both he and Gabe saw a determined look come into her face. "I need to do some reading on it, but I'm sure there are several options, even holistically that we can try. I'm not going to give up on her. I'm going to do everything in my power to save her."

They could see her medical background coming to the fore and Jon was glad, as he hoped the distraction of her mother's illness would make the transition easier for her to bear.

CHAPTER 11

Constantine Antonelli stood by the unlit fireplace with a drink in his hand looking out the window to his left. The grounds were unkempt and in desperate need of attention, but in the months since they'd been living there, he'd purposely told his men not to mow the grass or do anything to change the appearance of the outside. The house, which was located in the middle of the large property and about a mile in from the narrow dirt road, hadn't been lived in in years. The gardens surrounding it were flat and extensive but overgrown due to lack of care, giving the place a feeling of abandonment, and he wanted it left that way.

His twin brother Cornelius, who they called Neil, had acquired the hundred-acre estate in the Wasatch Mountains more than fifteen years before from one of his business contacts who was now deceased, and upon their arrival, Constantine had told Jimmy to 'terminate the services' of the caretaker who looked after the place. He was now resting comfortably in a grave out in the woods.

The house was fully furnished with antiques from a bygone era and had great bones. It had been a showplace in its heyday, so much so that Constantine was thinking of suggesting to Neil that he renovate it and use it for the business. It was so remote, it would be perfect for meetings or anything else to do with their trade. All that would have to wait, however, until his present crisis was over. He drained his glass and set it on the fireplace mantel, then moved over to stand by the window with his hands in his pockets.

Even though it had been months, he still couldn't get

over Giovanni's betrayal. Gio had worked for him from the first day he had started in the drug trade and they'd been close. Only his brother Cornelius and his cousin Frank were closer to him than Giovanni had been. He'd also been loyal to the core, so Constantine had never thought he would have turned him over to the Feds. He was also shocked to learn that Gio had kept a kill book from the beginning of their association. In retrospect, he supposed he couldn't blame him. At any time, something could have happened to cause problems between them, so having the 'kill book' as insurance was smart on Gio's part, although it was now proving detrimental to him.

Constantine knew it was having to execute the kid that had turned Gio against him. His enforcer had had no problem killing his lover, Lucinda, but had been vehemently opposed to killing the little girl, the result of Constantine's one-night stand with the beautiful model. Gio had been so opposed to doing it in fact, that Constantine had considered sending Jimmy Wexler, his other enforcer to do the job, but Jimmy had been in Miami doing another execution for him and he'd wanted Lucinda silenced quickly.

When Jimmy called and told him he'd accomplished his task earlier than expected, Constantine decided to send him out to L.A. where Gio had already gone and told him to make sure Gio carried out his orders. It was a lucky thing he had, as Jimmy's warning about the tape and the Doctor had given Constantine enough time to make a hurried departure from the east coast to the estate in Utah before the Feds had come calling.

It was unfortunate that, although Jimmy had been able to retrieve the recorder, he hadn't known about the book or seen the Doctor pocket it. He had seen her talking to Gio and recording the conversation so all he had done was taken

135

the device from her pocket and thought to silence her in case Gio had said anything incriminating. It was only when he'd listened to the tape after she'd escaped that he knew they were in deep trouble.

Gio's betrayal had not only shaken Constantine but had caused him to begin to question the loyalty of everyone around him. If Gio could give him up, then any one of his other men could. Of the three men he had brought with him, he trusted Wexler the least. The man had no soul and would cheerfully kill his own mother if the price was right.

With that in mind, Constantine had called him into his office at the estate a few days after Gio's death and made him an offer he couldn't refuse. He told Jimmy that if anyone propositioned him to get rid of Cornelius, Frank or himself or paid him to betray them to the Feds so they could take over the syndicate, Jimmy should come to him with the evidence and he would pay him double what they were offering. Wexler was fine with that.

The others who were with him and who were a part of his trusted inner circle besides his cousin Frank were his chauffeur and bodyguard Paulie and his chef and valet Adolpho. He didn't expect any of them would betray him, however, as they knew he was their meal ticket. He had saved Adolpho's life once and he was unswervingly loyal to him, and although Paulie was good at what he did, he was just a thug. He didn't have the smarts for much else.

Cornelius lived in South America and ran that end of the business. He had come up to the States when he'd heard what had happened, however, and was looking after things on the East Coast in Constantine's absence. Frank was acting as the go-between, making trips out to Cornelius and back to Utah in addition to taking care of the drug deliveries as he usually did.

Constantine's musings were cut short when Lahali, his South African born wife, entered his study with their two sons. She was a beautiful woman, a mixture of her Zulu mother who was half black and half Asian and her white English father. She was fair but with a tan blush to her complexion and had a slight hint of her Asian heritage around her eyes. Her hair was straight, long and light brown, almost the color of latte, and he loved to run his fingers through its silky softness when they were in bed at night. He had married her five years before and she had given him what he'd always wanted, children. They had two sons. One was three and a half and the other had just turned two and she was now seven months pregnant with their third child. She was very tall, almost six feet, but she carried herself with a regal bearing and elegance despite her protruding belly.

Every time he looked at Lahali, he felt his love well on the inside, and couldn't believe he had been foolish enough to get involved with Lucinda. She'd been a hot young thing he had been introduced to at a party he'd attended while in L.A. on business three years before. She'd stroked his ego and his pride, clearly telling him without words that she was available, and they'd spent the night together. He thought that would have been the end of it, but three months later he'd gotten a call from their party host and mutual friend to get in touch with her. That was when she'd told him she was pregnant. When the child was born, Constantine had sent Gio to break in quietly and get some evidence from the hairbrush of both mother and daughter and had discreetly had a paternity test done. She had been right; the child was his.

After a while she asked him for money as her career had

tanked, and in the last few months before her death, she'd become increasingly demanding. Constantine had had enough of her whining and threats and had sent Gio to kill her and the child. That decision had precipitated a chain of events, however, he could never have anticipated.

As he looked at Lahali now he was glad he had brought her to this remote location before she'd gotten wind of what had happened. He had enough problems without an unhappy wife to contend with. She came up to him with their youngest son Michael in her arms and leaned in for his kiss on the cheek. He put the back of his hand to the spot and caressed her smooth skin. It soothed him somewhat, and stirred a desire in him for more, causing him to place his lips on hers in a quick but fiery onslaught.

"How are you, beautiful?" he asked, "and how's my little football player?" He placed his hand on her stomach and rubbed it gently.

"We're both fine," she assured him.

"How are my two troopers?" he asked his sons next, taking Michael from her and ruffling Dominic's hair.

"Fine, Daddy," his oldest answered. Michael wriggled to get out of his father's arms, so he placed him on the floor and both boys went over to the toy box in the corner to pull out something to play with.

"Want to tell me why we're here, Constantine?" Lahali asked him softly.

For months she had been quiet about their hurried departure from their mansion on the New Jersey coastline.

She knew his occupation, of course, but this had been the first time in five years that what he did had affected her in any way. She had purposely not asked any questions, but after six months with no plans to go back home in sight, she felt she needed to get some answers.

"Giovanni sold me out to the Feds, and we have to stay in hiding for a while," he said.

"Why would Gio sell you out?" she asked in astonishment, "you two were as close as brothers."

"I have no idea," he lied. "I only know he gave them enough evidence to....," he didn't finish the sentence, mindful of the boys who were playing not far away, but he knew Lahali would get the picture.

She looked closely at Constantine who looked away. Michael had toddled over to him with his toy car and he got down on the floor with him.

Lahali knew this man better than he thought she did and knew he was only telling her the partial truth. He was twenty-two years older than her and at fifty-five his dark brown hair was beginning to gray around the temples. He was a handsome man, with brown eyes and a slightly olive tone to his fair complexion that spoke of his Italian heritage.

They had met at a winery close to her hometown of Johannesburg where she was working as an accountant and she had been swept off her feet when he'd shown an interest in her. It was only after their marriage, his second after having lost his first wife many years before, that she had discovered what he really did that made him so wildly wealthy. It took some getting used to, but she decided that as long as she wasn't involved in his business dealings, she could live with it.

Now here they were, hiding from the FBI and she pregnant with the two little ones to shield and protect. She was grateful that Constantine had allowed her to bring Elsa, her old friend and advocate who was sixty-two and had been with her family since she was a baby. She had been Lahali's nanny and now helped her look after the children, just as she had looked after her when she was little, and Lahali loved her as much as she had loved her own mother.

Aside from Elsa, Constantine had brought only three men with him, and except for Wexler, they were all from his trusted inner circle, just as Giovanni had been. Whatever had caused Gio to cave must have been something Constantine had done, she decided. Someone like that didn't just betray his employer and friend for no reason.

There were still too many unanswered questions and as she watched her husband playing with their two sons, she decided she needed to know more than the brief explanation he had given her. It was obvious from his inability to look her in the eye and his seeming distraction with the boys that Constantine was hiding something. She knew she would get no more out of him, however, so she decided to keep her eyes and ears open. Her children were everything to her and as she stood there watching the boys, she determined to get to the bottom of what had happened just in case she or they would be affected by it in any way.

CHAPTER 12

Two days after leaving Jacob's Mountain, Jon, Gabe and Marissa were in a small town in eastern Arkansas, as it had been decided they would drive the rest of the way to Tennessee. They had been flown as far as a small private airstrip in Texas where they parted ways with Anne. Marissa had shared a heartfelt hug with her protector as they said goodbye, thanking her for everything.

Anne had been her constant companion for months and their relationship had grown into friendship. Marissa had not only helped her with the baby blanket but had added to the layette by knitting a little sweater and booties to match, and Anne was touched by her kindness.

Just before they went their separate ways, Anne pulled Jon aside to speak with him while Gabe and Marissa went over to the car that had been waiting for them.

"I hope things work out for you and Marissa, Jon," she said with a wink, and saw his look of surprise.

"How long have you known?" he asked her.

"A while now," she said, "ever since you had pneumonia."

"That long?" he asked incredulously. "I thought you didn't have a clue."

"Ha," she laughed, "the two of you were eyeing each other like love struck teenagers, I would have had to be blind not to notice. I just played along as if I didn't know," she said.

"You're a dangerous woman, Anne Peterson," he said with a grin.

"So I've been told," she agreed with a laugh of her own. "I don't know how this will end, Jon, but she's a nice girl and I think she's perfect for you."

"You're something else, you know that?" he said, shaking his head.

"Yeah," she replied, "I do."

"Go on and get out of here," he grinned. "I'll see you when this is over, but until then, try to be good."

"I don't make promises I can't keep," she shot back, and they both laughed.

Once their goodbyes were over, Anne boarded the business jet once again, while Jon joined Gabe and Marissa in the car, and they drove off.

After switching cars twice more, they began taking a circuitous route through the southern states to their destination. Marissa chafed at the delay but knew she needed to be patient. She couldn't help her mother if she was killed by Antonelli's men after all.

They had travelled continuously that day and even through the night, with Jon and Gabe sharing the driving. They had stopped now at a hairdresser and told Marissa to go in and have her hair cut and colored. They had already gotten her several pairs of contacts in her prescription which had transform her sea green eyes into startling blue ones, and the change in her hair was all that was needed to complete her new look. Jon waited across the street, standing outside a grocery store and watching the door to the salon where Marissa had gone while Gabe had taken the rear of the set of shops.

Sometime later, Marissa sat in the chair looking at herself in the mirror and couldn't believe it. She had cut her hair into a boyish style, very short and close to her head, but with a few soft curls on her forehead to add a touch of femininity.

"My hair's twice as short as Gabe's and almost as short as Jon's," she thought and grinned.

She had decided to bleach it blonde as that had been her true hair color when she was very young. When she had left home, she wanted to erase every memory of her father who had the same hair color as hers, so she'd dyed it the deep chestnut it had been for years. She not only liked the fact that it removed any physical attribute that reminded her of Adrian Sparks, but she found she loved the color and how it transformed her. While she had been in their remote location, either Jon or Gabe had bought her the rinse she usually used. She figured, however, that reverting to the blonde she truly was would be a nice change and a lot easier for maintenance, as she would have had to color her tresses much more often if she left it short.

The salon had been empty while she was there, and she chatted amicably with the stylist. She shared nothing about herself, however, she just exchanged the usual pleasantries one would with a stranger. It was during their conversation that she noticed a door leading into the shop next door. The

143

hairdresser told her that her sister ran it as a clothing store, and they sent customers back and forth to each other all the time.

Marissa decided to visit after she finished with her hair. She had some cash so she wanted to see what she could find. She went in and was surprised by the variety of items available and the prices. She bought a slim fitting pair of blue jeans, a crisp sleeveless white blouse and three short-sleeved t-shirts in different colors. She would definitely need them for the warmer Tennessee weather. She also found a cute pair of large sunshades and decided to make her transformation complete in the fitting room at the back of the store.

When she emerged, she was wearing the jeans and white blouse with a long fashion necklace and earrings she had also bought, as well as the shades. She was startled when she glanced in the fitting room mirror after she'd changed and saw how different she looked, and she knew it would take her a while to get accustomed to her new appearance. She slipped the shopping bag with her new purchases and the clothes she had initially worn over her arm, exited the store and began making her way across the street to where she could see Jon watching the door to the salon.

The place was fairly busy with people out doing their mid-week shopping and errands, so deciding to see just how well she had made her transformation, Marissa crossed the road and walked right past him before going into the grocery store behind him. She came out a few minutes later and noticed his attention was still focused on the salon, so she stood behind him but off to his left a short distance away and watched him as he watched for her.

A few minutes later, she took off her sunshades and said, "Nice day, isn't it?" and he turned swiftly at the sound of her voice. His mouth gaped open when he saw her, and she grinned at his startled expression.

He inspected her after his initial surprise and smiled saying, "This is good. This is very good." He was obviously pleased with the changes he saw and got on his phone to Gabe, telling him to come around to his location.

When Gabe saw Marissa, he literally did a double take, just to make sure it was her then grunted and said, "I would have passed you and not known you. You did a good job."

That was high praise coming from Gabe, she thought as they went back to the car, got in and were soon on their way. They made their Tennessee destination by late afternoon. It was about fifty miles west of Chattanooga and took a while to find. Eventually they turned into large wrought iron gates with an impressive and scrolled archway overhead. The name of the property, Pleasant Valley, was written in gold letters across it with a large crest emblazoned between both words.

They drove down the mile-long drive leading into the property which was bordered on either side by enormous Southern Magnolia trees. The road was straight, but undulated in gentle waves up and down, so the house didn't come into view until they were about a quarter of a mile away. Jon immediately stopped the car and the three of them sat and stared in shock at the beautiful Greek Revival Antebellum mansion that stood before them.

"What the......," Gabe didn't finish his sentence.

145

"This is unbelievable," Jon said.

"You have got to be kidding me?" Marissa exclaimed when she had figuratively taken her chin up off the floor. "I never knew places as grand as this still existed."

The mansion was impressive with five imposing columns forming a bold and magnificent façade. The columns protruded forward before the massive double front doors creating a wide verandah, and they were not only huge in girth, but were three stories tall.

After their initial shock, Jon drove the rest of the way, going around the sweeping circular driveway before coming to a stop a little way from the front steps. He told Marissa to wait inside, then he and Gabe got out and Travis rose from a chair on the wide verandah where he had been speaking with a distinguished older man. He came down the steps to meet them, leaving the man sitting quietly and the three friends greeted each other. They conversed in low tones then, a few minutes later, Jon went over and opened the back door, inviting Marissa to come out and join them.

"Dr. Marissa Sparks," Jon said softly, "meet our boss and director, Travis,"

Marissa extended her hand. "Nice to meet you, Director," she said with an uncertain smile but a firm handshake. She took in his appearance as she greeted him and noticed he was tall with hair the color hers used to be, a deep chestnut and attractive green eyes. She estimated he was in his late thirties or early forties and was quite good looking.

"Travis, please Doctor," he said.

"Just Marissa, Travis," she said. "I don't stand much on formality," and Travis nodded.

"Okay, Marissa," he acknowledged. "We need to speak with you and let you know what's been decided," he added. "I know it must be difficult having other people making life altering decisions for you, but please know we are doing everything we can to ensure your safety."

"I understand," she said.

"Let's sit over here," he directed, and the three of them went to a lovely gazebo off the side of the driveway. It was surrounded by a profusion of chrysanthemums in full bloom and contained a built-in bench which ran the entire inner circumference of the little structure.

When they were seated, Travis addressed her. "Well, Marissa," he said, "I know you're anxious to see your mother, but I need to give you a little background first and then we need to talk about your new identity." She nodded so he continued, "You mother legally changed her name to Amelia Jordan about a year after she left home. She has been working here first as the housekeeper then the bed and breakfast manager for Judge Theodore Sterling and his daughter Sapphire for the past nineteen years. They run the bed and breakfast mainly because they like sharing their southern heritage with history enthusiasts. The family and staff love your mother; so much so, that when she became ill earlier this year, Sapphire began taking care of her. Amelia has been like a mother to her," and Marissa nodded again.

"Judge Sterling lost his wife when Sapphire was thirteen and employed your mother two years later. He has an exemplary judicial record and is now enjoying an early

147

retirement from the bench. Both himself and Sapphire know you are Amelia's daughter and a doctor but under a new name. They also know you're here with two agents and under their protection, but they don't know why, and we need you to keep that and any information about your case confidential.

"Judge Sterling suggested that we give you the cover of a nurse he's employed to take of Amelia, so the staff won't suspect anything. With that in mind," he continued, "we did some shopping for you and there are uniforms and other medical odds and ends in your room to make your part believable. I also got the information regarding her condition from her doctor as you requested.

"Jon, you will be posing as an author needing a quiet place to finish writing your novel and Gabe, you'll be Jon's friend and a widower recovering from the death of your wife. I'm sorry, pal," he said, "it was the cover that best suited our purposes," and Gabe nodded with his usual solemn expression. The part fit him well, Marissa thought, and that was probably why it had been chosen for him. He didn't have to pretend; he was living it.

"The staff is on duty from seven in the morning until three in the afternoon then they all go home," Travis added. "The Judge, Amelia and Sapphire usually have a heavy lunch and a light supper as the guests know they have to provide lunch and dinner for themselves. Judge Sterling said he'll tell the cook that lunch is included as part of the package. He says they sometimes do that for their long-term guests anyway.

"Now on to your new identity," he said, removing an envelope from his inside jacket pocket and giving it to her.

It contained a Social Security card and two hundred dollars in cash. She glanced at the name on the card and it said Isabelle Christianson. She liked it, thank goodness. She hadn't thought much about it until now, but she was glad it was something she could live with.

"Your house is under contract for sale," he continued, and Marissa's face showed her surprise that things had progressed so far so quickly. "Someone showed an interest in purchasing it within hours of it being put on the market and snapped it up immediately," Travis explained.

Marissa knew her home was a showplace. It had belonged to her grandparents and they had left it to her when they'd died. She loved decorating and had renovated the large four-bedroom home a little at a time, starting first with the bathrooms and finishing just the year before with a lovely gourmet kitchen.

"Your new bank account contains the money we got from the sale of your car," Travis continued, "and your furniture and personal items, minus anything displaying your old identity, are being held in storage for you and will be available for you when this is over." He paused then added, "You will understand why we won't issue a driver's license, passport, credit or debit card to you just yet, but as soon as things are resolved you'll receive them.

"I think that's just about everything," he said. He thought for a moment then remembered something he'd forgotten, "Oh one last thing. We thought it best not to let your mother know who you are just yet. It would involve too much explanation, and we don't want to distress her with your situation. When Jon called and told me how radically different you looked, we thought you might be able

149

to pull off a little acting while you're here."

Marissa agreed immediately as she too wanted to give her mother as little stress as possible. They hadn't seen each other in twenty years and with her new appearance she didn't think her mother would know her.

"Well, Isabelle," Travis smiled, using her new name for the first time, "let's go meet Judge Sterling." With that they all rose and left their meeting place to walk along the driveway then up the steps to the wide verandah.

Judge Sterling got to his feet as they approached and shook hands with Jon and Gabe. When it came to Isabelle, however, he took her hand in both of his and smiled.

"This truly is a pleasure, Isabelle," he said. "Your mother has mentioned you many times over the years she's been here, and I know more than anything that she's missed you."

Isabelle instantly took a liking to the Judge. He was warm and welcoming and his broad smile and laughing dark brown eyes were a testament to his sense of humor. He was also tall, slim and distinguished and she figured him to be in his late fifties. His almost black hair had a good smattering of gray at the sides but was full and offset his attractive face.

"It's very nice to meet you, Judge," she said smiling. "Thank you for taking such good care of my Mom."

"You're welcome," he said. "She's a part of our family you know," then added, "Sapphire looks on her as the mother she never had growing up as a teenager. Come," he invited, "let's go inside and I'll introduce you to my Sassy and you can see your mama."

150

He led them through the front door and into a short entryway which opened into a grand and massive reception room, complete with wonderful oil paintings, sculptures and flowers. The high ceiling was made up of intricately carved square wood panels that were simply magnificent because of their three-dimensional effect. Two wide staircases located to the rear of the room curved on either side of the space before meeting at the long wide landing above that overlooked the room below. Passageways on either end disappeared into the other areas of the upstairs that obviously included the bedrooms. Travis had already seen the 'Grand Foyer' as the Judge referred to it but Jon, Isabelle and even Gabe looked around awestruck.

"Kind of takes your breath away, doesn't it?" the Judge remarked with a smile, watching their response.

"That's putting it mildly, Judge," Jon said. "This place is incredible," he added, and the others nodded in agreement.

"We get that reaction from all our guests," he said smiling. "I'll show you around later, but I know this little lady is anxious to see her mama. You all might as well come along and meet Sassy."

He took them up the staircase on the right and down the passageway on that side. There were several rooms leading from it as well as another set of stairs at the end of the corridor which obviously led to the third floor. As they walked the Judge explained that they had moved Amelia from the housekeeper's quarters located beyond the kitchen and put her upstairs so Sassy could easily check on her at night without going all the way downstairs. He went to the last room on the left and knocked gently.

151

A soft female voice told them to come in and Travis, Jon and Gabe, by mutual consent, stepped back as they planned to wait outside. The Judge, however, stuck his head through the door first and asked his daughter to come out for a moment. When she appeared, they were all struck by her loveliness. She had jet black hair that cascaded down her back in wave after wave of soft curls and unusual amber-colored eyes and to say she was breathtakingly beautiful was putting it mildly. Even Gabe had a hard time not staring.

"Sass," the Judge said to her, "come and meet our new house guests."

He introduced Jon and Gabe first, she had met Travis earlier, then he turned to Isabelle and said softly, "And this is Amelia's daughter, Isabelle."

Sapphire took one look at her and folded her in a hug, and Isabelle couldn't get over the warmth and kindness in her embrace.

"Welcome, Isabelle," she said quietly, pulling back and looking at her with a big smile. "I can't tell you how I've longed to meet you. Your mama has spoken of you so much over these many years. I hope you don't mind," she added, "but I've kind of adopted her as my mama too."

Isabelle smiled and said, "No, I don't mind at all. I'm glad she's been in a place where she is so loved. She needed that so much in her life."

Sapphire nodded. "Can I call you Belle?" she asked. "Isabelle sounds so formal. Would that be okay with you?"

"That would be fine," Isabelle told her.

"Well then you must call me Sassy," she said. "My papa has called me that since I was a baby. Sass stands for my initials you see." Belle nodded, and Sapphire continued, "Your mama is sleeping right now, but let's go in and you can see her."

"As much as I'd like that," Isabelle said, "I think I'd better change first in case she wakes up. I'd like for her to see me in uniform right away."

"Okay," she replied. "Let me show you to your room then."

The men went downstairs while Sapphire led Isabelle to the room next door and showed her where the uniforms were hanging in the closet. She also showed her the attached bathroom and the box containing the other things Travis had provided for her. They stood talking for a few minutes until there was a knock on the door, and when Sapphire went and opened it, Travis came in with Isabelle's suitcase and handbag which she had left in the car.

After he left, Isabelle went into the bathroom to freshen up and change while Sassy continued to talk to her from the bedroom, bringing her up to date on her mother's condition.

"We've tried to get some information on alternative treatments," she said winding down after talking for a while, "but we haven't been able to find anything yet. We're thinking that maybe you would be the best person to get that type of information. The internet is like a maze."

"I know," Isabelle replied in understanding. "I've been thinking about alternative treatments too." She emerged

153

from the bathroom then in the scrubs which were so familiar to her. Granted, the ones she wore were either plain blue or green, but she liked the white top printed with butterflies and the dark pink pants. "I want to start doing some research as soon as possible," she said. "Maybe we can do it together since you know more about her current history than I do."

"I'd like that," Sapphire agreed as she led Isabelle out into the corridor, and they walked the short distance to Amelia's room.

When they were outside the door, Sapphire asked her if she wanted her to go in with her. Needing the support of someone else right at that moment, Isabelle told her she would, so they entered the room together.

Amelia Jordan looked small and frail lying in the bed. She had been propped up on a mound of pillows and was sleeping soundly. Her head, which had once had a bounty of flowing red hair was now completely bald but her face, although showing the signs of sickness, was still lovely at fifty-seven and looked peaceful in sleep. Isabelle stopped just inside the door and couldn't help but stare, her fingers going to her lips so she wouldn't cry out. After twenty years, she was finally reunited with her mother. It wasn't the reunion she would have wanted, but any reunion to her was a miracle. Tears coursed down her cheeks, and she asked Sapphire to excuse her for a moment. She went out the door, closing it behind her and almost ran straight into Jon who had come up to let them know supper would be ready in fifteen minutes.

He took one look at her and did what he naturally would have done for any woman in such distress. He took her in his arms and let her cry. This had nothing to do with passion of any kind, but compassion. That wasn't to say it didn't feel good to have her in his arms, it absolutely did, but his heart broke for her and as he held her, he prayed for her, whispering his petition to God out loud in her ear as he continue to let her spend her emotions.

When her crying jag was over, she eased away from him and took the handkerchief he handed her. "Better?" he asked, stepping back and allowing her to wipe away her tears.

"Yes, thank you," she said. She took a deep breath and explained, "I've had that stored up for a long time. I think I'm ready to go back in now. Would you go with me?" she asked, and he nodded, so she turned around and opened the door once more.

Sapphire looked at her with compassion and was surprised to see Jon enter behind her.

"I came to tell you that supper is about ready," he said softly, even as he looked over at Amelia.

"But I haven't had a chance to fix anything," Sapphire said, surprised.

"Gabe's pretty handy in the kitchen," he explained, turning his attention back to her. "He raided your fridge and pantry with your father's permission and is putting it together," he said. "I hope you don't mind?"

"Not at all," she replied. "I'm glad it's taken care of. Sometimes these days I am a little stretched."

"Well you have plenty of help now, so hopefully you can get a well-deserved reprieve," he said.

Sapphire smiled, "I don't remember what that's like anymore," she confessed. She turned to Isabelle who had gone over to her mother and was looking down at her. "She should sleep for at least another hour," she told her. "Some of the stuff she's taking tends to put her out for a time. Let's go eat and we can come back up later," she invited. "We'll leave the door open and there's a bell she can use if she wakes and needs anything," she added, indicating the long red velvet rope located just behind and to the side of the headboard.

They all went downstairs and into the 'Morning Room' as Jon heard the Judge refer to it. There was a round dining table in an alcove over to the left which looked out over a very large terrace. The house and grounds were so huge that Jon and Gabe knew it would take them and Isabelle a while to get the lay of the land.

Gabe had reheated some soup he'd found in the fridge and had made a salad and grilled ham and cheese sandwiches to go with it. There was also cake and ice cream with fudge topping for dessert. They all tucked in after the Judge had given thanks to God for the meal and for their new guests. Talk was light and centered around the mansion and its grounds and in no time at all, the meal was over, and Travis got ready to leave.

"Travis, why don't you stay over tonight," the Judge invited. "I'm not sure how far away you are but I know you'll probably have to overnight somewhere, even if it's at a hotel by an airport."

"You know, Judge, I think I might just take you up on that," Travis said, "as long as it won't be an inconvenience."

"Not at all," he assured him. "We always have rooms at the ready for surprise guests and people who come in off the road to break a trip for the night. Just so you know," he continued, "I've put up the 'No Vacancy' sign to keep visitors away, and we haven't taken any bookings for weddings or parties since Amelia got sick, so the place should be nice and quiet."

"Thanks, Judge," Travis said. "That will certainly help us keep track of who comes and goes. We're sorry we've turned your household upside down."

"Travis," the Judge said, looking him dead in the eye, "nothing's more important to me right now than seeing Isabelle safe and knowing she and Amelia can be with each other at this time. There are some things in life that are priceless, and this is one of them," he added, and Travis nodded in agreement.

The men went out onto the terrace while the women made their way back up the stairs. When they got to Amelia's room, they found her just stirring, but her eyes were still closed. Sapphire and Isabelle sat quietly talking for about five more minutes before Amelia opened her eyes and looked over at the women who were seated on a love seat in a corner of the room. She frowned when she saw that Sassy wasn't alone, and there was no doubt she was curious about the stranger in uniform who was conversing with her.

Both women rose and came over to the bed and Sassy made the introductions.

157

"Amelia," she said, drawing Isabelle closer to her side, "this is Isabelle. She's going to be your nurse for the time being; not that I won't continue to be with you," she hastened to add, "but she's going to be looking after you as well. Is that okay?" she asked.

Isabelle came forward, took her mother's hand in her unsteady ones and said with a smile, "I'm going to give you my very best care, Miss Jordan, if you'll permit me."

Amelia smiled at her then and said softly, "That will be fine. I've been worried that all this has been too much for Sassy," she explained. "It will be nice for her to get a break and be able to do her work and the things a young woman like her should be doing, but please," she continued, "call me Amelia. I don't stand much on formality."

"Well you just call me Belle," Isabelle replied. "I don't stand much on formality either."

They talked for some time then both women left Amelia alone for a short while. Sassy took Isabelle to the kitchen and showed her the schedule for her mother's food and medicine and they also carried up a light meal for her. They sat talking with her while she slowly ate, but she only managed to have the bowl of soup and half the sandwich before she pushed the tray away, saying she didn't have much of an appetite. Sassy took the tray from her and rested it on the chest of drawers opposite to take downstairs later, then she and Isabelle helped Amelia into the bathroom and assisted her in getting ready for bed.

When she was settled once again, Sassy took up the Bible from the night table and sat down to begin reading the Word out loud as was her habit for the last several weeks.

"Would you both please excuse me?" Isabelle asked feeling uncomfortable. "I would love to unpack if that's okay?"

"Of course, Belle," Sassy said immediately. "You go on and do what you need to do."

"I'll be back in a little while to say goodnight, Amelia," she promised before exiting the room.

Later, Isabelle lay in bed unable to sleep. To say it had been an eventful day was an understatement. She had changed her appearance, gotten a new identity and been reunited with her mother after two decades. Now as she had time to quiet down and reflect after the whirlwind, she thought about being in Jon's arms and his tenderness as she'd shed her tears.

It had felt so good to be comforted by him, and she'd been secretly touched by his praying for her. Being held close to him also ignited a longing in her that had been somewhat muted after her foolish mistake up in the mountains. Her longing, however, wasn't of a physically intimate nature. She longed just to be able to talk to him. She wanted to tell him about her life, her desires and her dreams, all the things she'd kept to herself since her grandparents had died and she'd had no one to share with.

Her grandparents had been wonderful mentors to her, especially her grandmother who had been born and raised in England. Isabelle shared a special bond with her as she had been so easy to talk to, and Patty Drummond in turn gave her granddaughter wise counsel on many of the things she would face in life. Her grandfather showed her by example what it was like to grow up with a real father, and they were constantly doing things together. He loved to go hiking and exploring the country on long drives, and he enjoyed watching English soccer. He roped her in to do things with him whenever she had a break from her studies, and they enjoyed each other's company. He also taught her to appreciate people from all walks of life and not to be intimidated by people who were higher up the ladder than she was, and his insight had been tremendously helpful to her in her chosen profession.

The one thing her Christian grandparents despaired about, however, was her stubborn refusal to listen to anything about God. She respected their faith by bowing her head at mealtimes and attending special services with them at Easter and Christmas, which they said were for family, but in every other way Isabelle ignored their efforts to bring her back to Christ. Eventually they told her they would pray for her and left it at that, but she knew they were grieved by her lack of love for the Lord.

When she had seen Sassy reach for the Bible to read to her mother, it had brought back memories of the times they had spent together as mother and daughter doing the same thing as she grew up, and between that and Jon's prayer, it touched a place in her heart she had long thought dead.

Eventually she grew tired as she lay there and turned over to sleep, determined to get some rest, but her thoughts went back to Jon time and time again and with her musings came the longing she had in her heart for them to be together.

She tossed and turned for some time until she quieted and finally felt sleep beginning to come upon her. "No use dreaming for what you can't have, Rissa," she said drowsily to herself. "No, not Rissa anymore," she corrected softly, "Isabelle. What a difference a day makes," she murmured just before she fell into a peaceful slumber.

CHAPTER 13

A week passed, and things fell into a comfortable routine. Isabelle took care of her mother during the morning and they got to know each other better. Sassy came and relieved her for a couple of hours during the afternoon, then they both spent time with her during the evening. The day rounded out with Bible reading and prayer which Belle left to Sassy after helping her get Amelia ready for bed. She usually went into the Morning Room with her knitting when she was off duty for the night and enjoyed listening to the Judge, Jon and Gabe talk while her hands worked.

During that time, Isabelle discovered that the plantation was a thriving enterprise and had activity taking place miles away from the mansion. The estate encompassed a little over four thousand acres and had a huge milking operation with hundreds of heads of dairy cows and goats. It also had an artisan cheese factory located several miles on the other side of Crescent Ville, the quaint little town which was ten miles from the estate.

The factory was a large-scale operation, employing many people from the area. It produced a line of specialty cheeses and Greek yogurt that was highly sought after by chefs, restaurants and the public alike. Their products were distributed to many stores and mainstream supermarkets around the country, and they accepted online orders for their more unique offerings. Even Jon, Gabe and Isabelle had heard of and purchased the brand from time to time.

Ted told them one night that it had been a small operation at first which had been started by his wife before

162

her death, but the cheeses had taken off almost immediately, so they had opened the factory off the property, increased the herds to match the demand and built a huge dairy on the northwestern boundary of the plantation. They had expanded even further since then and now the business was a major employer and supported not only the plantation, but many families as well. One would never know so much went on outside the mansion, however, as the surrounding hills and valleys were quiet and pristine with not an animal in sight.

They had also met Mrs. Gregory the cook, Prudence and Elaine the ladies who took care of the house and Patrick and Hanley who maintained the mansion and looked after the beautifully landscaped grounds. All of them, except for Mrs. Gregory, had been employed by the Sterlings for more than thirty years. The cook had only been with the household for a little over fifteen years after the bed and breakfast opened and Amelia had been promoted from housekeeper to bed and breakfast manager, but all the staff were treated like trusted faithful friends more than employees.

This particular afternoon, while Sassy was sitting with her mother and Jon and Gabe were busy on a conference call with Travis, Isabelle went out on the vast patio to stand at the balustrade and look out over the extensive grounds. The garden beds were terraced just below where she stood and were filled with roses of every description. A long line of steps to the far left which were bordered by dense hydrangea bushes led from there and down a wide expanse of sloping lawn, before stopping at a large pond encompassing several acres.

Its surrounding bank was filled with a profusion of trees and shrubs including several stands of weeping willows. The pond was home to ducks and other types of waterfowl including two majestic white swans, and Sassy had told her that the two 'beauties' as she called them were affectionately named Adam and Eve. Over to the left was, of all things, a maze with eight-foot high hedges, just like the ones found in formal English gardens and, beyond the pond, the land undulated between high hills in a wide valley that stretched out in the distance. The place was beautiful, and Belle could understand how her mother was able to find peace here.

Presently, she heard footsteps behind her and turned to see Judge Sterling coming to join her. She looked back over the panorama as he came up beside her, and they stood there for several moments in silence, both taking in the view.

"This place is so peaceful, Judge," she said. "It must be wonderful to have such an incredible family estate and legacy."

"It is," the Judge said. "I consider myself to be very blessed."

"This view is just amazing," Isabelle continued. "It has a way of quieting one's thoughts, for want of a better way of phrasing it."

"I know exactly what you mean," he agreed. "Sometimes I come out here after a long or stressful day to just unwind and center myself," and Isabelle nodded in understanding. She sensed he wanted to talk to her about something, but was hesitant, so she decided to give him some time to get out whatever he had to say. It wasn't long before he addressed her again, this time more tentatively.

"Belle," he said, "I've wanted to talk to you about the

past, that is as it relates to your mother, but I've hesitated since you've only been here a short while and have been through so much."

"You can talk to me anytime, Judge," she assured him, "I'm fine, really. I admit the first day or two was a little rough," she added, "but I'm settled now, so shoot."

He smiled. "Your straightforwardness reminds me so much of your mother," he said, and for the first time she noticed how his voice softened when he mentioned Amelia. Even the contours of his face gentled and his expression grew pensive, and it was at that moment it hit her.

"He's in love with her," she said to herself in wonder, her mouth almost falling open in shock at her discovery.

She thought back over the last few days, remembering the times when he had come in to see how Amelia was doing or when he had spoken of her and she figuratively kicked herself for being so blind. It had all been there for her to see if she had only cared to look. Granted she'd been wrapped up in her own adjustments, but she should have been able to pick up on the subtleties.

She was so stunned that without an ounce of caution, she blurted, "How long have you been in love with her?"

He looked at her startled, then his shoulders slumped, "Is it that obvious?" he asked.

"No," she said, gentling her voice, "I only just realized it."

"I've loved your mother for over ten years," he said, no

165

longer trying to hide his feelings. "I've wanted to marry her for nearly half that time but, although she loves me too, she says she's too terrified to try and find your father to ask for a divorce. Not only that, but she says she doesn't believe in divorce. She says no matter what he's done, she made her vow before God and she just doesn't feel right about breaking it."

"But why should that be an issue anymore?" Isabelle asked perplexed. "Surely with him being dead there's no reason you both can't get married."

The Judge looked at her in absolute shock. "What are you talking about, Belle?" he asked totally stunned. "What do you mean he's dead?"

"You mean you didn't know he was killed in the Amazon where he was a missionary?" she asked astonished. "How could you not know? It was all over the news when it happened."

"Isabelle," he said, holding onto the stone railing for support as if his knees would give way, "this is the first time I'm hearing any of this. Are you sure you have your facts straight?" he asked, unable to believe what she was telling him.

"I should hope so," she replied. "I was the one who had to identify his remains when they brought him back to the States and bury him."

"I think I need to sit down," the Judge said, and Isabelle noticed he'd become very pale.

They moved over to a grouping of chairs further back

from the balustrade and sat down facing each other.

"You don't look well, Judge," Isabelle commented with concern. "Do you have a heart condition?" she asked, as she reached out her hand to his and began to take his pulse.

"No," he responded. "I just have a little problem with my blood pressure from time to time that's all."

She found his heart rate to be quite rapid and he was still looking pale. "You stay here and don't move a muscle," she instructed, slipping into full medical mode. "I'll be right back."

She ran up to her room, picked up her stethoscope and the blood pressure monitor she kept there and was back downstairs and out on the terrace within minutes. She attached the cuff to his arm, took the reading and found it to be quite high.

"Do you take any medication to regulate your pressure, Judge?" she asked when she'd finished.

"Well yes," he replied, "but only when it's necessary."

"Is that what your doctor told you to do?" she questioned, looking at him intently, but he looked away and she had her answer.

"Now you listen to me, Judge Sterling, and you listen well," she said, as she began reading him the riot act. "I want you to take that tablet every morning, no ifs ands or buts, and I'm going to see to it that you don't miss one day," he opened his mouth to protest, but she just gave him a hard look and said. "If you love Sassy and my mother," she continued, "and I'm saying this with all due respect, you'll do exactly as I say, do you understand?"

The Judge looked at her with a stern expression that had intimidated many a criminal, witness and lawyer, but she just looked right back without flinching, not in the least bit bothered by his stony gaze.

"You're a mean little thing, aren't you?" he said wryly when he saw she wasn't going to back down, his expression softening into a grin.

She smiled back, "So I've been told by many a patient," she confirmed. "You have to understand, Judge, that as a cardiologist I've seen a lot in my profession," she said. "I've seen people who'd never been sick a day in their life die suddenly or become severely incapacitated from either a heart attack or a stroke. That always makes me sad," she explained, "because they didn't see it coming. I get incensed, however, when people know they have an issue and refuse to take their meds. That's when I get really mean."

"I didn't know you were a cardiologist," the Judge said in surprise. "Travis only told me you were a doctor."

"Well I am," Isabelle said, "so you can't pull the wool over my eyes and tell me any nonsense," she added.

"Okay," he said in defeat, "you win."

"Good," she responded. "And I'm going to take your blood pressure morning and evening," she added, much to his chagrin. He opened his mouth to protest again, but at her look he closed it and said instead, "Alright, now if you don't mind, could you please tell me about your father?"

"Not yet," she said. "Where do you keep your pills?"

He told her where to look in the kitchen cupboard and she went in and fetched them along with a glass of water and watched him put the tablet on his tongue and wash it down. Once he was through, she took his pulse and pressure one more time and although both were still elevated, they had come down a bit from where they were before, so she decided it was fine for their conversation to continue.

"Okay," she said as she settled back to tell him the story. "Now I'll tell you what happened: I got a call from his missions' board one Saturday afternoon near to Thanksgiving."

"How long ago was this?" the Judge interrupted.

"Nearly three years now," Isabelle said, "just about eight months after I lost my grandparents. Anyway," she continued, "they said they'd been searching for me for nearly two weeks before they finally tracked me down. They said they regretted to inform me that my father had been killed at the village where he'd been serving in the jungles of South America. As I was his next of kin, they wanted me to come and claim his body and arrange for his burial. I later learned that he'd so enraged two of the tribesmen there that one night they went into his tent and slit his throat." The Judge winced at her description.

"The missions' board tried to keep it quiet, but word got out about a week after the funeral. It was a five-day wonder when it happened. I don't understand how you and Mom never heard about it."

The Judge sat deep in thought. "Come to think of it," he said, "that's the time I was in Hong Kong visiting my sister and her husband. They'd been begging me to visit for years, so I went over to surprise her for her fiftieth birthday. I was gone about ten days. It must have happened while I was away. Sass was attending college in North Carolina at the time, finishing her master's degree, and Amelia doesn't watch much television so that's probably why we missed the story.

"You know, Belle," he continued, "Amelia never spoke ill of your father; not even once, but I knew she hadn't had it easy. Would you tell me a little about what you both went through?" he asked. "If you'd rather not talk about it, I understand. I just want to get a better grasp of what happened."

As he requested, Isabelle spent the next half-an-hour telling the Judge the story she had told Jon but went into more detail so he would know fully what her mother had been up against.

"I don't blame her one bit for leaving him," she said. "I only wish she'd taken me with her or kept in touch, so we wouldn't have become separated. I know her last night in the house was probably what precipitated her departure," she added. "He gave her a particularly brutal beating and she could hardly walk the next morning."

"I knew things must have been bad for her to leave him," the Judge said, "but never in a million years could I have imagined anything like what you've just described," he shook his head in disbelief. "No wonder she was terrified he would find her. What happened to you after she left?" he asked then.

Isabelle went on to relate to him what she had done, told him about her flight to her grandparent's house and a little about her love for them and about her education.

"They were so wonderful to me, Judge," she said winding down. "My grandfather showed me what it was like to have a real father, and my grandmother was just like my Mom."

"How did they die?" he asked.

"They were on a trip to the Far East and got food poisoning," she said sadly. "They both died within hours of each other."

"I'm so sorry, Belle," he said, "but I'm glad you had them in your life," he added. "I'm glad they were able to help you erase some of the memories."

"Me too," she agreed.

"You must have been devastated when they died," he continued, "especially as you didn't know where your mother was."

"Yes, I was," she said. "They were the last relatives I knew I had at the time. I didn't know if Mom was alive or dead and as far as I was concerned my father no longer existed. I hated him so completely," she declared with absolute frankness. "You know, Judge, the only reason I went in and identified his body was because I wanted to make sure it was him and he was gone for good. I wanted to know for certain I didn't have to look over my shoulder anymore," and the Judge nodded. "Besides me and the priest," she continued, "only two members of the missions'

171

board were at his funeral. That alone was testament to the legacy Adrian Sparks left behind.

"I stood there after the others had gone and watch them inter him," she added remembering. "When the workers had capped and sealed his tomb, I turned and walked away without a backward glance. It was finished. I had done my duty. Initially, I was just thinking of cremating him and throwing his ashes in the trash," she said bitterly, "but I knew my mother wouldn't have wanted that, so I gave him a full burial instead. The thought of him rotting in darkness seemed like a fitting end anyway. I know what I've just said has probably shocked you," she added, "and I'm sorry, but I can't and won't lie about my feelings towards him. I hate him to this day."

"I understand, Belle," he said. "You don't have to explain. You both went through a horrendous experience and healing from something like that takes time."

The Judge understood, right or wrong, why Isabelle felt the way she did. He also knew from Sassy that she never stayed with them for Bible reading and prayer at the end of the day, and it grieved his heart to know she had apparently turned away from God because of her earthly father.

"Lord," he said as he sat there with his eyes open. "I'm going to pray for this young lady. I know the experiences we go through, especially in our formative years, not only shape us but can lead to anger, hurt and bitterness. Lord, You bore even that for us when You died on the Cross; You bore it all. Father, You're such a good and loving God. Please help Isabelle to know that and to give her life back to You I pray, in Jesus' name, amen."

He knew they needed to change the subject, so he decided to break the ensuring silence and speak his heart, "Belle, I love your mother very much," and she nodded. "I know you've been through a lot and I know you haven't known me very long, but I want to ask you something."

"You can ask me anything, Judge," she said, deliberately pushing the memories aside and focusing on her host.

"I wanted to know if you'd have any objection to my asking your mother to marry me?" he inquired. "I promise you I'll take good care of her," he added sincerely.

"I have no objections whatsoever, Judge" she said with a gentle smile, "I think you'll make a wonderful husband for my Mom," then growing serious she continued, "I don't know how much time she has left or if we'll be able to find the right treatment for her, but I want to see you both grasp life and run with it. I want to see you both happy for however long that will be."

"Thank you, Belle," he said, "and please call me Ted," he invited with a smile. "After all, if we're going to be related, we might as well drop this Judge business."

"How about I call you step-papa?" she teased, grinning.

"How about just Ted?" he grinned back, and she laughed.

He was so glad they had recovered from their earlier difficult conversation, and he went on to tell her that he would propose to her mother later that night.

"There was a newspaper article that came out shortly

after everything happened," Isabelle informed him. "Why don't I give you the approximate time it was published, and you can research it and maybe print it for her to see. That way she'll just think you came across it and not become suspicious about how you got the information."

"That's a good idea," Ted acknowledged.

They sat talking for a long time and when Isabelle asked how her mother had come to work for him and Sassy, Ted told her that side of the story.

"Our housekeeper who was also a sort of governess to Sassy had gotten married and gone to live in another state," he said. "I'd been looking for her replacement for about two months when I got a call from your mother in answer to an ad I'd run in the local paper that morning. I was really desperate by this time. We hadn't opened the bed and breakfast yet," he explained, "that came later, but I was working full-time, and Sass was only fifteen and needed proper supervision. I'd interviewed several people sent to me through an agency, but they were all unsuitable. They were more in awe of the mansion than interested in the job.

"Anyway, I agreed to see your mother and asked her to meet me in the courthouse cafeteria for coffee. It was more convenient for me that day, and I figured there wouldn't be the type of distraction there that interviewing her at the mansion would cause." Isabelle nodded in understanding.

"I got to our appointment a little late, but I'd told her where to meet me and when I stepped in and saw her sitting there, I knew she was exactly the type of person I was looking for. We met and chatted for a while, but I noticed she kept watching the door and seemed uncomfortable,"

Ted said remembering.

"Eventually, I asked her point blank who she was running away from, it was so obvious. She looked at me with tears in her eyes, thanked me for the coffee and my time and rose to leave, she was so sure she wouldn't get the job. To be honest I didn't feel too confident about employing her either. She was a stranger to me, and I had Sassy to think about." Isabelle could picture the scene in her mind and knew she would have felt the same way if she had been in Ted's position.

"What happened then?" she asked.

"Well, just as abruptly as she got out of the chair," Ted continued, "she sat back down, looked me in the eye and told me she was running away from her husband, that her name wasn't the one she'd given me and that she wouldn't blame me for not employing her, but she needed the job. She went on to explain that although she had a degree in Art History, she'd gotten married straight out of college and had no work experience. She said, however, that she was a responsible Christian woman and I wouldn't regret hiring her. She just spoke to me with complete honesty, Belle, and that's what started turning the tide for me.

"We discussed her dilemma and she told me she just needed a place to work and feel safe. I asked her why she was running away from your father and she told me he abused her, but not much more than that. I asked her if she had any children and she told me she had an eighteen-year-old daughter, but that you were living with her parents. She said she didn't want to cause trouble for you or for them with your father so that's why she'd decided to head east and as far away from you as possible."

175

"He did come around to my grandparents' place about a week after we'd both left," Belle said. "His jaw was wired shut and he could hardly talk, but he asked my grandfather for us. Grandpa told him he hadn't seen us, which was technically true. I went straight from the bus station to a good friend of theirs because they didn't want me at their place in case he came looking. He hung around for about three days watching the house, but my grandparents knew he was there. About two weeks after they'd seen him for the last time, they picked me up, and I went to live with them."

"Well it seems he must have left there and begun trailing Amelia," Ted said, "although that's just supposition on my part. After our initial discussion, she didn't talk about him much."

"What finally made you decide to hire her?" Isabelle asked, so glad to be able to get some information about what had happened to her mother at that time.

"I felt God's urging in my spirit," Ted explained, "and I just couldn't get over how right she was for the job. To know she had raised a daughter was another plus. She would know exactly how to look after Sassy. Eventually, I told her I would try her, but I wanted to help her change her name legally, not only to protect her, but the protect Sassy as well. She agreed and within a short time she became Amelia Jordan and she's been with us ever since."

"Ted, I want to thank you again for taking a chance with her and for treating her so well," Isabelle said with sincerity. "She went through so much, and I'm glad she found you and Sassy and could finally have some peace."

"There's no need for thanks, Belle," he said. "Your

mother has added so much to our lives. She's wise beyond her years, and her perspective on things and on life has helped me a number of times."

"When do you want to speak with her?" Isabelle asked.

"How about after she has supper?" Ted suggested. "I'll research the article then go and see her."

"Sounds like a plan," Isabelle said, and they went on to talk about other things.

****

Later that evening after Ted had spoken to Sassy, he went up to Amelia's room. Isabelle had given her supper which she had just finished eating and when Ted came in, Isabelle took the tray downstairs in order to give them some privacy.

Ted sat in the chair by Amelia's bedside and held onto her hand. She smiled at him and allowed her love to shine from her eyes. "How are you, Teddy?" she asked. She was always careful never to address him that way unless they were alone.

"I'm doing fine," he said. "You look perky this evening," he commented.

"It's been one of my better days," she agreed.

She'd only been in bed for the last month and a half because she was feeling too weak to stand for long periods. She was not responding well to the new medication she was taking either, and it added to her fatigue. Her oncologist had promised to change it on her next visit if things didn't improve, but he wanted her to give it a chance first.

"Amelia," he began, "there's something I discovered today, and I want to talk to you about it."

"What is it?" she asked curiously, searching his eyes as he looked at her. He hesitated a moment, so she said, "Just tell me, Teddy, I'm okay, really."

"Your husband is dead, Ame," he said. "He died almost three years ago," and Amelia's eyes widened in shocked disbelief.

"Are you sure?" she asked.

He nodded and removed a copy of the newspaper article from his pocket. He read it to her then gave her so she could see it.

"You mean all this time he was dead, and we never knew?" she asked stunned, and Ted nodded again. "We could have gotten married before all this and at least have had a few years together." Her eyes filled with tears and she looked away, shaking her head. "Life can be so utterly unfair."

"Ame, there's absolutely nothing stopping us from getting married anyway, you know," Ted said. "I love you and I want to be your husband."

"No, Teddy," she said emphatically, looking back at him and then away again. "I don't want to be a burden to you, and I don't want you to suffer through the pain of losing another wife. I love you too much to do that to you."

"Amelia," he said, taking his hand and lifting her chin, turning her face so she could look into his eyes, "do you think I wouldn't suffer whether we were married or not?" he asked. "I want the right to be able to hug you close at night, to know I can speak on your behalf and take care of you. Please Ame," he pleaded with an earnestness she couldn't ignore.

"Are you absolutely sure?" she asked with doubt in her voice.

"I've never been more certain of anything in my life," he said, "and Sassy couldn't contain herself when I told her I was coming up here to propose. I've waited so long, sweetheart," he continued, "please don't say no."

Amelia smiled then and said with love pouring from her eyes. "Okay, Teddy, alright, I'll marry you."

She saw him relax then he moved from the chair and came to sit on the side of the bed. "Now isn't it nicer to see me here than in that old chair?" he asked her with a mischievous grin.

"It would be a lot nicer if you'd propose to me properly, Theodore Sterling, and then seal it was a kiss," she said boldly, and he threw back his head and laughed.

He got down on one knee, looked her in the eyes and said, "My sweet, Amelia, I love you. Would you do me the honor of becoming my wife?"

She grinned at him and said, "Of course I'll marry you, Teddy. What took you so long to ask?" she teased, and laughing he got up and sat on the bed once more.

He quieted down, and they looked into each other's eyes, both unable to believe that the moment had finally come, then he lifted her tenderly into his arms and kissed her for the first time.

"You taste just as sweet as I knew you would," he murmured before capturing her lips once more. "I love you so much, Ame," he said when they came up for air.

"And I love you," she said, running her fingers through one side of his hair. "I love you with all my heart. Could you do me a favor, Ted?" she asked.

"Anything," he replied.

"Could you please kiss me again?" she begged, and he was only too happy to comply.

****

They were married two days later by Ted's best friend and fellow judge Jerry Warner. Besides Jon, Gabe, Isabelle and Sassy, only Jerry's wife, Laura, and the mansion's faithful staff were in attendance. Amelia refused to take her vows sitting down, so Ted put his arm around her waist, and she put hers around him for support during the ceremony.

Mrs. Gregory prepared a sumptuous meal for after. She also baked and iced a two-tier cake for them, decorating it with pink and white roses from the garden and Amelia declared that nothing they bought from a bakery could have been prettier.

Later, Belle and Sassy transferred Amelia's things into the massive master bedroom suite on the third floor and as

Amelia was very tired, they got her ready for bed early then left her with her husband. After seeing the two women out and closing the door, Ted went back into the bedroom, got into the bed then took his new bride in his arms.

"Are you okay, my precious?" he asked, and she cuddled against his chest with her arms around him.

"I'm fine, Teddy," she replied, "just a little tired. Why don't you get ready for bed," she suggested, so he got up, undressed, brushed his teeth and put on boxers and a t-shirt, which was his standard sleeping attire, then slipped back into the bed with her.

"Now, why don't you help me undress and we can get up to a little fun," she smiled, and he pulled back, looking at her in shocked surprise.

"Amelia," he said, "I didn't expect us to do anything like that, not in your weakened condition."

She looked at him with the forthrightness she'd gained since leaving her home all those years ago and said, "Theodore, do you want to make love to me or not?"

"Yes, of course I do," he began replying, "but…."

She interrupted him, however, before he could finish, "And I want to make love to you," she declared, placing her hand on his cheek. "I want to know what it's like to make love to someone because I love them and because they love me. I want to feel what it's like to give myself to someone not out of duty but out of a deep longing and desire for intimacy with them.

"I don't know what the future holds for us," she added, "whether I'll survive this or not," but I don't want to waste a moment of it not doing things because I'm cautious and careful. I've spent too many years of my life doing that, so please Ted," she pleaded, taking her hand from his cheek and running it into his hair, "please make love to me."

He pulled her gently to him then and kissed her with the longing of ten pent up years and she kissed him back with equal heat. Then he did just what she asked. With infinite care, he helped her to undress and they made love to each other with all the passion and joy they were feeling in their hearts before she fell asleep in his arms.

"She's right," Ted said to himself as he cuddled her close, "this isn't the time for us to be cautious. This is the time for us to live and love as if there's no tomorrow."

CHAPTER 14

Cornelius Antonelli stood on the aft deck of his luxury motor yacht, The Aide-De-Camp, and watched as the Captain brought her into Jupiter Inlet then bear right onto the Indian River. He loved the yacht and used every opportunity to take it out on the water. He'd had business in Miami that morning and had sailed down to his meeting instead of taking a car. He was very pleased with the outcome of the deal he'd transacted and thought that if it wasn't for the trouble with Constantine, life would be great.

He had been encouraging his twin of late to go down to his home near Vera Cruz in Mexico and run the business at that end until his current dilemma was resolved, but Constantine wouldn't hear of it. He said he didn't know a word of Spanish or his twins' contacts there, but Cornelius knew it was really Lahali and her pregnancy that was keeping his brother in the States. He had told Constantine to leave his wife and the boys with Frank and head for safer climes, then she could join him after the baby was born and things had settled, but he wouldn't even entertain the idea.

Cornelius looked at the mansions along the intra-coastal as he was sailing by, but he wasn't really seeing them. He was thinking of the love Constantine had for Lahali and his children and couldn't help but be relieved he had remained single. Women messed with a man's brain and made him do stupid things, even the most intelligent ones as he considered his brother to be.

A good example of that was when Cornelius had asked Constantine why he had done something so senseless as to cheat on Lahali if he loved her so much. His twins answer had surprised and amused him all at the same time. He told Cornelius he had been missing his wife and needed relief from his pent-up frustration, so as Lucinda was hot, willing and available, he'd used her to satisfy his needs.

Cornelius heard the crew scrambling about and turned around to see his berth coming up on the starboard side. Within a short while the yacht was docked, so he disembarked and went over to the golf cart that was waiting for him. He got in then drove himself away from the pier and across the road to his mansion which sat facing the Atlantic Ocean.

Whereas Constantine loved his wife and children, Cornelius loved real estate, and had several homes in different countries around the world. This house and acreage in Florida was his favorite, however, and in times past he would sail from Vera Cruz to vacation here and go fishing off the Bahamas. Constantine, Lahali, the children and quite often Frank would visit him when he was in residence and while he, his brother and cousin discussed business, Lahali and the boys spent their time on the beach.

Cornelius parked the cart by the front steps and went inside, not stopping until he was on the expansive patio that looked out over the Atlantic. He went down the steps and walked out onto the beach near to the water's edge then, pulling his phone from his pocket, he called his twin.

"Hey, Neil," Constantine answered, "how did the meeting go?"

"Very well," he replied, and he filled him in on the discussions.

"Excellent," Constantine responded. "When are you going to make the delivery?"

"I'll tell Juan to move the stuff the day after tomorrow," he replied.

"Okay," Constantine said. "I'll send Frank down to take delivery."

"Anything new on your case?" Cornelius asked him.

"Not a thing," he replied. "I've pulled in just about every favor and no one knows anything. It's at times like this I miss Ralph," he said, speaking of the informant he'd had at the Bureau. "He was a greedy leech, but he always delivered."

"It's surprising Crew can't help us," Cornelius said, speaking of their childhood friend who was now in Washington D.C.

"Remember he told me months ago that the Bureau made some big changes when Ralph was found out and arrested," Constantine said.

"I remember," Cornelius responded, deep in thought. "That new department they have appears to be good," he added. "It's like a ghost. No one knows where it's located or anything about it."

"They must be the ones who have her stashed," Constantine reflected. "I get the impression they're like the Area Fifty-One of the Bureau. The thing is if we don't know who works there, it's a dead end. You can't buy someone off or extort them if you don't know who to buy or extort."

"You know, you just gave me an idea," Cornelius smiled as the thought struck him. "We've being going about this all wrong, Con. We need to stop doing the usual and go outside the box this time, and I have a pretty good idea what our next move should be."

"What are you thinking," Constantine asked. Cornelius was one of the smartest men he knew so he was always interested in hearing his thoughts.

"All this time we've been hunting the cub, Con," he said with a grin. "I think we need to start hunting the lion instead," and went on to outline his plan to his twin.

"That's genius, Neil," Constantine replied with a grin of his own. "Just brilliant."

"It will take a bit of creativity on Crew's part, but it just might work," Cornelius said.

"You call him and see if he'll be willing to help us," Constantine encouraged. "I've already sent Jimmy off on a fact-finding mission."

"To do what?" Cornelius asked curiously.

"I hear the Doctor's mother disappeared about twenty years ago and hasn't been seen since," Constantine explained. "I know it's a long shot, but if Jimmy can find her, maybe we can use her as bait. I haven't thought it through completely," he added, "but let me see what he can dig up. I like your plan better, but it's always good to have a Plan B."

"How are you going to use the mother as bait?" his

186

brother asked.

"I don't know, but right now I'll try anything," Constantine declared. "My only hope is finding the Doctor and silencing her for good, and if either one of our plans work, I'll be home free."

CHAPTER 15

Gabe stood at the balustrade of the expansive patio in the early morning light looking out as the scenery before him began coming to life. This place was just beautiful, and he found himself being drawn to it. He could really breathe here, and he wondered what it was that made it so different. In many ways Jacob's Mountain had far more dramatic and magnificent vistas, but there was something about this place that brought a peace to his soul he couldn't explain.

He found himself thinking more and more about Gina and their life together since he'd been here, and he also thought about his family and how much he missed them. He knew in his heart he was just existing. His days had a predictable sameness that was safe, but at the same time meaningless, and although he was tired of living the way he was, he felt too numb and hopeless to make the changes that would alter his life.

He sometimes watched people running after things like the latest gadget or car and wondered what on earth was wrong with them. Didn't they realize they could get something today and tomorrow be gone from this world without having the chance to enjoy it, just like his precious Gina? What was the point of it all?

He thought of her now, remembering their last night together and his heart ached him. They'd been so happy, and she'd been so excited about giving her life to Christ that they'd talked into the early morning without a thought that it would all end in a few short hours. Nothing could have prepared them for that next day and the devastating events that had robbed her of life and put him in this pit, and for that reason Gabe looked at happiness as a waste of time. Nothing that was sweet or brought true joy lasted forever.

With great effort he put his morose thoughts back in their compartment in his brain and firmly closed the door, determined to focus on the lovely morning and the day ahead. He found that if he didn't deliberately take control of his depressing thoughts, they would pull him down into a sea of blame and regret and he just didn't want to go there.

He drained his coffee cup and rested it on the balustrade, continuing to watch as the mist began to lift in little increments and bring the pond into full view. He thought of going inside and pouring one final cup of coffee before throwing out the rest and washing out the container, but he decided to stay a little longer. He'd wait a few more minutes until the valley came into full view and the sun bathed everything in light before heading indoors.

A short while later, he roused himself and decided he'd better go in and deal with the carafe. Sapphire Sterling always came down at about six o'clock to make enough coffee to last through the morning, and he made sure not to be around when she came into the kitchen. He was usually back in the Morning Room where he and Jon had set themselves up for their watches long before she came downstairs and, except for supper, he didn't see her much through the day which was fine with him.

Just as he was about to pick up his cup, he heard a slight noise and turned to locate the source of the sound. To his surprise, he saw Miss Sterling as he always called her making her way out to him with a coffee cup in hand, sipping the brew which he could see steaming, and he kicked himself inwardly for lingering so long.

"Great," he said with sarcasm under his breath, "I'm late and she's early."

She joined him at the balustrade and said, "Good morning, Gabe. I took the last of the coffee. I hope you don't mind."

He turned back to look out at the scenery once again and said, "That's fine. I just finished my last cup."

"It's a joy for me to drink this," she stated. "I usually have to suffer through the weaker brew preferred by everyone else unless I make a cup for myself in my studio." He didn't answer so she turned and looked out at the early dawn and continued to sip from her cup. "Wasn't the wedding lovely?" she asked. "I'm so glad to see Papa and Amelia able to marry after all this time."

He grunted but said nothing, and she looked over at him to see what was wrong. His face was solemn but not unapproachable, so she continued, "I'm just happy to see them happy, even if the future is uncertain. I know you're here working," she added, "but are you enjoying your stay?" she asked, trying to draw him into conversation.

"I've been in worse places I suppose," he replied cryptically.

"He's not one for talking much is he?" Sapphire thought as she continued to enjoy her coffee and look out at the newly dawned day.

She always tried to speak with each guest and make them

190

as comfortable as possible. They entertained so many visitors that it had become natural for her to talk to them and pull them out of their shell by asking a little bit about where they were from, what they did for a living and if they had everything they needed. It was something she did all the time.

"The history of this place is fascinating," she went on, ignoring his lack of response, thinking he must just be tired after a long night. "I'd love to share it with you sometime if you're interested. It….," she would have continued, but just then Gabe turned to her, and he looked so annoyed she stopped what she was saying and stared at him with a puzzled expression.

"What do you really want, Miss Sterling?" he asked in a biting tone but gave her no time to answer. "I can assure you I'm not looking for a relationship with anyone, so if that's what you're after, you may as well just sashay your little southern fanny back inside and leave me in peace. I'm tired of women hitting on me."

Sapphire was so shocked that her mouth fell open and the cup she was holding slipped from her fingers and shattered on the floor between them. Within seconds, however, she recovered from her complete surprise and felt anger erupt through her body, turning her face red and causing her to lose her temper.

"Of all the absolute nerve," she said. "Do you think I'm coming on to you?" she asked incredulously.

"If the shoe fits," was his dry response.

"Now you listen to me you insufferable, egotistical cur,"

191

she said, her temper becoming so inflamed she didn't guard her tongue, "I'm still at this moment recovering from the last encounter I had with one of your specie and a relationship with you or your kind is the last thing in this world I want. I'm thoroughly sick of the lot of you.

"It's a pity the human race can't survive without you," she continued, spewing out her contempt, "oh what a joy that would be. You can rest assured I have no designs on the likes of you Gabe whatever your name is. Arrogant jerks are not my cup of tea," and with that she turned and stalked away, but not before he caught the remark she made in fury under her breath, "Conceited pig."

Gabe's mouth gaped as he stared at her retreating back, and a few moments later he heard the kitchen door slam behind her. He thought back to when she had come out onto the terrace earlier and lowered his head in shame.

"Gracious, have I really sunk so low?" he asked himself.

Sapphire Sterling hadn't said or done one thing to promote the kind of response he had given her, and he felt like a toad. He had no idea why he'd gone on the attack like that. She had every right to be angry, but he was also surprised by her temper. She was always so quiet and serene that he'd had no idea she was so full of fire. One thing he knew for certain was he had to apologize to her. He hated apologizing to anyone, but he knew he needed to this time.

He bent and picked up the shattered shards of crockery she'd left behind and took himself back to the kitchen to dispose of the pieces, regret weighing his shoulders.

"I'll do it in the morning," he said. "That's just about the only time I'll be able to find her alone."

****

The following morning Sapphire made her way down the back stairs at the usual time, being extra careful to make sure the kitchen was empty before she entered.

"At least that arrogant cad is nowhere in sight," she whispered to herself, then felt contrite. "Please forgive me, Father," she said. She'd been asking God to pardon her a lot since her encounter with Gabe the morning before, but she became totally incensed every time she remembered his unfounded accusations and had been issuing scathing remarks at him in her thoughts ever since.

She found the coffee pot empty and clean, so she figured he must have already finished his final cup of the morning. She put on the weaker brew to begin dripping then went outside and up the steps to the terrace after looking around the wall that separated it from the kitchen's back door to make sure she'd be alone.

She looked out over the lovely morning and drew in a deep breath. She loved this time of day. She always felt she was the only human being awake in the world at this hour. The dew was wet on the grass and flowers, and there was a slight haze over the hills and valley which stretched out before her.

She stood there wanting to calm her tumultuous emotions and regain her usual serene demeanor, so she decided to think pleasant thoughts and made herself dwell on her father and Amelia. In just a few short days it was as if their love had bloomed, and it was simply beautiful to

193

watch. Amelia had begun to rally, and her father doted on her as they spent every waking and sleeping moment together.

Isabelle was always nearby in case her mother needed assistance, but much of the time Ted was there to see to Amelia's every need. She knew Isabelle gave them plenty of privacy, but made sure Amelia took her meds and had her meals on schedule. The rest of the time she spent working on her knitting. Sassy wasn't really needed at all, so she spent long hours in her studio catching up on her work as an illustrator.

She was just thinking of going to check if the coffee was ready when she heard a noise coming from the direction of the kitchen, and she looked around to see Gabe coming towards her with a cup of coffee in each hand and a small plate balanced on top of one.

"Oh, this is just perfect," she said to herself in exasperation. "I thought I wouldn't have to see him today."

She turned to make her way inside via the Morning Room door when he called to her, "Miss Sterling, please wait." She hesitated a moment, trying to decide what to do, but it was enough time for him to reach her, and he held out a cup to her saying, "It's strong, just the way you like it. I saved it in the microwave for you."

She looked at him suspiciously and asked, "Why?" before adding, "I suppose you'd like us to sit and chat so you can tell me how fantastic you are?"

"Ouch," he replied. "You really have a sharp tongue you know, but I deserve your anger," he acknowledged. "Please

194

take the coffee so I can put down the plate," he asked, and she did as he requested, eyeing the contents of the dish as he rested it on the wide balustrade.

"What's that?" she asked, noticing the little pale tan squares on it.

"A peace offering of sorts I guess," Gabe said. "I, uh," he paused then continued. "I'm sorry for what I said to you yesterday. You were right," he added, "I was being an arrogant jerk."

"I said that?" she asked, her eyes widening.

"Word for word," he replied.

"I was so angry I don't even remember what I said," she replied, her southern drawl deepening. "You made me madder than a wet hen. Why did you accuse me of coming on to you?" she asked. "I wasn't you know."

"I know that now," he said hanging his head. "I tend to dive headfirst down people's throats these days," he confessed. "It's a bad habit. I've had so many women throw themselves at me in the last six years I just thought you were another in the long line," he explained. "I really am sorry." He held out the plate to her and told her to have a piece.

She took one of the confections in her fingers and asked, "What is it?"

"It's maple fudge," he replied, "one of my few indulgences."

"I haven't had fudge in years," she said, taking a bite. She

195

closed her eyes and savored its creamy smoothness. "This is good," she acknowledged. "Thank you."

"You're welcome," he said, glad she seemed receptive to his offering and his apology.

"Why six years?" she questioned out of the blue.

"Pardon me?" he asked, not quite following.

"You said that for the last six years women have been hitting on you," she said, reaching for another piece of fudge which she was enjoying between sips of coffee. "Weren't they hitting on you before that?"

He looked out on the scenery and said quietly, "No, not really. I was married then."

She glanced over at his profile, saw a profound sadness there that was impossible for him to hide and suddenly she knew.

"She died, didn't she?" Sapphire said, more of a statement than a question, and he nodded. "I'm so sorry, Gabe," she said, unconsciously resting her hand on his arm, but she removed it immediately when he flinched. "Life sucks sometimes, doesn't it?" she said, not expecting a response. She turned from him and looked out over the morning. "What was she like?" she asked after they were silent for several moments.

"Like?" he questioned, not quite sure what she was getting at.

"What was she like?" Sapphire repeated. "Tell me about

196

her," she said. "Don't you talk about her much?"

"I don't really talk about her at all," he stated, looking at her to see if she was genuinely interested or just being inquisitive.

He noticed the compassion in her eyes as she said, "Why on earth wouldn't you talk about someone who you obviously loved and who meant the world to you? My Papa talks about my Mama to this day and she's been gone nearly twenty-five years."

"No one except Jon speaks to me about her," he stated, hoping she would get the hint.

"Well no wonder if you're always pushing people away," she said reasonably.

"Could we move on please?" he asked, not wanting to get in trouble with her again by telling her to mind her own business. "I'm really not up to having this discussion right now."

"Okay," she said, "but I don't see why not."

"How about you tell me what one of my kind did to you?" he threw the question at her.

"I ...," she paused. "Touché," she said, looking down at the ground, "I get your point."

"Oh no you don't," he said. "You're not getting away that easy. What unpardonable sin did my gender do to you to make you hate all men?" he asked, looking at her.

"I don't hate all men," she said pensively, and he could see the deep hurt in her eyes, "just the ones who marry you when they already have two wives who aren't dead and who they haven't divorced.

Gabe looked at her in shock. "You're kidding right?" he asked.

"No, Gabe," she replied, "I'm not kidding. Do you have any idea how humiliating it is to have someone marry you so they can get their hands on your money and….," she paused but didn't continue.

"Sapphire," he said, a rare expression of compassion coming to his eyes, "I'm so very sorry," and she nodded before looking away.

"We make a fine pair, don't we," she said a short while later, turning back to him. "You want nothing to do with women and I want nothing to do with men."

"Sounds like the basis for a great friendship if you ask me," he said, raising his cup to hers.

She knocked hers against his in agreement and said with a smile, "That's just what I was thinking."

They went on to talk about other things, their former fuss forgotten in light of what they'd shared. It was a beginning of sorts for both of them. Gabe finally found someone who he didn't view as a threat and was easy to talk to. He missed his sisters and Sapphire was a good substitute. Sapphire, on the other hand, now had the chance to relate to a man who was her contemporary without having to worry about a come on or an ulterior motive, someone she could share herself with in complete openness without fear of any kind.

They were able to relax and relate to each other with the confidence of knowing there was no chance of any romantic involvement, and it brought them the sense of peace in friendship with the opposite sex they had needed for so long.

CHAPTER 16

One evening a week later, just after they'd had supper, Sassy invited Isabelle up to her studio so they could continue doing their research on a treatment for Amelia. They had started working on it together just a few days after Isabelle arrived and had narrowed down the possibilities to two. An hour later, they made the decision to go with a doctor in Nashville who was using a less aggressive chemotherapy treatment and Radiation and getting very good results. He also had nutritional plans for his patients and used other holistic methods and both Isabelle and Sassy liked that a lot. They knew there was no guarantee as each person was given their own specially formulated 'cocktail' when it came to chemotherapy, but in all the options they'd explored, they felt this doctor's approach was the best.

"Let's run everything by your dad and see what he thinks," Isabelle said when the decision was made. "If he approves, I'll get Travis to make the arrangements for us to go and see Dr. Forbes," she added. "I think you and your dad should go, but I'd also like to be there. That way I can ask him the questions you both wouldn't know to ask."

"Can you leave here to do that?" Sassy asked.

"I'm not sure," she responded. "I need to find out, but I could just go as her nurse and not as her daughter. I need to be there, Sass," she said firmly. "This is my mom."

"I know," Sassy replied, as she shut down her laptop and closed the lid. "If you can go, then you should just go with Papa, and I'll stay here with Amelia."

"Are you sure?" Isabelle asked,

"I'm positive," Sassy replied. "Amelia will need one of us and I'd prefer if you go."

"Okay, thanks," Isabelle replied. "We can show Ted the literature you printed off tomorrow first thing and see what he says."

"Want some coffee?" Sassy asked getting to her feet.

"I can't drink the strong stuff you like, Sass," she replied.

"Don't worry," she said, "my coffee maker up here uses individual pods," she said going over to the table that had the machine. "I can give you green or raspberry tea or even apple cider if you'd like."

"I love hot apple cider," Isabelle smiled.

"Sounds good to me too, coming right up," she said and proceeded to make some for both of them.

Meanwhile, Isabelle looked around the studio as it was her first time there. They usually sat at the Morning Room table to do their research, but as Jon and Gabe were working on their own computers there, Sassy had suggested she and Isabelle work upstairs instead.

"You have such a lovely workspace, Sass," she said as she looked at the many and varied pieces of artwork on the walls. "You are so talented. These are fantastic."

"Thank you," Sassy said, shyly.

"What do you like to illustrate the most?" Isabelle asked.

"I love doing children's books," Sassy said. "They're my passion really. I work almost exclusively on them these days."

"That must be so much fun," Isabelle replied. "My job is so serious, but I love it and I particularly love surgery." Sassy made a face and she laughed. "Look at it this way," she encouraged, "You use pens, colored pencils and markers to do your work and I use a scalpel to do mine. Not only that, but I could never do what you do. I can't draw to save my life."

"And I hate hospitals," Sassy grinned. "Just the thought of going there gives my heart the flutters, so I guess we're even. God gives each of us our own talent I suppose," she added, as she removed one finished cup of cider from the machine and put in a new pod to fill the other.

A few minutes later, she brought the two steaming cups over to her desk and Isabelle joined her. Sassy noticed her stepsister had clammed up the minute she had mentioned the Lord and decided to ask her why she was so set against anything to do with God.

"Belle," she began tentatively, "can I ask you something of a personal nature?"

"Sure," Isabelle responded looking at her curiously. "What's up?"

"Why don't you want to have anything to do with God?" she asked. "If you don't want to talk about it, I understand," she hastened to add, "but Amelia told me long ago you were a Christian. What happened?"

At her question, Isabelle looked away, the memories of the past coming in like a flood. "I...., well...., I did love God once," she confirmed hesitantly, then continued with a show of anger "but He made Mom leave me. If He really loved me, why would He do that?" and immediately Sassy nodded in understanding. Isabelle was angry with God.

"Belle," she said. "I know how you feel better than you think."

"How?" she asked. "You've been raised in a loving home all your life, Sass. How could you possibly know what it's like to feel alone, bereft and abandoned."

Normally Sassy never spoke of her experience to anyone. She kept it and her feelings about it tightly locked inside. She was surprised she had actually shared it with Gabe the morning he apologized. She felt to do so now might be helpful to Isabelle, however, so she put her pain aside and decided to tell her the story.

"Belle," she said. "I'm going to share something with you, but I want you to promise me under your doctor's oath that you won't tell a soul."

"Of course," she said, curious as to what it was that Sassy wanted to tell her. "You can trust me to keep your confidence, Sass, I promise."

"Okay," Sassy said, then began her story. "Well, when I was finishing up my master's degree, I was living away from here. Actually, I was in North Carolina. Anyway, while I was there I met this guy......"

Half-an-hour later, Sassy came to the end of her tale, and Isabelle sat completely stunned by what she had revealed.

"Sass, I...," she paused, unsure of what to say. "I'm so very sorry," she said, using the exact words Gabe had used, before leaning over and pulling Sassy to her in a warm embrace as they sat facing each other, hoping to comfort her.

"I know," Sassy replied, when they pulled away and she had tears standing in her eyes. "I felt so many emotions after it happened, Belle," she continued. "at the time I didn't know why it happened to me, but later I saw so perfectly that I wasn't wise in my actions and I paid dearly for my naiveté."

"What happened to him?" Isabelle asked.

"I have no idea," Sassy replied. "Papa hired a private investigator to find him but there wasn't a trace. The investigator only found two marriage certificates in his real name, not the name he had given me."

"How did you feel about God after?" Isabelle questioned.

"Just like you, I was angry with Him at first," Sassy responded, "but when I looked back, I could see clearly that He had given me many warnings when I was seeing Greg. I was so in love, however, I ignored them all. If I'd listened to Him, Belle, I would have avoided all the pain I went through," she said, shaking her head. "When I realized it was my disobedience that had caused everything to happen, I asked God to forgive me and clung to Him fiercely after that. Only He got me through that terrible time, believe me," she concluded.

"Did Mom ever tell you anything about her past?" Belle asked then.

"She spoke about you many times," Sassy said, "but not about your father. I only knew she was married and left him because he abused her, nothing more. I didn't want to pry either. It didn't seem right."

"Well, let me tell you our story," Belle said, "Hers and mine," and she spent the next forty-five minutes giving Sassy the details.

"Gracious," Sassy exclaimed when she was through, her hand covering her heart in shock. "What an absolute nightmare."

"Nightmare isn't the word," Isabelle replied, unable to hide the bitterness in her voice. "He made our life a living hell."

"I thank God He took both of you out of it," Sassy said, and Isabelle looked up startled, Sassy's words somehow affecting her heart.

"Why did He put us in it in the first place," she shot back, and Sassy looked at her with sad eyes.

"I don't know, Belle," she said. "I can't answer that. You're going to have to seek Him about that yourself."

"I don't think that will happen," Isabelle replied stubbornly.

"I know you're angry," Sassy said, "and I can truly understand why, but I know God is good and loving and I'm going to pray for you every day and ask Him to show you just how much He loves you."

Isabelle's anger suddenly deflated as she looked at the lovely young woman before her. Like her, Sassy had been through so much but still loved the Lord despite her adversity. Isabelle knew she wasn't at that place and may never be, but she appreciated Sassy's concern and prayers. She also felt a kinship with her stepsister which had only deepened over the last two hours and was thankful she had come into her life.

"I don't know if it will do any good," Isabelle said with a smile, "but you go ahead and pray if it will make you feel better."

"Hold onto your hat then, sis," Sassy replied with a grin of her own. "I promise you're in for a wild ride," and they both laughed together.

CHAPTER 17

A few mornings later, Jon closed his laptop and stretched. He'd been up early trying to catch up on his reading assignments and had just finished. He looked over at the time on the clock radio and noted it was ten fifteen, so he got out of bed and straightened the sheets before putting on the quilt, making sure it was neatly placed. He made his bed automatically as soon as he arose, and he knew Gabe did the same. He'd heard Prudence and Elaine comment once that they'd never had neater male house guests and it was a pleasure to have them there.

The staff also loved Isabelle. She looked after everything to do with Amelia's needs, even doing her laundry, and tried to put as little work on them as possible. Elaine also discovered she had diabetes since they'd come to the house, and when the older woman admitted that poking her finger gave her the willies, Isabelle helped her to take her blood sugar every morning and advised her on her diet. She also made sure Elaine took her pills daily, and everyone admired the patience she had with her.

Jon heard noise coming from outside and went over to the window that overlooked the hills on the north side of the house. Hanley was busy tinkering with the hedge trimmer which appeared to be giving trouble and Jon watched as Patrick went over to give him a hand.

He looked out on the scene, but his thoughts drifted again to Isabelle as it often did, and he prayed as he stood there for God to heal her hurting heart and bring her back to Him. He loved her so much it was like a constant ache, but it was the fierceness of his feelings that bothered him the most. He sometimes wondered if his reaction was strong because he was just attracted to her, and she was out of reach. Before he had given his heart to the Lord, no woman had been off limits to him, and he seldom got a rejection when it came to the opposite sex. He had enjoyed their company and their physical affection without boundaries or commitment, and he knew they enjoyed him too.

Whenever he examined his feelings for Isabelle, however, what kept coming to him was that he wanted her for keeps, not just as a casual fling. He wanted to marry her and be with her for life and that was what convinced him that he was truly in love with her. What also convinced him was that as a single Christian man, he would be as dumb as dirt if he allowed a beautiful believing woman like Sapphire Sterling to pass him by, but to him she might as well have ten heads and two teeth, she didn't stir one thing in him. He only had eyes for his precious Belle.

He sighed, turned away from the window and went into the bathroom to wash and start his day. He needed to have breakfast and speak with Travis, so he had to get a move on. His love for Isabelle would be with him all day anyway, so he put his thoughts aside, turned on the water for his shower, stripped off his clothes and stepped under the spray.

Later that day, Jon went looking for Isabelle as he'd had news from Travis. He found her in the cozy living area of the master bedroom suite on the long 'fainting couch', as he'd heard them refer to it, knitting up a storm while Amelia was asleep in the bedroom. The Judge had used the opportunity to go into the small town of Crescent Ville a few miles from the house for supplies and to check on things at the factory.

208

"Can I see you a minute please Belle?" he asked, so she put down her work and followed him out into the hall, closing the door behind her.

"What going on?" she asked.

"Travis has made arrangements for you and the Judge to see the specialist in Nashville about Amelia tomorrow," he said quietly. "I'll let Ted know as soon as he returns, and I'll make arrangements with Sapphire to sit with your mother. Gabe and I will go with you while Travis plans to come over and stay here."

"Why is Travis coming," she asked.

"Just as a precaution," he said vaguely, then went on, "We'll have to leave around six in the morning to make the appointment in Nashville."

"I'll be ready," she assured him.

He looked at her then with his love for her standing in his eyes. "I'm praying for you and for her," he said, nodding towards the closed bedroom door.

Her eyes filled. "Thank you," she said, looking at him with longing. "I…," she almost told him she loved him but held back the words.

He nodded, however, and seemed to understand because he said softly, "Me too."

With that she turned and went back inside, and he turned to go down the stairs to start making the arrangements for the following day.

"All I want to do is love her, Lord," he prayed to his Heavenly Father as he walked. "Please work on her heart for me?" he asked before he pushed the thoughts to the back of his mind so he could concentrate on the task at hand.

****

They made the trip to Nashville and back the following day. They had spoken in generalities on their way to the appointment, and about Amelia's treatment plan on the way back. Isabelle and the Judge were impressed with Dr. Forbes, who they had gone to see, and they appreciated his pleasant demeanor and his unhurried attitude as he patiently explained everything to them and answered their questions. They had an enjoyable journey. Gabe seemed to be in a more approachable mood than in times past, so when they did speak, he joined in on their conversation in a more relaxed manner than usual.

They made it back in the late afternoon and found Sassy in the kitchen getting some tea and crackers for Amelia and Travis in the Morning Room on his computer. Isabelle went upstairs to visit her mother and give her the box of pretzels she had bought for her at the hospital gift shop. As long as she could remember, her mother loved the chocolate covered snack with its delicious play of both salty and sweet.

Amelia looked at the box in surprise when Isabelle handed it to her and asked in wonder, "How on earth did you know these are my favorite?"

Isabelle didn't want to lie so she just said, "A little birdy told me."

210

Amelia smiled and opened the box, took out one of the treats covered in rich milk chocolate, gave thanks and bit into it with relish. "How did the consultation go?" she asked as she munched on the sweet.

"It went well, and we think Dr. Forbes is definitely who you should go with," she replied, "but after supper we'll tell you everything if that's okay. There's a lot of literature to go through with you. You can tell us then what you want to do."

"That's fine," Amelia said.

"Would you like me to sit with you for a while?" Isabelle asked. "Sassy will soon be back with your tea."

"Absolutely not," Amelia said emphatically. "You just run along a find something fun to do," and taking another confection out of the box said with a cheeky grin. "I need to have a private moment with my box of pretzels if you don't mind," and Isabelle grinned back before telling her she would see her later and left the room.

Amelia watched her nurse's retreating back with a frown on her face. "How did she know?" she asked mystified, looking at the box she held. "I haven't had these since I left home."

She'd given up the confection and anything else that reminded her of that difficult time in her life the moment she went out on her own. Her parents would send them to her in the mail for Christmas and on her birthday, and she'd had to hide them away from her husband, taking them out and sharing them with Marissa when he was out of the house. He'd forbidden her from having anything to do with

211

her own family, and if he'd seen them, he would have wanted to know where she'd gotten them from.

"Maybe I told Sassy I liked them and forgot I mentioned it," she said as she munched, but it continued to trouble her nonetheless.

Isabelle meanwhile thought about her mother as she made her way to her room. The quiet woman she'd grown up with had certainly changed since they'd been apart. She laughed often, spoke her mind without apology and was more assertive and confident. She had become her own woman, and Isabelle likened it to watching a butterfly. Amelia had come out of her cocoon and unfolded her wings to reveal her glorious and unique markings, and Isabelle couldn't help but marvel at it.

"What a transformation," she thought as she reached her room and went in. It was a joy to see her mother free and able to express herself without censure, and her heart lifted every time she thought of the happiness Amelia had found living with Ted and Sapphire.

****

That same evening after supper, Isabelle, the Judge and Sassy all sat around in the master suite sitting room with Amelia, who was lying on the fainting couch. Jon, Gabe and Travis took the opportunity to meet on their own and the plan was for Travis to leave the following morning. Isabelle and the Judge outlined the doctor's recommendations to Amelia, and when they were through, she agreed with them that this was the way to go. The Judge assured her he would make all the arrangements for the process to begin as soon as possible and promised to go with her for every visit.

There were no guarantees, but Amelia knew everyone was praying for her, and she was willing to trust God and try this new course of action.

****

A week later, Isabelle rose from a restless sleep. She glanced at the electric clock and saw it was only a little after one in the morning. She was having a headache and knew it was because she had been knitting too much. Her eyes felt strained and tired, so she decided to fix herself some tea and take some pain pills. She didn't want to create a disturbance or alert Jon who was on watch, however, so she made her way barefooted to the back stairs generally used by the household staff and which led directly into the kitchen below. She opened the door at the other end of the second-floor corridor, went down the staircase and within a minute she was opening the door into the kitchen.

She was surprised to see the light on as she entered but figured Jon may keep it that way at night to make it easier to replenish his coffee cup. When she made her way fully into the room, however, she saw him standing at the counter nearest the stove making what looked like a sandwich. He turned at the sound of the door and stopped his task when he saw her. These days she dressed very conservatively, especially after that fateful night some months back, so she was well covered in a t-shirt and long knit pants.

"Hi," Jon said. "Couldn't sleep?"

"No. I ….," she paused and looked up at the antique copper baking pans lining the top of the cupboards, anywhere but at him. His eyes were taking in every detail of her attire, even as he asked his innocuous question, and it sent her pulse racing. "I have a headache and came to get some tea, but it's okay, I'll just go on back upstairs."

She began turning towards the door, but he hurriedly said, "No!" then in a calmer tone continued, "let me make it for you."

She nodded and watched while he filled the kettle and put it on to boil without the whistling cap on the spout so as not to make any noise. He took down a cup, placed it on the counter, then put a tea bag in it and a little sugar the way he knew she liked it. When he was finished, he turned to her as she stood just inside the door.

"Why don't you have a seat?" he said, indicating the kitchen table which had one of its short ends against one wall with chairs on the other three sides.

"Ah, I think I'll just take it back upstairs when it's ready," she said.

She was in trouble and she knew it. She felt a surge of longing grip her body that was hard to ignore and when she glanced at him, she saw an answering look in his eyes. They stared at each other, their love plainly displayed on their faces, neither one able to look away. He crossed the room and came to stand in front of her, then reached up with both hands and cupped her cheeks before sliding his fingers into the short curls on either side of her head and bringing his lips to hers in a soft but searing onslaught.

She wrapped her arms around his neck and responded eagerly to his passionate searching, inflaming him even more, and it took every ounce of his will power to pull away and just hug her tightly.

"I love you so much Sparky," he said. "I just can't fight it anymore."

She pulled away from his embrace so she could look into his eyes, "Sparky?" she asked.

"Yes, Sparky," he said, his eyes filled with unconcealed desire. "I call you that because every time I see you, Belle, you light my insides on fire."

She blushed to the roots of her hair and he pulled her to him again, raining little kisses on her face and neck, causing her to shudder with pleasure.

"Do you really love me?" he asked as he went to the pulse point at her throat.

Swallowing she said softly, "Yes."

"Say it," he murmured even as he continued his invasion on her senses.

"I really love you, Jon," she whispered. "I love you so much it aches."

"Do you want me as much as I want you?" he asked, having left her pulse point, and he now had his lips working just at the base of her earlobe.

She caught her breath and said, "Yes."

"Say it," he repeated as his lips began to roam once more.

215

"I want you," she said breathlessly. "I want you so badly. All I can think about it you."

She was fighting with all her might to regain her senses; one of them had to. "Jon, we shouldn't be doing this," she said. "Suppose someone finds out?"

He pulled away and looked at her, his eyes smoky with passion. "Are you going to tell?" he rumbled seductively, his eyes filled with such fire that she lost her will to care.

"Only if you don't kiss me again," she whispered, and he proceeded to do as she asked.

Her sweetness was an intoxicating elixir he couldn't get enough of, and he didn't hold back as he captured her mouth again, running his hands slowly over her body.

When they came up for air she said, "I love you, Jon, but we've got to stop before we won't be able to. I don't want you to get in trouble."

He knew she was right, so he held her in his arms and allowed their passion to cool. After a few minutes, with great difficulty, he pulled away completely and went over to the stove, removing the kettle which sat their boiling. He made the tea for her, finished the sandwich then poured coffee for himself and invited her to sit at the kitchen table in the chair opposite him. He put the sandwich between them and offered her a half which she took.

They ate and talked and between the two things were able to get their emotions back on an even keel. When they had finished the meal, he made more tea for her and poured more coffee for himself, and they talked for another hour.

He shared himself with her and told her all his hopes and dreams while she did the same. When the clock showed two forty-five, she reluctantly got up to go to bed. She would never be up on time if she didn't, but how she hated leaving him.

"How's the headache?" he asked as he saw her to the door that led to the stairs. He had given her some pain pills from out of the kitchen cupboard and she had taken them after she'd eaten.

"A little better," she said, "not as fierce." She looked at him then and decided to speak her heart. "Jon, I want to ask you something, but I'm not sure it's such a good idea."

"What is it?" he asked.

"Can we do this again?" she whispered. "I don't mean the first part," she said, blushing furiously, referring to their passionate exchange. "I just want to spend time talking with you. There's so much of myself I want to share, and I want to share it with you."

"I'd like that," he said without hesitation. "How about we make it a date at midnight every night? I promise to keep my lips to myself," he smiled, and she smiled back.

"Okay," she said, turning and opening the door. "Until tomorrow then," she murmured softly, and he nodded before she went through to the back staircase, closing the door quietly behind her.

He left the house after she had gone and did a quiet surveillance of the immediate grounds then went back inside and into the Morning Room. As he got to the couch, he fell on his knees and began praying earnestly to his Heavenly Father.

"Lord, this is Your wayward son again, asking for forgiveness," he said. "She's like forbidden fruit, Lord. I know Your Word concerning being unequally yoked, Father; I know Your Word, but I just can't seem to get her out of my system. Why, Lord?" he asked, truly perplexed. "I know I wasn't a model human being before I met You and I still mess up and seek Your forgiveness even now, but this thing I have for Isabelle is beyond my ability to comprehend.

"I was totally satisfied without a woman in my life, Lord, You know that," he continued. "Why allow her into my heart if there's no future for us?" he asked. "Now I've gone and told her she can share her thoughts with me without even asking You. I know I've already made the arrangement with her, but is it okay for us to share with each other at nights, Father? How do You want me to handle this whole thing? Please guide me God," he prayed. "I'm in desperate need of Your forgiveness, direction, mercy and grace, in Jesus' name, amen."

Jon remained still after his prayer. He'd learned early on in his Christian walk that if he wanted to hear from God he needed to stop and listen for His voice.

"Trust Me," he felt the Lord impress on his heart. "Open her eyes to Me."

Immediately Jon knew the direction God wanted him to take with Isabelle. He wanted him to take care of her soul instead of his own fleshly desires.

"I will Lord," he promised. "I'll do everything I can to bring her back to You, and I promise I'll keep a check on my passion too. I'll meet with her strictly for You. Thank You, Father, in Jesus' name, amen."

He rose from his knees after a while feeling better. He had a roadmap to follow and he was going to make sure to adhere to God's word from now on. He didn't know what the future held for them, but he would trust God for all of it. He would put his wants, dreams and desires aside and chase after Isabelle's soul instead. With the decision made, he picked up his Bible and began searching for passages he could use to win Isabelle back to the Lord. He was determined not to go outside of his Father's will again. His relationship with God was just too important and precious for him to compromise.

****

Isabelle sat opposite Jon at the kitchen table. This was their fourth night together, and it had become their habit to share a sandwich and a warm drink and talk. He hadn't touched her again, and she knew it was because of his commitment to his Heavenly Father. He had spoken to her about them not touching the night following their passionate encounter and explained that he wanted to respect her and honor God in any relationship they had. She told him she could live with that.

He had been very quiet since she had come into the kitchen earlier, however, and she knew he wanted to talk to her about something serious but was having a hard time approaching her about it.

"What's on your mind, Jon?" she asked in her usual

direct way. "I know something's bothering you."

He smiled. "You're beginning to know me too well," he said. He looked at her, took a deep breath as if to speak, but exhaled it and couldn't go on.

"Do you want to talk to me about God?" she asked, and he looked up startled.

"How did you know?" he asked, before casting his eyes down at the table. "I've been trying to broach the subject with you since last night, but I haven't been able to find the right words."

"Jon," she said, "look at me." When he raised his eyes to hers' she said, "I want us to promise each other something right now. I want us to promise that we'll never be afraid to approach each other about any subject, even if it's controversial or painful or might promote an argument. I want us to be open and honest with each other in love. Would that be okay with you?" she asked, and he nodded his agreement. "Good," she said. "Now tell me what's on your heart."

"I wanted to know if you'd be open to us reading the Word together and discussing it," he revealed. "We can talk about other things too," he hastened to add, "but I want to open the Word of God to you once again. We could share about ourselves over our meal," he went on to explain his idea, "but I would love for us to share in this way too. It's important to me."

She looked down into the cup in front of her, and after giving it some thought she said, "I think that would be okay."

"Really?" he asked incredulously and couldn't hide the look of hope in his eyes.

Looking up and seeing his expression, she smiled and said, "Yes. I think I'd like that."

So every night thereafter, when they got together, they talked and shared in the Word and Jon was happier than he had been in months. Isabelle was willing to listen with an open heart, and he knew God was working to bring her back to Himself.

****

A few nights later, Gabe came awake suddenly and shot up in bed in a cold sweat. When he became aware of his surroundings and reality took hold, he put his face in his hands in relief and took several slow breaths to try and calm his racing heart. He'd been dreaming and it had turned from something pleasant into a nightmare.

He'd dreamt that he was riding with Gina in the foothills near their home, and they were laughing and having a great time. Suddenly the scene switched to the morning she died and to the moment when the bomb went off. He saw her ascending into the clouds from the flaming wreckage of his car while he began falling into an abyss that seemed to have no end. He was reaching out to her while she was reaching out to him, but they were being pulled further and further away from each other. It was clear to him that Gina was heading to heaven while he was on his way to hell, and it was in the midst of falling that he came awake.

A few minutes later, when he had calmed and his emotions had settled, he looked over at the clock and saw it was only one thirty-five. He had another two and a half hours before he had to relieve Jon, but he knew he'd never get back to sleep, neither did he want to, so he decided to get dressed and keep his friend company.

He got up and after doing his ablutions and brushing his hair, he dragged on his jeans, t-shirt and shoes, strapped on his ankle holster and left his room. He went down the stairs to the Morning Room and, finding it empty, he made his way towards the kitchen, figuring Jon was getting his usual mid-watch coffee and sandwich.

As he got close to the door, he heard Jon talking and wondered who he could be speaking to at this hour.

"Probably his folks," he reasoned, knowing that timewise they were around fifteen hours ahead give or take, and it would be afternoon down-under in Australia. Just as he reached the door, however, Gabe heard him say, "I'm telling you, Belle, its right there."

"I don't see how you can say that," he heard Belle respond, and Gabe stopped in shock.

"What on earth's going on?" he asked himself.

Both Jon and Isabelle knew the rules about no private contact, yet here they were alone with each other at nearly two in the morning doing who knew what. He was surprised at Jon. His friend was always willing to listen to reason, but it seemed that love had made him take leave of his senses.

Gabe was about to go in and confront them when he heard Jon say, "Look, it's getting late and you need to get some sleep. When you have a little time today, go back into

Matthew and look at the entire chapter. Maybe then you'll understand what I'm getting at. The verse doesn't make sense in isolation, but when you read the context in which it is written, I think you'll understand what I'm trying to show you a lot better."

"Okay," she conceded, "but I still think you're wrong."

"We'll see," he heard Jon say. "Let's close in prayer."

Gabe heard Jon pray, asking God to continue to open His word to Isabelle and shortly after he heard when they both said, "amen".

"I know things seem a little confusing," he heard Jon say, "but I promise you it will become clearer as you read."

"Okay," Isabelle said. "I promise I'll read it with an open heart as you like to tell me," and Gabe heard the smile in her voice. "See you later," she added, and Gabe heard the door to the stairs open and Jon bid her goodnight.

Gabe quickly made his way back to the Grand Foyer and into the Music Room located across from the Morning Room. A short while later, he saw Jon enter the Morning Room then head out the door to the terrace to do one of several walk arounds they did as part of their protocol each night. Gabe decided to wait for him to return then give him a few minutes before going in to meet him. He didn't want Jon to know he had heard anything.

He sat in one of the comfortable chairs as he waited and thought about what he had discovered. He realized that he had totally misinterpreted why Jon and Isabelle were meeting. His best friend wasn't with her for a clandestine reason involving anything physical. He was simply looking after her soul, and it blew Gabe away.

He knew Jon loved Isabelle with all his heart yet, despite this, he was willing to put himself in a vulnerable position in order to open the word of God to her. Even with all the heartache that might come, he was pursuing her for God and not for himself.

"Peeps," Gabe said to himself, shaking his head, "you are something else."

He heard Jon come back inside and went to join him five minutes later, but in the days to follow, Gabe kept thinking about the dream he'd had and about Jon sacrificing his feelings to help Isabelle. It also caused him to begin looking into himself and where he stood with God. He knew with certainty he wouldn't be heading to heaven when he died, but he also wondered if he deserved to go there after what had happened to Gina. It was his fault she was gone after all. Didn't he deserve to be punished for that? There was so much he needed to think about and consider, but he was reluctant to talk to Jon and ask for his wise counsel. His friend had enough to deal with regarding Isabelle, he reasoned, so Gabe decided to wait for a better time.

CHAPTER 18

Constantine sat in front of the fireplace in his office watching the flames dance in the opening while soaking up the warmth. Under normal circumstances it would have been too warm for a fire, but the weather had been doing strange things lately and seemed to be intent on giving them the unexpected. It had rained for nearly a week, getting on everyone's nerves then a cold blast had shot straight down from Canada bringing unseasonably cold temperatures.

The house was frigid as the furnace wasn't working properly and only anemic warmth was coming from the vents. Getting a repairman out to look at the unit was out of the question, so he'd gotten Paulie to buy several ultra-safe child-proof space heaters to heat the house. The place was like a barn, however, and the heaters didn't work effectively in the main living areas, so he'd told Paulie to put one in each bedroom, and they used the three fireplaces to try and bring warmth to the rest of the house.

Lahali had gone up to put the boys to bed so the place was quiet, and he sat brooding about what to do. It was now the beginning of October, and it would get bitterly cold in the next few months so their temporary refuge wouldn't be ideal to live in at all. He was giving serious consideration, therefore, to Neil's suggestion of going to South America and running things at that end while his twin took care of things here. Lahali was almost to term, however, and he wanted her to have the baby before undertaking anything so demanding, so he was hoping either Cornelius' plan or his would work. His brother had called and told him that their friend Crew wasn't around but would be back in a few days, so they would have to wait.

He was glad, therefore, that he had put his own plan in place. Months before, he'd had one of his men pose as a reporter and canvas the hospital where the Doctor had worked in L.A. as well as a clinic where she volunteered her services in the inner city. It was at that time he'd learned that Marissa Sparks' father and grandparents were dead, and she had no other living relatives. The only possible exception was her mother who had disappeared when the Doctor was a teenager and hadn't been heard from since.

When that piece of information reached him, he began toying with the idea of sending Wexler to see if he could locate the Doctor's mother so he might have some leverage with which he could bargain. He had shelved the plan, however, as he wasn't exactly sure how he could use her. When things began to look hopeless, he'd decided to put his plan in action, but Wexler hadn't gotten back to him with anything yet. He wouldn't pull his enforcer from the assignment, however, until he was sure Cornelius' plan would work. After speaking with his twin and hearing his idea, Constantine felt it was his best option; but if it failed, it was smart to have another course of action available. He would figure out how he would use the mother in due time, that is if Wexler could find her. His back was against the wall and he was getting desperate, so he would try just about anything to keep his freedom.

He continued to nurse his after-dinner brandy and look at the flames. His thoughts went back over the last several months and he knew he couldn't complain. Business was still bustling thanks to Neil and his cousin Frank, who had just gotten back from the east coast. He had returned with two suitcases full of cash which would tide them over for another few months. He really could live like this indefinitely, but he was chomping at the bit to get back to handling his affairs personally. Cornelius knew the business in South America inside and out, had contacts that Constantine knew nothing about and spoke the language fluently, so he really was the best person for that end of the business. Constantine hoped, therefore, that one of their plans would work. Other than relocating, it was probably the only chance he had left.

****

Lahali tucked the boys in and kissed each one. She had already read to them and sung their good-night song as she usually did, and they had given her their usual fierce hugs before settling back on the pillows. They were her life and she loved them and her unborn child unconditionally.

She was weary of living in this isolation, however, and with the birth of their baby only weeks away, she was anxious to be in a place with a nearby hospital where she could give birth. Constantine had thought to rent an apartment in the nearest small town and have her do a home birth there, but she had been adamant that she didn't want the baby birthed under such rough conditions with only a mid-wife in attendance. If anything happened, they would have to drive many miles to the nearest hospital, and she refused point blank to even entertain the idea.

No matter how hard Constantine had tried to convince her she wouldn't budge, so he'd made arrangements for her to stay in a hotel with Elsa and the boys in Salt Lake City a week before the baby's due date and have Frank go with them. Lahali was always willing to go along with whatever her husband proposed, but when it came to her little ones, she was like a bear, so Constantine respected her wishes.

227

She made her way now to the kitchen to rinse the cups the boys had used to drink their nightly milk and fill them with water. She usually left the full cups on the chest of drawers to save herself a trip downstairs at night if they woke up and wanted a drink. As she reached the swing door leading into the kitchen, she heard voices coming from the other side and realized that Frank and Paulie were talking, probably about Frank's trip to look about Constantine's business. She usually just went about her tasks and didn't allow herself to pay much mind to the men, but she heard Paulie mention Giovanni's name and that caused her to pause and not enter the room.

The door had a bad habit of not swinging perfectly closed and the two-finger width gap left it open just enough for their conversation to be overheard if someone was inclined to place their ear at just the right spot to listen.

"Do you blame Gio for not wanting to off Constantine's kid, Frank?" she heard Paulie ask. "I mean, why not leave the kid alive and only kill the mother? For Pete's sake, she was only two years old." Lahali's fingers went to her mouth in shock.

"Yeah, well he did it, didn't he?" Frank replied. "Kinda lucky he didn't have to live with it on his conscience too long. Jimmy said he was pretty torn up in the accident. It's a pity he gave Constantine up at the last minute though," Frank continued. "We would all have been sitting pretty instead of wasting away here. Did I tell you I saw Rita while I was there?" he asked. "We had a good time she and I," he chuckled at the memory.

"I'm tired of this hole," Paulie said. "I haven't had me a woman in too long. Any word on the good Doctor?" he

228

asked, and Lahali leaned closer to hear.

"They can't find her," Frank said. "Seems the FBI has her stashed real good. They've been after Constantine for years, so you can imagine they're taking every precaution to make sure their star witness is safe and sound."

"Well if Jimmy can find her mother and we can use her as bait to flush the Doc out of hiding, maybe our stint here will be over," Paulie commented.

"We can only wish," Frank said. "I can't imagine how Constantine will use her to get the Doctor to come forward, but he has friends in high places, so we'll see."

"Since we're talking, Frank," Paulie said, "tell me honestly, did you know Gio kept that kill book?" he asked.

"I had no idea, or I would have told Constantine," Frank replied. "Jimmy has a sharp eye. I don't know how he missed the Doctor pocketing it."

"She's a brave woman if you ask me," Paulie commented.

"Brave or stupid," Frank said acerbically, "take your pick."

"Well we know they have it," Paulie stated. "Constantine's contact knew that much even though they've kept that piece of information out of the press."

"I can't get over how he knows that but has no idea where she is," Frank mused, "even with that new department they now have, he's high enough to be able to get that kind of information, but he says he doesn't know and can't ask."

"How high up is he?" Paulie asked.

"I'd have to kill you if I told you, Paul," Frank said, giving him a look that said better than words he meant it.

"Okay, okay, don't get your shirt in a knot," Paulie said, knowing he'd overstepped. "I won't ask again."

"You'd better not if you know what's good for you," Frank declared.

They went on to talk of other things, but they'd given Lahali the answers to all her questions in a single two-minute conversation. Constantine had cheated on her and had sent Gio to remove the evidence.

She thought back to Giovanni and how he loved being with her boys. He had been a big playmate, and they had loved to wrestle with him and take rides on his back. It had always fascinated her that a hardened criminal such as he could be so gentle and loving to her children, but he had told her in one of their rare in-depth conversations that he loved the innocence of children. He'd said that they weren't yet exposed to the harshness of life, and if it was within his power, he would never allow them to lose that purity.

She had learned early on that his childhood had been extremely difficult. He had an unfortunate face, one which showed the battles he had been in all his life, starting from his early days on the street. His stint as a boxer hadn't made any improvement to his rough looks and when she had first met him, she had been terrified by his frightening appearance. She had gradually gotten accustomed to his presence, however, and when Dominic was born, and he had seen him for the first time, his face had gentled into a smile. She only ever saw that look when he was dealing with her children and she had trusted him more than any of Constantine's other men when it came to her sons.

Having to kill the child must have been why he had given Constantine up to the Feds, especially if he knew he was dying. It must have been his way of clearing his conscience. That would explain everything.

She made her way back upstairs to the boys' room and, going over, she sat in the rocker in the semi-darkness, placing the unwashed cups on the ground beside her. She put the chair in motion and seemed perfectly calm as she rubbed her belly with soothing strokes. She was, however, experiencing a myriad of emotions that belied her peaceful demeanor: shock, anger, sadness and a whole host of other feelings that were hard to separate.

Constantine had cheated on her. It was the one thing she had been so sure he would never do. She had always treated him like a king, and willingly shared her body with him, never denying him his conjugal rights; moreover, she loved him, and he had demonstrated by his words and actions that he loved her too, so why had he done it?

What appalled her even more was that he could kill a child; a sweet little innocent who had done nothing more than been born to a man with no soul. She put her face in her trembling hands, so stunned she couldn't even cry.

Then, suddenly, a frightening thought occurred to her, and she stopped the rocker and sat up before lifting her head to looked out at the moon through the curtain-less window. If Constantine could kill his own child, his own flesh and blood, what was there to prevent him from doing away with her or even their children if they got in his way. The thought was terrifying and sobering all at the same time and, at that moment, Lahali understood that she had to do whatever she could to protect herself and her babies.

She sat back and set the rocker in motion once again, not thinking about her shock, her hurt, her anger or even her husband. She put their marriage and the love she had for him aside. This wasn't about that anymore. This was now about her and her children, so she turned her thoughts to survival and how she could save them and herself from the train wreck she could see ahead, whether it came from the FBI or from Constantine's own hand.

With that in mind, she continued to sit in the darkness brooding and thinking until something struck her that went from an inkling of an idea to something much more concrete. Feeling considerably better, she set about deciding the best way to go about what she knew she had to do and, forgetting everything else, she began to formulate a plan.

CHAPTER 19

Later that week, Isabelle went upstairs during her afternoon off to see if Sassy, who was sitting with her mother wanted to take a break. She felt at loose ends and decided she would rather be with them than with her own thoughts. She hadn't been knitting for the last few days in order to ease the strain on her eyes. The pain had subsided considerably since the night she had gone into the kitchen and found Jon there, but if she did too much, they would start aching again. She felt a week's break from her favorite pastime would do her eyes a world of good, but it left her with nothing to do. She had almost reached the third floor when she saw Sassy coming towards her. They met just as she reached the top of the stairs.

"Hi," she said. "Is she sleeping?"

"Yes," Sassy replied. "She fell asleep about fifteen minutes ago. Jon's with her as usual so I'm just going to get something cool to drink and come back," she added.

"Jon's with her?" Isabelle asked curiously. "I didn't know he visited her," she said.

"Belle, Jon comes up almost every afternoon as soon as she falls asleep and prays for her," Sassy explained. "He has since the day after you all arrived. Didn't you know that?"

"I.... ah ... I had no idea," Isabelle replied, stunned by the revelation.

"The only time he didn't come was right after Amelia

and Papa married, otherwise, he seldom misses a day. He really is a very nice man and a strong Christian," Sassy concluded. "Anyway, let me go get my glass of juice before he's done," she added as she continued down the stairs. "I'll be back in a jiffy."

When she was gone, Isabelle made her way quietly toward the master suite. The door was slightly ajar, so she pushed it a little wider, went through the sitting room and stood just outside the bedroom door, taking in the scene before her. Jon was on his knees at her mother's bedside with his hand resting softly on Amelia's head. His eyes were closed, and his lips were moving silently in prayer. The sight so overwhelmed her, that she quickly and quietly moved away from the door and, once outside, went downstairs to the second floor and sought the shelter of her own bedroom. When she was inside and had closed the door, she went over and lay face up on the bed.

Since they had been meeting together, Jon had demonstrated a love for the Lord which was hard for her to ignore. He also had an insight into the Word that often left her in awe. He lived out his faith by example too, just as he was doing right now, and it impacted her more than she could ever say.

She lay there for a full fifteen minutes, thinking about her life since her mother had left. She thought of how blessed she'd been to have had sweet grandparents who had taken such good care of her and given her love, a home and an education. She thought about the safe place God had placed her mother, about the miracle of finding her after twenty years, about the Judge's love for her and their recent marriage. She then thought about the wonderful man who had come into her own life, and about Sassy's words of how thankful she was that God had removed Isabelle and her mother from the situation with her father.

At that moment, the truth of what her stepsister had said pierced Isabelle's heart as nothing else could have and she sat up in shock as everything came into sharp focus for her. She understood in an instant that God hadn't abandoned her at all. He had in fact been making the rough paths smooth in her life and in the life of her mother all along. He had been with them every step of the way. How could she deny it when the evidence was right in front of her? At this revelation, she did something she hadn't done since the day she had come home and found her mother gone. She slid off the bed, got down on her knees and began to pray.

"Lord," she said, "if I'm still truly Yours, please make my relationship with You real to me again. I'm so sorry, Father," she whispered, "please forgive me. You didn't abandon me, I abandoned You. I turned my back on You and all You did was love me in return. I'm so sorry." Isabelle knelt in complete submission to her Heavenly Father and poured out her heart to him. Then she said the words that would recommit her life to her Lord and Savior.

"Dear Lord Jesus. I believe in You. I know You are the Son of God and I know You are my Savior. I believe You died for my sins and rose from the dead and that You now sit in Heaven at the right hand of God. Please forgive me for everything, Lord, and cleanse me from all unrighteousness I ask. Thank You, Father God so much for continuing to love me and give me blessing upon blessing despite my rebellion. I love You with all my heart and thank You so much for rescuing me from myself. I recommit my life to You from this moment and forever in Jesus' precious name, amen."

She didn't say anymore, she just bowed her head quietly and in the next instant, she felt a warmth and peace come over her entire body and knew that God was right there with her. Overwhelmed, she rose from the floor, threw herself across the bed and began weeping great gulping sobs into her pillow so no sound would reach outside her door.

"You're here, Father," she said. "I feel Your presence." She knew that God had never left her, but she now knew that she was back in fellowship with Him. "Glory to You Father," she said, laughing and crying all at the same time. "Praise Your Holy Name. Jesus, Jesus," she said over and over again, "my sweet Jesus. Thank You. Thank You for Your forgiveness and restoration. Thank You for Your love and Your mercy. Thank You for Your compassion and grace. Thank You Lord." She continued to weep tears of joy and pour out her love and gratitude to God, feeling happy and absolutely free in her heart, and she knew that only her restored relationship with her Heavenly Father had done it.

Sometime later, Sassy knocked on her door and asked if she was coming to supper. She told her she'd be right down and got up. She washed her face, brushed her hair and changed out of her rumpled clothes then left her room with a much lighter heart. She decided as she went down the stairs, however, to keep her recommitment to God to herself for a little while. She just wanted time to savor her experience with Him before she made any great announcement to anyone else.

"First order of business is to get myself a Bible," she said to herself as she reached the Morning Room door. She had been using one in her study with Jon that she had borrowed from the mansion's library where there were copies of the precious Book in several translations, but now she wanted her own. She decided to ask Gabe if he would go into town

236

the following day and do some shopping for her. She had loved Christian music, so in addition to purchasing the Bible for her and a devotional, she would ask him to get her some CD's which she could play on the small portable CD player that was in her room. She just wanted to soak herself in praise and worship music. She had missed it so much.

"I'll ask Gabe straight after supper," she promised herself, as she joined the others at the table with joy in her heart. She was once again on her way to being a strong woman of God, and she couldn't wait to see where He would take her next.

****

Later in the evening, Isabelle found Gabe in the library looking through the paperbacks on one of the bottom shelves trying to find something to read. Thankfully he was alone and when she came in, he looked up and rose from his stooped position.

"Hey, Gabe," she said. "Can I talk with you for a minute?"

"Sure," he said. "What's on your mind?"

"I wanted to ask you to do me a favor tomorrow," she said tentatively, then continued. "I wanted to ask you if you'd do a little shopping for me."

"No problem," he said. "What do you need?"

She hesitated so long that he looked at her curiously. "Well," she paused, suddenly bashful to make her request.

He frowned, "Is it something of a personal nature?" he asked, trying to figure out what was wrong. He saw she was floundering, so he added, "Anything you need I will get for you, Isabelle, you know that. Just tell me what it is."

He saw her visibly relax then she said to him shyly, "I'd like you to buy a Bible for me, and a devotional and some Christian CD's." She saw the stunned look on his face and smiled saying, "That's right, Gabriel. This lost sheep has given her heart back to the Lord."

"That's great, Belle," he said, and even though his face showed no emotion he added, "I'm glad for you."

"You are?" she asked, surprised by his remark.

"I am," he said simply. "Jon's example is tough to ignore, isn't it? When he's around it's kind of hard to push the Lord aside," and she nodded.

"He's such a good man, Gabe," she said, speaking her heart. "I'll love him till the day I die, whether he's with me or not. I don't think I could love anyone else," she confessed, and knew she was talking to someone who could relate to what she was saying. Gabe nodded that he understood.

"Does he know?" he asked her in his usual quiet way, and she shook her head.

"Not yet?" she said. "I only got through praying a little before supper. I'll tell him soon," she continued, "but right now I want to savor my reconciliation with the Lord for a little while. It's still so new and I just want to keep it to myself until I'm ready to share it."

"I'll keep your confidence," he said.

"Thanks so much for everything you've done for me over the last several months, Gabe," she said. "You've put your whole life on hold to protect mine and I can't tell you how much that humbles me. One thing I'll tell you right now is that I'm going to pray for you as long as I live. I'll pray that God will bless you more than I ever could."

Gabe held his head down at her comments. "I'm glad Jon found you, Belle," he said in a rare open moment. "I'm hoping things work out for both of you. I was married once," he admitted, "but when my wife died it was so painful that I'd rather stay single from now on. That doesn't mean I don't want to see others happy."

"Gabe," she said with a twinkle in her eye, "I'm going to do something that may shock you, but don't hold it against me, okay?" she asked. "I'm only doing what a sister would do."

He looked at her warily but nodded and she reached up and kissed his cheek. "You're a very special human being, Gabriel," she said, "and I thank God for you."

With that she turned and left the room, and when she was gone, Gabe touched his cheek where her lips had been and suddenly felt a tiny response in his heart.

"So are you, Isabelle Christianson," he said to the empty room. "So are you."

****

A week later, Isabelle was busy in her mother's room

239

putting away the laundry while Amelia slept. She usually washed and dried Amelia's things, while Prudence or Elaine ironed or folded her clothes and put them away. Everyone had been doing extra duty, however, as both ladies had succumbed to a nasty virus that had been going around and some of their family members were also sick. They'd been ordered by the Judge, therefore, to stay home until they were completely well, as he wanted to isolate Amelia from any risk of contracting the illness.

She had started her new chemo treatments and was responding very well, much to everyone's relief, but it was imperative she keep away from illness of any kind. Even her fruits and vegetable had to be cooked as she wasn't allowed to eat them raw for fear of contamination, and everyone was very protective of her.

Meanwhile, the Judge had been busy in his study. He worked now as a consultant and was often contracted to do jobs by several large law firms throughout the country. He spent time at the dairy or the processing facility several mornings each week, but he loved the law and enjoyed working as he did now, especially since he didn't have to leave home to accomplish his passion.

Isabelle and Sassy spent time with Amelia when Ted was busy, and as they looked after her and were often together, they also grew closer as 'sisters'. Now they were taking up the slack in the absence of the two household helpers, and even Mrs. Gregory had had to stay a few extra hours that day. She had finally left for home, however, just as Isabelle was on her way upstairs with the laundry basket.

In the short time since she had recommitted her life to the Lord, Isabelle had made changes to her daily routine which had her rising early to do devotions, and she stayed in her mother's room at night while Sassy read from the Word. After the first two nights, Sassy expressed to her how happy she was that Isabelle was joining them for Bible reading. It was then Isabelle told her that she had given her heart back to the Lord but asked Sassy to keep it to herself for the time being. She also thanked her for her prayers and Sassy in turn told her how delighted she was that Isabelle had given her life back to Christ before hugging her enthusiastically.

As she worked now, Isabelle softly hummed one of the songs on the inspirational CD Gabe had purchased for her. She had found a copy of it on the double collector's edition which contained thirty praise and worship songs, both old and new. This tune had been one of her favorites during her younger days and as she put away the last of the nighties her mother wore, she came to the end of the song and did a quick dance move to punctuate the final notes, chuckling quietly and shaking her head as she did so. Sometimes she just couldn't contain her happiness at having her personal relationship with God restored.

She went into the bathroom with a stack of towels for the linen cupboard there and came back out. She looked over at Amelia who had been sleeping soundly when she had entered earlier and found that she was awake and looking at her. She smiled, put down the empty laundry basket and went over to her.

"Are you hungry?" she asked, knowing that it was almost time for her afternoon tea.

"Not really," she replied, sitting up. "Could you fluff the pillows for me please?" she asked, and Belle did so, placing

241

several more behind her back so she would be comfortable.

"Let me just run down and put the kettle on," she said. "I'll be right back," and she turned to head out the bedroom door.

She was half-way there when Amelia said, "Do you want to explain why you're hiding from me Rissa?"

Isabelle was so stunned that she stopped and couldn't move.

"Who's Rissa?" she asked, turning to her, trying to see if she could bluff her way out of the discovery.

"Let's get one thing clear, young lady," Amelia said in a voice that was absolutely familiar to Isabelle from her teenage years, "I may be sick but I'm not stupid. It took me a while because I couldn't figure out the blue eyes, but I know you're my daughter. Now why the disguise and why are you hiding who you are from me?"

Her lips trembling and her eyes full of tears, Isabelle rushed over to the bed. She sat down at the side and gently scooped her mother into her arms saying, "Oh, Mom. At last I can hug you."

They both began to weep, and they hugged and cried for a long time, whispering soothing words and words of love in a chaotic jumble that spoke of their happy reunion. When at last they were spent, Isabelle sat back and gave Amelia a wad of tissues from the box on the night table then took some for herself.

"What gave me away?" Isabelle asked. "I was so careful."

"Nothing at first," Amelia said, "but then little things struck me. The chocolates for one, I hadn't had any of those since leaving home, then the turn of your head or a familiar phrase, but the eyes kept throwing me off. When I saw you make that little move at the end of your song, just now, that's when I knew for sure. You always use to sing that song in the living room when your father wasn't home and do that little thing at the end."

"I didn't even remember that," Belle admitted, "and you were supposed to be sleeping." They smiled at each other.

"Want to tell me what's going on?" Amelia asked.

"I need to talk to someone first," she said. "I'll tell you everything, but I can't until I speak with Jon."

"You mean that nice man who comes and prays for me every afternoon?" she asked. "Don't look so surprised, honey," she said when she noticed that Isabelle was looking at her in shock. "A lot goes on around here that you all think I don't know, but as I said earlier," she smiled, "I'm sick, not stupid."

"Oh, Mom," she said laughing and hugging her again.

"Go ahead and do your asking then bring me my tea and we'll have a talk," Amelia said firmly when Isabelle had pulled back. "I'm tired of being kept in the dark."

"Okay," Isabelle replied, rising to her feet. "I'll be back in a few minutes."

She found Jon and Gabe in the Morning Room playing a game of chess at a small table there. From the looks of it,

243

Gabe was creaming him, but Jon seemed determined to fight a losing battle.

"Ah, guys," she said, and they looked up from the board. "We've got a problem."

"What's up?" Jon asked, pushing back his chair and standing.

"Sure you don't want to finish your game," she teased and he grinned.

"I'm sure," he said, and she watched as Gabe shook his head and got to his feet too.

"Saved from certain defeat," he said in his usual dry manner before turning to Isabelle. "What's going on, Belle?" he asked.

"She knows," was all she said.

"Who knows what?" Jon asked.

"Amelia knows who she is," Gabe said as a statement and Isabelle nodded.

"How do you do that?" Jon asked in exasperation, looking at Gabe then back to Isabelle. "How did she find out?" he asked.

"Let me give you her quote," Isabelle said. " 'I may be sick but I'm not stupid'," and Jon laughed despite the seriousness of the situation. "She wants to know why I'm hiding from her. I told her I'd have to come and talk to you first before I could explain."

244

Jon took his cell phone from his pocket and made a call to Travis. He spoke with him for a few minutes, then he hung up.

"Okay," he said. "Let's get the Judge and go talk to her. Come on Ice," he turned to Gabe, "she may as well meet the entire protection detail."

They all gathered in the master bedroom suite, including Sassy, and Isabelle told her, Ted and Amelia what she could of the story. She only gave them the brief facts, however, that a patient had confessed something to her at the hospital where she worked, and she was in protective custody until she could testify in court. She also told them she was unable to give them specific details as she was under a gag order from the Bureau, and that she would have to remain in disguise probably for the rest of her life. Coming to the end, Isabelle looked over at Jon for him to finish up.

"Amelia," he said. "It's very important that you use Isabelle's new name at all times. The daughter you knew twenty years ago is for all intents and purposes no longer living."

"I can relate to that only too well, Jon," she said. "I had to do the same thing, so I know how to guard that secret." He nodded in understanding. "What happens from here on out?" she asked.

"We continue as we are," Jon said, "but what I didn't mention to you Judge or to you Isabelle is that we are also here to protect you Amelia, just in case our suspect gets wind of your existence and starts looking for you too. He might think to use you to get to Belle."

245

Ted nodded. "That's been my thought from the beginning," he said. "He wouldn't be the first to try something like that."

It was then Isabelle remembered that Travis had come to stay at the house when she, Ted, Jon and Gabe had gone into Nashville to see the doctor, and now she understood why.

"As long as we're vigilant," Jon continued, "I think we'll be okay."

Ted had sat with Amelia in his arms while Isabelle told her story, but now he eased himself from beside her. He kissed her cheek then told her he had to finish up in his study as the deadline for submitting his work was fast approaching, and she told him she was fine so he should go ahead. Sassy and Gabe also left to start supper and Isabelle went to get the tea she had promised her mother and forgotten. Jon turned to leave as well, but Amelia called out to him and he came over to her bedside.

"Thank you for all the prayers, Jon," she said and chuckled at the surprised look on his face.

"How long have you known?" he asked in disbelief.

"From just after you came here," she said. "I woke up earlier than usual one afternoon wondering whose hand was on my head," she explained. "I opened my eyes briefly and saw yours closed in prayer. I've listened for you every day since then, and while you've been praying for me, I've been praying for you."

Jon was so touched that he had to clear his throat before

he could respond. "Thank you, Amelia," he said, bending to kiss her cheek. "You are an extraordinary woman."

"Oh, I'm no big thing," she said. "You just take care of Belle for me," then she added with a cheeky grin, "I love her just as much as you do."

Jon just stood there shaking his head. "How on earth did you know that?" he asked. It seemed he had been asking her that a lot in the last few minutes.

"Your eyes follow her wherever she goes," she said, "and when you talked about her just now, there was a softness in your voice that only love could place there. Ted always did the same things, so that's how I know it for what it is."

He chuckled and said. "I think you've been brought completely up to date, Amelia. In the future, I'll know better than to try and hide anything from you."

"So are you going to pursue her when this is over?" she asked.

"It's complicated," he said. "The main reason I wouldn't be able to is that she has turned her back on God and wants nothing to do with Him. I love her very much, but I cannot compromise my faith and encourage a relationship unless it's with another believer. Then there's the fact that she's my witness; that, coupled with her transfer into permanent witness protection would make it impossible."

"What's complicated for us, Jon, isn't complicated for God you know," she said, "and what do you mean she's turned her back on Him?" she asked.

247

"Maybe I shouldn't have said anything," he countered, "but please pray about it. I've managed to get her to start looking into the Bible with me, a sort of mini Bible study," he continued. "I'm hoping to help her to come back to Him." Amelia frowned, but said nothing. It was something to ponder when she was alone. "I have to make a phone call to my boss to let him know how things went," Jon said to her, "but Belle will be back soon."

"You run along," she said smiling at him, "and don't stop coming in the afternoons."

"I won't" he promised smiling back then left to make his call.

Amelia, meanwhile, continued to ponder his statement. She couldn't believe that Isabelle would do something like that. And what about the praise song she had been humming earlier. She would be sure to ask her, but right now she just wanted to thank God for bringing them back together and to work on keeping them all safe. She also wanted to bring the situation between her daughter and Jon before Him. She rather liked him for a son-in-law she smiled. She would just have to hold the whole thing up before the Lord and watch how He worked things out.

CHAPTER 20

Senator Lamar Johnson put on his coat and looked in the mirror by the foyer, straightening his tie and smoothing his low black hair. He turned his head from side to side, making sure his beard, which was cut close to his dark brown face, was neat and presentable. He had just come back from fourteen glorious days in the Maldives with his wife Crystal and he couldn't remember the last time he felt so relaxed. They loved to travel and enjoyed the fact that they were now able to do so whenever they got a break from their demanding jobs.

Crystal was an obstetrician and gynecologist who had her own practice, so it was easy for them to take off when he was free from his duties, just as long as he gave her a little advanced notice. She had already left for work, having received a call at around seven o'clock that one of her patients was at the hospital and very close to delivery. She told him she would just go straight to the office after instead of coming home, as her first appointment was at nine that morning.

Satisfied with his appearance, he picked up his laptop bag in preparation to leave for Capitol Hill, but his cell phone rang, so he fished it out of his pocket and checked the Caller I.D. He knew the number well, so he set down the briefcase and answered as he looked out the window beside the front door.

"Hey, Neil," he said, "how are you?"

"Hey, Crew," Cornelius responded, calling him by his childhood nickname, "are you back from hobnobbing with the rich and famous?"

"Yes, we got back on the weekend," he replied. "You need to take a trip to the Maldives, my friend, it's a paradise."

"I've already made a promise to myself to do a transatlantic voyage next year," Cornelius replied, "so I'll keep your paradise in mind."

"How are things with Con?" Lamar asked next. "I know you were trying to tell me something the other day when we spoke," he added, "but the connection was so bad I couldn't hear a thing."

"I know," Cornelius said, "I could hardly hear you either."

"So what's up?" Lamar questioned. "I still can't give you the information you want Neil," he said. "I already told Constantine."

"Don't worry about that," Cornelius said. "I have another idea, and this might be easier for you to do for us." He told Lamar what he needed and waited to hear what he would say.

"Well, since it's just a name, I should be able to get that for you," he agreed. "I don't want to see Constantine go to jail."

"You still remember how to run a con?" his friend asked.

"You know where I work and can ask me a dumb question like that," Lamar laughed. "My work is one con game after another, pal," and Cornelius laughed with him. "Give me a few days to set things up," Lamar said, his brain already starting to churn. "I'll call you back as soon as I have a name, but you have to promise not to act on the information right away, Neil. I need a buffer so my bait won't remember our conversation."

"No problem," Cornelius replied. "We'll make sure to protect you every step of the way," and with that, they both hung up.

****

Cornelius put through a call to Constantine a short while after he had spoken to Lamar to bring him up to speed and his twin answered after the second ring.

"Hey, Neil," he said, sounding angry.

"Hey," he replied, "what's the matter?"

"Walter just messed up a delivery to one of our pushers and they're both in jail," he answered. "I should've gotten rid of him long ago, the stupid....," he went on to use a string of expletives.

"Are you going to get him out?" Cornelius asked.

"Yes, but I'll have Jimmy off him when he comes back," he said dogmatically. "I can't stand incompetence."

"I have some news that might cheer you up," his brother said.

"I could use some good news right about now,"

251

Constantine admitted.

"Crew's going to help us," Cornelius revealed.

"He is?" Constantine asked surprised, knowing their friend had told him there was no way he could get any information that would be helpful to them without arousing suspicion.

"Yeah," Cornelius said. "He says it should be relatively easy to get a name."

"Now I feel better," Constantine said, his anger forgotten.

"He wants us to sit on the information for a while though, so his bait won't remember their conversation and put two and two together," his twin informed.

"That's no problem," Constantine agreed. "As a matter of fact, why don't we run a bait and cover," he suggested, knowing his brother would know what he meant.

"That's an excellent idea," Cornelius replied.

"We'll wait a few weeks," Constantine said, "Then do something spectacular at the same time we act on Crew's information. We'll keep the Feds so busy he'll be totally in the clear."

"Any ideas?" Cornelius asked.

"You bet," he replied and gave Cornelius his thoughts. When he had finished, Cornelius grinned.

"That's just perfect," he replied.

"I'll set everything up with Jimmy," Constantine promised and a few minutes later, they hung up.

****

Lamar sat in the chair behind his desk two days later, running what he was about to do through his mind. The key to a successful con was to go over and over it until you couldn't get it wrong, and he had been doing just that for the last couple of days. It also required a cool head and quick thinking in case everything didn't go according to plan, and he had learned to perfect such a calm and relaxed demeanor when he was running a game, that no one ever suspected he was after something.

As chairman of the Senate Oversight Committee on Organized Crime, he knew the top people in just about every government department. He was good friends, however, with one of the Bureau's top men, Carson Silvera, so he decided to bait him for the information he needed.

He and Carson had met through their jobs and had hit it off well. They had lunch on a regular basis and even got together along with their wives for dinner or drinks occasionally. He really didn't want to use him, but he and the Antonellis went all the way back to his days on the street in L.A., and he just couldn't sit by and watch Constantine go to jail.

They were all very close, having grown up in the same neighborhood; as a matter of fact, he'd lived next door to the twins with his mother while Frank lived with his folks down the street. Frank's parents were always at each other's throats, however, so he spent a lot of time with his cousins. Eventually, when he was seven, Frank packed three pillowcases with his stuff, went over to Con and Neil's place and told their mother he wanted to move in with them if she and his uncle didn't mind. Knowing how difficult his home life was, his Aunt Angelina said she didn't mind at all, and sent her husband Amedeo to tell his brother and sister-in-law they were keeping their son for good.

Their parents all worked hard to make ends meet. Amedeo was in construction while Angelina was a home healthcare assistant. His mother worked as a cashier at a large discount store in the days and waited tables at a diner down the street at night. As children they were essentially unsupervised after school, and he and Frank were only ten years old, two years younger than the Antonelli twins, when they began their illegal activities.

Even at that young age, Cornelius had been great at strategy and it was he who usually master-minded their various schemes. While Cornelius took care of that side of things, his forte was running their con games as he acted well. Constantine and Frank were the fastest on their feet and excellent at picking pockets, so they were usually the ones who made initial contact with their victims depending on the game of the day.

As he thought about his friends, Lamar remembered the day they had decided to pull a game they called bait and sweep. It was relatively easy. One of them, usually Constantine or Frank would filch candy or some other item from the area by the cash register of the store they'd targeted. About ninety percent of the time the cashier would leave the register and run over to the front door and it was then they'd all raid either the register or the items on display and take off out the door before the store employee or

254

owner knew what was happening.

On this particular day, they went into a convenience store seven blocks over from their homes and Constantine, who was fourteen at the time, went into action. The owner did the unexpected, however, he called out to his wife to man the till, grabbed up a bat and gave chase. Knowing their plan was foiled, they left and eventually ended up at home, but Constantine didn't return.

They wondered if he had been caught and taken to the police station, but when his parents arrived that evening and he still wasn't home, they went to the station to report him missing. He wasn't incarcerated as he, Frank and Neil had thought, so everyone began searching for him. Eventually, close to two in the morning, his father had found him locked in an abandoned car in a vacant lot. He told them when his folks were out of earshot that he had hidden himself in the car trunk to get away from the store owner who was a good sprinter, but the lid had locked by accident and he couldn't get out. The floor of the trunk was rotted and had sections open to outside, but they were only large enough to keep air coming in.

The incident had traumatized Constantine, however, and from then on he was terrified of small or confined spaces. Places like closets, powder rooms and elevators completely freaked him out and he had to sleep with a light on at night.

They continued to run their games of chance, and Lamar became better and better with each con until one day, when he was thirteen, he came home to find the police waiting for him. He had actually thought they'd come to arrest him, but he quickly learned that they'd come to tell him that his mother had died at work. She'd apparently had a brain hemorrhage and had succumbed instantly.

His aunt who lived in Washington D.C. flew over right away, and after the funeral, she took custody of him and carried him to her home, hundreds of miles away from his friends. She was a good woman and a strong disciplinarian, so she soon got him on the straight and narrow. After he went to live with her, he never looked back and later went on to study law. Eventually, he went into politics and quickly moved from being a state legislator in Virginia to becoming a congressman and, three years before, he'd been elected to the senate. He had never forgotten his friends, however, and they'd kept in touch over the years. He regarded them as his brothers, and they treated him the same way too.

Even though they were close, he had stressed to them he wouldn't help them with their illegal activities because of his position, and although they had pressured him a time or two, he'd stuck to his guns. When he had heard of Constantine's trouble, however, he became concerned for his friend. Constantine had taken the fall for him once when Lamar was eleven and spent three months in Juvenile Hall because of it. Lamar would never forget it. He owed Constantine and he wanted to help him.

He glanced at his watch and knew it was time to leave for his luncheon appointment with Carson, so he put on his coat and went down to the lobby before exiting out the door and walking to the restaurant they had agreed on five blocks away. The day was sunny and cool and as he made his way, he ran the con through his mind again. He reached the bistro a few minutes later, went inside and saw Carson sitting in the last booth at the back over on the right.

His Bureau friend had just turned fifty and had graying blonde hair, hazel eyes and was at least six foot four. He was also trim and fit as he was an exercise buff. He hardly missed a day in the gym he'd set up at home and went running every morning before work.

"Lamar," he said, rising to meet him and they shook hands, "how was the trip?" he asked as they sat down across from each other.

"It was incredible, Carson," Lamar enthused. "You've got to take Lorraine some time."

"Maybe when the children are a little older," Carson said. "We're not flexible like you and Crystal remember." He and his wife had adopted four children, each from a different part of the world, including the United States. The oldest was just entering college and the youngest junior high.

"I've always admired you and Lorraine for taking on the challenge with your kids, Carson," Lamar said with genuine respect. "When Crystal and I found out we couldn't have children, we decided not to adopt."

"We wanted children too badly to let infertility stand in the way," Carson said. "They've brought more sunshine to our lives than we ever thought possible too."

"I know, pal," he said.

They both looked at the menu, placed their order with the waitress and talked as they ate, mostly about Lamar's trip before they went on to discuss business. They were having coffee and dessert by that time and Lamar decided to make his move and set the bait. They were well into a discussion on cases anyway, and it seemed the perfect time for him to bring up the Antonelli investigation.

"We have all the evidence we need to nail that lowlife for good," Carson said quietly, "but we still can't find him."

"He needs to pay for his crimes, that's for sure," Lamar agreed.

"If we could only get a location on him, we'd be able to get the judicial process started." Carson elaborated. "It's been months since the incident in L.A."

"How's the Doctor holding out?" Lamar asked next, building his set up.

"I have no idea," Carson responded.

"Are you serious?" Lamar questioned, genuinely surprised.

"Scout's honor," Carson replied. "I only know she's in the custody of our very best and they've been with her from the beginning, nothing more. Our new division is almost completely autonomous," he said, "and they're good, believe me."

"It must be hard to be on a protection detail that long," Lamar mused. "I don't think I could do something like that."

"When they sign up, their job description is outlined in detail and the time issue heavily stressed," Carson said then elaborated. "We mostly take on singles anyway or those who're divorced or widowed without small children as protection agents. That way we don't have any pinning wives or husbands or kids making them unhappy."

"Husbands?" Lamar questioned, feigning shock and ignorance. "I didn't know you used women in that capacity."

"Of course we do. It's protocol, pal," Carson explained. "We can't have an all-male detail protecting a single female witness."

"I guess not. I never even thought of that," Lamar countered, then let the trap fly, "I don't know if I was in danger like the Doc that I'd want a woman on my detail, protocol or not," he stated. "I can just imagine her firing at Antonelli's men if they came calling and stopping in the middle of the gun battle to scream blue murder because she broke a nail."

Carson laughed, thinking of Anne and her exemplary military record, "Not our girl," he chuckled, taking the bait. "She's definitely no wall-flower, pal. She's an ex-air force pilot and was with S.W.A.T. for a while before she came to us. She's the type who would chew off her leg to get out of a bad spot. I'd have her on my protection detail any day."

"If you say so," Lamar said dismissively. "By the way, the Committee has begun reviewing the O'Reilly case again," he carried on as if what Carson said didn't matter, but on the inside he was smiling. "Gotcha," he said to himself.

"Really?" Carson said surprised. "I thought that was closed," he commented, and with that they went on to discuss other things.

****

Lamar called Cornelius later that evening. "Hey, Neil," he said when his friend answered.

"Tell me you have it?" Cornelius said anxiously.

"I don't have a name, but I got enough information that, with your connections, I'm sure you'll be able to find who you're looking for," Lamar said.

"You're a genius, Crew," he grinned. "You haven't lost your touch."

"I told you, pal," Lamar chuckled, "I do this every day for a living. Listen, remember not to do anything with what I'm going to tell you for a while," he stressed. "I want to make sure I'm in the clear."

"Don't worry," Cornelius replied, "we won't use it for a few weeks; besides, Constantine is setting up a bait and cover to fade you out of the picture."

"What's he going to do?" Lamar asked.

"You'll know when it happens," Cornelius said mysteriously, and Lamar just shook his head.

"Okay," he answered, and went on to give Cornelius the information he needed.

"I can't thank you enough for doing this for us Crew," Cornelius continued. "Constantine asked me to pass on his thanks as well."

"We're brothers, Neil," he stated. "Don't mention it. I hope everything works out." and with that, they hung up.

CHAPTER 21

The morning after Amelia made her discovery, Isabelle sat talking with her while Sassy got some work done. It was such a joy to speak freely with her mother, and they had been getting caught up on all that had happened during the many years they'd been separated.

Belle told her about her flight from the house and about meeting her grandparents for the first time. She spoke about her life with them and about her work as a doctor and Amelia couldn't have been prouder when she learned that her daughter had achieved such a distinction. Then Isabelle gently told her of her parents' deaths and held her as she cried. Finally, she told her of her love for Jon and how it didn't seem possible for them to be together.

After a while, Amelia asked her, "Belle, sweetheart, how has your relationship with the Lord been?" She didn't betray Jon's confidence, she simply approached her as a parent who wanted to know how her daughter's spiritual walk was going.

Isabelle hung her head and didn't answer right away, then she looked at her mother and told her honestly, "When you left me, Mom, I left Him," and she could see the disappointment on Amelia's face. "I felt betrayed and abandoned and turned my back on Him completely. In my heart, even at a young age, I knew you wouldn't be able to stay with Father forever, but I always thought you would have taken me with you. It never occurred to me that you would go without me and send me off to strangers. It was the cry of my heart that somehow we could get out from under him, and when you did and left me, I was desolate." Amelia's heart became constricted as Isabelle spoke, and regret swept over her.

"Oh my darling," Amelia said, holding her hand, "I'm so sorry my selfishness did that to you. I had wanted to wait until you had finished your nursing degree, but I knew I couldn't survive a moment longer. Your father told me that last night when he had beaten me so badly that I could expect more of the same every evening for the next week."

"Why?" Isabelle asked. "What did you do to make him so angry?"

"He found a letter from my folks that morning in the mail," she said. "He had a meeting with the church board and had forgotten some papers he needed. He came back for them just as the mailman was putting the post in the box," she explained. "You know I always cleared it before he got home," and Isabelle nodded. "Anyway, he read the letter and was furious. Dad and Mom were begging me to leave him and come home and he realized from what they said that it wasn't the first time they'd communicated with me." Isabelle just shook her head as she could picture the scene.

"I knew I'd never survive if I stayed, I was in such agony I could hardly walk, so I made the decision to go," she continued. "The month before, Dad and Mom had sent me a money order, enough for plane fare for you and me to come to them in San Francisco if things became unbearable. I thank God that wasn't the letter your father found. That last morning, I cashed it, went home and packed my things. I wrote one note to him and one to you and was gone by ten o'clock. I knew I needed to get a good start to be able

263

to get away.

"In order to save cash," she explained, "I decided on us taking the bus, but I knew he would go to Dad and Mom first, so I called them and made arrangements with them to take you and I would head east. They agreed to hide you until everything had died down and take care of you and that was such a relief to me. I knew they were in a great position financially and could give you the kind of education that would enable you to fulfill your dreams of becoming a nurse."

"When Gramps asked me what I wanted to do and I told him," Isabelle interrupted, "he asked me why I wanted to settle on that when the whole medical profession was open to me," she smiled remembering. "Then he asked me if I could do anything I wanted, what would it be, and I told him I really wanted to become a doctor. I never told you that because I knew Father would never allow it and I also knew we couldn't afford it."

"I'm so glad, Belle," Amelia said.

"Mom," Isabelle said with a wonderful light on her face, "I want you to know that a few days ago I recommitted my life to the Lord," and Amelia melted with relief. "Jon has been going through the Word with me, and the other evening I realized just how good God has been to both you and I." Isabelle then went on to tell her the story. "I love our Heavenly Father so much, Mom," she said when she had finished, "and I'm only now acknowledging how much I've missed Him. The last few days I've been so full of joy, and I'm so glad to be walking with Him again. I know that danger might be looming, and the future is uncertain, but I haven't been this happy in years."

264

They were silent for a while then Amelia asked, "Were you the one who told Ted that your father was dead?" Isabelle nodded. "I wondered how he found that article after so much time had passed. Tell me what happened?" she asked, and Isabelle told her all that had taken place surrounding his death and burial.

"Belle," her mother said, "I'm going to tell you something that I've never told anyone else. Not even Ted knows all of it, but I'm telling you," and Isabelle nodded. "That man followed me for a year after I left home."

"He did?" Isabelle asked, totally shocked by her mother's revelation. "I thought he'd gone on the mission field almost immediately. He came around to Gramps and Gram's house looking for us a week after we'd left, just as you figured he would, but they told him they hadn't see us. That was true because they had me staying with a friend of theirs so I would be out of sight. They told me his mouth was wired shut so I think that's why it took him that long to come looking. I know he stayed watching the house after they spoke to him, and they knew he was there too. Gramps and Gram said he finally left a few days later."

"Well when he left you, he obviously went back home and picked up my trail. He tracked me like some kind of animal on the hunt," Amelia said vehemently. "He simply followed the bus route I had taken. I had no other way of traveling and I certainly wasn't going to hitch hike. Because I had no work experience and didn't even know how to use a computer at the time, the only jobs I could get was cleaning houses and waitressing at restaurants, but it wouldn't take him long to find me. God was so good though, Belle," she continued. "I never once spoke to him or had any kind of confrontation with him. I always saw him before he saw me.

265

"By this time, I had colored my hair and tried to change my appearance to make it more difficult for him, but nothing seemed to work. Then one day when I'd reached as far as Roanoke, Virginia, I saw him step through the door of the hotel where I was working. I ran out the back door, grabbed my things from the boarding house where I was staying and ran over to the church I'd started attending. I'd struck up a friendship with the pastor and his wife and as I knew they were leaving that day for Kentucky to visit their daughter, I asked them if they could give me a ride.

They dropped me off at a truck stop just outside of Louisville. I was so desperate and so determined to get rid of him once and for all that I did what I promised myself I would never do; I hitched a ride with a trucker and his wife. There was the Christian fish sign on both doors of their rig for one and as she was with him, I decided to take the risk. If she hadn't been there, I'd never have done it.

"Anyway," she went on, "they dropped me off in Chattanooga and I went into a diner to get something to eat and scan the local newspaper. The job here was posted and, as they say, the rest is history. One other thing," she said. "A few days after I left, I wanted to make sure you had reached Dad and Mom and that you were okay. When I called, they told me you were fine, but you were staying with some good friends of theirs for a few weeks. They tried to encourage me to come to them, but I told them no. I didn't want to bring them any trouble and I wanted you to be able to have some peace. I figured if your father came looking for me, I would lead him further and further away from you.

"After that initial call, I decided not to call Dad and Mom for a while so you could get to know them, be able to focus on your studies and begin to live a normal life. When I settled here and felt I'd given it enough time, I called one day and found that the house number had been disconnected. I couldn't reach Dad at work either and I'd left my address book in my hurry to leave so I didn't have their cell numbers. I had no idea where you'd all gone and that's why we became permanently separated."

"They retired and moved to L.A. to be with me less than a year after I moved out west," Isabelle explained. "That's where I was attending college. I lived with them off campus, then went on to medical school there. I was at the end of my cardiac surgical residency when they passed. I was devastated," and Amelia nodded with tears in her eyes.

Isabelle looked at her mother then and decided to share something that had been bothering her.

"Mom," she said pensively, "I don't know if I can forgive him. For the last few days that has been on my mind more and more and I know God wants me to deal with it. I just don't know if I can."

"It took me a long time, Belle," Amelia confessed, "years in fact, but God finally helped me reach a place of forgiveness and peace. I know He will do the same for you if you ask Him for His help, sweetheart. He only wants to know you have a willing heart and He will do the rest. Do you want us to pray about it right now?" she asked, wanting to help her daughter.

"Yes, Mom," Isabelle said. "I'd like that very much," so they joined hands and spent some time in prayer.

CHAPTER 22

Jimmy Wexler stood outside the church in Cincinnati, Ohio and looked up at the simple structure. It was painted white and was long and rectangular with a plain bell tower extending from the roof at the front. The only thing that gave it presence was the beautiful stained-glass windows that graced the sides and front of the building.

Within a day he had traced Marissa Sparks to the Los Angeles university where she had done her medical training. He had discovered that she'd been raised by her grandparents, who were both deceased, but he hadn't been able to make the connection with her origins before then. He decided, therefore, to use his charms on the sweet young thing who worked in the university office. He loved when his work was pleasurable. Within two days he had gotten the information he needed, so it was only a matter of silencing his willing sweetheart by creating an unfortunate accident and making the long drive up from the west coast.

After his first day in the Doctor's hometown, he had gotten the scoop on where she had lived with her parents, but he needed more to go on, so he had formulated a plan that had brought him to this moment.

He looked at his reflection in the glass covering the signboard outside the church door to make sure his glasses were in its proper place and grinned at his new appearance. He had taken one look at himself in the mirror the night he had arrived in town and knew he couldn't convince anyone he was legitimate. His hair was slicked back with gel, and his tight jeans and t-shirt showed off the muscles he worked hard at honing each and every day.

He looked more like a snake oil salesman than a writer he'd concluded, so with his new career in mind, he'd gone about making his appearance much more believable. He'd washed the gel from his hair and gotten it cut at the local barber and that, along with a daily shave, instead of one every three or four, took care of his face while the glasses gave him the studious look he was after. He had also gone shopping and purchased a long-sleeved shirt and tie along with a pair of dress pants and shoes, and as he stood there grinning at himself, he thought that for the first time in his life, he looked respectable.

He didn't know much about God or how a Christian should act, so for the next couple of nights he'd sat in front of the television in his motel room watching and listening to every show he could find on the two Christian channels he had access to. He felt confident he now had enough of the vernacular down to make his performance believable, so he'd made his way to the church that morning to carry out his plan.

He straightened his tie one last time, adjusted his new laptop bag into a more comfortable position in his hand and went through the doors into the sanctuary. The interior was dim and cool and carried the hush that all churches did. Before him and above the altar were three spectacular stained-glass windows which mimicked the ones he'd seen earlier, and there was the faint smell of lemon wood polish in the air. It had probably been used earlier on the fancy carved and raised dais he knew was referred to as the pulpit, which was ahead of him to his left, and as he walked down the aisle with pews on either side, he felt uncomfortable.

There wasn't a soul in sight, and when he reached the front row of benches, he stopped, trying to decide on his next move. Just then a man in his mid-thirties came out of a door at the side. He had on a clerical collar and a black shirt and pants and, seeing Jimmy, he crossed to the front of the altar and came up to him smiling.

"Welcome to Wings of Faith Community Church," he said, extending his hand. "I'm Pastor Jeff Mason. How can I help you?"

Jimmy grasped his pastor's hand in a firm grip and smiled too. "Good morning, Pastor Mason," he replied. "My name is James Devoroe and I'm a writer."

"That's an interesting profession, Mr. Devoroe," the pastor said. "Is there something I can help you with or are you here on a spiritual matter?"

"Actually, I'm writing a piece on a former pastor here, Adrian Sparks," he said.

"I see," Pastor Mason responded. "That was a little before my time, I'm afraid, I've only been the pastor here for the last three years."

"Oh," Jimmy said, putting on a disappointed face. "I was hoping I could get some information to help me get a feel for what he was like," he explained, totally into his part. "Is there anyone else who you think might be able to help me?" he asked. "I find him an interesting subject to write about."

"The only person who may be able to help you is our caretaker, Old Bob," the Pastor said. "He's been here more than thirty years. He's now physically very slow and arthritic,

270

but he gets the job done better than any young person who's come on board to help him," he smiled. "He should be resting in his quarters around back," he said. "If you make a left when you get outside, the office is next door. You'll find his apartment to the rear and the entrance is on the right side of the building," he directed.

"Thank you very much, Pastor Mason," Jimmy smiled, shaking his hand again.

"You're welcome," the pastor said. "Best wishes on your book."

Jimmy left the sanctuary, and as he was making his way over to the church office, his cell phone rang.

"Yes, sir," he answered when he saw Constantine's number on the Caller I.D.

"Jimmy, where are you?" Constantine asked.

"I'm in Ohio," he replied.

"You have anything for me?" his boss asked.

"No, sir," Jimmy responded.

"Listen," Constantine continued, "I need you to hire a shooter for me. Someone expendable," and went on to outline his plan. "Do you think you can find someone who would be unable to resist the cash?"

"I know two who would probably take the job," he answered immediately. "One used to be a sniper."

"Get him," Constantine said immediately. "I'll tell you when and where I want the job done."

"No problem," he replied, and they both hung up.

Jimmy was outside Old Bob's door within a few moments and after giving himself a minute to plan his approach, he knocked on the door.

"Come in," he heard a voice call from the other side, "it's open."

Jimmy went into the apartment and was surprised by its neat appearance. The room encompassed the entire width of the back of the office building and was a quarter of its length making it quite roomy. Except for the bathroom, the living and sleeping area was one big space with a tiny kitchenette off to the right, and a bed which had been carefully made to the left. Sitting in a recliner in front of a television in the living room section and stroking a big black and white cat was a tiny figure who looked to be in his early seventies.

"What can I do for you?" he asked, not rising from his chair, and Jimmy figured it would probably take too much of an effort for him to do so.

"I'm sorry I don't know your full name, sir," Jimmy said respectfully.

"It's Bob," he replied. "Just Bob."

"Hi, Bob, my name is James Devoroe and I'm a writer," Jimmy held out his hand and gently took Bob's extended one, being careful not to grip it too tightly. It was crippled with arthritis.

"Nice to meet you young fella," Bob said. "Why don't you have a seat and tell me what I can do for you."

"Well, Bob," Jimmy said, sitting as he'd been instructed, "Pastor Mason said you may be able to help me. I'm a writer and I'm doing a piece on a former pastor here, Adrian Sparks. I was wondering if you could give me a little insight into the man; what he was like, how he conducted himself, that kind of thing."

"Ha," Bob laughed, surprising him. "Why on earth would you want to write about that pious old hypocrite?" he asked. "He had the most cockeyed idea of Christianity I've ever seen."

"I just think his story would make good reading," Jimmy said.

"All that piece of writing would do young fella is give Christians a bad name," Bob said. "Best you find yourself someone else to write about," he advised.

Jimmy had to think fast, "Bob, I've been a Christian for twenty years and written about both the good and the bad in my business," he explained. "I'm not writing this story to give Christians a bad rap as much as using Adrian Sparks as an example of how Christians shouldn't live and act. I plan to write about three different pastors," he elaborated as the idea came to him. "Two of them were good, righteous and upstanding men and then Adrian Sparks." He had no idea why Old Bob disliked the Doc's father, but he read between the lines and hoped he was on the right track.

"Well," Bob said slowly, "since you put it that way, I'll tell you what I can. Just don't put your source in that article," he cautioned, pointing a crooked arthritic finger at him.

"I won't, Bob," Jimmy said readily, smiling inside that he had read the old man right. "My sources are always confidential," he assured him and saw Bob relax.

"There was really no love lost between Sparks and me, that's for sure," Bob said, as he began his story, and Jimmy spent the next two hours with the old man.

By the end of the tale, Jimmy got the picture of a man that only a mother could love, or maybe not. He couldn't blame Jolene Sparks for leaving her husband only, if it was him, he'd have made sure to kill him first. Out of the whole two hours the most interesting detail Bob had given him was that sometime after Mrs. Sparks had left, she'd sent him a money order from somewhere in Tennessee. The name of the place had been illegible, but the 'TN' had been clearly visible.

As Jimmy rose to leave, he considered doing away with the old man, but he took one look at him and changed his mind.

"I must be getting soft," he said as he left the church and made his way back to his motel on foot.

He felt, however, that it was best not to do anything to arouse suspicion. It would make for a clean getaway without any unnecessary heat. He had bigger fish to fry and a big bonus at the end of this anyway, so he left Bob alone. It was a good fifteen-minute walk to his motel and his car, but it gave him time to ponder his next move. He didn't know exactly where to start, but one thing he knew for certain, and that was he was off to Tennessee.

CHAPTER 23

Gabe stood at the balustrade in the early morning light looking out at the new day. He was waiting for Sassy as was their morning routine, but he had made his way outside way before their usual meeting time. He had come so far since arriving at Pleasant Valley that he almost couldn't believe it. He felt at peace here, even though there was the looming possibility that Antonelli might be able to locate Isabelle and Amelia despite their best efforts.

On mornings like this, he found himself thinking about the Creator of the universe, and as he looked out, he again acknowledged that all this couldn't have happened by chance. He knew God existed. He knew it just as surely as he knew that Gina was in heaven. He just knew.

He thought back to her and to their life together, particularly their last night. He remembered her praying for him just before they had cuddled close to sleep and her words had never left him. She had asked God to make Jesus real to Gabe just as He had made Him real to her, and God had done just that. He had been thinking more and more about the Savior of the world for weeks now.

He recalled a time before when he had heard part of a sermon Jon had played when they'd been on a witness protection assignment together. Jon had been listening to it when he had come to relieve him from his watch early and had asked him if he would mind if he finished listening to it before taking off for bed. Gabe had told him no and sat there while the sermon played down. It was near Easter, two years after Gina had died, and the speaker was talking about Jesus in the Garden of Gethsemane and at the time Gabe could relate well to the Savior's travail.

For some reason this morning, he felt particularly close to Gina's Heavenly Father and to His Son. He had been cold and numb for so long, as if every ounce of light and happiness had been sucked from his body. Now he no longer felt that way. Very slowly he could feel himself beginning to respond to life and the world around him and he knew that God was healing him from the dark place he had been for so long.

His thoughts turned to the people in his immediate sphere, and he found he was now able to look at others and feel emotion rather than the blank nothingness he'd had since Gina's death. He liked Ted and Amelia immensely and Sassy was so comfortable to be with. He was glad that Jon had found someone to love after all this time of being alone and he also found he liked Isabelle. Despite their rocky beginning, he felt that she really was the one for his best friend.

It was unclear if they would ever have a future, but he knew that once Jon learned of her recommitment to Christ, he would do everything in his power to make sure they could be together. He thought of himself and how happy he'd been when he'd been married, but he knew in his heart he would never go there again. The rending that had taken place when Gina had died had just about killed him, and it was a pain he vowed never to put himself in a position to experience a second time.

He saw Adam and Eve, the two majestic white swans swimming beside each other as they crossed the pond in the rapidly dawning light and the mist that had covered everything when he'd first come outside had almost completely lifted. He had just thought that Sassy wasn't going to make their morning rendezvous when he heard footsteps behind him, but when he turned to greet her, it

277

was Jon who was walking towards him from the direction of the kitchen with a cup of coffee in his hand.

"What are you doing up?" he asked his friend. "You usually don't surface for another few hours."

"I came awake after two hours and for some reason I couldn't go back to sleep," he said, coming to stand beside Gabe and sipping from his cup. "By the way, I met Sassy in the kitchen, and she said to tell you she wouldn't be able to make it this morning. She said she needed to spend extra time with the Lord."

"Oh," Gabe said. "I had wondered."

"You have anything you want to tell me?" Jon asked with a grin. "She's a nice girl."

"Sorry, Peeps," he said, "you're definitely barking up the wrong tree."

"You like her, don't you?" Jon asked.

"She's okay," Gabe said, "but we're like siblings, that's all."

"How did that come about?" Jon asked. "You usually avoid women like the plague."

"Well one day when I accused her of coming on to me, she called me an arrogant jerk and a conceited pig. We've been friends ever since," he explained, and Jon laughed out loud in the early morning light.

"She really said that to you?" he asked, unable to control

278

his amusement.

"Word for word," Gabe said, using one of his favorite expressions. "Seems she has an aversion to men the same way I have an aversion to women. We're perfect for each other."

"Why doesn't she like men? Jon asked, finding this new turn of events with Gabe interesting.

"I'd be betraying a confidence if I told you," Gabe said, wanting to give Sassy the privacy he was sure she wanted regarding that particular event in her life. "She was badly hurt, Jon," he continued, "and although I don't know the whole story, I know enough to want to get my hands on the disgusting creep who did that to her."

Jon nodded. He felt the same way every time he thought of Antonelli and what he wanted to do to Isabelle.

They stood in comfortable silence for a while, soaking up the peaceful atmosphere when Jon felt a tug in his heart to speak to Gabe about his Heavenly Father. The urge was so strong that he couldn't ignore it, and he silently prayed for God to guide him before he spoke.

"Gabe," he said, "you believe in God, don't you?" He decided not to beat around the bush but just approach his friend directly.

Gabe was silent for a long time. "Yes," he said, not looking Jon's way.

"He's calling you this morning, isn't He?" Jon asked, feeling a certainty in his heart that could only have been put there by God.

"I don't know about 'calling' as you put it," he said, "but I have been thinking about Him," he acknowledged.

"Ice, what's holding you back from accepting Jesus as your Savior?" Jon asked.

"I don't know how," Gabe said, surprising him.

"You mean all this time you've wanted to give your heart to Him and never thought to ask me?" Jon asked in astonishment.

"I knew I could ask you anytime, Peeps," he said. "I just wasn't ready. Now I am," and Jon was so shocked he almost dropped his cup. This was why God had woken him up. He had arranged this divine appointment between him and Gabe. This conversation was meant to be.

"We can do it right now," Jon said. "Let's go inside," but Gabe didn't move.

"If you don't mind, Jon," he said, "let's do it right here. Somehow, I feel closer to God out here."

Jon didn't hesitate but rested his cup on the balustrade, got down on his knees and Gabe followed suit. Jon described to him the plan of salvation and made sure to give Gabe the reference from the Bible that supported what he was saying. He quoted for him Romans 10 verses 9 and 10. "If you openly declare that Jesus is Lord and believe in your heart that God raised him from the dead, you will be saved. For it is by believing in your heart that you are made right with God, and it is by openly declaring your faith that you are saved."

When Jon had finished, he rested his hand on Gabe's shoulder then led him in the 'Sinner's Prayer' which was based on the verses he had quoted, and in less than a minute, Gabe became his new brother in Christ.

They got to their feet and as Jon knew Gabe wasn't a demonstrative man these days, he put out his hand for him to shake. Instead, Gabe pulled him into a bear hug, slapping him on the back several times.

"I've come a long way, Peeps," he declared. "Thanks for your example, your friendship and your prayers."

He released him and they both looked at each other, then for the first time in six years and much to his shock, Jon saw his best friend Gabriel smile.

Sassy watched from the upstairs window by the landing leading to the third floor and stood there crying her eyes out. For some reason she felt she needed to spend extra time praying for Gabe, but she'd had no idea why. She'd been praying for him ever since their first heart to heart talk, asking God to heal him and save him, so she couldn't understand the urgency she was feeling. As she was passing the window at the top of the landing, however, she felt compelled to look out and watched as Jon and Gabe talked. She stood there praying for them without really knowing how to focus her prayers, but when she saw them get down on their knees, she knew exactly what was happening and fervently went before her Heavenly Father.

She heard a noise behind her and looked around to see Isabelle come up beside her. When her stepsister saw her tears, she became concerned.

"Sass, what's wrong?" she asked.

Sassy couldn't answer for the emotion so instead she pointed out the window. Belle looked out, saw the men on their knees with their heads bowed and, moments later, watched them rise to their feet and Gabe wrap Jon in his arms. Her fingers went to her mouth when she realized what had just happened, and she felt tears sting her own eyes. She looked back at Sassy and the next minute they were both hugging and laughing and crying all at the same time. Jon had prayed for his friend for so long, and it was a beautiful moment to watch. Isabelle knew she needed to tell him soon that she had recommitted her life to the Lord, but she would leave it for one more day. Today belonged to Gabe and she couldn't have been happier for him.

****

The following night, Isabelle made her way down the back stairs for her usual time with Jon. He was already there when she entered and had already made the sandwich and the hot drinks and was waiting at the table for her. He gave thanks to the Lord for the food when she joined him, and they both began eating and talking. He was still excited about Gabe's salvation, and they talked about it for a while before they went on to other things.

When the meal was over, she stood and went over to the stove to fix more tea for herself, and when she asked Jon if he wanted more coffee, he came over to the machine with his cup.

"Jon," she said as she waited for the water to boil,

"before we start tonight's study, there's something I want to tell you."

"Sure," he said. "What is it?" he asked, putting his cup down and leaning his hip on the counter facing her.

She looked at him with love shining from her eyes, then came right up to him and put her hand on his cheek in a gesture that surprised him. They'd been very careful to keep a good physical distance from each other during the last few weeks.

"Thank you, Jon," she said looking tenderly into his eyes. "Thank you for your prayers and for your love. You have been so patient with me and all that's done is made me love you more. I wanted to tell you that earlier this week I gave my life back to the Lord, and I'm so full of joy at being reconciled with my Savior."

She watched as, incredibly, his eyes filled with tears and he pulled her to him in a tight embrace that nearly cut off her breathing but felt so good. When he pulled back, she could see the tears on his cheeks, and she used her fingers to wipe them away.

"Tell me," was all he said, his voice rough with emotion, and she told him everything that had happened. "I'll get you a Bible first thing in the morning," he promised, but when she smiled and told him that Gabe had already gotten one for her, he just shook his head. "Belle, I can't tell you how happy you've made me," he said. "I've been praying so long for you guys, especially Gabe. I almost gave up on him, but God wouldn't let me. Now here it is that both my prayers have been answered in the same week. God is so amazing," he declared. "I love you so much, sweetheart," he went on to say before he pulled her to him again, but gentler this time and they stood that way for a few minutes, not saying a word. He just held her and prayed a blessing over her.

Eventually he kissed the top of her head and let her go. She made her tea and they went back to the table to start their study, but this time was different for Jon. This time he knew he didn't have to try and pick and choose the passages that would best speak to Isabelle's lack of faith, and it was with joy that he showed her some of his favorite verses while she in turn showed him some of hers.

Later, when he was alone, Jon praised his Heavenly Father for all that had taken place in recent days. His heart was full of joy and he just couldn't contain his praise for God. He then turned his attention to Isabelle, and he asked the Lord to make a way for them to be together. He again felt God impress upon his heart to trust Him, so he decided to wait until he had the freedom to try and work something out.

"I'll not do anything until you tell me, Lord," he promised. "I'll wait for your leading."

CHAPTER 24

Jimmy had been searching fruitlessly for two weeks. No one had ever heard of Jolene Sparks. He couldn't blame them for not remembering her even if they had met her. He was, after all, chasing a nearly twenty-year-old trail. He had covered every bus stop, city and town since reaching Memphis and was now in Chattanooga. He had decided on his way here that this would be his final stop. If the trail was still cold, he would go back to Constantine and tell him he couldn't find her. He would have given up long ago, but Constantine's promise of a hundred-thousand-dollar bonus was a powerful incentive for him not to quit.

He had been pounding the pavement from early that morning and, around eleven o'clock, decided to go into a diner for something to eat and to rest his feet. The place was relatively empty, so he found himself a seat in a booth at the back and, after placing his order, picked up the local paper to browse while waiting for his meal. The waitress brought him coffee and he sipped it while reading up on local events.

His food arrived a short time later, and he started eating with gusto. He hadn't bothered with breakfast in order to get an early start that morning, so he was hungry. He was halfway through the meal and almost at the end of the paper when he saw something that made him stop with his fork in mid-air. There at the top of the second to last page was a small column of legal notices. He had seen them in newspapers all the time and had never given them a passing thought, but the one at the very top caught his eye and shot an idea into his head that he couldn't ignore. It was about a name change for a man named Rafer Panhelligan. It seemed

285

he'd decided to change it to Rafer Pennington, and the notice was advising the public of his new moniker.

"That's it!" he said to himself.

He'd been going about this all wrong. She must have changed her name. It would have been the easiest way for her to hide from her husband. He grinned to himself and attacked the rest of his meal. He felt confident he was on the right track. All he needed to do now was make a little trip to City Hall to see if he could find what he was looking for. If he didn't, he would back track to the places he'd been before and do the same thing. If Jolene Sparks was still in Tennessee, he knew it was only a matter of time before he would find her.

He got up when he was finished and set the tip on the table before heading to the cashier at the front to pay his bill. Just as he placed the change in his pocket and walked out the door, his cell phone rang, and he knew from the number it was Constantine.

"Yes, Mr. Antonelli," he answered.

"Jimmy, I have a job for you," he said without preamble.

"I'm still tracing the Doctor's mother....," but Constantine didn't allow him to finish.

"Forget that," he said abruptly. "We're implementing Plan A, the one I told you about," and went on to outline to Jimmy what he wanted him to do. "I'm texting her location to you now," he continued. "When you have her, let me know. I want you to take her to Cornelius in Florida, but not to the estate. He'll tell you where to meet him, so call him when you're close to the state line. Also tell your shooter it's a go and he must do the job tomorrow. Don't take her until he's finished."

"I was promised a bonus if I found the Doc's mother," Jimmy said. "Does it apply to this new assignment?" he asked. He wasn't about to throw away his additional paycheck, especially when he was this close.

"Don't you think of anything else?" Constantine asked him in annoyance.

"No," Jimmy said simply and heard an expletive on the other end of the line.

"You'll get your bonus," Constantine said, trying to hold on to his temper. "I'll arrange it."

"You'll have her by the day after tomorrow," Jimmy confirmed and disconnected the call.

CHAPTER 25

Lamar stood in the Capitol's Rotunda talking with his friend and fellow senator from West Virginia, Gene McKay. They had just finished attending a joint session of congress and a few of the senators and congressmen were gathered in twos and threes talking or giving interviews to reporters. Many others were still in the house chamber while some had already left for their offices. He and Gene had been talking about the session and, deciding to grab a bite together, they left the Rotunda and made their way out through the public entrance, talking as they went. Just as they got outside, they heard two loud pops in rapid succession.

"What on earth was that?" Gene asked, as everyone on the street seemed to pause what they were doing to listen.

"It could just be a car," Lamar said, speculatively.

"Or a gun," Gene hasten to add.

"I don't think….," but Lamar wasn't able to finish because just then the Capitol Police came rushing outside.

"We're in lock down, we're in lock down," they shouted. "Shots fired; shots fired. Everyone inside immediately."

"What on earth….," Lamar began again, but suddenly there was a hail of gunfire that shut him up completely, and he went running back inside the Capitol with everyone else.

Within twenty minutes, word came in that Congressmen Grossman and Prichard from Missouri had been shot and

288

killed as they were going into their office building and the shooter was dead. Everyone was shocked and deeply saddened by the news, and the entire city was reported to be in lock down with no one being allowed to enter or leave even the buildings.

Lamar was just as shocked, and he called Crystal immediately to tell her he was okay. He knew both men well and spoke with them often. He and Crystal had even entertained them a few times at their home, and she was in tears when she heard of their deaths.

Two hours later he stood talking with several of his fellow senators when he heard a chime indicating he had a text, so he turned away from his colleagues, brought up the message on his phone and saw it was from Cornelius. He figured he was checking to see if he was okay in light of the afternoon's dramatic events, but when he looked at the message, he only saw two letters with an ampersand in between, 'B&C'.

"Dear Father in heaven, no," he whispered to himself, and he went weak at the knees, the blood draining from his face. "My God what have they done?"

He fell into the nearest vacant chair, completely overwhelmed, because it was then he knew. Constantine and Cornelius were about to act on the information he had given them, and they had taken two innocent lives to cover him.

CHAPTER 26

Anne leaned back in her office chair and rubbed her eyes. It was well past seven o'clock, and she had just finished her investigative assignment and emailed Travis her report. She had been assisting him with the mountain of paper and investigative work he had, and he'd told her how grateful he was for her help. He was in fact working late, just as she was, and she could see him in his office on his laptop. There were other agents working too, but she decided she'd had enough for one day and began tidying her desk in preparation to go home.

"I need to call Leann and check on her," she reminded herself.

She kept in close contact with her daughter as her son-in-law Derek was an engineer with the navy serving on a nuclear submarine. He was due back State-side the following week, and the young couple were looking forward with excitement to his home-coming and to the birth of their first child in just over two weeks' time. They were also happy that this was Derek's last deployment, as he was mustering out of military service for good. It meant they could be together permanently, and they were looking forward to having a normal life.

"I'll call her when I get home," she decided, as she put the last of the files in the top drawer and locked it. "She's probably just leaving work too." Leann was a lawyer, and sometimes worked long hours, but she had promised her mother she would take off the last week before the baby was born and rest.

Anne pulled her handbag from the bottom draw of the desk and was just making sure she had everything when her cell phone rang.

"This is Anne," she answered, not bothering to look at the Caller I.D. as she pulled her keys from the front pocket of her bag.

"Momma," she heard a sob from the other end of the line and knew it was her daughter.

"Leann are you okay, sweetheart?" she asked, instantly concerned. "What's wrong?" The next voice she heard wasn't that of her daughter, however, and she went cold when the man introduced himself.

"Hello, Anne," he said as if they had known each other for years, "I'm Cornelius Antonelli."

"What the hell….?" she was so shocked she abruptly got to her feet.

"Now, Anne," he said, "it's not polite to swear."

"What do you want?" she asked automatically.

"Let's not play games, Anne. You know what I want," he replied.

"If you're asking me for information on a certain Doctor, I don't know where she is," she stated, even as she hurried into Travis' office, pushed the door almost closed so as not to make any noise and put the call on speaker.

Travis looked up startled, saw the stark terror on Anne's

face but didn't understand what was going on. She placed her finger to her lips, and he knew immediately he needed to be quiet and listen.

"It isn't polite to lie you know, my dear," he went on in soothing tones. "Reliable sources tell me you are on her protection detail."

"I was on her protection detail, but not anymore," she replied. "I was removed weeks ago when they moved her to another location, and I don't know where she is."

"That does pose a problem, doesn't it?" he mused, "but if you value your daughter's life," Cornelius said with steel in his voice, "I suggest you use your position inside your ghost organization to find out where they have her."

"Look, Mr. Antonelli," she purposely said the name and saw Travis' mouth fall open, "what you're asking is impossible," Anne stated firmly. "There is no way I have access to that type of information. Her location is only known by three people and we know not to ask questions."

"Maybe you need to hear your daughter suffer a little, then you'll cooperate," he said, the cordial tone leaving his voice.

"Don't hurt her," Anne said quickly, then with resignation added, "I'll get you what you want, but I'll need twenty-four hours."

"Well done," he said. "See what a little coercion can accomplish?"

"You listen to me scumbag," she said so calmly one

would never believe her insides were cold with shock and fear, "if you touch one hair on her head, you're a dead man, do you understand me?"

He laughed and said, "I needed some amusement today, Anne, thank you for that."

"Let me make you laugh again," Anne said, this time with fire. "If you hurt her or my grandchild, I'll make it my life's mission to hunt you down. You'll never be able to sleep in peace, or go anywhere without looking over your shoulder, I promise you that."

"We shall see, Anne," he said. "I'll be in touch," and he disconnected the call.

Travis was on his feet the minute Cornelius hung up and came around from behind his desk.

"How on earth did he get onto you?" he asked dumbfounded. "How could he possible know you were connected to the case?"

"I don't know," Anne said, her voice cracking with emotion. "All Leann knows is that I work with the Bureau; nothing more. When I'm on a case I tell her I'm on assignment and she can reach me by phone. I've not breathed a word to a living soul about being on Marissa's detail and now my child is in danger because of me." She was shaking so badly her legs couldn't support her, and she collapsed into the chair by Travis' desk.

"Anne," he said with conviction, coming over and placing his hand on her shoulder, "we are going to do everything in our power to get her out."

"Someone's betrayed us, Travis," she said, looking up at him in despair, tears coursing down her cheeks. "Someone's betrayed us and used my pregnant daughter as a pawn."

"I know," he said, a fierce anger taking hold of him.

"It's not anyone here," she said through her tears. "I would trust them all with my life."

"Me too," Travis agreed. "This is someone else," he said with confidence and Anne nodded. "I don't know who it is, Anne, and I don't how they knew to target you, but I make you a promise right now. I'm going to find out who did it, expose them for the Judas they are and throw the book at them."

CHAPTER 27

Travis sat at his desk looking out the window at the Atlanta skyline, taking a brief respite from planning how he and his team were going to get Leann Peterson-Jarvis away from the Antonellis' clutches. He'd been awake for over twenty-four hours and still hadn't made any headway in finding out who had leaked Anne's name to Cornelius Antonelli. He knew the Judge, Sassy and Amelia couldn't be involved as they never knew Anne or that she had been on the case. Jon had questioned Isabelle too and she told him she hadn't said a word to anyone at the house.

Meanwhile, Washington D.C. was an absolute mess in light of the killing of the two congressmen, and the Bureau was completely swamped from every angle. The city-wide curfew had been lifted, but investigators were busy trying to find out who was behind the shootings. They knew someone had hired the gunman as that was his trade, but they were stumped as to who could have done it and why.

Travis had called a staff meeting earlier and he questioned his personnel on whether or not they had said anything to anyone about the Antonelli case. They had all said no, and he believed them. Everyone knew the danger to themselves, their families and their fellow agents if Elite One was compromised. They all knew of Gabe's experience too, even though it had happened years before, and it had taught them all better than words just how dangerous working for the Bureau could be.

He started to think then about people outside Elite One. It had to be someone who knew about the case and the agents who had been deployed to protect Isabelle, and it was then it hit him. Only two men fit the bill and he sat there in shock. He knew the Antonellis' tentacles were far reaching, but he was stunned at just how far they appeared to stretch.

He shook his head in amazement then looked over at Anne. She had finally passed out from exhaustion on the couch in his office. He had encouraged her to take one of the 'hotel' rooms as they called the two self-contained suites they had at the office and rest there, but she'd said she was okay and wanted to be near the action. It was only after she had finally sat down and leaned her head back that she'd fallen asleep.

She had been hounding him to let her get Leann out herself by arranging an exchange, her life for her daughter's, but he was reluctant to do it. He'd looked at every other angle, however, and found each one problematic, so he was giving her request serious consideration and had been running through some plans in his mind while she slept.

As he sat there, he remembered a conversation he'd had with her once. He'd known she was divorced but otherwise didn't know much about her family. She spoke of Leann constantly, but never mentioned her daughter's father until one day his name came up, and she told him the story.

She'd met Leon Peterson in the army, and they had hit it off right away. After a whirlwind courtship, they were married, but they encountered one major issue within the first few weeks. She said they were too much alike. She told Travis that whenever they had an argument, they were like two cars that met in the middle of a one lane bridge, neither one would back down. Six months later, when she was three months pregnant with Leann, he looked at her after a quarrel they'd had and said, 'This isn't going to work, is it?'

and she'd told him no.

As quickly as they'd married, they divorced, but they still lived in the house together. When their daughter was born, they gave her a portion of both their names and looked after her just as if they were still husband and wife. Anne had several years left in her obligation to the Air Force, but Leon's tour of duty was over, and he hadn't re-enlisted, so as she continued in the service, he looked after their child while working as a computer programmer.

When Leann had just finished junior high, and Anne was working for the Bureau, Leon met and married his wife Pearline and they moved down the street. Anne and Pearline got on like a house on fire, however, and Leon often said he didn't stand a chance when the three ladies in his life ganged up against him.

Eventually, Leann moved away to college, Leon's job transferred him to Denver and Anne continued working with the Bureau. She made sure to take time out every year to visit with Leon and Pearline, however, and that was where she had been when she was assigned to Marissa's case. Leann now lived in King's Bay, Georgia where her husband was stationed and Anne, Leon and Pearline were so excited about the birth of their first grandchild.

Travis looked over and saw Anne stirring, so he went outside and got her a cup of coffee and a donut from the lunchroom. When he returned, she was rubbing the sleep from her eyes and gratefully accepted his offering.

"Have you heard anything more?" she asked after she'd taken a few sips.

"No, nothing new," he replied.

"Travis, I need to be the one to do this," she stated with determination.

"I know," he said, cementing his decision and surprising her.

"We don't have much time to arrange things," she added. "You have any idea how you want us to do this?"

"I do," he replied. "Let's get the team together and I'll tell you," and with that they went to work.

CHAPTER 28

Anne stood looking out the window from her hotel room located on the outskirts of one of the largest theme parks in Orlando. She was about to do the single most dangerous thing she had ever undertaken, and she was thinking about Leann, the last twenty-four hours and the plans that had led to this moment. She knew the chances were slim that she would make it out alive, but that didn't matter to her. Leann was her life and if she had to die so that her daughter and grandchild could live a full life with Derek, Leon and Pearl, then so be it.

She remembered with warmth in her heart her call from Jon and Gabe that morning. They had spoken with her encouragingly then Jon had expressed concern for her soul should anything happen to her. She had assured him right away that she had known the Lord from she was a little girl. She had learned about Jesus from her Mama and prayed every day. She told him she just didn't wear her faith on her sleeve like he did.

The room next door to hers was the staging area for the mission, and the entire Elite One team was on board in various locations across three states. She was never more grateful for the love and support shown to her by her co-workers. They were in many ways a family and the minute they had heard what had happened to her daughter, they had determined to do everything possible to rescue Leann, After all, it could have happened to any one of them and they were keenly aware of that.

She had dressed carefully for the meeting she was about

to have. She knew they would want to make sure she wasn't wired or carrying a weapon, so she wore a pair of dark gray leggings that sucked tightly to her slim but muscular legs and a navy colored sleeveless blouse with gray flowers that stopped at her thighs. It was made of chiffon and very transparent but had a separate navy tank underneath for modesty that clung to her torso, stopping at her hips.

She had also swept her long braids on top of her head and had pinned them securely and tightly so they wouldn't fall. She was very fit, a must for her job, and she worked out daily and swam in her pool every morning before work. She had been a medal winning swimmer during her youth and loved the water.

She thought back to her conversation with Cornelius Antonelli the day before and couldn't stop thanking God that the mob boss had agreed to the exchange. He'd called her just after Travis had deployed a team of agents to a decoy house set up on Lake Marion in South Carolina. Gloria was playing the part of Marissa while Jennifer and two other agents would act as her protection detail.

When she'd heard her cell phone ring and saw Leann's name on the Caller I.D., she'd signaled Travis and the others and the office went quiet.

"How are you, Anne?" Cornelius said personably, "I trust you've had a productive twenty-four hours."

"I have," she replied. "Before we go any further, I would like to speak with my daughter."

A few moments later, Leann came on the line, "Momma," she said, the fear and trauma obvious in her voice.

"Sweetheart, have they hurt you?" Anne asked.

"No, Ma," she said, and Anne sighed with relief when she heard the reply. She and Leann had a code they'd used from she was a little girl and they were out in public or in a sticky situation. If Anne asked her if she was fine and she was, Leann would call her Ma.

Cornelius' voice came back on the line then and he said, "Now, let's get down to business. Where is she?"

"Not so fast," Anne replied. "I have a proposition for you."

Cornelius laughed, "I don't think you're in a position to negotiate anything, Anne," he said.

"Au contraire," she replied, "I think I am. You want the information I have, and I want my daughter safe and sound."

"It appears we're at a stalemate then, doesn't it," he said, before adding menacingly. "but maybe if you hear her cry out in agony, you'll change your mind."

"No, I won't," Anne replied in a matter of fact tone. "You and I both know you're not going to let her live after I give you what you want. That's not your usual M.O."

"I might for the fact that she's pregnant," he replied.

"You'd have to have a soul for that," Anne said, and he laughed.

301

"So what's your proposition?" he asked with amusement.

"We make an exchange," Anne stated, "my life for hers."

"Hmm," he said as if pondering what she was suggesting. "Why would I want to take the risk when I already have a perfectly good hostage?" he asked.

"Because I have the information you want," Anne said, "including how the team operates, their protocols, the layout of the grounds. I am a more valuable hostage."

"That is a persuasive argument," he agreed after a few moments, "but how do I know you'll give me the correct information."

"After I tell you where the Doctor is," Anne said, "you can keep me around until your men check things out. They will be able to verify what I've said. When you see I've told you the truth, maybe you can search around inside somewhere and see if you can find that heart God gave you at birth and let me live to see my grandchild."

"It seems I underestimated you, Anne," he said then. "I take it you have a place in mind where this exchange should be made?"

"No, I don't," she replied. "You choose. I only want it public and I want to ask my boyfriend to come with me and take Leann after her release."

"Okay," he agreed, then went on to tell her where and when they would meet the following morning. "Just make sure you don't have an army waiting or I'll have no problem making my men open fire. They'll not only take out you and your daughter, but men, women and children as well."

"You have my word I'll come alone," she confirmed. "I don't want anyone else involved; it's safer that way. I'll only have my boyfriend with me, and he'll wait for Leann at a specific location," she said. "When I know they're safe, I'll go peacefully with your men."

"Agreed," he said. "They'll meet you and bring you to me," he concluded then abruptly disconnected the call.

They'd had to scramble to have everything in place, but they had gotten it done. She had stressed to Travis several times that she would meet Cornelius' men alone. She only wanted him to ensure Leann's safety. They were using Ray Stafford, one of Elite One's Lead agents as Anne's boyfriend, and he'd been instructed to meet Leann and tell her that her Ma had sent him. That way she would know it was safe to go with him.

Anne heard a knock on the connecting door and told whoever it was to come in.

"All set?" Travis asked, and she nodded. "You know you have a lot of people doing everything possible to help you and Leann, Anne," he reassured her, "and many praying too, including me."

"I know," she said smiling wanly. "Thanks, Travis."

"Let us know the minute we can come get you," he said optimistically, but they both knew the chances of that were slim to none and this was probably good-bye.

"I have everything to live for, Travis," she assured him, "and if I get an opportunity, no matter how small, I'll take it."

"I know," he replied. "It's at times like this I wish political correctness and regulations weren't a factor or I'd give you a hug," he added.

"Let political correctness and regulations take a hike," she said coming towards him. "I could use a hug," and she embraced him tightly while he hugged her back. "You're a great boss," she said pulling away, "and I love you, Jon and Gabe like the brothers I never had."

Travis swallowed, "We love you too," he concurred. "Now let's go whip Antonelli's butt and get you and Leann home safe."

CHAPTER 29

Isabelle listened to her mother's chest and back with her stethoscope then Amelia settled back on the pillows. She had received another round of chemo two days before and was extremely weak, but they were all thanking God she was doing much better with the new treatment. Isabelle folded the instrument and put it in the pocket of her slacks then went around straightening the room. Her mother followed her with her eyes and breathed a prayer of thanksgiving to God that they were back together. Sometimes she just couldn't believe it.

"Want me to get you some tea?" Isabelle asked coming over to her, and she nodded, too tired to give a verbal response. The injection she had received early that morning to boost her white blood cell count was causing her a lot of pain too, so she just lay still with her eyes open.

"The pain's severe, isn't it?" Isabelle asked, already knowing the answer and Amelia nodded. Isabelle then used her hand to rub her mother's bald head in soothing strokes and began to pray for her, the simple words falling effortlessly from her lips. She finished her petition to God then said, "When I come back, I'll give you a gentle massage and we'll see if that helps."

Amelia gave her a nod and a tired smile, then Isabelle left to get the tea. It broke her heart to see her mother in such physical distress, but she knew she now had a fighting chance to overcome the cancer. The lump that had been removed had in fact contained the cancer entirely with none of the surrounding tissue or lymph nodes being compromised, but the cancer had been the aggressive kind and the consensus of the doctors, even Dr. Forbes, was that chemo and radiation were necessary.

Isabelle went down the back stairs and into the kitchen. It was Saturday and the staff were off, so she quickly made the tea, took up a pack of cookies to go with it and went back through the door that led to the second-floor stairs, closing it behind her. She was about to move off when she heard Jon enter from the door to the main house. He was talking on the phone and she heard him call Anne's name. She began to step towards the staircase when she realized she was stuck. The corner of her roomy top had gotten caught in the door as she'd closed it and before she could open it to free herself, she heard Gabe enter and Jon finish his call.

"The operation has begun," Jon said to Gabe.

"How's Anne?" Gabe asked.

"Travis says she's like a brick," Jon said. "If it were me and Antonelli had my daughter, I don't think I could be so calm," and Isabelle had to stifle a shocked gasp.

"So what's the plan?" Gabe asked.

"Same as Trav told us earlier," Jon said. "Anne exchanges herself for Leann and gives Antonelli the decoy information. He says our team is already in position. Trav wants to give Anne every chance to make it out, however, so our guys won't fire unless engaged."

"How on earth could Antonelli have gotten Anne's name Jon?" Gabe questioned. "I've been racking my brain, and I have a suspicion but it's a little hard to believe."

"I've been thinking about it too," Jon said.

"You know, Jon," Gabe said, "only the members of Elite One and the two top brass know who works for our division and who was assigned to Isabelle's case."

"You think it's one of the brass, don't you?" Jon countered.

"I do," Gabe confirmed. "It has to be either Luke or Carson," he said mentioning Travis' immediate boss, Luke Hanson and Carson who was Luke's boss. "I know it's not one of our people."

"Travis feels the same way and so do I," Jon concurred. "They have always been tight lipped and they're loyal to the core," he added, "so either Antonelli got to one them or they said something to the wrong person."

"What's Travis going to do?" Gabe questioned, as Isabelle heard the fridge door open and bottles rattling. "Give me a cola will you?" he instructed Jon.

"He says he's going to deal with it when the situation with Anne is over and things have settled a bit with the shootings of the congressmen. D.C. and the Bureau are in a mess since it happened," Jon informed him, "He's as mad as a hornet over Anne, however, and no matter the outcome, he says someone's head is going to roll over it."

Isabelle then heard the fridge door close and the two men walk out. She carefully opened the door, dislodged her top, closed it softly again and made her way back upstairs.

She was absolutely stunned by what she had heard and began to think back on her conversations with Anne. Leann would be just a couple of weeks away from delivery, and now her life was in danger. She felt her emotions rising to the surface and knew she needed some time alone, so when she got to the third floor, she went past the master bedroom and on to Sassy's studio. When Sassy told her to come in after her knock, Isabelle entered.

"Sass," she began, "are you busy?"

"I was just thinking of taking a break," she said, rising and stretching before coming over to her. "Did you need something?" she asked.

"Could you give Mom this tea for me?" Isabelle asked. "I need a little time to myself, maybe half an hour. I also promised her a massage, but…." Her lips began to tremble, and she knew she with certainty she was going to be overcome by her emotions.

"Something wrong?" Sassy asked, taking the tea from her to do her bidding.

"I just need….," Isabelle was choking on her tears.

"You take some time to settle yourself," Sassy said. "I know it's hard to watch her suffer so much," she added, obviously getting the impression that Isabelle's upset was over her mother's condition.

Isabelle only nodded before she fled out the door and down to her own room where she locked herself inside. She let the tears come then, great gulping sobs that she stifled as best she could. She went over to her bed and got down on her knees.

"Why, Lord?" she asked in despair. "How much longer before evil stops winning?"

She was completely overwhelmed then and just cried. She'd been curious when Jon had asked her if she'd told anyone that Anne had been guarding her, but when she had said no and asked him why, he'd just said they were checking on something and it was okay. Now she knew the awful truth.

"God, suppose Antonelli finds out where I am?" she questioned her Heavenly Father. "I don't care about myself, but I don't want Mom and Ted and Sassy in danger."

She continued to sob out her despair, praying for God to intervene when suddenly she felt a peace she couldn't understand begin to invade her soul and calm her tumultuous emotions. She knew it had to come from God, so she knelt there quietly soaking up His comfort.

"Trust me," she heard her Heavenly Father speak to her heart.

"But what about Anne and her daughter, Father?" Isabelle questioned.

"I have them," He said, and she deflated with relief.

She knew there was absolutely nothing she could do, either for Anne or Leann or for even those here at the house. They were all in God's hands. Whatever the outcome, they were His and He was taking care of every bit of it, so she began praying for the situation with Anne with the confidence she knew God wanted her to have. God was sovereign and it was hard to let go, but she decided then and there to leave it in His hands. She was powerless to do anything to help, but she could pray. She would pray like she had never prayed before and leave the rest to God. Only He could change the circumstances and give them a miracle.

CHAPTER 30

Anne sat inside the busy restaurant, sipping coffee and watching the door. She had arrived twenty minutes earlier than her agreed upon meeting time and, due to her training and experience had spotted two of Cornelius' men not long after she'd entered. One was sitting by himself pretending to read a newspaper just to the right of the entryway, and another was standing with his cell phone to his ear looking out the window a little way over from her table. The reader had been on the one-page advertisement and hadn't turned the page since she'd arrived, and the one on the cell phone hadn't uttered a word. They seemed to be of Hispanic heritage which didn't surprise her. She knew Cornelius operated out of South America, so these were probably his men and not Constantine's.

Even though she hadn't felt like eating, she'd ordered a big meal when she came in and forced down every bite. She didn't know what lay ahead and knew she would need her strength. She drank the last of her coffee then rose and carried the tray with the disposables over to the trash receptacle. She tossed the items inside, placed the tray in the designated spot, turned around and saw Leann come through the door accompanied by two men.

The sight of her child brought tears to her eyes, but she drew in her breath to calm her emotions. She would need every bit of her focus during the next few minutes. She went over to them and Leann fell into her arms, despite one of her captor's efforts to keep them apart.

"Have they hurt you, my precious," she whispered.

311

"No, Ma," she replied, "but I'm worried for you."

"I'll be fine," Anne said reassuringly.

"But you're exchanging your life for mine," Leann whispered in despair.

"None of this is your fault, Leann," Anne stressed as they pulled away from each other. "Whatever happens, please promise me you won't blame yourself," she said, placing her hand on her daughter's cheek and Leann nodded. "Milton is waiting in the ice cream parlor across the street and two doors up from here. Go with him and don't look back. I love you," she said.

Leann frowned, obviously not knowing who Milton was or what was going on. "I don't...," she began, but Anne gave her a quick hard stare, so Leann took her cue and said instead, "I don't want to leave you."

"Just do as I say and don't go fretting about me," Anne continued. "You just take care of yourself and the baby. I love you, sweetheart."

"I love you too, Momma," Leann said, choking on her tears.

"Go on now," Anne said gently, "and don't look back," she reiterated in a firmer tone.

Leann let her go and went through the door. Anne saw her cross to the other side of the busy street and watched her enter the ice cream parlor. A minute later, she saw her come out of the store with Ray and head down the street.

312

"Let's go," one of the men who seemed to be in charge addressed her in heavily accented English.

"Not yet," she responded firmly. "I'm waiting for a call. It should only take a few minutes. That way I know your boss hasn't double-crossed me."

The call came in and when Anne answered, Ray assured her they were safely away. It was his signal to her that they were being surveilled by Elite One's team members positioned around the area and Anne could go.

When she indicated she was ready, the leader took her by the arm and he and the others walked with her out of the restaurant then behind it where he told her to lift up her blouse. She did as he asked and he told her to turn around, then felt her torso over the tank top to make sure she wasn't wired. It was obvious by her tight clothing that she wasn't carrying a weapon, so he didn't search her further. When he was satisfied, he took her cell phone from her, tossed it in a nearby dumpster and the four of them led her from behind the building.

Anne knew at that moment the time had come for her to meet her enemy, so she whispered a prayer, "Father, I commit my spirit into Your hands," and within seconds she and her captors were swallowed up by the crowd.

****

By late afternoon, Anne found herself locked in a smuggler's hold on board a fifty-foot cabin cruiser off the Florida coast. It was dark as there was no porthole in the space, but she was grateful for the faint light coming in from tiny cracks around the 'door' in one wall. The room was located near the prow of the vessel and was only about seven feet long, six feet wide and six feet high. It was accessed through the forward stateroom to the right of the bed. The panel on which the lamp was attached was a false wall and when it was removed it revealed a narrow, steep flight of stairs. She'd had to go down backwards, like descending a ladder because it was so precipitous and tight.

As she sat in the darkness, she thought back to what had happened when she'd left the theme park. She had been taken east, then north by car to an R.V. parked at a rest stop on Interstate Ninety-five. It resembled a sleek, modern bus, but the sides could expand outward when the occupants were at their destination. The men who had brought her remained outside after instructing her to go in, and when she'd gone through the door and up the steps, she saw three more men waiting inside, two Hispanic and one Caucasian. The fairest one who she knew right away from photographs was her adversary, came over to her and she examined his features. He was tall with low cut dark brown hair, brown eyes and an olive hue to his complexion and was a little older in appearance than the picture she had seen of him. He was an attractive man, but his eyes lacked warmth, which didn't surprise her.

"Well, Anne, we finally meet," Cornelius said cordially.

"You will forgive me if I'm not as excited to meet you as you appear to be to meet me," she said sardonically, and he laughed.

"I understand, Anne. All is forgiven," he assured her, before he turned to the other men who were with him. "Let me introduce you to my right-hand man Juan-Carlos," he said, pointing to one of the men who was short in stature,

314

"and this is my enforcer, Rico," he added, pointing at the other man who nodded at her without expression.

"Wonderful to make your acquaintance," Anne acknowledged with feigned sweetness. "I feel so fortunate to be in the company of three such fine and outstanding dilincuentes," she added calling them criminals in their own language.

Cornelius laughed and so did Juan-Carlos, but Rico only looked at her with no emotion on his face.

"Well, Anne," Cornelius said, "let's forgo any more pleasantries and you tell me what I need to know, then Juan-Carlos will take you on a little voyage about three miles off shore and anchor there while Rico and my men check out your story."

She spent an hour with him, giving him the information she and Travis had crafted, then true to his word, Cornelius handed her over to Juan-Carlos and the men who had brought her, and they took her by car to a marina on the Halifax River. She had been placed in the smuggler's hold immediately and had listened to the cruiser start up then slowly make its way south. It was some time before she felt them turn east, then a short while later, when they were obviously in open water, they gave the vessel full throttle, veering south once more as they headed out to sea.

As she sat there, she was thankful she'd had the big breakfast and didn't feel hungry. They hadn't even offered her a drink of water. By her estimation, she had been in the tiny space for about five or six hours, but that was just a guess. It was hard to make an accurate determination in the enclosed conditions. She did notice, however, that the dim

315

light was getting dimmer by the minute, so she suspected it would be dark soon and she was glad.

She'd had no visitors to her tiny prison, and she kept thanking God for every hour that passed. She felt with certainty as she'd assessed the men earlier that Juan Carlos would be the one she'd have to watch. Two of the men who had taken her from the theme park had accompanied them and seemed harmless enough, as did the two men waiting on board the cruiser, but Juan-Carlos gave her the impression she wouldn't be leaving the vessel alive.

She was counting on him being the one to take her out as she was taller, and his lack of height was to her advantage. She had begun making plans as soon as she was alone and was only waiting for him to come to her. She wasn't about to let him harm her, but she was praying he would come alone and after dark. The execution of her plan would be next to impossible if he brought another man with him and it was daylight. She was looking at him as her means of escape, and the circumstances had to be just right.

****

Travis paced back and forth from one end of the hotel room to the other. He had teams deployed along the east coast, from Florida to South Carolina and was monitoring the situation with the other agents who were with him. He hadn't heard anything from Anne at all, and he was worried. He knew her chances were slim, but he hadn't stopped asking God for a miracle.

Leann was fine and in their custody, but she was, understandably, frantic about her mother. They had her in the suite next door where Annie had been earlier, along with

316

Cynthia Vargas, a female agent who usually worked in the office and not on assignment. It was all hands on deck for this particular operation and, in any event, everyone wanted to be involved in some way. This was very personal to the Elite One team.

He was standing at the window now double-checking that he had taken care of every possible eventuality, when his cell phone rang and he saw it was Steve McGinley, the senior agent he had assigned at the decoy house.

"Yes, Steve," he answered right away.

"We've got company, Travis," he whispered. "Five men, heavily armed just surrounded the house."

"Give me their locations," Travis said immediately, and he plotted on his map of the house and grounds where each of Antonelli's men were located. "Okay," he took a breath. "This is it, Steve," he stated, "I'll have Cliff move his team in behind them and we'll come at them from all angles. Remember, don't fire a shot until fired upon," he warned. "I don't know if Anne's still with us, but I want to give her every chance. If we engage them too early, they might realize it's a set up."

"We'll follow your instructions to the letter, Travis" Steve agreed. "Depending on the outcome, I'll hopefully talk to you on the other side of this," he added, and both men hung up.

****

Anne sat with her eyes closed, thinking about Leann and praying she was okay, that the trauma she had been through

317

hadn't affected her or the baby. She wished this nightmare had never happened, but it had, and she was ready to face whatever was to come, whether life or death. She had promised herself from the beginning, however, that she wasn't going to roll over and let them take her out without a fight, so she again went over the plan she had in her mind.

Fifteen minutes before, she'd heard the motor of a boat and she'd wondered with hope if it was a Coast Guard Patrol, but there was nothing to indicate anything was wrong. After only a few minutes, she heard the boat leaving, but was unsure what was happening.

It was pitch black in her little prison now as the sun had set several hours before, and she could hear Spanish music playing somewhere above. There was also raucous laughter and talking and she figured the men were letting loose and having a good time. She knew that by now, Cornelius had had enough time to verify what she had told him about the house on Lake Marion, so her time was probably growing short.

The thought had just come to her, when she heard footsteps and activity in the stateroom above. A short while later, her tiny room was flooded with light as the panel was removed and she could see Juan-Carlos crouching at the opening with a battery-operated lantern which he used to shine into the tiny space.

"Hello, Senora," he said, and he grinned at her, even as she rose to her feet. "Cornelius sends his regards and thanks for the information." Anne just stared at him and said nothing. "He also asked me to tell you that he searched around inside and tried very hard, but unfortunately he couldn't find his heart."

318

"You'd have to have one to find one I suppose, so I'm not surprised," she replied dryly. He appeared to be alone and she sighed inwardly with relief.

"You know, you don't act like someone who's about to be executed," he stated. "Most people usually beg for their lives."

"That's because I'm not afraid to die," she said right back, and he laughed.

"Everyone is afraid of dying, Senora," he answered.

"Only if they don't know where they're going," she responded. "The way I figure it, I'm going straight to heaven when I die, Juan-Carlos; but when it's your turn, you're definitely going to hell. I have no doubt in my mind."

He laughed again before he reached over and hung the lantern on a hook just inside the entrance.

"Let me make a deposit I just received," he said, "then we'll get the unpleasantness out of the way."

He reached behind and began throwing down several bulky packages wrapped in black plastic, about twenty-five in all.

"Work never stops, Senora," he explained.

When he had finished, he expertly swung down from the floor above, foregoing the stairs, and opened another secret panel that she hadn't noticed in the dim light. It revealed a cupboard, as tall as the space they were in but only about three feet square, and he began stacking the

319

parcels of what she assumed was cocaine inside, moving back and forth. He didn't carry a weapon, so Anne figured he was probably planning to kill her somewhere above and throw her overboard.

"How come you're not carousing with your buddies," she asked conversationally as he continued with his task. Meanwhile she began feeling between the long braids she had swept up tightly on her head and within seconds she found the pocketknife she had concealed among her tresses. She quickly and quietly opened the weapon, hid her hand behind her thigh and bided her time.

"Ah... they love tequila and cards, Senora," he replied as he worked, "but I have no such vices. I only love money, and lots of it," he explained, stopping to turn and grin at her before reaching for another package. "When I have enough, I'll retire and take on as many vices as I like."

"A criminal with a retirement plan," she smiled, pretending amusement, but the second he turned his back to her, she was on him, taking him completely by surprise. She caught his head from behind and in one swift movement, plunged the knife she had into his neck, killing him instantly; then, as she quietly lowered him to the floor she said softly, "Enjoy hell and retirement, Juan-Carlos."

She peeled off her chiffon blouse, wiped his blood off her hands and the knife with it then threw it on top of him with contempt. She took off her flat sandals and stuck them in the back of her tights, then quickly and quietly went up the stairs into the empty stateroom. She took the lantern from the hook, turned it off and secured the panel back over the opening, closing up Juan-Carlos' body and her prison.

She looked around and noticed Juan-Carlos' gun on the bed where he had apparently rested it, so she took it up and went to the door which was closed. She opened it a crack to reveal a narrow corridor ahead and, finding it empty, she went quickly forward after locking the stateroom door. Using caution and bending low, she peeped into two tiny bedrooms and a compact bathroom as she passed to make sure they were empty. She continued until she reached a short flight of stairs that led to the galley and lounge then stopped to listen.

The music was blaring, and the joviality of Cornelius' men could be heard coming from the large fly bridge above. The door had an inset glass window that enabled her to see into the next room, and as she peeped out, she saw to her relief that it too was empty. Within thirty seconds she was at the door leading out to the deck at the stern, and she knew this was the moment. If she could make it out and over the side, she had a chance, if not…. She left the thought hanging and opened the door.

She slipped out after making sure the deck was empty, closed the door quietly and plastered herself against the wall, the noise acting as a perfect cover for her. She went around to the narrow port side and tried to calm her racing heart. She looked carefully above her head just as a wad of tobacco juice came sailing over the side, missing her face by inches, and she grimaced.

"Yuck," she thought to herself with a shudder, then peered over and began perusing the boat, looking for the ladder which she had seen when she'd boarded earlier. It was fixed to the side of the cruiser and when she found it, she realized it was to her left, about three feet away from where she was standing.

She looked up once more, said a prayer, closed the knife and tucked it and the gun in her waistband then moved quietly over to the railing. She went over the side, found the rungs quickly and climbed down into the water, using her hands and upper body strength to lower her the rest of the way until she was submerged to her neck.

She looked out into the black abyss and saw the glow of lights on the shore in the distance. It would take all her strength she knew to make it, but she thought of Leann, her grandchild and her family and felt a determination take hold of her.

"What's impossible for man isn't impossible for God," she whispered. "Father, please give me the strength of Samson," she prayed, then as soon as the words left her lips, she pulled out the gun, released it into the water, looked up to check the position of the moon to guide her, then gently pushed off from the side of the boat and started the long swim towards shore.

****

Travis hung up from Steve after getting his latest report. All was still quiet. Antonelli's men were in the same position and his men were ready. It seemed the mob boss was biding his time before making his move, and Travis figured he would give the go ahead when activity at the house had quieted and everyone except the watch had gone to bed.

It was late now, around eleven o'clock, so he expected Antonelli's men would strike within the next hour. Leann had gone to bed exhausted thirty minutes earlier, but he had promised to wake her should he hear from her mother.

322

"Anne, where are you?" he asked softly as he looked out the window into the night. "God," he prayed what had become his litany, "please give us a miracle."

****

Anne crawled on shore then collapsed in the surf, too exhausted to go any further. It had taken her nearly two hours, but she'd made it.

"Thank You, God," she whispered breathlessly to her Heavenly Father. "Only You, God, only You," she said over and over.

She knew she was still in a vulnerable position, so she got up on all fours and crawled onto the deserted stretch of beach. Several yards ahead she spotted a flight of stairs that led to a boardwalk above, so she made her way over and concealed herself beneath it. She was completely exhausted, and although she was anxious to find a phone and let Travis know she was okay, she knew she would never make it up the stairs, much less to help without resting.

She had swum west at first, then when she was far enough away, she began swimming towards the northwest, figuring that if the men discovered Juan-Carlos' body and her missing, they would make a beeline for the shore. The swim took her more time, but she'd felt it was a safer option. She had kept an eye on the cruiser for as long as she could, but the lights coming from it had remained in place and she was thankful to God for that. The men were probably too inebriated to put two and two together yet and that was exactly what she'd hoped.

It took a half an hour before she had not only caught her

323

breath but felt she could move again. She was cold to the bone, however, and shivering in her wet clothes, her teeth chattering. She emerged from her hiding place and found an outdoor shower right at the base of the stairs, so she washed the sand off herself, took her sandals from the waist of her tights and slipped them on before slowly taking the steps one by one, her legs trembling with fatigue. When she got to the top, she noticed a group of lights about a quarter of a mile away and as she walked tiredly towards the buildings, she saw one was a restaurant, another a bar and grill, and the third a pool hall.

She got to the eatery a short time later and the place was busy. She was wet and cold, but she went right over to the cashier.

The woman behind the register took one look at her as she approached and said, "You always go swimming in your clothes?"

"Not really," she replied with a weary smile. "My boyfriend got angry and threw me overboard. It's a lucky thing I was near to shore."

The woman used several unflattering words to describe men in general then asked one of the waitresses to bring Anne some coffee. She was also starving, and as she had a single twenty-dollar bill in the concealed pocket of her tights, she vowed to order herself a meal the minute she'd called Travis.

Anne gratefully accepted the steaming cup when it was brought to her and wrapped her hands around it, the warmth making her fingers tingle.

"Thank you," she said to the kind woman. "Could I use your phone to call my brother?" she asked next, even as she pulled one of the take-out menus from the stand in front of her.

"Sure, honey," she replied and handed the cordless land line over to her.

Anne thanked her again then moved to sit on one of the chairs in the waiting area. She dialed Travis' cell and he answered on the first ring, "This is Travis."

"Hey, boss," she said quietly with a grin. "I'm at Big Bob's Barbeque on Melbourne Beach. Come get me."

"Anne," she heard him say, the relief palpable in his voice. "Thank You God, thank You God!" she heard him declare. Then he must have turned to the others in the room because the next thing he said was, "It's Anne and she's safe," and she heard a loud cheer. "Peter and Colin are north of Vero Beach near Sebastian," he informed her then. "Go find a quiet corner and hang tight. They'll be with you in half an hour."

****

Isabelle lay awake, unable to sleep. The hour was late, but all she could think about was Anne and the danger she was in. She had been in constant prayer for her friend. Everyone had gone to bed, and earlier Jon had told her he wouldn't be able to make their usual midnight rendezvous. She knew he was no doubt in constant contact with Travis about what was going on, so she wasn't surprised, but she only told him it was fine and didn't ask him why.

She knew she should try and rest, so she turned over in the darkness and closed her eyes, but just as she was getting comfortable, she heard footsteps in the corridor. Unsure if something was going on with her mother, she threw back the covers, got out of bed and went over to the door to see what was happening. Gabe's room was beside hers and when she peeped out, she saw Jon there, quietly knocking on the door.

She knew it was wrong to listen, but she was anxious about Anne, so she stood there hoping to hear some news about her.

When Gabe answered, Jon said, "Sorry to wake you, pal, but I had to come up and tell you this."

"What's happened?" Gabe asked.

"God is a God of miracles, Ice," Jon declared, "Anne made it out and she's waiting to be picked up."

"Thank God," Gabe stated with relief. "It is a miracle," he agreed. "Any idea how she did it?" he asked.

"Not yet," Jon replied, "but knowing Anne, it will be a good story," he said with a grin, and Gabe nodded.

"What's going on at the decoy house?" Gabe asked next.

"Antonelli's men have it surrounded, but all is quiet so far, Trav says," Jon replied. "He figures Antonelli won't give them the go ahead to attack until everyone's in bed except the first watch. Let's keep praying."

"I will," Gabe acknowledged. "God has given us one

miracle tonight, let's hope for two," he added before they said goodnight.

Isabelle quickly and quietly closed her door even before Gabe had shut his and she made her way back to bed. She lay there with tears of relief and gratitude running down her cheeks.

"Father," she prayed, "thank You from the bottom of my heart. As Gabe said, please give us another miracle tonight, Lord?" she asked. "I trust You it will be so," she said with confidence. Then she turned over, told the Lord goodnight, and fell into a peaceful sleep.

****

Travis looked at his watch and saw it was twelve fifty in the morning. He was anxiously awaiting word from Steve, but his phone had been quiet since the call from Peter that he and Colin had Anne and were on their way back to him. They would be there in another fifteen minutes he estimated, but his focus was now on his team at Lake Marion and the danger they were in.

Leann was overcome with emotion when he had gone in with Cynthia and told her that her mother was safe, and he couldn't stop thanking God for answering everyone's prayers. Now if only his team could have the same outcome, he'd be able to get some sleep. He'd been up for nearly seventy-two hours with only short naps in between and his body was craving rest.

On the stroke of one, his phone rang, and he saw Steve's number, so he answered quickly.

"What's happening Steve," he asked anxiously.

"It's over, Travis," Steve informed him. "We have two injured," and he went on to give Travis the names of the two agents and outlined their injuries. "None are life threatening, so don't worry," he assured him.

"What about on Antonelli's side?" Travis asked relieved.

"Two dead, two in custody and one missing," Steve told him. "Two of Cliff's men are in pursuit on foot, but we haven't heard from them yet."

"Let me know as soon as you do," Travis said, then went on to talk with him about logistics. When he hung up, Travis went over to the window and lifted his thanks to God. Things were still fluid, but under control and he was never more grateful to his Heavenly Father for the good outcome.

****

Cornelius hung up the phone, using a string of expletives to punctuate his anger. The captain of his cruiser had just called to tell him he had found Juan-Carlos dead and the Senora missing and he was seething with rage. He and Juan had been close friends and Cornelius felt his death keenly. Juan had been his right-hand and his left, having been a part of the business from the beginning, and Cornelius would miss him. The one solace he had was the fact that the Peterson woman was probably dead. No one could swim that far and make it.

He was about to place a call to Constantine with the latest when his cell phone rang, and he saw it was Rico.

"Yes, Rico," he answered.

"It was a set-up," his enforcer said breathlessly, and Cornelius got the impression he was running. "Two of our men are dead and two in custody."

"Where are you?" Cornelius asked him.

"Trying to get out of here," Rico said, "but the Feds are right behind me."

"What's the terrain like? Cornelius asked. "Maybe you can find a place to hide."

Just then he heard Rico utter an expletive and a voice call out, "FBI. Put down your weapon and put your hands on your head."

"Go with them," Cornelius told him. "Constantine has contacts who….," but suddenly he heard what sounded like more running, and Rico panting.

"Stop," he heard someone say, then there was a deafening noise in his ear followed by several shots from a distance, before silence.

He heard what sounded like footsteps, and it was obvious that Rico's phone was still live because he heard a voice say, "Check to make sure he's dead."

Another voice confirmed, "Yes, he is. Are you okay?"

"Yeah," came the reply. "He just creased me."

"Well, look who we have here," the second man said. "Rico Sanchez."

"You're joking," said the first. "It's a lucky thing I kept my head."

"No wonder he opened fire on us," the other stated. "Hold on a second, this phone is active. Hello?" the voice came at him from the other end. Cornelius remained quiet, however, and eventually the call was disconnected.

He sat stunned, unable to believe their plan had failed and he'd lost his two best men. He felt a surge of anger rife through his body, and in a fit of rage he took up the crystal decanter to his left and flung it across the room, shattering it to pieces against the wall. He then placed the call to Constantine he'd meant to place earlier, and his twin answered after the first ring.

"How are things Neil?" he asked. He'd been anxiously awaiting his call.

"The whole thing was a set-up, Con," he reported, "and I've lost Juan-Carlos and Rico."

"No!" Constantine said in total disbelief. "You can't be serious!"

"I've never been more serious," Cornelius replied, still shaken by the unexpected turn of events.

"You don't think Crew...," Constantine left the sentence unfinished.

"No," Cornelius replied. "I'm sure it wasn't him. It was

330

the Peterson woman," he said with certainty. "She had the Feds involved from the beginning."

"I hope you make her pay dearly before you kill her," Constantine said with venom.

"She's the one who killed Juan," his twin revealed. "She's missing, but I know she's probably shark bait. She was three miles from shore when she escaped. It looks like she swam for it."

"She probably figured she didn't have anything to lose," Constantine reflected.

"What are we going to do now?" Cornelius asked.

"It's back to Plan B I guess," his brother replied in disappointment. "Jimmy called and told me he just offed Walter in Virginia Beach and I told him to head back here, but I'm going to call and tell him to resume the search for the Doctor's mother. It's the only chance I have left."

"Okay," Cornelius said sounding defeated. "I'm going to head out to sea for a while till things quiet down. They have two of my men in custody and they'll probably be searching the entire Atlantic seaboard for me. Call me if you need me," he added, and the brothers said good-bye before they hung up.

Constantine called Jimmy right away and apprised him of the situation.

"I want you to resume the search, Jimmy," he said. "I need you to find the Doctor's mother."

"Is there another bonus involved?" Jimmy asked.

"You know, you're really beginning to tick me off," Constantine said angrily. "Tell you what," he continued in exasperation, "you find the Doctor's mother and bring her to me, and I'll pay you double what I promised. That's on top of what I just gave you."

"Consider it done," Jimmy responded with a smile and hung up the phone. He stretched out on the bed in the motel room he'd rented along Interstate Sixty-four, then turned out the lights. "I'll catch some sleep and leave here at sunrise," he decided. "If I'm lucky and I find what I'm looking for in Chattanooga, I'll soon be a whole lot richer."

CHAPTER 31

Lahali put the last of her clothes in the suitcase and closed the lid with finality. She had hidden away most of her valuable pieces of jewelry in the lining but made sure not to take too much to arouse Constantine's suspicions. They were part of her insurance for the future. He showered her with expensive trinkets all the time and she had two large jewelry chests and a standing armoire chocked full of items he had bought for her over the years. She felt confident that if he happened to look in any of them, however, he wouldn't notice that the most expensive pieces were missing.

She also had a bulging Swiss bank account he knew nothing about. He gave her a hefty allowance each month which she seldom used, and she'd opened the account without his knowledge some years before, just after she had found out his occupation. Over time, she had squirreled away most of what he'd given her in case she'd ever need it. She had handled money all her life and had felt at the time that to have the nest egg would be a smart move. Now she was so glad she'd followed her instincts.

She went into the boys' bedroom and finished putting their things in the suitcase she had gotten ready for them. Lastly, she put the layette Elsa had lovingly made for her new little one with the other items in a large diaper bag and zipped it shut. When she was finished, she left the room and made her way down to the living room. The boys were with Constantine and he was reading them a story. Dominic was sitting beside his father on the sofa and Michael was in his lap, leaning back on his chest.

The sight almost moved her to tears, almost. One thing she could never fault Constantine for was how much time he spent with his sons. For a criminal he made an excellent father, at least to the children he didn't feel were expendable. She imagined that he saw them taking over the business from him one day, and she was thankful that, if everything went according to plan, it would never happen.

It had taken days for her to reach this place of peace after she had learned the truth and initially, whenever he touched her, it took every ounce of her willpower not to flinch and push him away. Eventually she had convinced herself that if she wanted to pull everything off, she would have to get over herself and focus on being exactly as she had been before she knew what he was capable of.

She moved further into the room and sat quietly until the story was finished and, when it was over, she told the boys to find Elsa and see if she was ready. She knew Dominic would be able to handle her simple request while Michael would just go along as if he too had something important to do. When they were gone, Constantine came over to her and pulled her up from her seat. She was hugely pregnant, and she appreciated his assistance.

"Are you ready?" he asked her, wrapping his arms around her as best as he could. She looked at him and nodded. "Good," he said. "Frank is going to drop you at the hotel this morning then do some business for me. He should get back here sometime this evening, and I'll send him over when he brings me what I've asked him for. Will you be okay?" he asked concerned. He loved this woman and knew he would miss her and the boys for the week or two they'd be away.

"We'll be fine," she said, cupping his cheek with her palm. "Don't worry."

Now that the time for their parting had come, she wasn't sure if she could do it, but at that moment her unborn child moved in her womb and gave her the push she needed to seal the future.

Constantine also felt the movement and grinned, "Fiesty little fella, isn't he?" he commented.

"How do you know it isn't a girl?" she asked.

"Are you kidding?" he said. "That would spoil my plans for a whole football team."

"Not with this girl," she said smiling. "This is my last one."

"We'll see," he said, just before he kissed her passionately. "A few more of those and it will be interesting to see who wins."

They hugged each other close. For her it was a poignant moment. It marked the end of their marriage, the end of what was and what could have been. She had loved this man fiercely and that had been what made it possible for her to stay with him after she found out what he did for a living. The thought of his affair and his doing away with his lover and his child, however, had hurt her heart, astonished her sensibilities and touched a place in her that gave her the reality check she needed.

She felt like such an idiot. She had buried her head in the sand and thought that if she didn't know the details of his business dealings it wouldn't matter, it wouldn't directly affect her. Well here she was, front and center, living with the consequences of his and Giovanni's actions. She had finally been given the wake-up call she needed, and it made her ashamed that she had ever been a part of it.

The boys came back just then with Elsa in tow, and Paulie went up to the bedrooms and brought down the bags. There were more hugs and kisses, then they were in the car and waving good-bye. As the car moved off, the boys knelt on the back seat facing the rear windshield waving their little arms off, but Lahali faced forward and wouldn't look back. In any event she wouldn't have been able to see anything, because despite what she was about to do, her eyes were blinded by her tears.

CHAPTER 32

Travis leaned back in his chair looking at the ceiling in deep contemplation. He was thinking about the events of the last few days since Leann had been released and Anne had survived her miraculous swim. Like his brother, Cornelius Antonelli had disappeared. His men in the Bureau's custody hadn't cooperated with investigators either, as it seemed they were more afraid of their boss than spending the rest of their life in prison.

On the home front, Anne and Leann were still in protective custody and although Leann was probably in the clear, they had started work to transfer Anne into permanent witness protection. To further secure her from retaliation by the Antonelli brothers, Travis had arranged a news release stating that the body of FBI agent, Anne Peterson, had been found washed up on a beach near Sebastian Inlet in Florida. It said that she had been working on a case at the time, had died in the line of duty and no further information would be released.

Travis was intent now on finding out which of his two bosses had leaked her name to the Antonellis' and, with that in mind, he planned to leave for Washington D.C. in two days' time. He'd told his superiors that he needed to meet with them on an urgent matter and would be traveling up to see them, but when they asked what it was about, he hadn't given them any information.

He was just thinking of heading out for lunch when his phone rang. "This is Travis," he answered, again leaning back in his chair and listening for whoever was on the line.

337

"Hey, Travis, this is Jerry Parnell in L.A." came the familiar voice of his friend who was very high up the ladder at the Bureau's office on the west coast.

"Hey, Jerry," he said. "How are you?" he asked.

"Doing great, pal," he replied.

"What's up?" Travis asked.

"I have a caller on the line who insists on speaking with the agent in charge of the Antonelli case," Jerry explained.

"Any idea who it is and what they want?" Travis asked, curious that they should get a call after so long.

"I don't," Jerry said, "but I decided I would patch them through to you, just in case the call is legit."

"Okay, go ahead and put them through and thanks Jerry," Travis said.

As the transfer was being made, Travis prepared to receive another call which would probably lead to nowhere. The Bureau had fielded hundreds of similar calls over the last several months, and he didn't expect to glean any pertinent information this time either but when the transfer was completed, he answered.

"Hello."

"Are you the agent in charge of the Antonelli case?" a female voice with a foreign accent asked.

"I am," Travis replied.

"I......," there was a hesitation and then the woman spoke up with a little more confidence saying, "My name is Lahali Antonelli," and Travis nearly fell out of his chair.

"Do you have any way to prove your identity to me," he asked calmly while scrambling for a pad and his pen.

"You have a kill book in your possession which belonged to Giovanni Russo," she stated. "It was passed to a doctor on duty when he was brought in after his accident," and Travis knew she was who she said she was. The book's existence wasn't public knowledge.

"Mrs. Antonelli, this is a surprise," he said. "What can I do for you?"

"I would like you to give me immunity from prosecution and put me in your Witness Protection Program," she said. "If you agree to do so, I'll tell you where to find Constantine."

"Why have you come forward now?" Travis asked completely stunned, unable to believe they were finally getting the break they needed and from Antonelli's wife of all people.

"Ah....," she paused again before saying, "certain facts which weren't known to me have recently surfaced and that has precipitated this call," she said. "Look agent, whatever your name is...."

"It's Travis," he interrupted.

"Agent Travis," she continued, "I only have a very small window to work with here. I'm at a hotel in Payson, Utah, just outside of Salt Lake City, and I have my two children and my old nanny with me. I'm nine months pregnant and can deliver at any time. Constantine's cousin, Frank, will be back tonight to stay with us and I need to be out of here by then."

"Give me a number where I can reach you," he instructed, understanding the urgency of the situation, and after she did he said, "Sit tight and don't worry, Mrs. Antonelli. I'll get back to you shortly," and they both hung up.

****

By late afternoon, Lahali, the boys and Elsa were at a safe house in San Antonio, Texas in the hands of Travis and three other Elite One agents. It seemed impossible at first to have everything done in the very short timeframe, but they had been able to complete the arrangements and get Lahali into protective custody.

Travis told no one on his staff who Lahali really was. He'd only told them they had a new witness, gave them a fictitious name and had hopped on a plane with his agents within an hour of her call. He trusted his staff implicitly, but he was taking no chances with the information reaching his superiors. It was essential no one knew her identity, not only to protect her, but to maintain the element of surprise when they went in for Antonelli later. Just one little slip, and it could put everyone in jeopardy.

Lahali wanted to be debriefed immediately, so Travis sat with her in the living room of the safe house and took her

340

taped and written statement. Gloria and Elsa kept the boys occupied in the family room while three other agents guarded the premises.

"One last thing, Travis," Lahali said winding down. "Constantine has sent his best man to try and find the Doctor's mother so he can use her to flush out your witness. He's been gone almost a month. I don't know how far he's gotten in his search," she said, "but I'd be very careful with the Doctor if I were you. Out of all of Constantine's men, he was the one I feared the most."

"That would be Jimmy Wexler I take it," Travis said and Lahali nodded.

Travis looked at her, saw the profound sadness in her eyes and knew that what she had done had been extremely difficult for her.

"Thank you, Lahali," he said with genuine compassion. "I know this hasn't been easy. I want to get you moved from here as soon as possible to a more secure location," he continued. "That baby looks like it will make an appearance at any minute."

"I was supposed to have a week to go," she said, "but I've been having contractions for the last two hours."

Travis' eyes widened in shock. "Okay," he said. "Let's get you into some expert hands."

He called Gloria and handed Lahali over to her, telling her to call the Bureau's doctor in the area, then he went outside and called and arranged Antonelli's take down before placing a call to Jon.

341

His friend answered on the second ring. "Hey, buddy, what's happening?" he asked.

"Your case just got red hot, pal," Travis informed him quietly. "Lahali Antonelli just gave up her husband."

"You have got to be kidding me," Jon replied, completely floored.

"I'm not kidding," Travis said. He went on to relate what had happened since earlier that morning and they both spoke for some time. Finally, Travis told him about the new threat to Isabelle and Amelia. "You and Ice keep your noses to the ground, Peeps," he warned. "We're so close to wrapping this thing up, I don't want any problems on that end. Our men are going in for Antonelli tonight, but only Steve who is leading the take down knows who they're going in for. Not even the agents here know who they're guarding. I'm keeping this so tight the higher ups won't know a thing until it's over. I'll call and let you know how it turns out."

"We'll be praying," Jon said.

"We?" Travis asked. Jon never made an apology for his faith, but Travis was accustomed to him saying, 'I' not 'we'.

"Yes, my friend," Jon said, "we, Ice and I."

"You're kidding," Travis said in shock. "When did that happen?"

"A few mornings ago," Jon said. "He looks so at peace, Trav," he continued. "Don't tell him I told you. See the difference for yourself on your next visit."

"God is amazing!" Travis exclaimed. "I'll look forward to it," he added, truly glad for Gabe's breakthrough, and they both hung up.

Jon went to find Gabe and briefed him on what had taken place, then they went to find the Judge. Jon told Ted they had received information that there was a new threat to both Isabelle and Amelia but didn't elaborate. He only said they would have to be even more vigilant with the ladies, and Ted promised to cooperate with them fully to ensure that Isabelle and Amelia were kept safe.

****

Jimmy watched the house from his vantage point at one of the weeping willow trees by the pond. He had come earlier, before darkness had fallen, as he had wanted to get the lay of the land before he made his move.

He knew they ran the place as a bed and breakfast and figured that the two men he'd seen outside earlier must be guests. He saw only one other man, this one looking quite distinguished and figured him to be the Judge who owned the place. If there were women present, they must be inside as he hadn't seen any since his arrival.

As all seemed quiet, he made his way across the vast expanse of lawn, trying to keep to the shadows as much as possible. He made his way to his right and saw a door which, on further inspection, lead to the kitchen. It was locked but wasn't difficult to pick and he entered the room which was thankfully in darkness. He could see three doors leading from it in the pale moonlight, and on inspection he found that one lead to a bedroom and bathroom suite which looked unused as it was filled with miscellaneous odds and

343

ends, almost like a temporary storage area. The second led into the main body of the house while the third was the grand prize. It was apparently a servants' staircase leading to the upper floors.

"Just what I need," he said to himself with a grin. "Easy access up and down. Piece a cake," he added.

He listened carefully to make sure no one was using it at present, then being as quiet as possible, he slipped into the stairwell and closed the door softly behind him.

CHAPTER 33

Constantine sat in his office looking at the picture of Lahali and the boys which he had on his desk. He missed them already and they hadn't even been gone one night. He had called her a few times during the day and they had spoken but nothing to him beat her physical presence.

He got up and made his way over to the liquor cabinet, just off to his left. He poured himself a whiskey and stood nursing it as he thought of Jimmy Wexler. He was angry to the bone that his enforcer was working for him only out of greed and there wasn't a shred of loyalty in him.

Not only was the money and loyalty a factor, but it irked Constantine that Wexler was always guarded when he sent him on an assignment. Since he had been on the Doctor's mother's trail, Wexler hadn't once given Constantine an update, and he figured it was Jimmy's way of ensuring that Constantine didn't interfere. One thing Wexler had stressed when he had employed him was that he worked alone, and he wanted to do his job his way. Not many mob bosses would have accepted those terms, but Constantine knew Wexler was good at what he did, and he had to admit that Jimmy always delivered.

Adolpho called him to dinner and he left his office, taking his drink with him. The big glass window in the dining room looked out over the unkempt garden and, although it was dark outside, the full moon bathed the grounds in light. It would have made sense to draw the heavy drapes, but for Constantine's Achilles' Heel. It embarrassed him that he couldn't stand tight spaces or

345

anywhere too closed in, but ever since he had accidentally locked himself in the old car as a teenager, he had been claustrophobic.

He sat at the table and looked at the array of food in front of him. There were escargots in white wine to start followed by lobster bisque and an entrée of beef tenderloin, stuffed potatoes and vegetables. One thing he admired about Adolpho was his ability to provide him with the sumptuous fare he was accustomed to, even though they were in a remote location away from the city and their creature comforts.

He was half-way through the meal when he heard a car and figured it was Frank returning from Salt Lake City. He had asked him to do some business for him there and some errands after he'd dropped Lahali and the boys off. Lahali's birthday was three weeks away and he had wanted to get her a necklace and earring set he had admired just before he'd had to take off from the east coast. He'd given Neil the details a few weeks before and his twin had procured the jewelry and shipped it to a mailbox Frank had set up so they could receive packages and correspondence.

Constantine knew the business he had asked Frank to attend to would take him most of the day, but he was back even later than he'd thought. He decided he would let his cousin have dinner and bring him up to date on his activities then send him back to Payson to Lahali and the boys. He couldn't wait for her to have this baby. When he had called her earlier, she had told him she was so tired she wanted to sleep, so he'd told her he would talk to her later. That had been several hours ago, so he determined he would call her just as soon as he got up from his meal.

346

Frank came in and sat down at the table, and Adolpho brought him a plate he'd already served up in the kitchen then left him and Constantine alone. While he ate, Frank reported on what he'd accomplished on his behalf and also pushed the package containing the jewelry over to him. As Constantine had finished his meal, he opened the box and looked at the beautiful diamond and ruby necklace and earrings with satisfaction. He couldn't wait to see the look on Lahali's face when he presented them to her.

"You'll score a ten with that one, Con," Frank said smiling as he too sat back having finished his dinner.

"That's the plan," Constantine said grinning. "I always keep my girl happy, Frank," he said, "that way I know she'll love me for life."

Just then Paulie came running into the room panting as if he'd come a long way instead of from the back pouch where he'd been taking a smoke. He weighed nearly three hundred pounds, so the short sprint had winded him.

"Boss," he said, trying to catch his breath. "I see movement out by the shed. With the full moon, I'm sure I saw someone out there."

"Frank," Constantine said rising to his feet, "you and Paulie grab some heavy fire power and check it out. I'm going to secure this and take a look out front."

The men quickly dispersed, and Constantine went into his office with the jewelry. He had just placed it on the desk and opened the drawer to pulled out his semi-automatic pistol when he heard someone with authority say, "Federal agents," and the world exploded around him. There was

347

shouting and running, and it sounded like the fourth of July with all the fire power that was in play.

He grabbed his gun and raced out into the living room and through the dining room, turning out the lights as he did so, then he went into the kitchen. Adolpho was firing out the back door when he entered.

"It looks like we're totally surrounded, Boss," he said. "I just saw Paulie take a bullet to the chest. Frank is out behind the kid's play yard returning fire."

"You stay here while I check out front," Constantine said, his adrenaline through the roof.

He made his way back to the living room, keeping low as he did so. He had just reached the window beside the front door when he heard a cry of pain and a crash come from the kitchen and knew immediately that Adolpho was down. He heard automatic fire coming from several different directions and assumed Frank was still in play, but within another minute, the gunfire stopped, and he knew in that moment his cousin was gone and he was completely alone.

He hurried into the office and shut and locked the door in absolute panic, frantically racking his brain to see if he could think of a way to escape. The silence outside was almost as frightening as the gun fire a few minutes earlier, and he took a deep breath to try and calm himself.

He crouched and went over to his desk, reached behind his chair and closed the drapes. He left the light on, however, knowing he wouldn't be able to think clearly in the dark. He was one of the most powerful men in the country's underworld, but he had to have a night light in his bedroom and bathroom and the window coverings open at night or he couldn't sleep. He had told Lahali that he had the lights on for her benefit and that he liked to look outside from their bed at night, but he was unsure she believed him. He hated admitting his weakness, even to her.

As he wasn't visible from outside, he sat in his chair and thought about his life and all that had led to this moment. He took up the picture he had on his desk of Lahali and the boys and as he looked at them and touched their faces, he was glad they weren't in the house. He had done many heinous things, but he knew he was looking at the only thing that truly mattered to him; the only good and decent thing he had ever accomplished.

He thought of calling her but decided against it. He would write her a note instead, already having made up his mind what he was going to do. He would rather his boys think of him as just being dead rather than know their old man had been executed. He also knew he would never survive jail. Just the thought of the confined space made him break out in a cold sweat.

He put the picture back down carefully, pulled out a piece of paper and wrote his note to her, then sat looking at it and the gift he wouldn't be able to give her. He then thought of Neil and pulling out his phone, he speed-dialed his brother's number.

"Hi Con," Cornelius answered, "I was just going to call you."

"Hi, Neil," he said, and sadness gripped his heart at the sound of his brother's voice. "I... I.... I don't have much time, but I just called to tell you good-bye."

"Good-bye?" Cornelius asked bewildered. "Where are you going? Have you decided to move south as we discussed?"

"No," he said, calmly. "Everyone's gone, Neil."

"What do you mean everyone's gone?" Cornelius asked. "I know Lahali and the boys are in Payson, but where are Frank and Paulie?"

"I think they're dead," he said bluntly, "even Adolpho."

"What are you talking about?" his brother asked.

"The Feds are outside, Neil," he said. "It's over."

"Okay, okay," Cornelius replied, finally understanding what Constantine was saying. "Don't panic," he continued. "I'll work with Jimmy and we'll find the Doc. You won't spend more than a few weeks in jail at most, I promise."

"I can't do jail, Neil, even for a few hours, you know that," Constantine said.

"What are you going to do then?" Cornelius asked.

"Look after Lahali and the boys for me," Constantine said, and Cornelius suddenly understood with frightening clarity what his twin was saying.

"Con, no!" he said desperately. "You don't have to do that."

"Good-bye, Neil," he said with finality.

"Con, no!" Cornelius shouted, but Constantine hung up the phone and put his face in his hands.

Just at that moment he heard a knock on his office door. "Federal agents, Mr. Antonelli," a voice said with authority from the other side. "Your men are all dead and you're surrounded. Just come out quietly now."

Constantine knew the moment had come. He took one last look at his family and thought with sorrow about Frank, Paulie, Adolpho and even Giovanni whose actions had led this. They had been his trusted inner circle and now every last one of them was gone. The knock came again, and he knew his time was up, so he quietly picked up the gun from the top of the desk, put it to the side of his head and pulled the trigger.

****

Travis sat in the living room of the safe house in San Antonio, anxiously awaiting word about the operation in Utah. He knew it had begun but hadn't had any word in more than forty-five minutes. Lahali Antonelli had been in labor for several hours and the doctor was with her along with her nanny Elsa. Her boys were playing with some toys they had brought with them on the floor in the family room next door with Gloria keeping an eye on them.

Travis got up to get himself another cup of coffee when his cell started ringing and he answered it quickly.

"It's over, Travis," Steve said to him without preamble. "They didn't come quietly, so we had no choice but to engage them in a firefight. They're all dead," he continued, "and Antonelli committed suicide rather than be taken alive."

"Did we have any casualties?" Travis asked concerned.

"No," Steve told him, "and, miraculously, no injuries."

Travis listened as he was given the full report and hung up when he'd been completely briefed. Just then he heard the lusty wailing of a newborn baby coming from the room down the hall. About thirty minutes later the doctor came out, rolling down and buttoning his sleeves as he made his way to Travis.

"She has a beautiful baby girl," he told him, "and they're both fine."

Travis thanked him and watched as he turned and went back into the room. He stood looking out the living room window and thought with sadness about Lahali and her children. Antonelli had lived his life outside the law, chasing riches and destroying lives and deserved whatever punishment he received, but Travis wondered if he had ever realized that he'd had the greatest riches he could have ever wanted right under his nose in his wife and his children.

He knew he needed to let Jon know what was happening, so he went outside to place the call. He also knew that, in a little while, he would have to go in and talk with Lahali, because as much as he didn't want to be the one to tell her, she needed to know that as of earlier that evening, she had become a widow.

CHAPTER 34

After supper, Isabelle sat in the reading chair in her bedroom knitting. Amelia was taking an evening nap and she had decided to come and relax a while and enjoy her favorite pastime while listening to a Christian CD Jon had bought her earlier in the day. She had been knitting for quite some time, but as she was working on something complicated, she forgot the time and became lost in her craft. Eventually, she looked at her watch and was shocked to discover that she had been on her own for over an hour.

"Mom must be awake by now," she thought, putting down the wool and her needles. "I'd better go check her," she said, rising to her feet and heading to her bedroom door.

The medications her mother was taking often put her to sleep for a time, but when she woke up, she always wanted company, so Isabelle decided to go and spend some time with her. Sassy would probably come up in a short while, then they would both get her ready for bed.

She left her room, closing the door behind her, and made her way up to the third-floor master suite. As she did so, she thought about Jon and his small gift to her that morning. He had been doing little things like that for her lately, and every time she looked at him, she saw him looking at her in a different way. She felt he no longer saw her as off limits as he had when she hadn't been following the Lord, and she wondered if, by some miracle, they could be together after all.

She knocked discreetly on the door to the master suite

and, as there was no answer, she opened it and went inside. She always did that in case Ted was present. She went in, closed the door, made her way across the sitting room and approached the bedroom. She peeped in and saw that Amelia was still sleeping, so she thought to go downstairs and join the others for a while. She knew her mother would ring the bell when she was awake. She was just about to turn and leave when she felt cold hard steel against the back of her head.

She opened her mouth to scream but closed it when she heard a voice behind her say, "Do it, and you're dead. Do you understand?" she nodded slowly and, following the pressure of the gun on her skull, she went fully into the bedroom.

"Who are you? What do you want?" Isabelle asked softly so as not to wake Amelia.

"Who I am isn't important," the voice said. "I need a little information."

"What kind of information?" she asked, her voice trembling. She still hadn't been able to turn around to see who it was, but knew it had to be one of Constantine Antonelli's men.

"Who's the old broad in the bed?" he asked.

Isabelle wanted to tell him to have some respect, but she was shaking too much to even respond to his question. She felt the gun press harder into her head to the point of being excruciating.

"Answer me," the man said.

354

"Mrs. Sterling, the Judge's wife," she said.

"Who are you?" was his next question.

"I'm her nurse," she responded, while silently pleading to God for help.

"Why does she need a nurse?" he asked. "What's wrong with her?"

"She has cancer," Isabelle replied.

"You mean she's dying?" he asked, and Isabelle nodded even though it wasn't quite true.

Suddenly, in response to her prayers, she felt a calm come over her and she knew that God was with her. She was still terrified, but she could think a little clearer and was so grateful to her Heavenly Father.

"How long have you been here?" he asked next.

"Not very long," she replied. "Just over a month."

"You're not going to be of any help," he said. "Go ahead and wake her."

"No," Isabelle replied firmly. "She's very sick and I don't want her upset."

"Would you rather I kill you and wake her up myself?" he asked.

"You'd bring the whole house up here," she replied

355

defiantly, "unless you have a small army outside."

He raised the gun and used the handle to butt her on the back of her head. Isabelle saw stars and whimpered in agony.

"Shut up," he said. "I don't need an army," he continued, "I work alone. Now go and wake her," he demanded, pushing her forward.

Just then, they heard footsteps in the hall outside and a knock on the main door to the suite.

The man put his hand over her mouth and whispered in her ear. "You're going to answer it and get rid of whoever's there or I'll kill them, you got that?" she nodded, and he turned her around and led her over to the door, just as another knock sounded.

"Belle are you in there?"

It was Jon and she wanted to cry out and run to him, but the steady pressure of the gun kept her still. Her captor released her and, as she opened the door, he slipped behind it to remain hidden from view.

"Belle," Jon smiled when he saw her. "I have some unbelievable news," he said, with barely suppressed excitement. "Is she still sleeping?" he asked.

"Yes," she responded as normally as possible. "What's happened?"

"Antonelli's dead," he said. "Our guys raided his estate in Utah and took out his men. Seems the prospect of jail didn't appeal to him, so he committed suicide."

"That is good news," she responded. "I'm sure Mrs. Sterling will be relieved to hear that," and she saw Jon frown. "Do you want me to tell her or do you want me to call you when she's awake so you can speak with her?" she asked and moved her eyes to her right indicating behind the door. In seconds she saw when understanding dawned on Jon's face. He used his eyes and moved them to his left to confirm and she blinked once.

"I'll come up and tell her," he said, then dropped his hand to his side, made it into a fist and brought out one finger, then a second then a third and shifted his eyes again to behind the door and she understood. "How much longer do you think she'll be out?" he asked.

"Give her one more hour," she replied. "I'm sure she'll be awake by then."

"Great," he said. "I have some calls to make so I'll see you later," he added, and when he turned, she closed the door and heard his footsteps retreating down the hall.

Jon walked calmly down to the second-floor landing then raced to the staircase and went down the steps two at a time before rushing into the Morning Room. Sassy and Gabe were just setting up the chess board to start a game, and they both looked up as he came in.

"Ice, we've got company," he said without preamble.

"What do you mean?" Gabe asked. "I came in from walking the perimeter just two minutes ago."

"Not outside, pal." Jon clarified. "Someone's in Amelia's room and he has Isabelle," and Sassy gasped.

"How on earth did he get past us?" Gabe asked, reaching down to pull up the leg of his jeans for his gun. Both he and Jon hadn't worn their shoulder holsters since leaving the mountains but used ankle ones instead.

"He must have jimmied a door," Jon said. "While you were outside, I checked that everything was locked tight, but he must have come in earlier." He then turned to Sassy.

"Sass, I want you to go to your father," he said, knowing that Ted was in his study, "and I want both of you to stay in his study no matter what you hear going on in the house or outside, do you understand?" and she nodded in fright. "Please tell the Judge to let us handle this," he stressed. "I know he'll be concerned for Amelia and Isabelle, but we need to know you are both safe, so we can concentrate on the situation without any distractions, okay?" he asked, and she nodded again.

"We'll communicate with him via cell," he continued. "Please tell him to put his phone on vibrate."

She told him she understood and followed them out of the Morning Room. They saw her to the Judge's office, made sure she was safely inside and heard the door lock slip into place before they took off in the direction of the stairs, hoping they could help Isabelle and Amelia before it was too late.

****

When Isabelle closed the door after speaking with Jon,

358

she looked over and saw her tormentor for the first time, and it was only the Lord who restrained her from showing her shock and fear. She was face to face with the man she had seen in the Emergency Room all those months ago. The man who had occupied her dreams on more than one occasion, usually causing her to wake up in a cold sweat.

"This doesn't make sense anymore with the boss dead," he muttered, and it was obvious much to Isabelle's relief that he didn't recognize her.

"Looks like he should have sent that army when he sent you here," Isabelle said.

"The Antonellis have no idea where I am," Jimmy responded offhandedly, obviously rattled by the news Jon had brought and trying to reason out his next move.

"You'll never make it out of the house you know," Isabelle said with certainty.

"I will because you're coming with me," he informed her then, having made up his mind, and Isabelle began to protest. He grabbed her throat and squeezed it, however, then said, "Do as I say, or I'll kill the old lady."

He was holding her neck so tightly she couldn't breathe, and Isabelle began to see spots before her eyes. It wasn't until she started sinking to the ground that he released her, and she fell to her knees, sucking in several noisy breaths to try and get oxygen into her starving lungs.

He reached down and grabbed her by the arm, hauled her to her feet, put her in front of him then, with his left arm wrapped around her waist and his right with the gun at her head, he pushed her forward, telling her to open the master suite door when they reached it.

They moved towards the stairs and went cautiously down then straight ahead on the second-floor corridor, past her bedroom and several others before he made her open the door to the back staircase. Jon and Gabe reached the second-floor landing just in time to see Wexler's back as he went through and closed the door, so they knew he was making his way down to the kitchen. They didn't know what had happened to Isabelle and Amelia, however, so Jon sent Gabe down the stairs to the kitchen after their perp while he raced up to the third floor.

He found Amelia just stirring from her slumber, although she wasn't yet awake, but Isabelle was nowhere in sight. He pulled out his cell phone and text Gabe, telling him Isabelle was missing and asked him if he could see either her or their perp. Gabe text back that they had just gone out the kitchen door. Jon called the Judge and told him that he and Sassy should come up and stay in the bedroom with Amelia until either he or Gabe came and got them, then wasting no time, he ran back out the door and down the stairs to the second floor then over to the back staircase where he slipped inside quietly and closed the door.

****

Gabe followed Wexler and Isabelle, moving cautiously with the stealth he was known for. He saw Wexler looking around as he held Isabelle in a tight grip, and Gabe stepped back into the shadows so as not to be seen. He pulled out his phone and text Jon, telling him to go out the front door and make his way around to the terrace from the opposite side of the house.

When they reached the wide stone stairs leading down into the garden, Wexler took them cautiously, encumbered as he was with Isabelle ahead of him. By the time he reached the bottom of the terraced gardens, Jon had come quietly around the house up onto the terrace and stood among a group of small ornamental trees contained in three massive planters in a corner by the balustrade. There was a similar grouping on the other side where he saw Gabe hiding and Jon watched in the moonlight as Wexler and Isabelle continued to descend the steps. He signaled Gabe to make his way down towards them then made his move.

"FBI, Wexler," he said with authority. "Let her go and we can end this thing peacefully."

Jimmy quickly moved his gun from Isabelle's head and sent two shots in Jon's direction. Although he was well hidden, the bullets came close, and Jon ducked down for safety.

"Your boss is dead, Wexler," he continued. "You may as well not add another murder to your already long list. The jury may look kinder on you." Jimmy sent off another series of shots in Jon's direction, but he kept himself well out of harm's way. "You're not a very good shot, are you Wexler?" Jon taunted him.

While Jon kept him occupied, Gabe made his way back to the kitchen door and down another set of steps into the vegetable and herb garden. He went quietly down the path, then crossed over to where the terraced garden ended and hid himself in some shrubbery there. He got a good look at where Wexler was, but with Isabelle as his shield, he couldn't do much.

Just then Jon received a text from the Judge asking if he wanted him to turn on the flood lights which would illuminate the entire back yard, from the patio right down to the pond. Jon text him back to wait for his signal.

Jon text Gabe and told him to make his way down to the pond but cautioned him to stay well-hidden as the place was about to be lit up like the Fourth of July. Gabe acknowledged him and began quietly making his way down to the water, keeping behind the shrubbery which separated the kitchen garden from the rest of the lawn.

Jimmy stepped out onto the lawn. He had his back to the pond and was facing the terrace, using Isabelle as a shield between himself and Jon. He went slowly backwards towards the water and the willow trees, and when he was a third of the way down the grassy expanse, Jon gave Ted the go ahead and the entire place became illuminated like daylight.

Wexler looked around frantically, the suddenness of Jon's move catching him off guard and leaving him exposed. Just then Jon got another text from the Judge, and this time he was so shocked he made a call to Ted, barely speaking above a whisper.

"Judge, what do you mean Sassy is on the roof and has him in her scope."

"Jon," he said, "we never told you this because it never came up, but Sassy is an expert markswoman. She can shoot a hole in a quarter from ninety feet away."

"You're kidding," Jon said in shock.

"I'm not kidding," Ted said. "She's won many major competitions."

"Judge," Jon said quickly, while trying to get over his shock, "I appreciate what you both are trying to do but shooting targets and shooting people are two totally different things."

"She can do this, Jon," Ted replied. "She says she'll do anything for her sister, and that is a direct quote."

"Let me work on something and get back to you," Jon said and hung up before calling Gabe and relating to him what the Judge had told him.

"We need a plan, pal," Jon said softly. "This standoff isn't going to end peacefully. We need to be preemptive and strike first."

"Let me continue on down to the pond and come up behind him while you keep him busy," Gabe suggested.

"That would put you at too much risk, Ice," Jon said worriedly. "You would be totally out in the open."

"Not if you get Sass to give him a display of her prowess," Gabe said, and Jon nodded even though Gabe couldn't see him.

"Okay," he replied thoughtfully, "I'll have her create a diversion and enough noise to keep him distracted, then you come up behind him, but be careful." Their plan made, they quickly hung up and Gabe continued quietly down to the pond.

"Are you okay, Isabelle?" Jon called out to her while he was busy looking for the Judge's number on his phone. He didn't have Sassy's, so he needed to call him to relay the plan to her. Isabelle whimpered but was too afraid to speak. "Hang in there, honey," he said soothingly. "This will soon be over."

Just as he was about to make his call, his phone vibrated and when he answered he heard Sassy on the other end. "Jon," she said, "I have a clear shot. What do you want me to do?"

"Sass," he replied, "I don't want you to have to live with the consequences of killing anyone. Can you take him down without a fatal shot?" he asked.

"No," she responded. "I have a clear head shot. Anything else would risk Isabelle."

"Gabe and I have a plan that can avoid that," he said, then explained to her what they'd come up with. "Just follow my lead and do everything I say."

"I will," she said readily. "I'll listen for your cues."

They hung up and, as everything was in place, Jon put their plan in action. By this time, Jimmy was halfway to the pond and the cover of the willows, but Jon had no intention of letting him get any further.

"I'm not alone, Wexler," he said, again engaging the criminal in conversation. "My assistant has your head in their sight. Let her go and I'll tell them not to kill you."

"You're bluffing," Jimmy called back.

"You think so?" Jon asked. "Take a look at that birdbath to your left. Do you see the pots around it? You're going to see three bullets appear dead center of the flower that's painted on the red one."

Immediately Sassy went into action and made the shots with complete accuracy.

"Still think I'm bluffing, Wexler?" Jon asked, truly impressed by what Sassy had done.

"You send any shots my way and I'll kill her," Jimmy said, but his voice was uncertain as the display of accuracy had obviously rattled him.

"You can't shoot her if you're dead, Wexler, can you?" Jon asked with a bark of laughter, then called Sassy back.

"Make him dance, Sass," he instructed softly, and watched as Sassy sent off a quick succession of shots around Jimmy's feet causing him to shift frantically from one to the other, Isabelle's presence making him clumsy, almost causing him to fall.

Jimmy sent off several wild shots of his own, unable to place where the shooter was, sending bullets at the mansion in all directions. He felt like a trapped animal and had begun to panic. Meanwhile, Gabe made his way up from the pond in the open as there was nothing to provide cover across the wide green lawn. Sassy could see him making his move, so she kept sending shots, first into each pot that was visible around the birdbath and then a few just in front of Wexler's feet.

Gabe was within arm's reach when Jimmy must have

sensed his presence, because he spun around, just as Gabe launched a massive right fist which was supposed to connect with the side of his head. Wexler pulled back at the last second, however, and the punch caught Isabelle in the temple instead. She went down sideways like a toppling statue, inadvertently knocking the gun out of Wexler's hand and leaving him without his shield or his weapon.

Gabe dove on top of him, and when they landed on the ground, they became embroiled in a fierce struggle, both of them rolling back and forth. Jon was on the scene in less than a minute, and he lifted an unconscious Isabelle over his shoulder like a sack of potatoes, before hurrying off with her and going up to the terraced garden where he lay her on one of the paths before running back to assist Gabe.

Wexler, meanwhile, had managed to get the upper hand and now sat on top of Gabe, leaving him flat on his back and Jon saw with fright when the criminal reached down to his ankle and brought up a bowie knife from a sheath beneath his jeans. Gabe saw the knife when Wexler raised it to kill him and managed to grab onto the criminal's forearm with both hands when he brought it down just inches from his throat. Jimmy's arms, however, were like hams and Gabe's strength was outmatched. The knife came closer and closer to his neck and Gabe knew with certainty he couldn't hold out much longer.

Jon was running flat out to save his friend but knowing he couldn't get to Gabe in time, he brought up his weapon, quickly aimed, and fired. Wexler went limp and Gabe pushed his body off him then quickly sat up. He rolled the enforcer over but realized with relief he was dead; Jon's bullet having caught him in the forehead. He knew his friend had no choice but to deliver the fatal wound, and Gabe just sat there panting, trying to catch his breath while looking silently over at the man who had nearly taken his life. If Jon hadn't saved him, he would have been dead instead of Wexler and he was thankful to be alive.

"Are you okay?" Jon asked, running up, and Gabe nodded, still breathless, even as Jon did his own check of Wexler to make sure he was deceased. "I'm going to Isabelle," he said then turned and ran back up to the terrace.

Gabe continued to sit in the grass, however, the reality of his near-death experience having shaken him to the core, and he couldn't stop thanking God. Suddenly, the thought hit him that if this had happened a few weeks before he would have been happy to be done with life. Now that he had found the Lord, however, he wanted more than anything to live and see what purpose and plan his Heavenly Father had for him.

"You've come a long way, Michaels," he said in amazement. Then taking one last look at Wexler's body, he got to his feet, straightened himself and hurriedly followed Jon up to the terraced garden to attend to Isabelle.

CHAPTER 35

When Isabelle regained consciousness, she found herself on the couch in the Morning Room with Sassy beside her, holding a cold compress to her head. The house was swarming with local law enforcement officers and within a few minutes the paramedics arrived to take over her care. They took her to the hospital, and Jon made sure to send Gabe with her. They decided to keep her overnight for observation, so Gabe remained outside her door. Things were still fluid, and they wanted to make sure she continued to be well protected.

The next morning, Isabelle woke up to find Sassy at her bedside, and learned that Jon had brought her over after Isabelle was asleep. The Judge apparently thought it best for her to keep her stepsister company, but Isabelle suspected he wanted to get his daughter away from the unpleasantness at the house. It wasn't every day one had a dead body in one's back yard. Sassy told her she'd had the same thought, but it didn't matter as she had seen everything from the roof through her scope and had nearly lost her supper.

Gabe carried them home mid-morning after Isabelle was released. When they got to the mansion, they found Travis there along with Jon and it was obvious they were still wrapping things up.

When Travis saw them enter, he whistled and said, "That's a shiner to beat all shiners, Doc."

"Well," she said looking pointedly at Gabe, "what do you expect when you've been hit by a freight train."

"Belle, I said I was sorry," Gabe said contritely. "I really wasn't aiming at you. You sort of just got in the way."

"Lighten up, Gabe, I'm just messing with you," she teased. "As far as I'm concerned your punch saved my life, so this little temporary discomfort is worth it."

"What happened to your neck?" Jon asked gently when he saw the mottled colors on either side of her throat.

"He tried to choke me into submission up in the bedroom," she said without batting an eye. "Is Mom okay?" she asked. "I've been worried about her. This must be so upsetting."

"She's fine but worried about you," Jon said. "Let me take you upstairs to see her," he offered and indicated that she should go ahead of him.

When they were on the second-floor landing and about to climb the stairs to the third floor, Jon stopped her and gently took her in his arms as they were out of sight and earshot of the others.

"Are you okay?" he asked, placing a gentle kiss on her forehead and holding her close. She hugged him tightly, closing her eyes and relishing his touch.

"I'm good, Jon," she said. "I'm so relieved it's over."

"Me too," he said. He held her a little away from him and kissed her eye and her throat. "I'm so sorry about these," he added, referring to her bruises. "Gabe is feeling pretty bad about the blow he gave you."

"God made everything work together for good, Jon," she said firmly. "I know he feels bad, but I keep telling him not to be so hard on himself."

He continued to hold her, and they talked for a few more minutes before he kissed her softly again, this time capturing her lips. He was just about to pull her even closer when they heard an, "Oh my," from the direction of the top of the stairs. They turned startled and saw Sassy standing there with a surprised expression and a grin beginning to spread across her face.

"So that's the way the wind blows," she said, coming up to them as Jon and Isabelle stepped away from each other. "You both hid it well. I didn't know a thing until just now."

"Sass, you can't tell anyone," Isabelle implored. "It will get Jon in serious trouble."

"Your secret's safe with me," she said. "Let me take you up to see Papa and your Mama. Jon," she continued, "Travis needs to speak with you."

He left them and made his way down to the first floor where Travis and Gabe were in conversation. Travis briefed Jon on the latest developments and, presently, Gabe left them alone to begin writing his report on the incident.

When he had gone, Jon turned to his boss and said, "Trav, I need to talk to you."

"Sounds serious," Travis said concerned. "What is it?"

"It's a long story," Jon said, "and you're the only one who can tell me how it's going to end."

370

"Now you really have me worried," Travis replied. "What's wrong?"

"I'll tell you," he said, "but let's go in here," and with that he led him into the library and closed the door.

CHAPTER 36

On Thursday of that week, Travis' plane landed in Washington D.C. He'd had to postpone his trip to the nation's capital in light of the events surrounding the deaths of Constantine and Frank Antonelli and Isabelle's rescue from Jimmy Wexler. They had also been hunting hard for Cornelius, but the crime boss had somehow been able to elude them, and they were stumped as to where to look next.

Travis was met by an agent Luke sent over to pick him up, and as they made their way to the Bureau's headquarters, his thoughts were on what he was about to do. He had never had cause to doubt either of his bosses before, and he was having a difficult time believing one of them could be a traitor.

He had known both men for years and they were as straight as they came, but they were the only ones outside of his staff in Atlanta who had known the agents assigned to Isabelle's case; not only that, but all the staff at Elite One knew that Anne was no longer on her protection detail. Only Luke and Carson were unaware of that fact.

Travis had been tight-lipped about the case from the very beginning and used the authority given to him by these very men to carry out his job without telling them his every move. He had wanted the Antonelli syndicate closed down permanently and because of that, he'd asked them to let him do things with total autonomy and they'd agreed.

Twenty minutes later he was ushered into Carson's office and Luke was already there. Luke was tall, about six feet, and had red hair and blue green eyes. Travis shook both their hands and sat down, then chatted amicably with them. They congratulated him on his work regarding the case, and it was the perfect segue he needed to come to the point of his visit.

"Thank you both," Travis began. "It was a team effort, believe me and Jon, Gabe and Anne did an excellent job. I know you're curious about my visit," he continued, "but I didn't want to go into details until I was with you face to face."

"Sounds serious," Carson said.

"It is," Travis replied. "We've had a major security breach at Elite One, and it almost cost us some of our team members and an innocent, pregnant young woman."

"You have got to be kidding?" Luke said, he and Carson looking at Travis in absolute shock.

"I'm not kidding," Travis said.

"Any idea how the breach happened and who's involved?" Carson asked.

"I'm pretty sure," Travis confirmed.

"Well, are you going to tell us?" Luke asked, obviously anxious to know.

"It came from one of you," Travis said, and carefully watched the reaction of both men.

"No way!" Carson said emphatically.

"Now wait just a minute," Luke began, but Travis interrupted him.

"I have no doubt in my mind one of you is involved," Travis stated firmly. "Either the Antonellis got to you or you let something slip, but I know the source of the leak is right here in this room."

"That's ridiculous, Travis," Luke said, clearly offended. "I've been nothing but loyal to the Bureau since I began working here and I resent your accusation."

"So do I," Carson concurred, "and I can't believe you would make this type of allegation without proof.'

"Let me say this," Travis said clearly. "I trust and respect you both, and it has been difficult for me to believe either of you would deliberately compromise the department; that being said, if the Antonellis didn't get to one of you, and that doesn't appear to be the case, then you let something slip, I'm positive."

"Instead of making these wild charges," Luke said angrily, "why don't you tell us what happened?" and Travis told them the story, all of it.

"How do you know one of us is involved?" Carson asked. "One of your staff is probably the culprit."

"No," Travis said. "Only the both of you didn't know Anne had been removed from the case weeks ago and was working at the office with me. Antonelli told her in my hearing that he had it from reliable sources that she was on the case, not that she had been on the case."

"I didn't say anything to anyone," Luke said firmly. "We've known from the beginning that Elite One had to be impenetrable. Only Carson and I discuss the work you do with each other and no one else."

"Could your conversations have been overheard?" Travis asked.

"It's highly unlikely," Luke said. "We usually grab a bite somewhere and discuss things but only in vague terms, nothing that anyone would understand."

Suddenly Travis and Luke saw when Carson shot up in his chair, Luke's comment about lunch bringing back a memory to him.

"Dear Father in heaven, it can't be," he said, and they saw his eyes widen in realization.

"What is it, Carson?" Luke asked.

"I...I just remembered something," he said, looking at them with his startled expression, "but it's too fantastic for me to believe."

"What?" Travis asked, knowing he was about to get to the bottom of things.

"I had lunch with someone weeks ago and the case came up," Carson said. "It's the only time I've discussed things outside of talking to Luke," and he went on to relate the conversation. "Because of his position I didn't even think it would be an issue," he concluded, the despair evident in his voice.

"Who are we talking about?" Travis asked.

"Senator Lamar Johnson," Carson revealed, and both Travis and Luke looked at him in absolute disbelief.

"Senator Lamar Johnson as in the Chairman of the Senate Oversight Committee on Organized Crime?" Travis asked when he had picked up his mouth off the floor, and Carson nodded.

"I didn't give him Anne's name," he stated, "but I think I gave him enough of a profile that if he was fishing for something, he would have been able to find out who she was."

"That's impossible," Luke said, clearly blown away by Carson's revelation.

"Well, if it is him," Travis said, "the three of us have some work to do. This has got to stay right here."

"Let's get comfortable then," Carson stated, rising and taking off his jacket. "I want him nailed to the wall," he said in anger. "He's been my friend for years and I just can't believe he'd use me like this. If it is him," he continued, "the minute he's indicted, I'll tender my resignation."

"Let's not get ahead of ourselves," Luke advised him. "In light of who we're talking about, Carson, I'm not sure that will be necessary."

"We'll see," Carson said. "Luke go get your laptop," he instructed. "We're going to dig so deep into Lamar's past, we'll know what color underwear he wore on his sixth birthday."

376

****

By ten that night, they found the connection they were looking for. The Antonellis and Johnson had lived beside each other in their L.A. neighborhood back when he was a youth. They would need further proof, of course, but they'd made a good start. They called it a night and decided that in order to keep things tight, Travis would continue the investigation at Elite One's headquarters in Atlanta. His team was good, and they knew that if anyone could find a concrete link, they could.

****

On Saturday morning, Lamar sat at the breakfast table with Crystal. He had hardly touched his oatmeal but was slowly sipping his coffee.

"Lamar, will you please tell me what's bothering you," Crystal begged. "I've never seen you like this and I'm worried sick."

Lamar looked over at her concerned expression and knew he couldn't have loved her more. She was a pretty woman, with black shoulder-length hair which she wore pulled back into a simple bun at the back of her head. Her hazel eyes were beautiful and her best feature as they made a nice contrast with her medium brown complexion. He knew she was worried, but he just couldn't bring himself to tell her what he'd done. She'd always looked at him with such devoted love, that he didn't want to see her look at him with anything else.

"I'm fine," he lied.

"Will you please stop telling me nonsense and instead tell me the truth," she said in anger. "For days you've only been a shell of yourself."

"I said I'm fine," he reiterated soberly, looking away.

"Lamar," she said, gentling her tone and, reaching over, used her finger to turn his head back to her, "I love you, sweetheart. I've been so worried, and I've been racking my brain trying to figure out what's wrong with you. It's more than sadness over what happened, I know it is. Darling, please tell me, are you in some kind of trouble?" she asked looking him in the eye, and knowing he couldn't keep it in anymore, he lowered his head in defeat and nodded.

"Bad?" she asked, and he nodded again. "Jail bad?" she asked next.

"Yes," he confirmed softly, and her heart sank.

"Tell me," was all she said.

"No," he said firmly. "It's best you don't know, or should I say safer."

"What on earth does that mean?" she asked, a frantic expression crossing her face.

"Crys," he said. "I did something to help some friends and to cover for me they did something to create a distraction. I never in the world expected they would do anything like that, please believe me."

"What did they do?" she asked automatically, but he just shook his head. "What is it, Lamar. Tell me," she insisted.

"George and Matt," was all he said, and she fell back in her chair in absolute shock when the realization of what he was saying had taken hold.

"Dear Jesus," she called out to her Savior. She closed her eyes and felt her insides start to tremble. "What are you going to do?" she asked when the words could come.

"I don't know," he replied, unable to look at her. "I've been thinking about turning myself in. I'm sorry, Crys," he said. "I'm so very sorry," and she could hear the remorse and despair in his voice. "You don't deserve any of this, sweetheart, and I don't want you involved, so listen," he continued, "I want you to leave me. I want you to go somewhere far away and I'll face what's to come alone. I don't want you in danger."

"I'll do no such thing Lamar Kenneth Johnson," she said with quiet ferocity. "Thirty-two years ago, I made a vow to you before God, for better or for worse. I guess this is the worse part," she said, her voice cracking with emotion, and she gave him a teary smile.

He stood to his feet then pulled her up from her chair into his arms, and they shared a warm embrace. "I love you," he said.

"And I love you," she replied. "I love you, Lamar, and I make you a promise right now," she said, looking into his eyes. "I'm going to stand by you from beginning to end, and if it means you go to prison, I'll wait for you until the day you're released. I said my vows to you when we got married and I'll stick by them and by you," she declared. "Nothing you've done will make me compromise them, I promise."

"I don't deserve you," he said, choking with emotion. "Would you do me a favor, sweetheart, and pray for me?" he asked, and she looked at him in shock.

She had become a Christian nearly ten years before and went to church every Sunday morning, but her husband had adamantly refused to go with her, using work as an excuse. It had distressed her, and she had been praying for him for years. She looked at him now with sadness, because she knew that if he had been a believer, he probably wouldn't be in the fix he was in.

"Lamar," she said. "I think it's time you gave your heart to the Lord, so you can have a personal relationship with Him and be able to pray for yourself," she stated. "I'll definitely pray with you and for you, but you need to put your pride aside and ask Jesus into your heart."

"He wouldn't want me after what I've done," he said with tears on his cheeks.

"Don't believe that for even an instant," she stated firmly. "If He could want Paul who was literally orchestrating the imprisonment and murder of His people, then I know He wants you,"

"Sounds like the Bible has some interesting stories," he said looking at her as she held him.

"No," she countered. "The Bible has some interesting truths. Now are you ready to repent and invite Jesus into your heart?" she asked, and at his nod she said, "Then let's pray. When we're through," she added, "you can call and talk to Carson."

380

CHAPTER 37

Isabelle stood out on the terrace taking in the cool weather and late afternoon sunshine. It was an absolutely gorgeous fall day, and as she stood there, she thought how light and free she felt. It was such a relief to know she no longer had to live with the burden of someone trying to kill her.

She hadn't seen Jon over the last several days as he was very busy wrapping up the case, so Gabe was with her most of the time. They still felt that caution was needed until everything was sorted out and the possibility was very real that she would have to keep her new identity and remain in the Witness Protection Program permanently. She was still awaiting word on that.

She heard footsteps behind her and when she turned around, she was delighted to see Jon coming towards her. He was casually dressed in a pair of black jeans, a deep red turtleneck sweater and a black leather jacket. He came up to her and smiled before taking her hand and raising it to his lips.

"I've missed you," he said, letting her go.

"Jon, what are you doing?" she asked worriedly. "Aren't you afraid someone will see?"

"Don't worry about it," he said nonchalantly. "Let's go for a walk."

He led her down into the terraced garden then onto the

lawn until they reached a bench in the grass about ten yards up from the water's edge.

"I've never seen you in that outfit before," she commented as they sat down.

"That's because I've been home and working at the office," he explained. "There's been a lot to do."

"Oh," she said.

She had no idea where his home was or anything about that side of his life. She began to wonder if this was going to be their good-bye talk, the one where he would tell her it was over between them. If she was to be in the Program permanently, then it would be impossible for them to be together.

"Belle," he said growing serious, "I need to talk to you about something."

She took a deep breath. "I figured you might," she said soberly. "Go ahead and talk," she added, bracing herself for what she knew was coming.

"We feel it's best you stay in witness protection permanently," he said, confirming her fears. "Word on the street is that Antonelli's brother has taken his death and his cousin's hard and vows to take down everyone involved. The chances are slim he'll come after you, he's more interested in the person who sold Constantine out, but we need to be cautious just in case."

She nodded, unable to speak, her emotions close to the surface. She knew this meant it was over for them and the thought so distressed her that she got up and made her way a few yards down the closely cropped lawn to stand with her back to him.

He got to his feet and went to stand behind her. "Based on the information you gave us that Wexler said the Antonellis didn't know he was in Tennessee," he continued, "we've agreed that it will be okay for you to keep in touch and see your mother, but we've decided to give you another name change and relocate you from here to another state."

"Jon, I'm happy I can still be in contact with Mom and Ted and Sassy," she replied, "but I've just gotten accustomed to Isabelle and now you want to change it again, whatever for?" she asked in frustration.

"The Isabelle is fine," he assured her, turning her gently to face him and lifting her chin to look into her eyes. "We want to change your last name only, to my last name," he said smiling, "to Peoples."

She stepped back and her fingers went to her lips in shocked disbelief. She was trying to grasp what he was saying but was having a hard time believing it. Eventually, she swallowed and found her voice, "Is that a proposal?" she asked hopefully.

"No, Belle," he said seriously, causing her to doubt what he'd just said, "that wasn't a proposal." Her heart fell to her toes, but then she saw him go down on one knee, pull a small jeweler's box from his pocket, and he opened it for her to see the beautiful solitaire diamond ring inside before adding, "this is a proposal. My sweet Isabelle," he said with a smile, "I love you with all my heart. Will you marry me?"

383

She stood there with both hands on her cheeks just staring at the ring then at him, not saying a thing. This was so far from what she'd expected when their conversation began that she was stunned. She saw doubt run across Jon's face and realized she hadn't answered, so she took control of her emotions and said a heartfelt, "Yes! Oh, yes, Jon, I will marry you."

He slipped the ring on her finger with relief and looked up in time to see her eyes sparkling before she flung herself at him and they both went down in the grass. She lay on top of him and rained his face with kisses and he laughed out loud at her unrestrained affection, so glad they didn't have to hide anymore.

Ted, Amelia and Sassy stood at the window on the third-floor balcony watching the scene and they burst out laughing when Isabelle fell on top of Jon, while Gabe who was with them, lifted his lips in a rare smile. Just after he'd arrived, Jon had gone upstairs to the master bedroom suite and asked Amelia for her daughter's hand in marriage, then he had gone out to Isabelle. Amelia told Ted she wanted to see her daughter's engagement, so he'd helped her from the bedroom only to find Gabe and Sassy had also had the same idea. When it was over, they all turned away, each of them happy for this special couple who had been through so much, and Amelia declared as she held onto Ted that she was so excited she couldn't stand it, which caused them all to laugh again.

Meanwhile, Jon kissed Isabelle several times, then she slid off him and they lay beside each other and talked.

"How is it we can be together?" she asked. "I thought you were coming to tell me it was over."

384

"Normally, that would be the case," he said, "that's why I was going to resign?"

"You were?" she asked surprised.

Of course I was," he confirmed. "There was no way I was going to give you up over a job, Isabelle, no way," he said emphatically. "I was going to arrange for us to join my family and live in Australia."

"Is that where your Dad's from," she asked, and he nodded.

"Anyway, it turns out that God worked things out so well, Belle," he continued. "Because of the highly secret nature of our department, and because no one knows our location or where we live, what more perfect place to put a witness for protection than in the home of an agent who is already well hidden," and she grinned.

"God is amazing," she agreed. "Where will we live?" she asked next, finally feeling free to ask him some of the things she had been curious about.

"We'll live in a suburb of Atlanta called Pinewood Lakes," he said. "It's almost out in the country really, on the way here, so we'll be close to your family. I have a home there on the water," he explained. "Gabe lives three doors down."

"Will you be gone from home a lot?" she questioned.

"No," he said, "not anymore. Again, God came through for us, Belle," he continued. "Unknown to me, late last year, long before your case, Travis put in a request for a deputy director position to be created for Elite One," he revealed. "He's been literally swamped with work to the point where it's impossible for him to operate effectively, and he's been unable to take any decent time off at all.

"When I told him privately about us and that I was thinking of resigning, he told me about the position and that I was his first choice. So," he added with a smile, "you're now looking at the Bureau's newest deputy director and except for the few occasions when I would operate like how Travis does now, I'll be permanently in the office."

"Congratulations, Jon," she said, kissing his cheek. "I'm so glad you'll be home. I didn't want to be without you for long periods of time."

"I didn't want that either," he said. "The only thing I can't tell you is where I work or about my work, and you can't visit me at the office either," he added. "The location requires the highest level of clearance, and you not knowing will not only protect us, but will protect you as well. You'll always be able to get in touch with me on my cell," he assured her, "and I'll give you Gabe and Travis' numbers too."

"Will I be able to apply and work wherever I want?" she asked.

"Absolutely," he confirmed. "All the paperwork regarding your education has been taken care of."

They lay there for a long time, making plans and working out the details of combining two homes and two busy careers. Every now and then, Isabelle would glance at her engagement ring and shake her head, unable to believe how

God had worked everything out. There was no doubt in her mind that He was truly amazing.

****

Later that afternoon, Jon stood out on the terrace with his cell phone in hand. Gabe had gone into Crescent Ville to do some shopping while Isabelle was attending to Amelia, so he had some time alone. He needed to make a few calls, but he knew his first had to be to the Colonel. The phone rang twice before Jon heard his booming voice on the other end of the line.

"Hello, Jon," he said, obviously seeing his name come up on his Caller I.D.

"Hi, Colonel," Jon replied. "How are you and Mary?"

"We're both doing well, my boy," he responded. "How about you, and how is Gabe?" he asked. "Mary and I were never more happy than when he called us the other day and told us he'd become a believer. That was such wonderful news. I've been keeping you and your witness in my prayers too, son."

"Thank you, sir," Jon said, "and Gabe's doing so much better. Jesus is transforming him day by day."

"That's great, Jon," the Colonel replied.

"I'm really calling, Colonel, to ask you something," Jon said soberly

"I'm all ears," the Colonel said. "What can I do for you?"

"Well, sir, I'm getting married you see, and I'd love if you and Mary could come to the wedding." Jon said smiling.

He burst out laughing, however, when he heard the Colonel exclaim, "Glory to God! Yes! Thank you, Jesus! Hallelujah! God You're amazing! Yahoooooo!" Jon could picture the older man doing a jig, he sounded so excited. When he had calmed down, he asked, "So I figure she's given her life back to Christ?"

"Yes, sir," he replied.

"Has everything been resolved regarding her case?" he asked next.

"Yes," Jon said. "She's been put in permanent protection, but she'll be with me."

"God, You are incredible," the Colonel said to his Heavenly Father.

"Yes, He is," Jon agreed.

"When's the wedding?" the Colonel asked. "Mary and I wouldn't miss it for the world."

"The fifteenth of this month," Jon replied. "We need to get it done in a hurry."

"Will Philip and Jake be there?" he asked.

"I'm about to call them," Jon said, "but I knew I had to tell you first."

"Well you've made my day, Jon, you really have," the Colonel said. "When you have all the details worked out, just let us know and congratulations to you both. By the way, what's her name?" he asked.

"It's Isabelle," Jon replied, "and she's a cardiologist."

"Great," the Colonel said. "We couldn't show up for the wedding and not know the name of the bride now could we," he laughed.

They talked for a few minutes more then they hung up and Jon went on to make his other calls. His friends Philip and Jake were surprised and glad for his news and said they and their families would definitely be at the wedding, but they were curious as to how Jon and Isabelle had met. He only told them, however, that it was through work, and they seemed satisfied with that. He would trust these men with his life, but knew he had to use Isabelle's cover story with everyone from now on. It was how they would have to live for many years to come.

Just then he heard a noise and turned to see his fiancé coming out of the Morning Room door. She made her way over to him, and they smiled at each other.

"What are you up to?" she asked when she came beside him.

"Just making some calls," he said, pocketing his phone and pulling her into his arms.

He put his forehead against hers and just cherished the feel of her, thanking God in his heart that they no longer had to hide their love from everyone.

"You feel so good," she said, kissing him. "I'm so glad we don't have to hide anymore," she added, echoing his thoughts.

"I was just thinking the same thing," he agreed, kissing her back.

"There's so much I still have to learn about you, Jon," she said, looking into his eyes, "but I'm so looking forward to it and to being with you every day. Are you sure we can't elope?" she asked with a hopeful smile, and he grinned.

"Sounds like a fine idea," he replied, "but I don't think everyone here and my friends would approve. They're almost as excited as we are."

"That's true," she concurred. "Jon, God has been so faithful, hasn't He?" she stated, and he nodded. "Sometimes we don't think His ways make a bit of sense, but just look at us and all He's done to lead us to this moment."

"He really is amazing, sweetheart," he agreed, "and I can't wait to see where He takes us next," he said.

"Neither can I," she replied. "I'm just so happy to be His once again, and that now I'm yours too," she said.

"I'm glad too," he replied. "Maybe one day we'll be able to tell the story of our courtship to everyone, but right now I just want to snuggle with you," he said before bending his head and nuzzling her neck.

"That's fine by me," she said, running her fingers through his hair. "Being right here in your arms is where I always want to be."

Jon stood on the terrace outside the mansion at Pleasant Valley. It was a clear and beautiful day in the middle of December, and he was watching as Patrick and Hanley positioned the elaborate white gazebo down by the pond. It was his and Isabelle's wedding day and everyone was busy. They had planned to have their nuptials in the Grand Ballroom along with the reception, but when the weather made a warm and surprising jump into the mid-sixties, Ted declared it was comfortable enough for them to have the ceremony outside, and Isabelle couldn't have been happier.

Amelia had finished her last chemo treatment, and although she still faced radiation, she was doing exceptionally well. Dr. Forbes was pleased with her progress and so was Isabelle. Only time would tell if she had beaten the cancer for good, but they were all praying and trusting God it was so.

Jon had initially come out on the terrace to take a call from Travis who was on his way out to the festivities with Anne. He knew he needed to get back inside, but he took a few minutes to look out on the valley and think back over the last few weeks.

Anne had been placed in permanent witness protection, but still worked at Elite One. She wouldn't be routinely placed on any more protection assignments, however, as the plan was for her to work with Travis and himself. If they were short on agents she would fill in, of course, but she was happy just to be able to continue working with them.

She had been totally reinvented, however, with a new appearance, a new name and a new home. She had colored her hair jet black and wore it long and straight to her shoulders with bangs on her forehead, and her new metal framed glasses gave her a studious look which totally transformed her. She was now Andrea Holloway but said she preferred to be called Andy. Leann had given birth to a beautiful baby girl and Derek had moved his little family across the country to Oregon just as a precaution. Anne planned to see them when it was safe and possible, but she used video communication to keep in touch with them.

Cornelius Antonelli was still at large and his vendetta against those involved in his brother and cousin's deaths was becoming well known. Rumor on the street was that he was looking for Lahali and the children and for Jimmy Wexler as they'd all disappeared. Nothing had been released about Wexler's death when it had occurred, which was easy as he had no relatives, and Travis told Jon and Gabe privately that he had buried Lahali, Elsa and the children so deep, he didn't think Cornelius would ever be able to find them.

Lamar Johnson and his wife Crystal had also been put in protective custody. Lamar had confessed to his role in the Antonellis' attempt to coerce Anne into giving up Isabelle's location, but as soon as word about it hit the news, Lamar got a text on his cell with the ominous words, 'Dead men tell no tales'. He knew it was Cornelius' way of telling him to keep his mouth shut about the killing of the two congressmen, but he had already told investigators the story. They just hadn't given the information to reporters. The future of the senator was uncertain, but at least the Bureau now had an answer to the shootings that had baffled them for weeks.

Jon then looked up to heaven and smiled at the Lord. Gabe had been making good progress since he'd accepted Jesus as his Savior and was planning a surprise visit to his family for Christmas. How thankful Jon was to see his best friend literally coming back to life.

The Colonel and Mary, Philip and Gabby and Jake and Jessica had all arrived the day before with their children ranging in ages from six years to three months and it was wonderful to hear the sound of their chatter in the big house. Jon was so glad his friends had been able to come.

Just then his musings were cut short when he heard Gabe call to him from the Morning Room door.

"Hey, Peeps," he said, "you're needed inside."

"Thanks, pal," he replied over his shoulder, "I'll be right there."

He closed his eyes then and prayed softly, "Father, thank You so much for everything. I'm so overwhelmed by Your goodness. It was so hard to trust You when everything was so uncertain, but You took each difficulty, all that I thought was impossible and turned it around for good. I didn't compromise, Father, and You honored my faith in You and worked it all out. How incredible You are."

When he finished, he opened his eyes and took one more look at the valley then said to himself, "You better get a move on, Jonathan, you have a bride waiting," and with that, he turned and made his way inside.

****

Isabelle stood in front of the mirror in her bedroom a few hours later, checking to make sure everything was in place. She tucked a wayward curl from her short hair back into place then examined the dress Sassy had helped her into just a few minutes before. It was ivory and had heavy beading from the off the shoulder sweetheart neckline down to the waist where it joined a pencil slim skirt that ended just at her knee. She wore high-heeled pumps in the same shade and matching pearls at her neck and ears.

As she stared at her reflection, she thought how different her life now was. She had changed so much in the past nine months, as not only did she have a renewed relationship with God, but she looked and felt so different.

She remembered earlier when she had gone to answer the front door as everyone was rushing about and opened it to Travis and a woman who she didn't know at first. They stared at each other for a few moments then Travis introduced them with a grin, calling them each by their new name. It was only after he told Anne that this was Jon's fiancé that her mouth fell open in shock at Isabelle's new look. When she in turn exclaimed that she couldn't believe it, Isabelle recognized the voice and they literally fell laughing into each other's arms, so glad to see each other again.

Isabelle smiled at the memory as she stood there. Gabe had come up five minutes earlier and told Sassy when she'd answered the door that they were ready, so Isabelle had sent her with him as she wanted a few minutes to herself. She closed her eyes then and prayed, thanking God for His goodness and once again asked Him to bless her marriage to Jon and her new life. When she finished, she felt ready to go downstairs to her future, so she opened the door, crossed the corridor and began making her way down to the Grand

Foyer.

As she descended the stairs, she saw Sassy waiting for her at the bottom as she expected but was surprised to see Gabe beside her. She thought he would be by Jon's side at the beautiful wrought iron gazebo, so she was curious as to why he was there.

When she reached the last step, Gabe looked at her with a full smile that came easier to him these days and said, "You look beautiful, Isabelle."

"Thank you, Gabe," she replied.

He seemed to have something more to say but was reluctant until Sassy prompted, "Go ahead and ask her, Gabe. She won't bite you know."

"I beg to differ," he argued. "I've been on the receiving end of her bite and believe me she's mean," he said, and Isabelle knew he was referring to the time when he had cut his hand.

"I'm only mean when you deserve it," she said with a raised eyebrow. "What can I do for you, Gabriel?" she asked smiling.

He straightened his tie, cleared his throat and said, "Belle, I wanted to know if you would allow me the honor of giving you away to my best friend today?"

She looked at him as tears stung her eyes. This man had come so far in the time she had known him. She had wanted her mother to give her away but was accepting of the fact that the walk would have been too taxing for Amelia. She had planned, therefore, to make the journey to Jon alone, but as she looked into Gabe's eyes, she knew she wanted him to do this for her. He had, after all, been there from the very beginning of her relationship with Jon, and they had all been through so much together.

She came down the last step, put her hand on his cheek and said, "Gabe, I'd be honored to have you give me away today."

He took her hand from his face and put it in the crook of his arm then smiling, Sassy went out onto the large patio to start the long walk down through the terraced garden to the guests waiting below. When she was half-way there, Isabelle and Gabe started down after her.

Jon stood waiting for his bride and was wondering where Gabe had gone, but when he saw her on his friend's arm, he thought how appropriate it was that Gabe should give her away to him. When they reached his side, Gabe put her hand in his following the Judge's instructions, then went beside Jon to take his place as best man.

As the ceremony began, Isabelle stood before the Judge and exchanged vows with Jon with a grateful heart to God. He had worked everything out so that she and Jon could be together, and she was simply amazed at His goodness.

****

Later, they received a surprise from Ted, her mother and Sassy. They learned that there was a honeymoon cottage on the property located on the far side of the pond and hidden from view by the weeping willow trees that almost surrounded it. It was where many a bride and groom had spent their first night together when they had their wedding at the mansion, and it had been prepared for Jon and Isabelle.

The cottage was Victorian in style, with a porch which had a wooden railing, white fretwork and overlooked the pond. Jon placed the key in the lock, and they opened the door to a wonderful large one-bedroom space equipped with a kitchen and every modern convenience one could want. Everything was hidden behind antique cupboards and furnishings, and when they made their way into the bedroom, they discovered a beautiful antique four-poster bed which had been turned down and sprinkled with fresh rose petals.

Jon immediately turned to her after closing the bedroom door and took her in his arms. "You look so beautiful my Belle," he said, smiling down at her and lowering his head for a kiss.

She stayed his move, however, with her finger on his lips and said seductively, "Let me undress you first. I want to see what I got for Christmas."

The minute she finished her sentence, she began divesting him of his clothes, starting first with his tie, causing desire to shoot through him like lightning. She systematically removed his jacket, shirt, undershirt and belt, tossing them on the armchair in the corner of the room, then he stepped out of his shoes and socks so she could remove his pants, all while they looked at each other with longing.

"My turn," he whispered.

He put his hands behind her neck and removed her pearls, stealing a kiss as he did so. Then he took out her earrings and, after he had dropped them on the night table, he pulled down the zip at the side of her dress.

"You won't find me in much, you know," she said, looking at him seductively, then added, "as a matter of fact, I have very little on underneath."

He had finished his task, but she held on to the top of the bodice to keep the dress in place. "Let me see," he cajoled, pulling her even closer and using his lips on her neck to begin his gentle persuasion.

She smiled and relished his touch. "Are you sure you want to have a look?" she asked teasingly.

"Do I breathe air, woman?" he murmured, fully engrossed in working his lips along her collarbone, "Of course I want to see what's under there. Come on," he said pulling away, his eyes sparkling while tugging at her bodice, "give me a peek."

"What will you give me if I do?" she flirted, her eyes looking at his lips then back up to his eyes.

"As much of what you're looking at as you'd like," he replied, giving her a little sample to convince her.

"Okay, step back and I'll show you," she said with a grin, and when he had done so, she released the dress and it fell to her feet, leaving her in only two lacy bits of underwear and her high heels.

Jon stared and swallowed. "Wow!" he exclaimed, and

she giggled but didn't move. "You...., ah...., well," he cleared his throat, finding it difficult to speak, "you....," then he took a deep breath and said, "you know, for an innocent young lady you are quite the hussy, Mrs. Peoples."

She laughed, then stepping out of the dress and her heels, she came towards him, "Yes, I am," she agreed, causing him to laugh. "Let me show you," she said when she reached him, putting her arms around his neck, and her intimate contact sent his breathing, his pulse and his senses wild.

He kissed her then with the hungry passion she had come to expect from this man, and she kissed him back, so glad they were no longer restricted from enjoying each other fully.

"You taste so good my sweet Isabelle," he said, leaving her lips and whispering in her ear. "I love you so much and I want to make love to you so badly, but I need to ask you just one question first."

"What?" she asked, as she dropped little kisses on his chin and worked her way down to his neck.

"Where on earth did you learn some of your moves?" he asked. "That little bit of provocation up in the mountains made me believe you were a woman of experience."

She stopped her exploration and blushed before saying, "I knew you were going to ask me that one day." He looked at her with a raised eyebrow. "When I tell you, you're going to laugh," she said, hanging her head shyly.

"Try me," he encouraged, lifting her chin so she could

look into his eyes as he waited for her answer.

"Well, you see," she said, "my first act of rebellion after leaving my father's house was to buy a two-inch-thick novel which would have given him a coronary if he'd seen me with it, and read it while I was on the bus to my grandparents." Jon looked at her and nodded for her to go on. "To say it was steamy would be an absolute understatement," she continued. "I don't know how the cover wasn't on fire, it was so lurid.

"When I reached California and was leaving the bus station, I dropped it in the trash where it belonged and never picked up another one again," she said, then sliding her hands up his bare chest and running her tongue across his closed lips she added, "That doesn't mean I don't remember a lot of what I read."

Jon stepped back, looked at her in disbelief then threw back his head and roared.

She giggled. "I told you you'd laugh," she said.

"You little tease," he said. "Do you know how close I came to taking your innocence that night, Isabelle?" he asked her seriously when he'd wound down. "When you told me that you'd never made love to anyone, I was shocked; delighted mind you, but shocked nonetheless. Now you're telling me that you got your moves out of a book?" he asked incredulously.

"Well it was two-fold really," she replied. "I knew clinically what your response would be and used what I'd read to aid me in getting that response."

"Was it really that cut and dry for you?" he asked softly, pulling her up against him once again and running his fingers up into her hair then dropping little kisses on her face.

"I can assure you, sweetheart, that after your first kiss, every ounce of clinical flew out the window," she said, her breath coming in little bursts at what he was doing to her. "What I feel for you Jon has nothing to do with that," she whispered. "I love you so much, and I'm so hot for you right now." She shifted her mouth to his once more and kissed him with pent-up eagerness. "Jon, can I ask you to do me a favor, please?" she pleaded when they both came up for air.

"Anything," he said, his body on fire after what she'd said and done to him. He just couldn't believe that this sexy and passionate woman was truly his.

"Please let's stop talking and make love," she said, taking his hand and leading him over to the bed. "When it comes to intimacy, I'll always be bold and brazen with you, honey," she added, climbing in and moving over to make room for him to join her. "Do you think you can live with that?" she asked him as he settled in and turned on his side to face her, going up on one elbow.

"I'll always be delighted to be on the receiving end of your brazenness my darling Belle," he stated, looking lovingly into her eyes and cupping her cheek with his hand, "but as this is your first time, how about allowing me to take the lead, would that be okay with you?" he asked.

She nodded, so he did what he had wanted to do for such a long time. Very gently, but with some bold moves of his own, he took his beautiful bride into his arms and made

401

her his wife.

THE END

DISCUSSION QUESTIONS

1) Have you ever been tempted to compromise on your faith? What did you decide and what was the outcome of your decision?

2) Can you think of a difficult moment or time in your life when you had to rely completely on God and His promises and precepts? How did things turn out?

3) Have you ever been angry with God? How did you handle your feelings? Did you run to Him or away from Him?

4) The book mentions compromise several times and for differing reasons. See if you can find them and discuss compromise in the various areas mentioned.

5) Have you ever seen God work out a difficult situation in your life to perfection? How did that affect your faith and ability to trust Him?

AUTHOR'S PROFILE

SARAH-JANE MCDONALD wrote her first book at the tender age of twelve. After a long hiatus, she picked up writing again and now spends much of her time weaving stories and plots for her readers to enjoy. She also hosts an award-winning program on Christian internet radio called Sarah-Jane's Corner and writes an inspirational blog. Sarah-Janes loves to quilt and paint and makes greeting cards as a ministry to others. She is active in her church and contributes her artistic skills to various projects there throughout the year. She lives in Florida with her husband, and they have two grown sons.

Sarah-Jane would love to hear from you. You can contact her via email at: sarahjanemcdonaldfl@gmail.com, and be sure to check out her website: sarahjanemcdonald.com.

Made in the USA
Columbia, SC
16 June 2023

17844456R00248